AF400685

For Laura and our boys, Max, Josh, and Tommy

FRAUDULENT INTENTION$

By Scott P. Hilsen

authorHOUSE®

AuthorHouse™
1663 Liberty Drive
Bloomington, IN 47403
www.authorhouse.com
Phone: 1-800-839-8640

© 2011 Scott P. Hilsen. All rights reserved.

No part of this book may be reproduced, stored in a retrieval system, or transmitted by any means without the written permission of the author.

First published by AuthorHouse 4/22/2011

ISBN: 978-1-4567-3704-7 (sc)
ISBN: 978-1-4567-3705-4 (e)
ISBN: 978-1-4567-3706-1 (dj)

Library of Congress Control Number: 2011901543

Printed in the United States of America

Any people depicted in stock imagery provided by Thinkstock are models, and such images are being used for illustrative purposes only.
Certain stock imagery © Thinkstock.

This book is printed on acid-free paper.

Because of the dynamic nature of the Internet, any web addresses or links contained in this book may have changed since publication and may no longer be valid. The views expressed in this work are solely those of the author and do not necessarily reflect the views of the publisher, and the publisher hereby disclaims any responsibility for them.

PROLOGUE

There are a lot of lies going around – and half of them are true.
-- Winston Churchill

The Deal

The polished blonde anchor woman readied herself as a camera man signaled the countdown. When he held up a fist, her script started to crawl up the teleprompter.

"In business news, local Atlanta bank SouthPoint announced today that it is acquiring Miami-based Internet Connections for $750 million. ICon, as it is known, is an internet payment processor and aggregator of internet credit card transactions. The deal will give the traditional SouthPoint bank an arm into the ever-expanding internet commerce industry. It has received a warm reaction from Wall Street."

She turned to face a side camera. The screen split between her and an image of a written press release.

"In a statement released earlier today, the Chairman of the Board of Directors of SouthPoint, Hunter McMillan, said 'we are excited about the acquisition of ICon. We view the deal as a partnership that makes both companies stronger as we march side by side into the arena of internet commerce. With ICon's industry leading technology and SouthPoint's strong and conservative balance sheet, we think we have put together the best combination to ensure maximum value for our shareholders.'"

The screen cut again to a close up as she continued the story.

"However, some analysts criticized how fast the deal was done and are wary that the decision may have been a rash short term move just to pacify edgy shareholders. In fact, the annual meeting of SouthPoint's shareholders is scheduled to take place soon after the ICon acquisition, which a source tells us was planned in order to drive the stock price up right before the shareholders meet to pass judgment on management. Only time will tell. Now let's go over to Kurt to tell us how the Braves did last night . . . ."

CHAPTER ONE

Three Months Before The Deal

Bill Dixon's fingers trembled on the keypad trying to enter his password as quietly as possible. The offices of ICon were dark and he was alone huddled in his cubicle. The air conditioner had been turned down overnight, and the single story building began to bake inside. He wiped his glistening forehead with the sleeve of his golf shirt and blinked to focus. Although he had spent countless hours at his desk at ICon over the past three years, he never realized how loud he typed until he was the only one in the large room of work stations. Only the hum of sleeping computers interrupted the silence. He glared nervously at jagged shadows that were inching across the walls from his co-workers' screensavers. Bill knew that he was alone, but his eyes were not so sure.

He rubbed his tired face and felt his unshaven cheek scuff at his hand. Dark crescents had seeped under his eyes from his recent restless nights. His thinning brown hair was now splashed with silver, and small crevices meandered across his forehead like tiny dry riverbeds. At forty-eight years old, he had expected gravity to catch up sometime. But the weight of the stress he was under over the past few weeks heralded its early arrival.

With each key stroke, his chest pounded so loudly that he was sure it amplified outside of his body. His computer, however, was impervious to his anxiety. It seemed to take an eternity to meander through its log on procedures, and all he could do was clench his jaw and wait. Finally, after a series of blips and flashes, a rectangular logo encasing the word *ICon* emerged onto the screen. A small hourglass turned slowly in the center signaling that the computer was still waking up. He noticed his hurried breathing for the first time, and inhaled deeply to try to calm down. Tiny sparkles of perspiration reemerged and dotted his balding forehead.

A moment later, his familiar home page flashed onto the screen with a window waiting for a username and two passwords. He quickly typed in *WillD* and his first password, *Trouper*, the name of his first childhood dog. The second password changed every ten seconds and was displayed on his employee identification card. The ID card had an embedded microchip that continually received a different six digit number from a satellite signal. He pulled the ID card out of his pocket and, for a moment, stared at his grinning face looking back. The card read *William C. Dixon, Senior Computer Programmer, Internet Connections, Inc.*

Three years ago when the photo was taken, both his hair and his face had been fuller. He remembered that first day at ICon and the excitement of getting involved in a start-up internet company at the ground level. ICon was an internet payment processor, which connects small websites to large credit card companies like Visa. Similar to PayPal, ICon's computer system operated a secure pay page that customers of the websites accessed to input their credit card information for a transaction. Once entered, ICon processes the credit card information, transmits it to the credit card company to be approved, and then sends the approval to the customer - all in the blink of an eye.

He joined ICon after twenty five years of being just another name on a bulging corporate phone list. He had decided that it was time to take a risk. Sixty years old was still twelve years away, but as he sighed over his thinning brokerage account statements he knew that his silver years were approaching quicker than his investments were increasing. So he quit the big company and borrowed against his 401K to buy a piece of hope. As an initial investor and employee in ICon, he might have a last chance at wealth if the start up company grew as big as his dreams. Now, looking down at his grinning photo on the ID card, he wished he knew then what he knew now.

He softly entered the digital number that appeared temporarily on the ID card and eased down the Enter key. Again the hourglass spun. Before it had turned three times, the *ICon* logo disappeared and a background photograph appeared of him in a loud Hawaiian shirt draped with a flowery lei. He was standing arm and arm with his wife Cindy who was grinning broadly behind large designer sunglasses. Every morning when he saw that picture of his twentieth anniversary, he grinned. This time, however, he stared right through the tropical setting to an array of icons that lined the beach at the bottom. He slowly raised his head to peek over the cubicle as he glanced around the office. No one.

He jockeyed the mouse to access the computer server that housed ICon's operating software that ran the payment processing engines. The only way to access the secure server was through his computer at ICon, and the only time that he could do it without being watched was after hours. As he scrolled through the programs, his scanned the lines of computer source code that were racing down the screen. He had written most of ICon's software over the past three years. To the untrained eye, the speeding data looked like unintelligible computer gibberish. But after a lifetime of programming, the computer source code was clearer than English to him. Computer code devoutly follows strict rules and patterns, unlike the inconsistent tenets of most written languages. His eyes darted through the passing data as he frantically searched through the programs. He was hunting for a parasite program that he suspected someone had buried somewhere deep in the multitude of electronic data.

"C'mon, c'mon, where is it?" he whispered to the oblivious computer monitor.

For the past several weeks, he had been assigned to work on a secret corporate project. ICon's biggest client, Modos Operations, needed a special computer program to process international transactions faster, and Bill was told that no one else could know what he was working on, not even his wife. According to ICon's President, the veil of secrecy was necessary to keep ICon's competitors in the dark about the new technology, and he promised Bill that he would be paid handsomely for his discretion. But it wasn't long until he figured out the real reason for the confidentiality . . . and the danger of what he was involved in. It was not really about speed or technology, it was about deceit.

Again, he looked around the empty offices, which glowed in the blue hue of computer screens. A bead of sweat traced down his temple, and he wiped it with his shoulder as he continued to scan through ICon's innermost computer system. He was sure that the secret programming work he was assigned to do was just a front for a surreptitious scheme. He suspected that someone had installed some kind of spyware in ICon's operating system because he had detected a slight disturbance in the processing rates. But when he tried to examine the source code during the day, he could tell that his cursor was being shadowed. Someone was watching him. He had to get in after hours.

It was past midnight and his stomach tightened with stress. He still had a thousand lines of code to scan and his head was getting blurry. Bill blinked hard to clear his eyes. Just as they began to refocus, he saw what he was looking for. Strange computer code with awkward formatting. As soon as he saw the first lines of the foreign code, he let go of the mouse abruptly. The data stopped instantly and glared back in black and white. He leaned closer to the monitor, and his eyes narrowed while he scrolled slowly through the spyware that had been added covertly to ICon's operating system.

He could tell right away that this was not the work of an amateur. The program was complex and it fit seamlessly into ICon's system. It was like a cancer that had metastasized onto the source code, the source code that he had written. Someone knew exactly what they were doing, and he shuddered at the thought that the operating system that he created had been violated. He could feel his breathing quicken as he scanned the spyware trying to figure out what it did and who could have written it. Again, he wiped his glistening brow and shot a glance at his watch. He had to get out of there. Although he was an employee by day, he clearly was a trespasser that night.

After ten minutes, he had read the whole spyware program. "Jesus," he muttered and sat back in his chair, stunned. His mind raced through the implications of what he had just found as he stared blankly at the computer monitor.

Suddenly, he heard voices on the far side of the room. A shock of adrenaline raced through him as he lunged down on the floor under his desk. He listened for the direction of the voices, but the sound bounced around the cubicles making it impossible to track. He looked up and saw that his monitor was still displaying the program. While on his knees, he reached up and guided the mouse to close down his computer. After a few clicks, he saw the familiar background picture of he and his wife in Maui, and he leaned back down under his desk praying that he would not be found.

There were at least two men and it sounded like they were on both sides of the room. The exit was behind them and they were blocking his escape. He was trapped. They were getting closer, and his heart was pounding louder. He inched further under his desk feeling an array of computer cords pressing hard against his back. Bill held his breath, unable to do anything as the men approached.

Before he knew it, the voices were right above him and he could feel the presence of the men. All of a sudden a tattooed arm reached down towards him. Just as he was about to lurch forward in self defense, the man grabbed his trash can and whisked it out from under the desk. Bill froze. In an instant, the trash can reappeared empty and wobbled in front of him from being dropped down. He slowly looked out from under the desk and saw the back of the man's cleaning crew uniform as he walked towards the next bay of cubicles.

His chest ached from holding his breath, and he gasped as he finally let the air escape. He tried to calm himself by breathing deeply, and he pulled his striped golf shirt to his face to wipe away the sweat. After a few moments of panting, he eased himself out from under the desk and peeked slowly over the cubicle. The room was quiet again. This was his chance. Bill slipped out of his cubicle and snuck across the room towards a hallway that led to an employee exit. At the exit door, he tapped his ID card on a black pad on the wall, and a small green light flashed. He gently opened the door and slid out of the building.

A full moon brightly illuminated the humid Miami night as he dashed in the shadows of palm trees to his car hiding in the back of ICon's parking lot. He looked around before opening the car door, and then quickly got in. No one had seen him. He eased the late model Volvo out of the parking lot and glanced up at the rear view mirror to confirm his escape. In the mirror, he watched the single story office building emblazed with the ICon logo grow smaller as he drove away.

Standing on the roof of the office building, a guard dressed in a black jumpsuit watched the red tail lights of the Volvo disappear around a corner. He snapped a cell phone from his belt that was clipped next to a gun holster, and he punched in a phone number. After four muted rings, a sleepy voice answered.

"Hello."

"Sir, we have a problem at ICon."

* * *

The worn brakes of the aged Volvo whined as Bill slowed the car and parked next to the curb on the corner in front of his ranch-style house. He turned off the ignition and leaned back in the seat, trying to process what to do next. The residential street was quiet except for the incessant buzz of cicadas that seeped through the closed windows of the car. He ran his fingers through his thinning hair. He had to tell someone about the spyware program that he found, and it couldn't wait until morning. It was just past 1:00 a.m., and Cindy was long asleep.

After a few minutes, he reached for his Blackberry. At least he would send an email to Mick. Mick Sertoff was a computer programmer who worked with him at ICon. They had known each other long before ICon, and Bill hired him as the company started growing. Mick was the only one at the company who he could really trust.

After he typed the email, he re-read it almost disbelieving what he had discovered on ICon's server. He sent the email to Mick and he felt a sense of relief as he watched the message disappear from his Blackberry. Now he was not the only one who knew.

He yawned deeply as the adrenaline began to subside. Tomorrow morning he would confront ICon's President and demand that the program be removed. If he had to, he would call the authorities, but there was nothing else he could do that night. He rubbed his tired eyes and he nonchalantly looked out of the car window as he reached for the door handle. The grill of a late-model pick up truck racing towards him was the last thing he saw as it slammed violently into the driver's side of his car. A horrific crash sounded, and everything went dark.

CHAPTER TWO

All men are frauds. The only difference between
them is that some admit it. I myself deny it.
– Henry Louis Mencken

Six Months Before The Deal

From the darkness, the lights flashed on abruptly. The sudden mechanical churning of the jetliner's wing flaps sliding into position startled the sleeping passenger. The Spanish man rubbed his eyes and blinked several times before moving, making sure he remembered where he was and where he was going. A muffled voice of the pilot squawked over the intercom, incoherent from the poor equipment and the vibrating airplane.

A twinge ached in his shoulders from being asleep for most of the red-eye flight. Raul Ramon sat up and scratched the side of his head that had been leaning against the closed plastic window shade. His dark hair was swirled tight in a neat pattern and hugged his caramel colored face. The hint of a clef adorned his strong jaw, and he had a mysterious attractiveness that could hold onto a female's gaze.

Chatter grew into the cabin as the pilot slowly brought the Iberian plane down to earth. Raul slid the shade up and the oval window was engulfed in the huge plateau of Barcelona nestled between the Mediterranean and the Collserola mountains. After fifteen minutes of bumping on turbulence, the plane touched down with a thud in Spain.

As Raul strode through the contemporary airport, he squeezed his attaché case firmer as if a marauder was close on his trail. The corridors were awash with voices from a hundred dialects like a sea of people in constant motion. He knew the place well, having spent countless hours hiding in the shadows of anonymity waiting on a contact. This time was different, a little bit anyway. He tried to relax. No one knew he was here, and his job was not near as dangerous as before.

The sliding doors of Barcelona International Airport sprang apart as if repelled by magnetic force, and the warm metallic air welcomed him to Spain. The scream of a departing airplane temporarily drowned out the traffic of taxies and buses lurching in front of him. He squinted in the morning sunlight, causing the thick scar above his right eyebrow to purse. The traveler put on thin dark sunglasses that partially covered the scar, and he glanced along each curb for the car.

A placard in the window of a dusty black sedan signaled that it was his ride. As he approached the car, the window slid down.

"Señor Garcia?" said the aged disheveled driver as he got out to greet his passenger.

"Si," Raul uttered responding to the false name he had given the car service. The driver scampered out of the car and reached for his bags.

"I'll hold onto this one," he said in Spanish gripping the attaché case.

"Of course," the drive said obediently and buried the other bag in the trunk.

Raul opened the car door and stood momentarily bidding farewell to Barcelona. He would have to miss the city's intoxicating nightlife this time, but he knew that he would be back.

The car eased into the bustling tide of taxis and pulled away from the airport.

"How long is it to Andorra la Vella," he asked from the backseat.

"A couple of hours or so, senior . . . and mostly uphill." The driver chuckled hoarsely. "Don't worry, my Francesca is a workhorse," he added tapping the cracked dashboard.

The trip through the Catalonian region had grown colder as the elevation rose with the Cadi Mountains. On the other side lay the Principality of Andorra, a small country encased between France and Spain, sitting high atop the Eastern Pyrenees. The isolated little country would be unknown except for the tourists that flock to its cascading ski slopes and the uber rich that are drawn to its tax haven. The private banks of Andorra protect secret funds while its powdery slopes entertain their owners.

Raul wiped the frost from the inside of the car window revealing the snow-jagged mountains slowly passing by. For the last hour, the crackly roads danced alongside the winding waters of the Valira del Nord, a frigid creek that joins the Valira d'Orient to form the Gran Valira River running through the capital city of Andorra la Vella. As the car wrapped around unending curves, he knew he was getting near. Storefronts selling skiing equipment began to dot the landscape, and thin rectangular highway signs told of the impending destination.

"I told you my friend that I would deliver you safely to the slopes," the driver proclaimed breaking at least an hour of silence. "Or maybe you come on financial matters?"

He glared at the driver who sheepishly peered away from the rear view mirror realizing that his passenger was not in the mood to have a conversation.

As they entered Andorra la Vella, the winding Avinguda de Salou highway pierced the towering peaks that looked down on the city as if to protect the fortunes that lie among its walls. The bustling city stretched out in the valley between the towering mountains, which gave context to the church steeples that dotted the skyline. Cars raced in opposite directions on both sides of the river, as it split the city in two. Although there were touches of a once quaint village, downtown Andorra la Velle shone with new sleek structures. The only modern luxury that Andorra la Vella lacked was an airport.

"You can drop me off at the Banca d'Andorra," Raul said pointing up ahead. "On Carrer del Prat de la Creu, across from the Govern d'Andorra."

"Si Senior," said the driver glancing up in the rear view mirror for an opening in the traffic. The car made its way through the thoroughfare and snuggled up to a curb in front of the four story curved building.

Raul handed the driver €120 Euro and stepped out onto the sidewalk. The crisp mountain air chased away the stale odor of the car. He heard the rapids of the river forever rushing in the channel along side the street. He was glad to have arrived on time. The bank had opened five minutes earlier.

"Gracias," he said as the driver placed the single bag next to him.

The last time he stood on the sidewalk in front of the Banca d'Andorra he was there to make a withdrawal. A withdrawal of secret funds deposited there by the U.S. Drug Enforcement Agency. His clandestine assignment had been one of many that took him to financial institutions throughout Europe, which were more than eager to hold money that the DEA used across the globe to bribe government officials, to pay informants, and to buy drugs. He had been a courier, but he preferred to think of himself as a conduit. A money man. This time was different, though. He wasn't acting for any government, officially or unofficially.

The lobby of the Banca d'Andorra greeted him with a warm embrace. This was not the kind of bank that customers dealt with a teller and used deposit slips. There were no automatic teller machines and no giveaways to open a checking account. Other than the name of the establishment on the wall, there was nothing that even indicated it was a bank. Appointments were required and anonymous account numbers were issued.

"Hello, how can I help you?" The dark-haired receptionist asked in Catalan knowing the answer. She sat behind a sleek marble countertop.

"My account number is 12803, and I have a meeting with Senior Ribes."

She nodded and glanced down as she pressed several keys on a hidden keyboard. As she did, her low cut blouse invited his gaze.

"Senior Ribes, there's a customer to see you. 12803."

He tried to glance away when she looked back up. "He'll be right down. Can you please enter your pass code into the computer?"

He almost missed the keyboard built into the stone counter.

"Of course." He typed in his pass code and heard an approving tone chime on the receptionist's computer.

"Thank you. Can I store your luggage during your stay?"

"I'll hold onto this one, but you can take the bag," he said favoring the attaché case, which he had not let go of since Barcelona.

Within minutes, the smoked glass door behind the receptionist swung open and a well-dressed graying man emerged. His glossy black tie matched his slicked black hair.

"Hola, it is good to see you mi amigo." The banker's arm was extended almost from the minute he opened the door. There was honesty in his smile, but not as a friend, more as an indebted business colleague.

Raul reached out and grasped the banker's hand. "It has been a while. I hope the years have treated you well."

The men disappeared behind the door, but not before Raul glanced back at the receptionist to catch another glimpse of her chest.

The banker led his guest down an art deco hallway to a corner office.

"I heard you changed professions. I have to admit, I miss your client's business." The banker motioned towards a smooth white leather chair in his office. A picture window framed the snow-capped peaks that appeared to lie in arms length of the building.

"You can only stay in that business for so long. Either you leave voluntarily or you don't leave at all." Raul's scar bounced above his eye as he smirked. "Let's just say that the money is better, and safer, in my current line of business," he added emphasizing *safer*.

"And your new endeavors involve credit cards?" the banker questioned tapping a computer disk on his desk, but not really expecting to get a fulsome answer.

"My employer has a need for clean numbers . . . to be used legitimately, of course. As I said on the phone, your bank will receive full payment for all transactions."

"I'm sure we will. And I'm sure our agreed-upon deposit will be sufficient to cover any . . . ," the banker delayed purposefully, "slippage in payment. You know, my friend, U.S. banking law requires me to report the issuance of credit card numbers in batches such as this to American customers. Money laundering is a big issue, especially with your government after 9/11. Your country's Patriot Act is not very friendly to establishments such as this."

Raul was well versed in banking law. He did not travel all the way from Miami to be thwarted by mere legislation. Nor did the banker sneering at him from the other side of the desk expect that his customer had come unprepared.

He released his grip on the attaché case and rolled the clicking dials of the lock with his forefinger. The hinges slid apart and the pins recoiled with a sharp sound. Out of the dark case, the former DEA conduit pulled $500,000 in U.S. currency, wrapped tightly in $100 bills.

"This is for the deposit," he said stacking the bricks of money on the edge of the banker's glass desk. "And this is for you to take care of any *unfriendliness* that you may encounter." He placed four additional stacks conspicuously next to the computer disk.

The banker grinned and eased back in his chair, eyeing the orphan stack of bills in front of him. "See, now that is why I miss you so much my friend." He slowly pushed the computer disk towards its waiting recipient. "One thousand sequential credit card numbers issued from the Banca d'Andorra, each with a fifty thousand dollar limit. I hope you don't use them all in one place," the banker laughed and raked the additional stacks of bills into his middle desk drawer.

"Don't worry," Raul quipped back. "I'm not in the narcotics business anymore."

"Oh, but you are," the banker said with an air of wisdom. "Credit is the new opiate of the masses, no? It brings the same euphoria as a drug, while leaving you as destitute as an addict. The only difference, of course, is that credit cards are harder to get these days." He winked sarcastically towards his guest and handed him the computer disk. "I hope you and your employer enjoy great prosperity."

Raul rose and tucked the disk into his attaché case. "It's been nice doing business again. Next time, I'll buy you dinner."

"That's what you said last time," the banker said waving his finger in jest.

The two men smiled and shook hands firmly, both thinking as they had in the past that it probably would be the last that they ever saw each other.

Back on the sidewalk, Raul raised his sunglasses to his eyes as his warm breath billowed in the cold breeze. From across the street, a two hundred year old stone-columned church reflected in the dark lenses. He had completed the transaction as promised. Unlike the last time he left the mirrored doors of the Banca d'Andorra, he was at ease. This time, he departed with only a non-descript computer disk packed safely away. Last time, it was two hundred thousand dollars in unmarked bills hidden in the linings of his coat. For a moment, he missed the excitement of his former job. But only for a moment.

He pulled out his cell phone and tapped the screen to send an email. He addressed the email to t.vickerson@icon.com, and typed *Just left the bank, I got the card numbers.* He sent the message and grinned wryly.

As he looked up, a tall blonde woman passed in a tight ski outfit and furred boots, no doubt on her way to contribute handsomely to the Andorran economy. Her shapely figure quickly replaced the church's reflection in his sunglasses. Raul gazed fervently at her, and then followed her down the sidewalk.

* * *

Half a world away in Miami, Florida, the pavement glistened in the street lights from the sheen left over after a midnight drizzle. Palm trees swayed in the warm night breeze along the road in quiet Coconut Grove, which was lined with swanky condos of Miami's affluent young professionals. A sharp crescent moon peered down from the Southern sky.

The faint screech of tires broke the calm of the night, and the sound of a car engine revving grew louder. A red Mustang suddenly lurched around a curve in the road and sped through the sleeping neighborhood leaving behind the booming base of dance music.

Troy Vickerson glanced down at the illuminated dashboard. 1:58 a.m. He grinned. It had been a wild night at the club, and it wasn't over yet. He gripped the polished steering wheel with his left hand and with his right hand he stroked the soft thigh of the brunette sitting in the passengers' seat. Krista, or maybe Kristen, he wasn't sure. He glanced over at her and she gave him an inebriated smile as she swayed her head to the loud beat.

He pulled the car into a parking space in front of his condo building, which was partially hidden in the dark by lush foliage and mango trees. They walked down a crushed shell path towards his condo, and she giggled loudly as she hung on his muscular arm trying not to trip in her high heels. He held her up and one of the straps of her sequined blouse fell down her arm exposing half of her tanned breast. They laughed together as they stumbled in from a night of partying.

As soon as Troy shut the door behind them, he pinned her against the wall and they kissed deeply. His large hand ran up the side of her bare leg and snaked under her mini skirt. She arched her head back and her brown hair draped down as she pressed into him. He kissed the nape of her neck and their lips met again in a long passionate embrace.

"Come in here," he said as he took her hand.

She managed to kick off her heels as he led her down the hall into the bedroom. Troy pulled off his skin tight t-shirt revealing a muted tattoo of a sprawling dragon hovering on his left pectoral. He lifted her onto the bed and pulled off her mini skirt in a smooth and well practiced motion. As she lifted her blouse over her head, she heard the soft hum of a motor. She looked curiously and saw Troy holding a remote control. At the foot of the bed, a large screen was slowly rising from a thin cabinent.

"Whoa, what's that?" She asked.

"It's my window to the world," he smirked.

When the screen reached its apex facing the bed, it illuminated and displayed a menu with oversized icons.

"Cool," she said as she laid on her stomach facing the screen.

He lit a cigarette as he stepped out of his pants and gazed at her toned body. Her white laced panties outlined the small curvature of her bottom and contrasted against her bronzed skin. Her soft auburn hair played down the curve of her bare back and over the side of her breasts, which bulged against the bed.

As she watched the screen, Troy glanced at his IPhone on his night table. "Damn," he muttered under his breath. He had been expecting an email and was starting to get frustated that it hadn't come yet.

Reaching in the drawer of his night table, he removed a smooth oval object. He placed it lightly on her bare back.

"What's that?" she giggled.

"Watch," Troy said. He moved the oval computer mouse slowly down the small of her back. She grinned and stared at the screen as he glided the mouse around her back to access the Internet.

He clicked to a porn website and a video appeared of couple beginning to undress each other. Troy tossed the mouse onto the bed and leaned in from behind her kissing the back of her neck as he eased off her panties. She moaned lightly.

Suddenly a short tone sounded from his phone and he quickly rolled over to reach for it. He squinted at the digital clock on his night table. It read 2:37 a.m. Eastern time.

He held the phone in his thick hand which made it look like a toy as he slid his finger over the screen. The display skated smoothly to the left showing his email in-box. The first email in the list stood atop the others and was in bold. As Troy read the one sentence email, a grin spread across his chiseled face.

"He got the credit card numbers," he said to himself under his breath.

"Huh, what is it?" she asked still transfixed by the couple on the video.

"It's nothing."

Nothing to her anyway. But for Troy, the email meant that his new client, the largest client of ICon, could continue to pump money through the company's veins. In just nine months, ICon went from being a small player in the internet payment processing industry, to the leader of the pack. Troy's commissions unimaginably cracked seven figures, and his blood rushed with cash. After years of poking around in the dirt, he had finally tapped into the financial gush of the biggest, most lucrative industry on the Internet. The one industry that is larger than the revenues of Microsoft, Google, Amazon, eBay, Yahoo!, Apple, Netflix and EarthLink . . . combined. Adult entertainment.

Every second, almost 30,000 Internet users view an adult entertainment website, and the United States has the dubious honor of far exceeding every other country by hosting nearly 250 million pornographic websites. Like no other industry in the world, adult entertainment fits seamlessly with the instantaneous, largely unregulated, and private reach of the Internet where sex and money combine into a combustible mixture of power. The age of e-commerce split open Pandora's Box for pornography, and a hail of fortunes rained down. Troy had his hands out hoping to catch one.

He gazed at the couple on the screen as he took a long pull off of his dying cigarette, and he buried it in an ash tray. He exhaled slowly sending a whirl of smoke across the moon lit bedroom. As he slowly glided his hand up her leg, she breathed deeply gasping at the screen. He gently squeezed her tight bottom and she moaned closing her eyes. But Troy remained fixated on his new client's website . . . along with the 30,000 other people doing the same thing on the Internet that particular second.

CHAPTER THREE

If you tell the truth, you don't have to remember anything.
-- Mark Twain

One Month After The Deal

"I'm leaving the office soon, I promise. Just a few more things to look at and I'll call it a night." Thomas Nelson hoped he was telling his wife the truth. "I love you, too."

As he eased the phone into its cradle, the General Counsel of SouthPoint Bank glanced out his office window high above the empty city streets. The Atlanta skyline sparkled in the clear Southern night, framed by his faint image in the window. His reflection concealed the graying sides of his short cropped hair cut, but the dark shadows on the window seemed to exaggerate the circles under his eyes. Although he was staring down fifty years old, he wore his age well and had a boyish face that maturity cannot hide. For a moment, he focused past his image and caught the twinkling of tiny lights in distant office buildings. Other people working late just like him, probably gazing out of their windows and wondering who was looking back.

Thomas had the perfect temperament to be the chief lawyer of a publicly traded financial institution, which required the ability to present an outwardly stable persona while being a nervous wreck inside. For a General Counsel, worry is an unlimited natural resource because legal problems can rear up anytime and in any way. He learned to shield the anxiety by erecting a gruff exterior, which led some to consider him to be a bit crotchety and unapproachable. But after glass or two of good single malt Scotch, his professional veneer peeled away and exposed a sensitive and vulnerable foundation.

The day before had been Thomas' fifth anniversary as General Counsel of SouthPoint, a mid-sized bank steeped in conservative tradition. The mainstay of the Bank had been safe loans to established businesses. Underwriting was not just a process to be completed, but, as its training manual proclaimed, a philosophy to believe in. Unlike many of its competitors, SouthPoint had shied away from virtual businesses. The kind of company that existed only in the ethereal world of the Internet. Unknown customers and virtual profits.

That was not the SouthPoint way, however. Conservatism was religion at the Bank, and borrowers that did not have front doors could not be trusted. *Bricks and mortar make a company strong and its revenues long.* He had heard that mantra countless times in board meetings from craggy silver-haired directors. And, for the most part, they had been right.

After years in the law firm rat race, Thomas had been ready for some conservatism and maybe for a little religion. At the law firm, every year was another beginning. A new beginning to the incessant count of billable hours, and a new beginning to the tally of dollar collections. At the end of the year, the partners clawed for profits by divvying up the pie, wiping their mouths, and readying for the next feast. He was ready to get off of the roller coaster.

SouthPoint had been a good client of his at the law firm and after he helped the Bank go public in an initial stock offering it hired him as its General Counsel. As a new publicly traded company, the Bank needed an experienced in-house lawyer familiar with the intricacies of the federal securities laws and the traps of Wall Street's expectations. He traded in his fickle partnership draw for a stable salary and stock in the Bank, and he did not miss for a second having to bill by the minute.

Thomas peered back down at the stack of papers staring up at him from his mahogany desk. Just a few more to go he thought to himself trying to summon up the stamina to finish. He was reviewing exit questionnaires that departing employees were asked to fill out when they left the Bank, voluntarily or involuntarily. What did you like and dislike about your job? How were your working conditions? How were you treated by your supervisor? The questionnaires were reviewed first by the human resources department and any of them that raised legal issues made their way five floors up to his in-box.

In most of the questionnaires that graduated to the legal department, the former employee complained that he or she had been discriminated against in some fashion. The typical allegations were based on age, race or gender, but every once in a while he was entertained by the creative. A bank teller once said that instead of being habitually late three months out of the year, as she was so accused, she really was fired because she had a religious objection to Daylight Savings Time. A branch manager said that he was discriminated against purportedly because of his love of women, or as he described it, heterosexual discrimination. Apparently, his "condition" required him to spend hours of "therapy" on the Internet's more colorful websites. Thomas could only imagine the exit questionnaires that human resources thought better than to send to him.

More and more, he found, employees who were shown the door claimed that they were whistleblowers protected by law from being fired. In 2002, Congress reacted to the Enron and Worldcom fiascos by passing the Sarbanes-Oxley Act. Among other things, the statute granted federal protection to employees of public companies who were treated adversely because they reported or threatened to report corporate wrongdoing. The employee would get reinstated and get back pay, and the company could face stiff penalties. The law was designed to shield employees against retribution by crooked executives.

The word "whistleblower" itself connotes a gallant champion of honesty calling out bad actors. In some cases, this moniker suitably fits the person; but in most cases, it is a charade. The statistics show that these self-proclaimed whistleblowers are often employees who were terminated for a perfectly legitimate reason, but who think incorrectly that they will be protected if they point the finger at someone else. Nevertheless, a public company has to treat every whistleblower complaint seriously, and usually anytime something has to be handled seriously, there are lawyers.

Thomas flipped the page as he glanced at his watch. One more to go. He'd be home in time to kiss his wife good night. He would be a man of his word, this time.

His eyes darted across the first page of the questionnaire, jumping first to the employee's position, location, and hire and fire dates. Those data points gave him the context that he needed to scan the answers to the following twenty questions. Most of the former employees answered the questions by just checking either the "yes" or "no" boxes, but a few of the more prolific former employees added commentary. He read the last questionnaire.

Position: Accounting Manager
Location: Miami
Hire Date: 9/23/09
Fire Date: 11/8/09.

Thomas unconsciously held his breath for a moment when he read *Miami*. Miami is where SouthPoint's newest acquisition is located. It was the second time in the past month that his nerves resonated with anxiety about the deal. The first time was the night of the deal, not a great start.

Thirty days ago, the SouthPoint Board of Directors approved the purchase of ICon, a private internet payment processing company. ICon helped small websites get started and it operated a secure "pay page" for the websites that enabled their customers to buy products using credit cards. It was an unprecedented move for the Bank. ICon was an opaque company. Its customers were small websites that existed only in the netherworld of the Internet, and their customers were anonymous credit card users sitting at computers anywhere in the world. The deal was well outside of the Bank's business model and far from Thomas' comfort zone.

But the directors of the Bank had been getting increased pressure from shareholders to push the stock price higher after it had remained stagnant for years. What once was a small Southern bank guided by patriarchs of conservatism was being yanked into the reality of internet commerce by hungry institutional shareholders. Other banks in SouthPoint's peer group were gobbling up internet payment processors and other web-based financial upstarts, and the effervescent capital of these large shareholders would not stay at SouthPoint for long. Threats of proxy contests and takeover bids finally edged the Board of Directors towards modernism, as well as self preservation. Whatever happened behind the oak doors of the boardroom, SouthPoint collectively was holding its breath that the ICon acquisition would not implode.

Thomas re-read the employee's position and tenure. An accounting manager who was only hired for three months. Great, he thought. An accounting issue, and in Miami on top of that. In his experience, he knew that it is never a good sign when an accounting employee leaves in a short time.

Name: Patti Tomanski
DOB: 3/24/67

Well, it probably is not a race or age issue he surmised. He started to read the questionnaire and noticed immediately that this was not in the typical form. Patti Tomanski answered virtually every question with a careful string of comments in perfectly neat handwriting. He quickly glanced at the second and third pages, and realized that he was going to have to spend some time reading her tome.

Were you encouraged to make suggestions or help process improvements? After checking *yes,* Tomanski added *I tried to improve the accuracy of the company's financial statements but I was told by my boss (Jane) not to because they were fine the way they were.*

Did you know where you stood with the company? Patti checked *no* and added *I thought I was doing a great job and getting things done faster than expected, but I was fired two days after a glowing review.*

Were your working conditions satisfactory? The box was marked *yes,* with the comment *Because I truly thought I would be a long term asset, I decorated my office.*

Did you think you were fairly compensated for your duties? Patti responded affirmatively and added *I took a $25k pay cut for this job because I thought it was a solid company.*

These were not the typical responses of an aggrieved employee who had just been fired. There was something else going on, Thomas thought. The next response began to provide an answer.

How would you describe ICon as a place to work? Thomas shuddered when he read the perfectly straight handwriting. *I would describe it as a very deceptive place to work. No one trusts anyone. Even though I was an accounting manager, I was told not to talk to anyone about my job and not to contact SouthPoint directly.* She had to write in the margins because the single line did not afford enough space.

It got worse.

What were the 3 biggest obstacles to productivity in your last 6 months with ICon? Patti's response was a paragraph with her words growing smaller as they approached the bottom of the page.

> *Most people in the accounting department just recorded things without understanding the costs that flow through the accounts or some of the fundamental operations of the business, yet these are the people recording all of the financial information. Also, upper management seemed very secretive and deceitful. Many people in upper management would give conflicting stories until they could agree on one – I thought it was suspicious and difficult to work in that environment. You never knew what was right.*

Before turning to the next page, Thomas pulled out Patti's personnel file from the pile that accompanied all of the exit questionnaires. Maybe she was inexperienced and didn't understand how an accounting department functioned. There are internal controls to ensure that employees' duties are segregated, and that restrict certain people from having access to accounts or reconciliations. She may have just not understood that.

He opened her file and saw that the first page was her resume. Bachelor of Arts in Accounting and Finance at the University of Illinois. She graduated *cum laude*. After college, she worked in a small accounting firm in Springfield for a couple of years, and then passed the CPA exam. For the next three years she did audits of public companies at KPMG in Chicago, and after that she was in the internal audit department of Technyx, a publicly-traded electronics company. A handwritten note was scrawled in the margin by someone in human resources: *Moved to Miami to be close to mother.* He skipped to the bottom of the page and read her hobbies: *History, Cooking, and Piano.* Not the typical pastimes of an employee who is usually characterized as unstable and untrustworthy.

"Shit," Thomas grunted softly with his increasing stress. She was not a young accountant. She was not mistaken about the accounting process. Having labored in the audit department of a Big Four accounting firm, Patti would have known if something was not right. And the one thing that she must've learned from working in internal audit is to tell when someone was hiding the truth. He grimaced and continued reading the questionnaire.

After reading a few more similar responses, he saw the bombshell. At the bottom of the last page of the questionnaire, Patti added the following postscript:

> *P.S. I was very suspicious of a ton of money that was paid to a foreign company for fees. I could not find out what they were for before I was let go, but it looks like they relate to international transactions. Just a note that someone may want to check it out because I believe they may be fake transactions. Plus, it makes ICon look like it is doing better than it is.*

"Shit," he said again louder. He rubbed his dry eyes with the palm of his hands and blinked hard realizing that the Bank had a problem. A big problem.

After spending a moment to cool down his simmering panic, Thomas scanned through his electronic contact list. He stopped on Jake Morgan at the law firm of Levi & Everett. He knew that making the call would set in motion a force that he could not control. It was a process that would exist outside the scope of his authority, yet it was designed to scrutinize those under his auspices. He knew that SouthPoint would have to hire a law firm to conduct an internal investigation of ICon. It was unavoidable, and it was the law thanks to Senators Sarbanes and Oxley.

Once allegations of fraud are made, a host of federal and state laws are triggered that mandate an appropriate response. An internal investigation usually was the right response. He cringed at the painful prospect of what roaches might scurry when the rocks are lifted, but he also knew that no matter what the consequences, SouthPoint's management had a legal obligation to its shareholders to investigate the situation and to discover the truth, as difficult and as expensive as that may be.

Jake Morgan was not only the preeminent fraud investigator in Atlanta, he also was Thomas' former law partner. Jake would know exactly what to do, and he would know how to do it fast. SouthPoint's shareholders were meeting in less than a week, and the recent ICon acquisition was sure to be on the tips of thousands of tongues.

"Shit," Thomas said for the third time, this time with resignation. He took a deep breath, and then picked up his phone.

* * *

The coins on the marble night table began to dance as the Blackberry next to them vibrated. After another buzzing, the tune to Beethoven's Fur Elise echoed in the dark bedroom. Jake Morgan reached blindly from the bed, knocking the change off of the table, but capturing the singing cell phone. He squinted at the bright screen, seeing the phone number for SouthPoint Bank.

"Hello, this is Jake," he said in a hushed voice as his wife pulled the covers over her head.

Jake sat up and rubbed his eyes. He brushed his wildly strewn blonde hair out of his face. Even after years of work, marriage, and a child, he had managed to keep fit by clinging onto his daily jaunts to the gym. Perhaps the only remnant of his long ago single life that still remained was his morning workouts. At a slim five feet nine inches, Jake never threatened to be a body builder, but he had so far avoided the softness that comes with middle age.

"Jake, this is Thomas. Sorry to wake you, but I need you to look into something for me."

He had represented SouthPoint in various matters ever since his former law partner had become General Counsel of the Bank. Most of the legal work was preparing filings with the Securities and Exchange Commission, drafting public disclosures, and giving corporate governance advice to the Board of Directors. They had worked side by side on the Bank's initial public offering, and there was not another lawyer at Levi & Everett who knew more about SouthPoint than Jake.

"Sure," he said pausing to get his bearings. "What is it?"

"Well, we might have a whistleblower situation at ICon." Jake could detect a cringe in Thomas' voice when he mentioned the name of the newly-acquired subsidiary.

"A former accounting employee claims that there are fake transactions going on down there. It's not really clear. She was fired shortly after she started and she's alleging some kind of fraud with international transactions."

Jake used the illumination from his cell phone to find the legal pad and pen that lived on his night stand. Over the years, he had developed a unique skill of writing in the dark as the constant chatter of thoughts kept him awake. Some of his best ideas came to him as he lay in bed, and scribbling notes eased his mind that the particular pearl of wisdom would not be lost by morning. This time, however, he flipped on a small night light and scratched SouthPoint across the top. As he listened to Thomas, he added:

accountant fired @ icon
fake transactions
whistleblower?

"How did you learn about it?" Jake asked, his mind now revving up in full gear.

"I just read her exit questionnaire. The Bank sends them to everyone who leaves or gets fired."

"Does ICon know?"

"Not likely. The questionnaire is sent directly to the former employee from the Bank's human resources. I doubt ICon even knows about the process yet."

After a slight pause, Jake asked "does she seem credible?"

"Uh huh. I don't like it. I don't like it at all. Man, I told the Board that I didn't think the ICon acquisition was a good idea."

"Yeah, well you were just standing in the way of progress," Jake joked.

"Look, maybe it's nothing. But I want you to go down there, talk to her, talk to Jane Weaver the CFO, and see whether there's anything to this."

"Sure thing." Jake had conducted dozens of whistleblower investigations. Most turned out to be a disgruntled employee who refused to accept the blame for his own poor performance. Most employees also did not understand the process and got in over their heads when company lawyers began to investigate.

"I'll call in the morning and get a flight to Miami."

"No, we'll take the company plane down. Meet me tomorrow morning at seven at Peachtree-DeKalb airport."

"Gotcha," Jake said. "See you then."

Jake glanced over at the figure shifting under the covers. His wife's muted voice escaped. "What's up?"

"It was Thomas. There's a possible whistleblower at SouthPoint. I've gotta go to Miami in the morning." He answered his wife while rubbing her back somewhere beneath the sheets.

Jake squinted at his Blackberry and found the phone number for his practice group leader at the law firm. He needed an associate to come on the trip with him, someone to take notes during interviews and, more importantly, to be a witness to anything that was said. He fiddled with the phone and soon heard the ringing on the other end.

"Hello, this is Jim," said his weary colleague.

"Jim, this is Jake. Sorry for the late call, but Thomas at SouthPoint just called. Looks like they may have a whistleblower in Miami, and I have to go down in the morning to look into it. I need an associate to tag along. Is there anyone on the team that can meet me at 7:00 at PDK?"

"Uh, sure. Let me think about who has some time, and I'll have someone meet you there."

"Thanks much, Jim."

Jake leaned over and changed the alarm from 7:00 a.m. to 5:30 a.m. He eased back down in bed knowing that it would be a while before his racing mind settled down.

* * *

The door creaked as Jake tip toed out of his bedroom and pulled the door softly behind him. A red nightlight glowed in the hallway waiting for the morning sun to rise. At the end of the hallway, a crooked sign with a skull and cross bones hung on a door warning that all trespassers would walk the plank. Jake took the risk, and he quietly intruded into his five year old son's room. A mop of wavy blonde hair peeked out from the pirate-themed comforter that was tossed wildly across the bed. One leg protruded from the covers. Jake gently tucked his son's little leg under the covers and he leaned down to kiss the sleeping boy.

"See ya soon pal."

The moment made him pause. It evoked a memory that he had forgotten long ago of his father kissing him goodbye early in the morning as he went to work. Jake remembered the warm feel of his father's touch and the comfort of knowing that he was being taken care of, protected, and loved. His father was his hero, and it was never more apparent to him until that moment he looked down at his own son. Jake blinked away a tear. It was his turn to be the hero for a little boy.

Frost on the manicured lawn shimmered in the headlights of Jake's black Land Rover as it glided slowly down the sloped driveway. The stacked stone Tudor behind him was nestled high among ivory dogwood trees and azaleas that would bloom with color as soon as the sun awoke. He and Jenny had moved into the tony Buckhead suburb of Atlanta shortly after he made partner at the law firm. The house was everything they had wanted. A quiet neighborhood with a cul-de-sac filled with kids. Enough bedrooms to grow into. A pool in the back. A baby grand piano for her, and a gym for him. They made an offer the day the house went on the market, and Jenny's bulging belly gave comfort to the aging couple who sold it to them that the house would soon again be filled with children's voices.

They met at Levi & Everett. Still vivid in Jake's mind was his first day at the law firm. He was sitting in his new barren office with nothing on the walls and only a firm telephone directory on his desk. Then he saw Jenny walk past his office. In an instant, her profile burned into his mind and, without thinking, he jumped up around his desk and leaned out of his office door. He saw her as she glanced back and then she turned the corner and disappeared. There he was standing alone in the office hallway. His first day on the job and he had just fallen in love. He thought to himself that he would never see her again. Fortunately, he was wrong.

It turned out that she worked for the law firm. That day began his quest for her heart. It took him a year of friendly flirting to convince her to date a lawyer. At the time, she was more interested in guys in black leather jackets than in business suits. But after seeing her bad-boy suitors come and go, he finally cornered her and asked "when are you going to realize that I can make you happy?" A lawyer is trained not to ask a question that he does not know the answer to, and Jake knew the answer. They were engaged within a year.

Levi & Everett was one of the oldest law firms in Atlanta, steeped in tradition and engrained in the community. It was the result of an improbable union at the turn of the century between a Jewish defense lawyer and a Protestant plaintiff's lawyer. Neither could get a job at the bigger firms of the day, so they decided to go in together. From humble beginnings, the firm had grown to over one thousand lawyers spread across the country.

Gold elevator doors opened to the main lobby on the fiftieth floor of the Midtown Atlanta high-rise, which greeted clients to a rich cherry wood decor. High above Peachtree Street, the floor to ceiling windows afforded expansive views from the shining steel structures of Downtown Atlanta to the foothills of the Blue Ridge Mountains. Its partnership rolls boasted former senators, governors, and judges. And the seven figure salary of its senior partners was the envy of other lawyers in town.

Law school seemed to be preordained for Jake, and he learned early in life to use quick wit to compensate for his fledging stature. More than once he skillfully talked his way out of a situation that his mouth had precariously gotten him into. The defining moment for him came as an adolescent when he accepted a dare to ring a large bell perched on a pole in the yard of the neighborhood scrooge. Just as Jake reached up for the bell and was about to consummate the challenge, the grumpy neighbor suddenly jumped out from behind a tree and caught him red handed.

The chase that ensued between the ten year old boy and the fifty-five year old man ended on the front porch of Jake's house. His father opened the door to see his son in the grasp of his neighbor who promptly accused Jake of ringing his antique yard bell. Jake, however, coolly looked up at the man and in his first ever cross-examination he asked the leading question "You didn't hear a bell ring did you?" For a split second, the man forty-five years his senior was stumped. Jake was right, he had not rung the bell despite his attempt to do so. Although that technicality did not exonerate him and his father swiftly sentenced him to his room, Jake realized in that fateful moment that being smarter could mean being stronger.

Being smarter, however, sometimes means avoiding the stronger. But Jake seemed drawn to conflict. In high school, while his clowning earned him popularity, his sharp tongue threatened his longevity. When a bully-prone linebacker of his high school football team was picking on a hapless freshman, Jake heckled the athlete about his uncanny bowed legs. The freshman was saved, but Jake quickly found himself pinned against his metal locker. Just as he saw the enraged football player's fists start to clench, Jake blurted out that the temporary gratification from pounding him into the locker would not make up for being benched from the homecoming game for fighting in school. The thug paused just long enough for Jake's plea to sink in. It was a close call, but Jake hobbled away with all of his teeth. He would have many similar encounters with those who used their brawn to intimidate the weak.

That innate sense of fairness, coupled with an uncanny tendency to endanger his personal wellbeing, drove him towards the law. But it took him a while to decide whether he wanted to advocate the law using a pen and paper or a gun and badge. The adrenaline that he felt from confrontation, whether with an angry neighbor or a high school tyrant, never subsided. He wanted a career that had the thrill of risk with the safety of escape. So at the end of his senior year of college, he had two choices. Law school or the Federal Bureau of Investigation.

Throughout the years, he often wondered what would have happened if he had chosen to strap on a gun to work for the United States Government. But the excitement of being an FBI Special Agent finally gave way to the practicality of being a lawyer and, more importantly, the indebtedness of his student loans. That little boy who argued his first case on the front porch of his house was ready to upgrade the venue to a courtroom.

He remembered his first day at L&E gently stroking the name plate inscribed with gold letters outside the door to his office. The empty office would soon be filled with flying paper and ubiquitous binders of documents carpeting the floor. But on that opening day as a lawyer his glossed mahogany desk supported only a phone and a lonely blotter. After all the late nights, final exams, and student loans, Jake had arrived.

It did not take him long to find his forte. In his first year as a junior associate, he was working late one night mired in a lengthy document review – a rite of passage for young lawyers – when he inadvertently discovered an email that would launch his career. His assignment had been to review the emails of one of L&E's biggest corporate clients that had been sued for failing to pay a few thousand dollars of severance to a former employee. It was an inconsequential case for the client, but just the kind that a junior lawyer could cut his teeth on.

As Jake was thumbing through one of the boxes of documents that were stacked in his office, he found an innocuous looking email that had been sent from the company's Chief Financial Officer to the company's President. The email read: *We need two more runs in the bottom of the ninth. Looking for more hits.* The baseball reference caught his eye, but it was the timing of the email that spurred his curiosity. The email had been sent at 12:05 a.m. on March 24th. He pulled out the single sheet of paper and stared at it. Something was not right. Baseball season does not start until April and, in any event, there certainly are not any games being played in the ninth inning after midnight. It might have been because he had just swallowed his third cup of coffee, or maybe it was because he was not eager to read more mind-numbing emails about severance payments, but for the next five hours he scoured all the boxes of documents looking for emails about baseball.

When one of L&E's partners strode past Jake's office early the next morning, he was astonished to see the young lawyer sleeping on the floor among a forest of paper. When the senior lawyer woke him up, he was even more amazed by what Jake had found. In all, there were twenty seven emails referring to baseball between the two company executives, but they were not talking about sports. Instead, by comparing them with the company's financials, Jake figured out that the executives were using baseball terms as code words. *Runs* meant millions of dollars and *hits* meant reserve accounts that they could use to falsify the company's income. When all of the emails had been decoded, Jake had unwittingly discovered a two year scheme to fraudulently inflate the company's earnings by tens of millions of dollars.

The massive internal investigation that ensued involved the Securities and Exchange Commission, the U.S. Justice Department, the Internal Revenue Service, and – to Jake's delight - the FBI. Newspapers ran stories for weeks about the fraud, while the local news repeated video clips of the two executives cowering to the cameras as they entered the federal courthouse with their lawyers. The investigation rekindled the kind of adrenaline that he craved as a youngster, and he found the perfect practice that mixed sophisticated deception with criminal drama. He studied forensic accounting at night and became a Certified Fraud Examiner, mastering the techniques of interrogation and investigation.

Whenever a client suspected fraud or other wrongdoing, Jake was called in, most times confidentially and with little notice, to investigate the allegations and report to the directors of the company. The viability of the company frequently hinged on what his investigation revealed, and the careers of many executives imploded when he uncovered their fraud. Although he did not have a badge or a gun, he had the full authority of the corporate charter behind him. He was part lawyer, part detective, and part executioner.

Jake's arrival at L&E could not have been timed better. He rode the wake of the corporate accounting scandals of the early 2000s, and sailed the wave of option backdating investigations and securities fraud cases that followed. The white-shoe law firm represented some of the biggest companies that got entangled in financial misdeeds. After the eruption of Enron, WorldCom, and others, the tremors of the Sarbanes-Oxley Act were felt in board rooms across the country. The law heightened the scrutiny placed on corporate directors to find fraud, and their new-found legal exposure led to hair-trigger reactions to investigate any inkling of wrongdoing. Jake's phone lit up as allegations of fraud blew up.

The morning sun was inching over the horizon, and the Atlanta streets already were covered with hustling cars. Jake drove as he took a measured sip of his coffee, slipping it back down into the hidden cup holder. Peachtree-DeKalb Airport was on the north side of town and was the sanctuary for the corporate jets of the Atlanta elite. Sleek fuselages lined up in rows waiting to jaunt those sitting atop the organization chart around the country. No baggage check, no security lines, no boarding by zones. It was curbside to Gulfstream in a few steps. A very civil way to travel he thought to himself as he turned the Land Rover onto Airport Boulevard and drove under the winged archway.

CHAPTER FOUR

There are some frauds so well conducted that it
would be stupidity not to be deceived by them.
-- Jason Lee

Two Weeks Before The Deal

The Miami heat bore down on the SUV as the team from SouthPoint arrived at the lush headquarters of Internet Connection, Inc. The clean single story white building spread out in front of the parking lot masking its depth. The center of the building welcomed visitors with expansive glass doors framed by palm trees. The ICon logo blazed across the top of the front entrance.

The SUV pulled into a visitor's space and all four doors sprung open soaking the interior of the vehicle in the warm humid air. Thomas Nelson exited the drivers' side and saw SouthPoint's targeted acquisition for the first time. They had come for a meeting with ICon's management, primarily to engage in due diligence for the acquisition and partly to size up their prey. The charge from the Board of Directors was to wrap up the deal quickly because the Bank's annual shareholder meeting was just forty five away. Adding ICon's revenues to the Bank's income statement would give the bottom line a nice boost, and the directors could cool shareholders who were simmering for profits. Thomas paused gazing at the building. As the Bank's lead lawyer, it was his job to worry about what could go wrong . . . and he already was worried.

SouthPoint's CEO and President, Gary Cassel, got out of the passenger's door and straightened his tie. He was large all over and his personality fit his size. He was from Cochran, Georgia, nearly dead center in the middle of the state and far from what most would call civilization. Growing up on fried chicken and gravy-laden biscuits, he was the biggest at his age . . . at every age. Size seemed to matter growing up, and he quickly became well known and well liked.

After playing football for Georgia Southern University just down the road in Statesboro, Georgia, Gary founded the Central Bank of Georgia and became its majority owner. Lending to farmers and shift workers at the local paper mills proved profitable, and the bank grew to be Georgia's largest financial institution outside of Atlanta. The bank attracted various suitors over the years, but Gary refused to sell. Finally, SouthPoint Bank made a deal that Gary could not resist. SouthPoint acquired Central Bank of Georgia in the high nine figures and Gary moved to Atlanta to be SouthPoint's Vice President and Chief Operating Officer. His down-home style and back slapping charm soon won over the SouthPoint's management, and the Bank's soaring profits quickly won over the Board of Directors. Even as an adult, size still mattered and within two years Gary was SouthPoint Chief Executive Officer.

"Whew, I think we overdressed," he said fanning himself and pulling at his collar. "I'm sweating more than a long tailed cat in a room full of rocking chairs." It was an accurate description despite its lack of originality.

Out of the side car doors emerged Sheila Stevenson, Vice President of SouthPoint, and Vic Tomlinson, Chief Financial Officer of SouthPoint.

Thomas searched for the back door latch and lifted the hatch above his head. Each of the officers reached in to grab their respective brief cases, all except Gary who depended on the others to bring what he needed.

He turned towards ICon as he squinted in the sun. Shielding his portly face from the sun, he said "remember folks, let's treat 'em like third cousins. They may on the family tree, but you never know what knots they have in their branches."

Sheila looked over at Vic and shrugged her shoulders as if to tell him that she had no idea what Gary's Southern euphemism meant. Vic grinned back and shook his head in agreement as he handed her briefcase to her.

The lobby of ICon was part tropical forest part living room with couches that seemed too plush to ever be able to get out of. Off-shore fishing and yachting magazines were lined neatly on glass coffee tables, and a large piece of abstract art clung to the wall. The SouthPoint executives mingled next to the table as Thomas crossed the lobby to check in with the overly-bronzed receptionist. After ten minutes, an equally striking brunette approached the group and asked them to follow her to the office of Alan Arnold, ICon's Founder and President.

The meeting at ICon was planned just six days before. Gary had received a call from an investment banker who was gauging SouthPoint's interest in buying an unnamed internet payment processing company in Miami. The timing was curiously fortuitous because SouthPoint was confidentially surveying acquisition targets. The week before, Hunter McMillan, the silver-haired Chairman of SouthPoint's Board of Directors, had laid down the edict that SouthPoint had to diversify into internet commerce immediately or the very foundation of the Bank would be threatened.

While some of the directors initially balked at McMillan's antics, they knew that he controlled the majority of the Board and they knew better than to stand in his way. McMillan had watched keenly as SouthPoint's competitors acquired internet payment processors, and then boasted record earnings to the delight of Wall Street. SouthPoint's stock, however, lagged as it held firm to its conservative lending base and hesitation to diversify. Less than complimentary analyst reports about the Bank began to fan SouthPoint's smoldering shareholders, and McMillan finally convinced the Board to retain an investment bank to help SouthPoint look for an acquisition. The strategy seemed sound on its face, but McMillan had another agenda. His grip on the majority of the Board was in jeopardy and he needed some insurance.

"Mr. Arnold," the brunette said as she knocked on his door that lay ajar.

"The people from SouthPoint are here."

"Come on in." Alan Arnold leapt from behind his glass desk and rushed to meet his presumptive new business partners. His hand was outstretched and Gary was the first to accept the handshake.

Alan was in his late sixties, tanned in every crevice, and his salt and pepper hair reached down his neck and dabbed at his shoulders. A thin gold rope chain hung loosely around his neck. His open shirt and jacket defined Florida business casual, but the price tag of his Christian Dior outfit was anything but casual. A jeweled Rolex hung loosely on his wrist.

A transplant from the steely side of Newark, New Jersey, he had flown south twenty years ago to strike it rich under the Florida sun. He blended seamlessly into the eccentric sub-culture of relocated New Yorkers to North Miami Beach. If one were to listen with his eyes closed to the northern accents in North Miami Beach, he would think that he was in the heart of Brooklyn only to find himself in a bagel shop on Flagler Boulevard. Money from the north flowed like the inter-coastal waterway down the shoreline of Florida, and Alan followed the trail of early bird specials that led to less than diligent older investors. He got involved in everything from selling variable annuities to time shares. Each time he came into some money, he dumped it into the next venture hoping that it would be the big one. More often than not, however, he kept chasing the brass ring.

His glimmer of brilliance finally came in the early-90s when internet commerce began to boom. The major retailers rolled out fancy websites with promises of instantaneous shopping gratification and overnight delivery. With one click, a consumer could enter a credit card number and instantaneously be approved to buy anything the store offered, in any location in the world, at any hour of the day. But the credit card companies only offered accounts to large, established retailers. For small retail websites, the true start ups, however, the flow of electronic commerce was not as fluid. They did not have merchant accounts with credit card companies and, as a result, their customers could not use credit cards to shop online at small websites.

Alan and a few other entrepreneurs saw the need for an intermediary to aggregate the credit card transactions of these small websites and to provide the bridge between their customers and the credit card companies. The intermediary would host a "pay page" for the small websites so that their customers could link to the credit card companies. The transaction would be approved or denied by the credit card company, and the intermediary would charge a fee for each credit card transaction that was processed. To the customer, this happened seamlessly and instantaneously.

A cottage industry of internet payment processors was born, and it was like printing money. Overnight, thousands of mom and pop websites sprung up selling everything from hand made baskets to religious t-shirts. To survive in the internet world, all of the start ups had to accept credit cards, and to do that, all of them needed access to the major credit card companies. ICon and other payment processors raced to enter into contracts with the credit card companies to allow the processors to aggregate the transactions from these small websites and to filter them through electronic pipelines to the credit card companies. The *quid pro quo* for the money that the payment processors earned was the responsibility and the liability to monitor their websites clients for fraudulent transactions and criminal activity.

ICon was not SouthPoint's first choice, but it was available. Because Alan had infused much of his own money into starting up ICon, the company was not highly leveraged. It seemed to have a relatively strong hold on the South Florida market, even though there are no geographical limitations in the internet industry. As critical to the SouthPoint board was that Alan seemed to be a motivated seller. Alan was ready to cash out and live his remaining years under the golden sun. But Thomas was leery about Alan's motivations. Then again, it was Thomas' job to be leery about everything.

"It's nice to put a face with a voice," Gary said smiling and shaking hands.

"This is Thomas Nelson, our General Counsel, Sheila Stevenson our Vice President, and Vic Tomlinson our CFO." They each took turns greeting the President of ICon.

"Please, sit down, and thanks for coming." Alan motioned to a glass table in the corner of his expansive office. "We're excited about the deal and I hope that the due diligence will go as planned. We've set up a data room down the hall with all of the documents and information on the list that we got from your financial advisor, and there are a few computers in there for the electronic stuff. The room is available to you and your team for as long as you like, and we'll have our folks around for any questions."

The bookshelves flanking the table were littered with mementos from various travels. There were pictures of Alan smiling with local celebrities, and a large photo of him and Bill Clinton standing next to a golf cart. The credenza behind his desk boasted a model of a yacht, which given its prominent position, was clearly his pride and joy.

"Before I turn you all loose, I thought that it would be helpful for you to meet our executive team and for them to give you an overview of ICon and its operations. I know you've probably heard a lot about us from your advisor and read through our presentation materials, but ICon's most valuable asset is our people and I want you to meet them early in the process and feel comfortable that we're the right business partners for SouthPoint. They should be gathered in the executive conference room whenever you're ready."

"That sounds great, Alan," Gary said. "I'm sure you likewise have heard that SouthPoint is looking for the right fit, and we've heard good things about ICon."

The group rose and began leaving the office.

"Nice fish," Vic said pointing to a picture of Alan standing next to a massive marlin hanging upside down on a lift.

"I caught it off the coast of Bermuda last fall. It took me two and a half hours to haul it in. It fought like hell."

"Man, I bet that was a blast. I wrestled with a pretty big sailfish when I was in Cancun a while back. My son and I were on a fishing trip and he thought it was the greatest thing in the world. It was one of those fishing charters, so they just told me when to jump into the harness and hold on. It was almost embarrassing. He thought I actually caught the fish. I'll tell you what though, there was nothing like seeing my son's face the first time that baby took air." "That's good stuff," Alan said patting Vic on the shoulder as they walked down the hall. "I wish my son and I did more of that." There was a hint of remorse in his voice.

The ICon executives were huddled near the coffee station as Alan led the SouthPoint team in the conference room. Everyone went through the permutations of introducing themselves to one another, making sure not to miss anyone.

"We've got coffee and bagels if you're interested."

They mingled as the visitors got coffee and then sat at the elongated table, each team taking opposing sides with Alan ceremoniously at the head. A laminated binder with the ICon and SouthPoint logos was placed perfectly in front of each chair.

"Well, I'm happy to say that after all of the expressions of interest, and after our respective chaperones reviewed the invitations, we're finally here on our first date." Alan said with a smile as the others on both sides of the table chuckled.

"I know that you all are dying to immerse yourselves in reams of spreadsheets and documents as you conduct due diligence, so we'll get started. Our VP of Sales, Troy Vickerson, will kick it off by giving you some details about our operations and business model. The materials you got from our investment banker provided a good overview, but Troy can put some meat on the bones."

The pun was intended, as Alan gestured to the thick muscular man sitting next to him. Troy's suit was stretched around his bulking frame, which he clearly donned just for the occasion. Either his physique had been synthetically enhanced, or he had begun lifting weights when he was five.

"Then Jane Weaver, our CFO will go over last year's financials and will discuss our projections for next year. You've got the financial statements in front of you, along with our pro formas. To steal a little of her thunder, we just closed our books on last year and we had our best year ever. Our revenues were over $250 million."

"Sorry Jane," Alan added as he winked to the attractive brunette who politely smiled back.

"Troy, you're up."

Troy stood and walked to the opposite side of the table from Alan, where a laptop and projector were waiting. He moved the mouse and an ICon logo appeared on a drop down screen.

"Without ICon and similar internet payment processors, internet commerce would be almost nonexistent." He paused to give his statement significance. "Virtually all business done over the Internet is through credit card transactions, however only a tiny amount of the millions of websites doing business have merchant accounts with the major credit card associations like Visa and MasterCard, or companies like American Express. A merchant account allows the merchant to send electronic credit card transactions directly to the credit card companies for approval. These accounts are reserved for major retailers and service providers. Think Home Depot, Sears, and AT&T. So, what does that mean for the rest of world? That means that most of the websites out there cannot get approval for credit card transactions directly from the credit card companies, and without approval, there are no transactions and no payments and no business. That's where we come in."

He clicked to the next slide of the Power Point presentation. At the top of the slide was a computer graphic of a large building labeled "Credit Card Company." A thick vertical arrow pointed down from the Credit Card Company to a photograph of the white ICon building in the middle of the slide. From the ICon building, there were twenty five thin arrows pointing down to small graphics of computer terminals.

"We provide a critical link between these small websites and the credit card companies." He motioned his sculpted arm from the bottom to the top of the slide. "We are the link to internet commerce."

Gary leaned over and whispered to Thomas. "He looks like the *missing* link." Thomas tried to hide a smirk.

"We have a portal which allows all of these non-merchant websites to route their credit card transactions to ICon. When a website's customer wants to purchase something, he will click on a link on the website and it will go to ICon's secure pay page. The customer enters his credit card information and then submits the transaction for approval. The transaction is sent to our proprietary computer platform, which we call Velocity, that receives the transaction, confirms that all necessary information has been entered by the customer, implements fraud-detection software, and then it sends the transaction to the credit card company for approval."

"Once approved, the transaction reverses course and flows back through ICon's system. If the transaction is approved, a message is sent directly to the customer who sees a 'transaction approved' notice, and a separate notice is sent to the website. The dollar amount of the transaction is then sent from the credit card company to ICon and, after we take out our fee, we wire the money to the website. Because of the sheer number of transactions taking place, we usually delay payment to the websites for five business days from the date of the transaction. That gives us time to make sure that we don't have any accounts receivables or other charges from the website that we need to deduct before we pay. The amazing part is all of this happens in seconds – from the moment the customer hits 'submit' to when he sees the approval notice. It's totally seamless and totally automated."

"What is ICon's fee based on?" Sheila asked as she was flipping through the binder in front of her. "The number of transactions or the amount of the transaction?"   "We typically get paid a per transaction fee. The normal range is seven to ten cents on each transaction. Our business is quantity based. It really doesn't cost us anymore in variable expenses to process a one dollar transaction as opposed to a thousand dollar transaction. The flow is exactly the same. In certain cases, though, if the website is selling high dollar merchandise but has a comparatively low number of transactions, like diamonds, we'll work out a different deal, maybe even a mix between a volume and a dollar amount."

"How does your normal fee compare to your competitors' fee?"

"Everyone is in the seven to ten cents range. The price is somewhat limited to that range because, don't forget, the credit card companies also are taking a piece, usually a bigger piece, maybe ten to fifteen cents. So together with the processor's fee, that can be almost twenty cents for every transaction. For small websites, that can be a big chunk and any more can get too cost prohibitive to operate. We have a wink-wink with our friends not to go out of that range for most customers."

He demonstrated a wink as if the SouthPoint team did not understand the reference. Thomas clenched his jaw at the antitrust implications of Troy's nonchalant comment. Something else to worry about, he thought.

Sheila continued her inquiry. "When do you record revenue on each transaction?"

"You can tell she's our CFO," Gary quipped to the amusement of the group.

Troy looked cluelessly towards Jane Weaver, ICon's lead accountant. "I think that one's yours," Troy said.

Jane sipped her coffee before she began. She was beautiful, a rarity for an accountant and not at all what the men on the other side of the table had expected. Her glasses teased them trying to hide her dark eyes.

"Technically, we earn the revenue as soon as we send the transaction to a credit card company, regardless of whether it is approved or not. The amount of revenue may differ, but some amount is earned. At the end of each day, I run a report in Velocity that tells me how many transactions we sent that day, how many were approved, and how many were denied. Each transaction is coded automatically with the internet protocol address of our client's pay page, so we know the specific rate for the client. The report then calculates the revenue generated for each client for each day, and we enter a journal entry each night recognizing the revenue. We record a receivable and book a bad debt allowance of around ten percent."

"Hmm, that's pretty high," Sheila remarked.

"Well, our clients tend to be small and, uh let me say, transitory." She shifted in her chair sensing Alan's unapproving gaze.

"We also keep a percentage for charge backs, which is when a customer later claims that he didn't make the purchase and asks the credit card company to refund his money. To protect ourselves from losing money when this happens, we hold onto a small percentage of the transaction amount. If there is no charge back within forty five days of the transaction, we give the rest of the money to the client. We don't record revenue on this piece because it's not ours."

"What if the credit card company doesn't approve the charge," Vic blurted out wanting more to engage in the conversation with Jane than to understand the process.

Jane looked over at Vic exactly as he intended. "Good question," she responded. He tried unsuccessfully to hide his grin.

"Our clients are obligated to pay us a small fee for each denial, usually about two cents per denial, but only after a certain number of denials occurs each month. I think the number is one thousand. To be honest, our variable cost for processing a denial is essentially zero, especially when you're talking about processing nearly half a million transactions a day. We don't incur the costs to manage a payment like we do if it's an approval. A denial really is just an electrical impulse. But, we want to dissuade our clients from filling up the channels with bad transactions and, believe it or not, the revenue we earn on denials is not insignificant."

She turned back to Sheila. "Maybe that's more than you asked for, but I knew that you were going to ask about it." She nodded to Sheila and they seemed to share an understanding between accountants.

Troy looked impatient as he was still standing in front of the screen. He made sure the women were finished before he returned to his presentation.

"So, we have a variety of products, ranging from our Platinum Package, which is a complete website design and construction, pay page, daily and weekly reporting of all transaction analytics and a premium discount on our fees."

He clicked to the next slide that showcased ICon's suite of products. "Our Gold Package includes a pay page, daily reporting of all transaction analytics, and slightly less premium discounts on our fees. And, our Silver Package is our pay page with weekly analytics."

"Does the website client have access to its pay page? In other words, can the website see its customer's credit card information?" Thomas asked.

"Nope. The pay page is totally secure. It actually exists on Velocity, our computer platform. Each person that accesses a pay page through the website sees a completely new and different pay page, so there is no way for one customer to ever see another customer's information, or for our clients to see any customer's information. The pay page exists just long enough to complete the transaction, even if there are multiple attempts. Once the transaction is approved, or the user terminates the session, that pay page is backed up instantly and disappears. The computer nerds can tell you exactly what happens with the information, but I think it's stored by the IP address of the user."

"Then how do the websites know who their customers are if they don't see the customer's information?"

"Maybe I should show you what a pay page looks like. It only captures the credit card information."

Troy clicked the mouse and the slide changed to show a screen shot of a pay page emblazed with the now-familiar ICon logo. Down the middle of the page were boxes for a user to fill in his or her name, address, credit card number, CVVC number, expiration date, and billing address. Below was a paragraph with tiny print explaining ICon's limitation of liability and requiring the user to check that all of the terms and conditions were read and understood.

"Before the user gets to this page, our page," Troy continued, "the website typically collects the name and address, the shipping address if it's different, and anything else they want to ask for. So they get all of the user's contact information. Only after that does the user get the option to click to our secure pay page to input the credit card information and to buy whatever the website is selling."

A well-dressed younger executive sitting next to Troy spoke up for the first time. "The Computer Secrecy Act, passed by the Florida Legislature several years ago, requires that we continually monitor these pay pages to make sure that all user information is protected. We have to report on an immediate basis any exceptions we find. Every month, the State sends in an auditor to verify that our system is secure. All of the back ups of our system have to be kept offsite in a guarded warehouse and inventoried. We even have to transport them under lock and key by armored car. You can imagine with all of the identity fraud out there, this is a very tightly regulated industry. And data protection costs a lot. It is by far the largest expense we have, about eighteen percent of all operating costs. The politicians in Tallahassee are trying to pass a law that would increase that to five years, and require full back ups of the data instead of incremental back ups. That would raise data storage costs almost twenty five percent. Believe me, it keeps me up at night."

"What more can a father ask of his son?" Alan interrupted gesturing towards the young man. "This is my son Cain who is our in-house lawyer. I'm happy to say that we have no litigation pending against us. It's probably because Cain here is such a bulldog, just like his mother."

Cain nodded back at the end of the table, slightly embarrassed. There was not much resemblance between father and son, neither in physical appearance nor attire. Cain had short hair slicked back neatly and he was dressed sharply in a pinstripe suit. Shiny cuff links peeked out from the end of his jacket, and his gold tie was cinched in a tight knot. The SouthPoint team knew that ICon's in-house lawyer was the President's son, but only after seeing him did they realize that there were no pictures of Cain in Alan's office.

"On the plus side," Alan continued, "we've donated generously to our duly elected officials on the *right* side of the issue and, from what we're hearing, the bill isn't going to pass. Apparently, voters' fear at having their data lost takes a back seat to their need to shop online." He forced a chuckle, hoping to change the subject away from the cost of doing business to something more appetizing for a company considering shelling out $750 million for ICon.

"Why don't we take a break? Troy, are you done?" Alan looked hard at Troy strongly suggesting that he answer in the affirmative.

Troy nodded, receiving the signal loud and clear.

"Good. Good. Restrooms are down the hall and you're free to use the lobby or the room next door to make calls or to beat down all the emails you missed."

The executives shuffled out of their seats. The SouthPoint team leisured their way out of the conference room and split in one direction towards the restrooms and one towards the lobby.

"What the hell Cain?" Alan barked after the conference room door shut.

"What?"

"We're trying to sell the goddamn company and they've showed up with a big fat checkbook. Bringing up the storage costs and the bad legislation is not helping."

Jane and Troy sleeked together out of the room as if trying to distance themselves from a sibling getting in trouble.

"It's all in the offering documents," Cain stammered in his defense. "They've obviously read it. I'm not telling them anything they don't know. And it would raise more questions if we just avoided discussing it at all. How would that look? I also think we should tell them about the other issue that's *not* in the documents," Cain retorted with a smart tone that only the President's son could get away with.

Alan slammed the table with his open hand and stared at Cain. "We talked about that dammit! Not a fucking word."

Cain glared downward in reaction to being scolded.

After a moment, Alan slowly unclenched and took a deep breath still staring at his son.

"Listen Cain, we're *this* close." His voice softened as he motioned an inch with his fingers. "We need this deal . . . I need this deal. So don't blow it. I know that you've been going through a lot lately, but just hang in there a little longer and you'll able to do whatever you want . . . *we'll* be able to do whatever we want. Okay?" Alan asked lightly gripping Cain's shoulder from across the table and nodding a question mark to him.

"Okay," Cain said looking back at his father. "Okay."

* * *

"You know that those things are addicting, right?"

Gary was standing in the lobby and looked up from his cell phone. Alan approached him with a smile from across the lobby.

"Hell yeah," Gary said, "but at least they don't leave lipstick on my collar like my last addiction." He cackled at himself and slid the phone into his jacket pocket.

"Why don't I give you a look around while the bean counters back there add up all the beans?"

"Sounds good to me. Due diligence is well beneath my pay grade anyway." His Southern drawl floated across the lobby.

Gary took an instant liking to Alan. Although Alan had a different style and swagger, he was an entrepreneur and a self-made man. In Gary's mind, that made him a peer.

The two men walked past the receptionist and stopped at a secured door with a blinking key pad. Alan swiped a pass card and entered a code on the key pad. The door buzzed and Alan led Gary into the heart of the operations center of ICon. There were rows of cubicles filled with employees, but it was oddly quiet other than the clicking of keyboards. A few people turned to look as the door opened, but most ignored the two executives walking down the hallway.

"These are our customer service reps. They handle issues that may come up with our clients, changes in their access agreements, upgrades to their websites, and all the typical schmoozing that we do for customer relations."

"Looks like you have a full house."

"More the merrier. Each rep usually services around twenty clients, and we have about five hundred clients."

"Who are *they*?" Gary asked pointing to several rows of people with headphones and computer terminals in a separate room encased with a thick glass wall and protected by another secured door. A video camera on the ceiling stared down at the door.

"That's our call center. We call it the fishbowl. They talk directly to the customer using the pay page. They might get a call if the customer is having a problem entering his information or having some issue with the approval process."

"How come they are segregated?"

"Because they have direct access to our customers' credit card information. They can see the pay page that a customer is accessing. They see everything from the person's name, address, credit card number, and what they're buying. As Cain said, this information is highly sensitive and we have to take all kinds of security measures. They've had complete criminal background checks, they get drug tested every two weeks, and they consent to allowing us to see their personal bank account records if we want. The computers that they're using are only connected to our Velocity platform. They do not have internet access, they can't send emails from in there, they can't print or copy any information, and there are no USB ports or external drives on the computers. Each day that they come to work, they are screened and can't bring anything in."

"Sounds like fun," Gary said sarcastically. "Why would anyone want that job?"

"Money, my friend. We pay them very well to swim in the fishbowl."

"Hmm, I guess so."

Gary glanced back over the field of cubicles and saw a thin man on the far side of the room eying him. He had wiry black hair and dark eyebrows. The man's stare was more than one of curiosity about a stranger in ICon's offices. He was watching Gary intently. Gary looked away, and then he instinctively peeked back to see if he really was the intended recipient of the man's glare. The man had not moved, nor had his stare abated.

"Do you have kids?" Alan asked as they walked past the glass room, oblivious to the exchange of glances between Gary and the probing man across the room.

"Huh?" Gary said, trying to shake off the uncomfortable stare. "Oh, two girls. Well they'll always be little girls to me. One's an accountant and one's an artist. They couldn't be more different from each other, but somehow they're *both* like their mother. I'll never understand it. Anyway, despite my youthful appearance," Gary paused as he tapped his gray thinning hairline in jest, "I have my first grandchild on the way."

"Congratulations Grandpa. The accountant or the artist?"

"The accountant. The artist is too busy looking for her inner Picasso somewhere in Paris."

Chuckling, Alan said "well I never had that problem with Cain. He was born with a briefcase in his hand. Motivation was never his problem. You know those kids who put up lemonade stands? Well, Cain was the kid who franchised the stands and had the other kids working for him. It took a while, though, for him to find his path. *That* he got from his dad. He's my only child. His mother and I split when he was five, and let me tell you, alimony is a pretty good form of birth control."

Gary laughed from deep in his belly.

"The father-son thing has always been important to me," Alan continued. "If you think about it, throughout time wealth and power have always been passed from father to son. Kings bestowed empires upon their sons. Tycoons tapped their sons to take over their fortunes. It may be genetic or just plain chauvinistic. But I've always felt this sense that I need to leave something for my son."

Alan paused as they continued to walk through the hallway. "To be honest, that's a big reason why ICon is in play. I want to capitalize on what I've built so that he'll have some security. Whether he stays on with the company or does something else, he'll have it much easier than I did. Maybe it's to make up for what I didn't give him when he was growing up, or maybe it's just to make me feel better. Either way, $750 million should do the trick," Alan joked, patting Gary on the shoulder.

"Come in here and let me show you something pretty cool." Alan gestured Gary towards a room with several large computer monitors. "This is our training room. Here, sit in that chair."

Gary sat down in front of one of the screens and Alan stood next to him. Alan typed in a password and the screen in front of Gary lit up. The word *Velocity* flashed onto the screen, and the graphic made it appear that the word was speeding across the screen. Gary watched as Alan moved the curser through various programs.

"Here we go," Alan said as he was clicking.

A moving three dimensional graph appeared with detailed graphics. An array of colored lines snaked horizontally across the screen, as if reading a patient's EKG. The lines carved mountain peaks and valleys as the graph's grid moved perpetually underneath. A thick black line recorded the volume of transactions being processed, while other colored lines displayed information about the transactions. Approvals, declines, average dollar amounts, charge back ratios. Each metric of ICon's business was being displayed. Various numerical counters on the screen clicked upwards, ranging from total daily revenue to year-to-date revenue. Every credit card transaction that was processed by ICon's computer system – hundreds of them each second – came alive on Velocity.

Alan leaned over to the screen that Gary was watching and pointed out the different metrics that were being displayed.

"This is the pulse of the company. I can see how we're doing on a real-time basis and I can get instant trending information down to the second. Day over day, month over month, year over year. Whatever I want to look at is here and is being recorded. I can tell which segments are out performing others, and drill down to a granular level. There also is a separate tab for every client, so with a click or two I can see the volume of their business streaming over any period."

Alan clicked a drop down menu with hundreds of client names in alphabetical order. He scrolled down and clicked on homeshowcase. com. The moving graph instantly changed to mirror homeshowcase. com's real-time performance.

"I can run any number of reports that will list the clients that are performing under or over budget. It's a great tool to see where we need to make tweaks and where we have problem areas. And, get this. I can also switch modes to pull up the streaming numbers for any of our sales reps. Every transaction that is keyed to a rep's client is displayed in the same way. Let's see how Carlos is doing today."

Alan moved the cursor to an icon on the menu and, after clicking another drop down list, the screen changed to display the current performance of one of ICon's salesman.

"As always, Carlos's numbers look good." Alan proudly watched the graphics. He of course knew that Carlos was one of ICon's leading salesmen and his performance would not disappoint.

"The best part is that there is no waiting until the accountants close the books to see how the business is doing, and no guessing at the end of the quarter about whether we're going to make our numbers. These are gross revenue numbers that you see there, but I have a good idea about our run rate on expenses, so I pretty much know where our net income is at any point. Only Jane and I have the pass codes to see all of this, and of course our IT guy. George Orwell would be proud, huh?"

Alan paused to let it all sink in for Gary. The computer system was without question the most sophisticated in the industry. Millions of transactions racing through Velocity every day. Each one being recorded, measured, and analyzed. Three dimensional graphs vibrantly illustrating every twist and turn of the business, of each client, and even of each salesperson. The almost unfathomable ability to instantaneously know exactly how the company was performing - twenty four hours a day, seven days a week. On top of that, algorithms programmed into Velocity constantly mined the historical data in order to produce near perfect projections about the future performance of the business, of each client, and, of course, even of each salesperson. Never missing a target; never blowing a budget; never over paying an employee. It was a CEO's wet dream.

In a private company with only a few owners, that kind of information can be leveraged and even exploited by the wishes - and the riches - of the owners. However, in a public company where millions of shareholders own the company, that kind of information is absolute power. The power to essentially control the stock price of a publicly traded company by never missing Wall Street's earnings estimates. For a CEO, it meant perpetual job security. If a company's stock price falls within a projected range of estimates, the stock market smiles on the stock. But if a company misses its earnings estimates, a stock price invariably will drop. And the further it drops the more pain that ensues. More than a few ticks down, and day traders may start to scamper. For the big publicly traded companies, that exodus would be nothing more than a rounding error. But for many other smaller companies, if shareholders begin to sell their stock it could trigger larger investors to pivot to another benefactor.

Gone are the days when frantic men with thinning hair and hoarse voices controlled trading from the littered floors of the stock exchanges. In their place are quiet and calm computer servers in cooled refrigerated rooms. Buy and sell orders are based on hyper-complex programs dashing through trillions of transactions. Human thought is dangerously too slow and sporadic to make real money. Instead, infinitely small microprocessors decide the fluctuation of hundreds of millions of dollars in trading. They buy and sell without thinking, and without remorse.

Once the momentum surges away from a stock, it sometimes is

unstoppable. In the blink of an eye, bad news about a company can turn a solid business into a burning Hindenburg. The first to go usually is the CEO who, more often than not, had no control over the stock price. Executives of public companies should install seatbelts into their plush leather chairs in the boardroom. The ride sometimes can be turbulent.

But the landing also sometimes can be soft. The lure of the capital markets is that with risk sometimes comes reward. No where else in the world or in any market of any kind can an idea launched in someone's garage sweep the globe and rake in billions. Momentum swings in both directions.

"So what do you think?"

Gary blinked at Alan's question, almost startled. His head had been swimming in the possibilities that this little company in Miami could open for SouthPoint. He had never seen anything like Velocity. The idea of being able to monitor ICon's performance in real time ensured that he would never miss his numbers and never let down SouthPoint's Board of Directors. Not seeing Hunter McMillan's craggy face snarl in the boardroom because of disappointing financial results was reason enough to do the deal with ICon. But the voyeuristic ability to watch as the dollars rolled in was addicting. He was hooked.

"Gawdamn, that's pretty slick." That was the most eloquent expression Gary could come up with to react to the flashing computer screen in front of him.

* * *

The Miami sun shimmered off of the sea and baked the myriad of bronzed sunbathers. The beach was alive with a circus of people, and the ocean breeze carried a symphony of sounds and smells. Looking around, Raul removed his sunglasses and wiped his brow, revealing his jagged scar above his right eye. A teenager on a skateboard whizzed by him and blurted out an obscenity to get out of the way. Raul had heard far worse, but he nevertheless heeded the youth's advice and joined the flow of people on the sidewalk.

After a few minutes, he spotted a concrete bench worn by the salted air. He sat down and stared out over the beach, not acknowledging the man sitting next to him on the bench.

"You're late," said the man next to him in an Eastern European accent. Despite the heat, he was wearing denim jeans and a black shirt. He had a hard pitted face that had seen too much.

"I was sightseeing," Raul quipped back sarcastically. A sun-kissed blonde woman in a tiny thong walked past. She had the kind of a body designed for the skimpy suit, and both men watched in silent respect as she walked away.

"My partners and I are growing concerned about some activity at the company."

Raul paused purposefully, still looking out over the beach. "I don't know what you're talking about, things are going fine."

"Don't fuck with me," the thick-faced man said reminiscent of Arnold Schwarzenegger in any of his action movies. "Who are the suits visiting ICon? You get one chance to tell me amigo." He emphasized *amigo* mocking his Spanish colleague.

Raul flirted with a couple of stories, but he knew that the threat was real. During his time with the DEA, Raul had come across men who were evil and others who only acted evil. There was a difference, and on more than one occasion his survival had depended on telling them apart. The man sitting next to him probably was in the latter category, but Raul knew that his partners were not. He had to dance carefully around the truth.

"Alan was meeting with a bank from Atlanta, something about a secured financing deal or credit revolver. Management wants to expand the platform and they're looking for financing alternatives. There were some people down for due diligence."

With a twinge of contrived frustration, Raul added, "Alan doesn't tell me everything, you know." He hoped his foreign counterpart would be satisfied with the half truth.

The man stared straight ahead and grumbled "nothing better affect our interests." After a pause to watch another bikini pass by, he continued. "How is the project?"

"Working as planned," Raul answered. "The ratio threshold has not been breached. There was a slight bug with the auto activation, but it seems to be under control. We've cleared a few months and the numbers are good, but we have to know when you're going to press so we can be prepared."

"You'll know what you have to know."

The man stood and walked away, leaving a rumpled copy of the Miami Herald on the bench. Raul waited a few moments, glancing up and down the crowded sidewalk. He picked up the newspaper and squeezed it to make sure it contained a thick envelope of cash. He stood, put the rolled up newspaper under his arm, and blended into the sidewalk traffic.

CHAPTER FIVE

*How many crimes are committed simply because
their authors could not endure being wrong.*
-- Albert Camus

The Night of the Deal

The sound of a steak knife tapping a crystal glass rang out over the chattering dinner table. The executives of SouthPoint and ICon came to a slow hush as Gary stood to make a toast. Just hours before, the same group had gathered around a different table and had signed the merger agreement. SouthPoint's bankers wired $750 million in cash to ICon's bankers in return for sole ownership of ICon. With the stroke of a few pens, all of ICon's employees instantly became SouthPoint's employees, and all of ICon's customers became SouthPoint's customers. The three quarters of a billion dollars bought all of ICon's assets and its hopefully long-lived revenue streams. It also bought ICon's liabilities - even those that were unknown to SouthPoint.

Liabilities, however, were the furthest thing from Gary's mind. He was well primed after downing a few Glenlivits, and he battled gravity to stand and make a toast.

"I'd like to say a few words," he paused trying to come up with the promised few words. "I don't really have anything to say, I just want to slow ya'll down a little on those $400 bottles of wine. After spending $750 million, this bar tab may put me under!"

Laughter filled the private room of the elegant City Club, one of Miami's most exclusive restaurants. The room was adorned with two crystal chandeliers bowing over a rich cherry table. Thick leather chairs circled the oval table, which was draped with a gold macramé cloth and set with ivory china. A wall of glass from floor to ceiling crowned the room and overlooked the bay. The masts of sailboats parked in the marina below reached up and pierced the view.

"Seriously . . . let me welcome the ICon team into the SouthPoint family. We're excited about the partnership and taking our combined companies to the next level. I have gotten to know Alan and his team over the past weeks and, in spite of Alan's wardrobe, I think we'll get along famously." The others cackled and raised their glasses.

Gary winked at Alan, who was clad in a half open Tommy Bahama shirt and thin Italian loafers. Alan's designer sunglasses were perched on his head, even though the sun had gone down long ago. He might have been mistaken for a kitschy tourist who mistakenly wandered into the corporate dinner. The manager of the City Club, however, warmly welcomed Alan with an embrace when the party arrived. Alan was well known at the restaurant, and his penchant for expensive wine was legendary.

At the far end of the table, Cain reached across and clinked his champagne glass with Thomas' glass. With the deal consummated, the two lawyers had each accomplished their client's objectives. But neither of them knew exactly what goals the other had. Lawyers are trained to advise against full disclosure to another side in a deal. There is an understood dance that is performed during negotiations. Lead a little, but don't get led. Try not to step on the other side's toes, but let them know when you're putting your foot down. It sometimes is difficult to know when the dance is over.

Thomas liked Cain in an odd, understanding kind of way. He was intrigued by Cain's drive and impressed by his business savvy. He clearly beat to a different drum than his father, and he seemed to be confident in the path that he chose. In many ways, he saw Cain as a younger, perhaps more ambitious, version of himself.

"Can I buy my new boss a real drink?" Cain asked pointing his frail champagne flute towards the bar downstairs.

"Absolutely," Thomas said. "You're well on your way to your first promotion."

The bar at the City Club was packed with the kind of beautiful people that made Miami an international hot spot. The women and the men seemed to be plucked for admission to the hopping scene, while the other diners could only gawk at the perfect bodies and striking smiles from their far off dinner tables.

Thomas followed Cain as he made a path through to the bar, thanking each person for safe passage. Whiffs of perfume swirled around them as they passed women fumed with Dior and Chanel. A light roar of laughter and conversation drowned out the faint beat of dance music overhead. As they approached the bar, Thomas could see that it was glowing with light blue and teal lights. Behind the bustling bartenders was a massive saltwater tank glimmering with technicolor reef fish.

Cain glanced down the shiny bar and spotted his friend. "Ray," he shouted over the crowd. A chiseled Latino behind the bar turned and smiled at Cain at the other end. He wore a tight black t-shirt that curved around his chest.

"What's shaking," the bartender said as he did a combination handshake and fist pump with Cain. "Last time I saw you, we were at the Diamond Club party. Man, those strippers were off the hook."

Cain chucked nervously and tried to ignore the unexpected social revelation. He introduced Thomas as the General Counsel of his new parent company, emphasizing *General Counsel*. Ray quickly understood the import of Thomas' title and Cain's obvious deference to his new superior. The grinning bartender extended his hand to Thomas and tried to brush off his faux pas.

"Nice to meet you. If you're a friend of Cain's, then you really do need a drink," he said sarcastically. "What can I get you?"

Thomas quickly realized that Cain complimented his rigorous business persona with an equally ambitious social life.

"McCallum, double barrel on the rocks, thanks," Thomas ordered.

"I'll take a Tanqueray and tonic," Cain followed. "Thanks Ray." Cain turned towards Thomas and leaned close to speak over the revelry. "It's all about who you know in this city. Forget the bankers and brokers. If you know the bartenders, you're set."

Thomas nodded with a smile as they both watched an immaculately tanned woman with tight curves saunter past them in a completely open-back dress. As if being true to an unwritten male code, Cain winked at Thomas with an understanding smirk. The intoxicating mixture of money, sun, and sex fueled Miami's economy and ignited its soul. And it was on full display that night. After gazing at the sights for a few more minutes, they walked back to the private room on the far side of the restaurant.

The executives of ICon and SouthPoint were now mingling together and getting to know their new business partners. A waitress in a tuxedo uniform walked between the groups serving crispy coconut shrimp on a silver platter.

Thomas tapped Cain on the shoulder and motioned across the room towards the platinum blonde woman in a skin tight black dress hanging on Troy's think arm. "So what's the story with Troy's date?"

The vacuum-packed dress squeezed her bulging chest together, and the hem line inched upwards revealing her perfectly tanned upper thighs. She had the kind of body that made it physically difficult for most men to look away, regardless of how pious one may be. But her body was more than an attribute; it was a source of revenue. Slinking around brass poles in Miami's most exclusive adult clubs earned her a healthy six figures a year.

"That's Fawn . . . obviously a stage name," Cain replied. "Troy likes to show off."

Troy cocked his chest and proudly had his meaty arm around her tiny waist. It looked as if with one swift motion he could toss her across the room. He relished in the gazes of the other men eyeing his catch. A wry grin was cemented on his thick face as his date was giggling at something Vic was telling them. It was painfully apparent that Vic was enjoying entertaining her.

"Troy had an ugly divorce a few years ago, and he's had a taste for the fast lane ever since. She dances at one of the strip clubs down in South Beach."

"Really," Thomas said as glanced over again with a renewed, although not unexpected, sense of interest.

The two lawyers stood next to each other, both still gazing at Troy's show-and-tell, while Vic continued his comedy routine. Vic was flailing his hairy arms around gesturing the visual part of a joke that surely would only get worse with the added dramatics. He was not doing a very good job of keeping his eyes off of Fawn's pillowy chest, but he clearly was oblivious to his obviousness. Troy scanned the room desperately for someone to come rescue them from Vic.

"Troy's a damn good salesman," Cain said after a moment. "You probably know from the commission reports that he's our top producer. He made more last year than our next three salesmen combined. You don't say 'no' to Troy . . . if you know what I mean. But if you ask me, he's really a street thug dressed up in a nice suit. He just knows the right people."

They continued to watch Vic's comedy routine and his antics kept Fawn from catching their glares.

"You know that he pulled in a whale last year that broke the scales." Cain added, taking the last sip of his drink.

Thomas finally pulled his gaze away from Fawn's showcase and turned to Cain.

"A whale?"

Cain answered but he kept looking at Fawn. "A whale is a client. A big client. In Troy's case, it was the biggest damn client."

Thomas hesitated before asking the question that nearly rolled off his tongue. *Which client?* His pause was not because the question was irrelevant, but because he should have known the answer. Here they were celebrating the closing of the biggest deal either had been involved in, long after the lawyers had sifted through the due diligence materials, and Thomas did not know the name of ICon's biggest client. Not a way to impress your newest in-house lawyer.

Thomas raced in his head through the multiple spreadsheets and reports about ICon's business that he had seen during due diligence. The conference room that ICon had set up for the SouthPoint team was filled with boxes and folders crammed with data about ICon's business. Thomas had peeked his head into the room on their first day at ICon the previous month, but it was up to the investment bankers to actually dig into the data and to interview ICon's management.

After the bankers emerged from the morass, they prepared an insanely overpriced PowerPoint presentation for Thomas and the others on SouthPoint's executive team. That presentation highlighted the key metrics of ICon's business and established a range of prices that would be fair prices for the company. It is called a fairness opinion, and the price tag usually starts in the six figures.

Thomas had studied the fairness opinion about ICon that the investment bankers sent him in a glossy binder with a sleek marketing logo that clearly no banker created. But he did not remember anything about a big new client, let alone *the biggest damn client*. Certainly a catch the size of what Cain described would have shown up somewhere in the presentation. If anything to make sure that SouthPoint knew that a big part of ICon's revenues were brand new. Thomas could feel his worry about the deal begin to percolate.

As he stood looking over the room of mingling executives, he silently cursed Hunter McMillan. Sitting in his cordovan throne as the Chairman of SouthPoint's Board of Directors, McMillan had been too far removed from the teller's window to remember what drives the banking business. *Bricks and mortar make a company strong and its revenues long.* When did that philosophy fly out of the window?

McMillan now cared only about Wall Street's expectations and the Bank's stock price. One of his favorite ways to stroke both at the same time was through acquisitions. SouthPoint buys a company that is making money and overnight the revenue is added to the bank's bottom line. Sell some of the new company's assets, terminate some of the employees, and the Bank makes a few more millions as pocket change. This cycle can continue until either the stock price falls or an acquisition implodes. And the speed at which McMillan had SouthPoint buy ICon seemed to hasten the latter result.

Thomas wished they had more time to have conducted the due diligence of ICon. Two weeks was not enough to be sure they caught everything. But McMillan had pushed the deal to close before SouthPoint's annual shareholder meeting, which was quickly approaching. McMillan was desperate for a favorable bump up in the Bank's stock price and he needed a quick infusion of revenue.

This year's meeting posed a different risk for McMillan. It was the year that his two closest confidants on the board were up for election. The terms of the directors were staggered so that on any one year only two directors are up for election. If the Bank reported profits again, his allies would be safe. And that meant his control would be cemented.

McMillan had long ago seen this shareholder meeting looming

on the calendar, and he had pushed the Bank into investments that broached the top of the Bank's risk tolerance. To Thomas anyway, McMillan was trying to drive up revenue in the short term at the expense of future profits. But what did Thomas know? He was just the in-house lawyer. Just the lawyer who was responsible for SouthPoint's latest acquisition, and whose ass was really on the line.

"Well, looks like Troy's living the American dream," Thomas said with a hint of sarcasm and a dash of envy. He made a mental note to find out about Troy's new "whale" – and why he was not told about it before SouthPoint opened up its checkbook.

"Let me give you a friendly tip that you didn't find in our private placement memorandum," Cain began. "If we keep that goon over there happy, the cash flow will come, and it will keep coming. But between you and me . . . ," Cain leaned in towards Thomas. "I'm not exactly sure what the deal is with Troy's new client. I wasn't involved in drafting the contract or working out the terms. I don't even know what websites it operates. It was all very hush hush between Troy and Alan."

It sounded strange to Thomas that Cain called Alan by his first name. There was an odd distance between father and son that no amount of due diligence could have detected.

Cain finally looked away from Fawn and faced Thomas. "Look, I'm not saying that there's anything wrong going on . . . I'm just saying." Cain intended his unfinished comment to convey a message to his new boss.

Thomas took a long sip of his cocktail. Just two hours after the deal with ICon, and Thomas' stomach already was tight with worry.

CHAPTER SIX

*Whoever is detected in a shameful fraud is ever
after not believed even if they speak the truth.*
-- Phaedrus

One Month After The Deal

The black Land Rover turned into the entrance of Peachtree-DeKalb airport just outside of metro Atlanta. Jake followed the signs to Corporate Aviation, which offered luxury services for a fleet of executive jets. As he turned a corner, he saw the shiny glass building ahead. A circular drive complimented the grand entrance with a covered canopy. He eased the SUV to a stop as a uniformed valet darted to his door to open it.

"Welcome Sir. Which flight are you on this morning?"

"I'm on the SouthPoint flight to Miami," Jake answered handing his keys to the energetic valet.

"Very good, I'll take care of your car. If you walk through the glass doors and go to your right, you'll see the departure lounge where you can get coffee or breakfast before your flight."

The thin glass doors to the airport sprung open and Jake walked through the gleaming lobby towards the lounge. There were no check in gates, no security lines, and no harried travelers running around. Instead, the corporate concourse resembled a four star hotel with every accommodation imaginable from business suites to massage services. The soothing sound of a spouting water fountain in the center of the lobby drowned out the whirl of airplanes. This was the poster child of the era of corporate excess, and the kind of executive perk that caused shareholders to boil. Jake had investigated countless abuses of similar benefits, but standing in the vast lobby he could not help but relish in the VIP treatment. This is how the corporate elite travelled.

Jake walked into the departure lounge and scanned the room for Thomas. Flat screen televisions dotted the walls blaring CNN in front of business-clad executives hacking away on laptops. At the far end of the room, a bartender was filling orders of orange juice and Bloody Mary's.

Jake spotted Thomas on a couch nestled behind a wrinkled Wall Street Journal. He made his way over to his client.

"Don't believe everything you read."

Thomas lowered the paper and saw his friend.

"Hey there," he said standing and shaking Jake's hand. "How come the only time I see you is when I have a problem?"

"Because that's the only time you need me anymore," Jake said with a chuckle.

When they were partners at Levi & Everett, they had spent hundreds of billable hours working together on cases, and countless non-billable hours working together on their golf game. You get to know a lot about someone when you share the pressure in a courtroom and the pain on a par five.

When Thomas walked into Jake's office at the firm and closed the door, Jake knew that an announcement was imminent. In a law firm, when someone walks in and closes the door, someone has either died or is leaving the firm. In some cases, the effect may be exactly the same. Jake had heard Thomas lament more than once over a beer about the pressures of a law firm and the demands of tracking every six minutes of your life.

For a lawyer who thrives for the biggest dollar cases with the whitest shoe clients, there is no better place to work than at a big law firm – as long as you are making money year over year. Like any other business, it is a numbers game. In a law firm there are only two main questions asked of each partner at the end of the year . . . at the end of every year. What were your billable hours over the last twelve months? And how much money did you bring in? Good results for your clients, of course, are important and are applauded. But answer those two questions favorably, and you can count on a healthy bonus and an upward trajectory.

The moment the hours dip or the collections sag, however, the anxiety starts to build. One slow year can be overlooked, but two years turns into a trend. The first sign of institutional displeasure comes in the form of a year without a bonus. The second sign is usually a reduced partnership draw. The third sign comes when the managing partner walks in and closes the door. Only those whose compensation depends on the tally of their hours can truly appreciate the stress of being slow.

After ten years, Thomas was ready to get off the ride – and Jake could not have been happier for him. He watched as his friend eased into the top lawyer post at SouthPoint, and eased into a smoother path for him. It was the right fit at the right time. So when Thomas walked into Jake's office that afternoon and shut the door behind him, Jake immediately began to grin.

"Well, we may have a problem with this one," Thomas said folding the newspaper. "Thanks for coming, especially on short notice. Are you alone?"

"No, an associate of mine is coming." Jake glanced around the room feigning that he was looking for someone in particular, but he really had no idea which associate had answered the late night call. "Why don't we wait outside in the lobby and we'll spot him . . . or her."

Thomas glanced over curiously at Jake's uncertainty, but Jake just kept walking towards the lobby hoping that he could outrun Thomas' look.

The serene lobby of Peachtree-DeKalb private airport was dotted with business people in sharp suits and coiffed hairstyles. There were no children tugging on strollers or vacationers mingling in flowered shirts. This was business, pure business. Only the sound of falling water from the fountain in the center echoed through the atrium. It seemed a thousand miles away from the hectic concourses of Hartsfield-Jackson International Airport, the busiest airport in the world just twenty-two miles to the south.

The smooth glass doors to the lobby slid apart and a harried young man scampered into the lobby. His unblemished briefcase gave away his inexperience, and his frantic stride gave away his tardiness. A striped tie flapped at his side and his briefcase clung behind him on its shoulder strap as if trying desperately to hold on.

Alex Perry had been an associate at Levi & Everett for exactly nine hours, most of which was spent learning how to work the phones and computer. He had not yet recorded his first real billable hour, and now he was racing through a private airport to join a partner who he had never met on a case he knew nothing about. Welcome to the big time he thought.

He hoped that he would recognize Jake from his picture on the firm's website. He glanced again down at his iPhone and saw the stiff picture of L&E's senior partner glaring back. The photograph clearly had been taken of a younger man, and not surprisingly, it had never been updated over the years. As he scurried on the polished tile floor, Alex silently prayed that the years had not changed Jake's appearance too much.

As if on cue, he saw two men walk into the lobby from the lounge. Alex's eyes instantly locked with the man on the right. That's him. Jake Morgan. It was that strange kind of fate that usually only happens in the movies. Jake's website picture had been taken a good ten years earlier, but his blonde wavy hair had stood the test of time.

Alex slid to a stop just three feet in front of the two men. But by the look of Alex's apprehensive expression, he was not convinced that his new Johnston Murphy dress shoes were going to take hold in time to stop. He caught his briefcase as it swung towards them, and he tried nonchalantly to stuff it behind his back. Thomas and Jake stopped abruptly in even stride surprised by the young man who suddenly skidded towards them.

"Mr. Morgan," Alex said catching his breath while extending his hand to Jake. "Sorry I'm running late."

Jake shook Alex's anxious hand. He clearly was the chosen associate, but Jake did not know his name.

After an awkward second of silence, the young associate keenly detected that Jake had no idea who he was. As Jake tried to stammer out an introduction, Alex quickly turned to Thomas.

"Nice to meet you, I'm Alex Perry." He turned to shake Thomas' hand.

Thomas regained his composure and reached for Alex's outstretched hand. "I'm Thomas Nelson. Welcome to the team."

Alex turned back to Jake who tried to recover. "Alex," Jake said emphasizing his name as if he had just remembered it. "You're right on time."

"Well, if we're all here, the plane is ready," Thomas said. "Follow me and I can bring you guys up to speed on the way down."

As they turned to walk towards the gate, Jake glanced back at Alex.

"Thanks for the save. And, for coming on short notice."

"You bet," Alex said enthusiastically. He had an easy smile that was instantly endearing.

Jake saw a glimpse of excitement in Alex's eyes that he remembered he used to get as a young associate. Being called on an emergency assignment and getting to fly to the scene in a corporate jet was just the kind of scenario that charged Jake. He remembered the anxiety as his nerves bristled at the uncertainties that lay ahead.

The three of them strode down the airport corridor as the rhythmic tapping of their shoes echoed on the marble floor. It was like a business march. Corporate solders on an official mission, armed with legal firepower and sharp intuition. Jake grinned just barely as he imagined the military analogy, and he felt a surge of the excitement that he still got with every new investigation.

The tarmac of the private airport vibrated under their feet as a jet wailed down the runway. The three men boarded the sleek jet that waiting for them at the end of a long carpet runner. The Georgia morning sun shone off the plane's silver belly giving the appearance that it already was in flight. Inside the jet, the three lawyers huddled before take off.

"Here are copies of her exit questionnaire," Thomas said handing copies to Jake and Alex. "Read what she says, but also look at her tone. She's not angry. She's surprised she was fired. She loved her job. It's been a couple of weeks since she left and I haven't gotten a call from a lawyer screaming that she was wrongfully terminated and demanding money. She just took her stuff and said 'thank you' for the time. And, oh by the way, in a damn post scrip, she says 'you also might think about checking out these fraudulent international transactions. Have a nice day.' That's what scares me." Thomas paused for emphasis, but it was clear that he wasn't finished.

He shifted in his crème colored leather chair facing Jake and Alex across the thin aisle of the luxury jet. Polished wood outlined the lavish cabin of the eight seat airplane. Each of the seats had a smooth wood table garnished with gold pen and paper holders, laptop sockets, and a marble inlaid cup holder. Down the center of the aisle was a soft blue carpet with gold scripted letters reading *SouthPoint*. Executive privileges.

"I don't know if she's some nut jerking us around, or if she thinks she's the Enron whistleblower, but you guys have to figure it out pretty damn quickly."

"I hear you." Jake nodded. He tried to read the first page but his client's words rang in his head. He dared not yet ask about the deadline for the investigation, but *pretty damn quickly* did not bode well. He had no idea what was to come, or how little time he really had.

"Let me read this over."

Jake and Alex swiveled simultaneously in their leather chairs to face the front of the plane. The chairs glided softly into position. Jake looked over and caught Alex running his hand across the shiny wood trim.

"This is a pretty nice way to travel, huh?" Jake winked at Alex who was still taking it all in.

Alex nodded trying to veil his anticipation. He watched out of the window as the ramp agent signaled the pilot. He blinked hard to make sure it was not a dream. He had come a long way to get there.

Just three months before, he was trying not to trip over his graduation gown at his law school class crossed the stage and proudly accepted their coveted scrolls. From where he had been, law school seemed a million miles away. His grandmother had raised him and older brothers while his mother was busy working two jobs. College, let alone graduate school, did not seem to be in the cards.

But computers always came easy to him. Not the video games that most of his friends were hypnotized by, but the programming behind the façade. The languages; the codes. Maybe it was the simplicity of ones and zeros, or maybe it was growing up with a mouse in his hand. In any event, it kept him out of trouble. Sort of.

Three months before high school graduation, he got caught hacking into his school's computer system. He was not attempting to change his grades or to cause any mischief. Instead, he was testing a password detection program that he had developed for the final project in his computer class. The irony was not lost on his high school's forward-thinking - if not benevolent – principal who had seen promise in Alex from early on in school and had taken him under his wing. Mr. Mann, or as the students called him The Man, met with Alex every semester to make sure that he was headed in the right direction. With no father at home and an overworked mother, that special attention from the principal was like a godsend to Alex. Without it, he likely would have followed his brothers' path and dropped out of high school.

During one meeting, Alex noticed Mr. Mann fumbling with his computer unable to make it do whatever he wanted it to do. Within an hour, Alex had not only cured the computer of a nasty virus, but he also wrote a simple database program that the principal could use to plot the test scores of every student. From that point on, Mr. Mann refused to let Alex slide in his academics and Alex made sure that the principal's computer never crashed again.

After graduation, Alex moved sixty-five miles east to Athens, Georgia, and earned a computer business degree from the University of Georgia. But the bright promise of the computer industry was darkened by the dot.com bust. After his college commencement, he found himself toiling for a couple of years as a systems analyst. Instead of developing innovative computer codes, he was being dispatched to all corners of the country as an over-qualified troubleshooter. During his first year, he spent a total of twenty seven days in his apartment. The rest of the time he lived off of room service and airplane food as he rode the jet stream from east to west, and then back again. At the ripe old age of twenty-five, the constant travel caught up with him and he did what many lost souls end up doing - he went to law school. Just three years later, he was sitting on a $70 million plane about to plunge into a fraud investigation and he had not even billed his first full hour as an associate.

Suddenly the engines began to whirl and the plane rocked in place. Alex gripped the smooth armrest. It was a far cry from the cramped flights in coach squeezed between two snoring salesman. He was on his way . . . but he had no idea what was waiting for him.

The Gulfstream pivoted at the end of the runway and paused for a moment as if taking a deep breath before running a sprint. The whine of the turbojets escalated as the engines fought the brakes that held it still. An instant later the plane lurched forward and accelerated like a sports car down the runway. It leapt into the air and the landing gear quickly tucked into the plane's belly. The jet cut through the golden morning clouds as the lights of the Atlanta traffic below inched slowly towards downtown. They were on their way.

* * *

"Holy shit," Jake muttered, flipping the last page of the exit questionnaire. He swiveled towards Thomas who was tapping feverously on his Blackberry. Alex was still reading, but he saw Jake turn and did the same.

"There are a ton of red flags in here. Internal control issues. Tone at the top issues. A lack of transparency. Not to mention that she could be a whistleblower who was illegally terminated under Sarbanes-Oxley."

"So what's the bad news?" Thomas asked sarcastically. His sleepless night wore on his face but not on his wit.

"The bad news is that this looks to me like it could be true – at least she thinks it's true." Jake said holding up the questionnaire. "This took a long time for her to write and she put a lot of thought into it. Why would you go to all that trouble unless you really believed it was true? She even wrote paragraphs about what she liked about the job. We certainly need to approach this with a healthy degree of skepticism, but this doesn't bode well." Thomas knew that Jake was not an alarmist, but he started to feel that familiar pain in his stomach again.

"What else do we know about her?" Jake asked.

Alex instinctively clicked his pen ready to memorialize any new information.

Thomas breathed deeply. "I was saving the worst for last." He pulled out the thin manila folder from his briefcase and started thumbing through it. "This is her personnel file. Here's her employment application. College degree in Accounting. She's a CPA. She worked at KPMG and then in internal audit at some public tech company."

"Damn," Jake could not hold back his comment. He stared out of the tiny oval window down towards Earth. It was quiet in the plush cabin, other than the muted hum of the jet engines. Alex bravely broke the silence.

"Why is that bad?" He asked.

"It means that she knows what she's talking about," Jake answered still gazing into space.

Thomas added, "and she knew that we would have to follow up on this. She's expecting our call. Here, look on the back." Thomas motioned turning over his copy of the exit questionnaire. "She even wrote down her cell phone number."

Jake flipped over the document and saw the number with a 305 Miami area code next to *Patti cell* in loopy handwriting.

"I'm still holding out hope that there was just some misunderstanding." Thomas tried to make it sound possible, but he didn't even convince himself.

"Well, you never know with these kinds of things," Jake said trying to console his nervous client. "A new employee comes in asking questions like an auditor and rubs someone the wrong way. We'll know a lot more when we talk to her. The one thing that is always true about these kinds of investigations is that whatever appears on the surface is never the full story. I hate say it, but you have to expect the unexpected."

As if on cue, the jet hit some turbulence and bounced on the air pocket. Alex dropped his pen and grasped at his arm rest, unaccustomed to the exaggerated feel of turbulence on a small plane. He looked sheepishly towards Jake and Thomas who did not interrupt their conversation.

"Is that all?" Jake said pointing to Patti's personnel file.

"Just this." Thomas tossed Patti's security badge on the polished table in front of Jake. The granular photo showed a sandy blonde woman in her late thirties with wireless rim glasses resting on her thin nose. Her hair was pulled back tight in a bun. She seemed to have a muted attractiveness. Jake detected an uncomfortable smile on her, perhaps someone not used to posing for pictures. He handed the security badge to Alex, wondering to himself if he was looking at the face of a saint or a sinner.

"Look, we have to keep some perspective on all this because even if there is something going on it may be not have a material impact on ICon's bottom line. And since ICon is consolidated into the Bank's financials and not reported separately, it might amount to just a rounding error to the Bank. I'm not saying that this questionnaire doesn't raise other issues, but I think first and foremost is for us to get a handle on whether this impacts the numbers the Bank publicly reports to Wall Street. How much do ICon's revenues contribute to the Bank's overall numbers?"

Thomas answered as if he had already considered the worst case scenario. "Well, ICon has been at about seven percent of the Bank's revenues since the deal, but the internal strategy is for it to grow aggressively over the next eighteen to twenty four months and, possibly, to transition some of the Bank's traditional banking customers to an online platform that ICon would host. I've seen some of the forecasts and management is planning for ICon to play a pretty big role in the Bank's future. If we have a problem down there, we gotta know - and now."

"Understood," Jake said nodding.

"So what are the next steps and how long can we keep this under wraps? I haven't told anyone about this yet, but at some point, I'm going to have to brief McMillan."

"The first thing is for us to meet with Patti, hopefully today if we can get in touch with her. Once we get an idea of what international transactions she's talking about, we can do some data mining and look deeper at those transactions, the size, which clients are involved, and the trending. We probably can get someone in the Bank's corporate finance department to request a report of all international transactions over a certain period in order to mask the one's that we're really looking at. That shouldn't raise anyone's eyebrows at ICon. We should see if there are any hotline call reports or other internal audit reports about similar transactions. We also may want to talk with someone in human resources to see if anyone else left the accounting department in the past two years."

"I'd do a background check on her just to see if anything comes up," Jake added. He paused to give Thomas a chance to jot down his thoughts.

When Thomas looked up, Jake continued. "We need to review her emails as soon as possible. If she was only there for a few months, there may not be too many. I'd like to know if she talked about any of this with anyone else. Do you know what happened to her computer?"

Thomas answered looking back down at his pad and writing. "No. The Bank has a policy of keeping the hard drive of some employees who leave, like executives. But it's an HR thing rather than legal. I only get involved if there is some dispute with the employee about termination, discrimination, things like that. Then I make sure an image is made of the laptop. But otherwise, I think that the hard drives are wiped and reused. I don't know what ICon does because we haven't had to address it yet."

"Well, we'll need to talk ASAP to someone in IT about the hard drive."

Alex chimed in not sure if as a young associate he was stepping on Jake's toes. "I think we should find out how often ICon's email server is backed up and suspend the rotation schedule so that nothing historical on the system is lost. It's a good idea to take a snapshot of the server now so we have a current copy of everything on there because, depending on the back up schedule, it's possible for emails to be deleted before being backed up. And, we should find out whether the electronic dumpster is set to a zero day default. If so, we should change that to guarantee that nothing can be deleted."

Thomas and Jake both glanced at Alex, surprised not by his interruption but by his knowledge. Jake was about to continue when Thomas asked Alex "what's an electronic dumpster?"

Alex edged forward to make sure they heard him above the background noise of the corporate jet.

"It's a term for a little known computer file that you can set up to capture emails that people try to delete. When you delete an email, it goes to the trash bin or deleted folder, right. If you then go into your deleted folder and again delete that email, the email is gone. There's no way to recover it from the system, unless by chance, the server was backed up while the email was in the deleted folder. That's not likely if someone wants to get rid of it."

He had their undivided attention as he continued. "So what you can do is add an electronic tag, actually a bit, to the email that prevents it from being deleted for a certain amount of time. If someone tries to double-delete the email with this tag, it's not deleted but instead it is sent to the electronic dumpster file and stays there until whatever time period you chose has passed, and only then does it get permanently deleted."

Alex paused to make sure they were following him. "The time period on most email servers usually is defaulted to zero days, so there's never any emails in the electronic dumpster. But, if you think that someone may try to delete emails, you can re-set that person's tag to, say 180 days, and any emails he tries to delete will be saved in the dumpster for six months."

Jake turned towards Thomas who clearly was impressed by L&E's newest associate. "Those are the kind of things we can do while staying in the shadows. And Alex is right, before we announce the investigation, there are some things like this dumpster that we can put into place." Jake tried not to let on that he had never heard about an email dumpster before.

"We want to control the process as long as we can and get as much information as we can. I don't think you need to talk with the Board about any of this until we've had a chance to interview Patti and to look at some of the data. You're not going to want to have a conversation with the Board until we get some answers first. I expect that we'll know more in the next forty eight hours or so."

"I thought you said to expect the unexpected," Thomas jested.

"You're catching on," Jake said with a wink.

The jet skimmed on the Atlantic trade winds straddling the Florida coast line below. A sharp beam of morning sunlight traced the interior of the cabin as the plane slowing banked to the right.

A soft, respectful tone rang twice in the cabin announcing the pilot's interruption. "Gentlemen, we're starting our descent into Opa-Locka Executive Airport, and we'll be landing in about twenty minutes. The weather is already seventy eight degrees heading to a high of ninety one. I'll need you to go ahead and switch off your laptops, cell phones, and PDAs. And yes, Mr. Nelson, this does apply to you."

Jake and Alex looked at Thomas, who laughed at the pilot's ribbing of him.

"Roy's been flying us around for years, and let's just say that we've had our differences about the potential impact that my little friend here," Thomas said holding up his Blackberry, "has on a state-of-the-art Gulfstream."

"Well, would you want him negotiating SouthPoint's next leveraged finance deal?" Jake chided his friend.

"I see your point. But, don't forget that I'm the client. I pay you to argue my side."

They chuckled . . . and then they both conspicuously turned off their Blackberries.

The jet gracefully descended between swaying palm trees and touched down in Miami. The plane slowed to the end of the runway and taxied towards the shiny executive concourse. Alex leaned towards his window and saw a man dressed in a sharp white uniform on the tarmac waiting next to a black town car with its trunk open. The plane approached the car and inched forward until the man held up his hand. Yes, this was a nice way to travel he thought.

Roy stepped out of the cockpit and opened the plane's door. A wave of thick warm air rushed and chased away the cooled interior of the cabin.

"I've got to meet with banker downtown, but I should be done around two o'clock," Thomas said loudly over the plane's engines as he tossed his briefcase into the open trunk of the car. "There is a business suite in the concourse that you can use to get in touch with our star witness. And you can get a courtesy car from the concierge."

Thomas' tie waved behind him in the breeze as he turned towards the pilot who was standing in the jet's threshold. "Roy, what time are we leaving?"

"Whenever you want to," Roy yelled. "Just give me an hour or so heads up so I can refuel and coordinate with flight control."

Thomas turned to Jake and Alex. "Send me an email when you know more, and we can plan on meeting back here this afternoon." They watched as Thomas climbed into the town car and headed off the tarmac.

* * *

Sitting in the plush business suite of the executive concourse, Jake pulled out his copy of Patti Tomanski's exit questionnaire and turned it over. He took a long sip of his coffee and glanced down at her cell phone number.

"Here we go, hope we get lucky," Jake said to Alex who was sitting across the table on the edge of his chair. He dialed the phone number she had written on the back, and readied his pen and pad.

The line rang five times. Just as Jake was about to hang up, he heard a click and a woman's voice answered. He sat up instinctively.

"Hello, this is Patti. Please leave me a message and I'll get back to you."

After the beep, Jake began. "Uh Ms. Tomanski, this is Jake Morgan. I'm a lawyer representing SouthPoint Bank, the parent company of ICon. I wonder whether you would have a moment or two to talk about your exit questionnaire. I happen to be in Miami today and if you have time I'd like to meet with you. You can reach me on my cell, which is 404-888-1809."

He hung up and looked over at Alex. "Well, we'll wait and see." He leaned back in his chair and put his hands behind his head.

"That was pretty impressive back there on the plane about the electronic dumpster. I gotta say that you taught me something new. Where did you learn all that?"

"I worked at an IT consulting company before law school. I mainly worked on applications and did a little programming. But before I left, I got into the computer forensics side, which I liked a lot. We did things like inspect employees' computers to find out whether they were stealing data, or posting confidential information online, or going to websites that they shouldn't – you know, at least at work."

"What made you want to go to law school? That's not the typical choice of computer types."

"Well, I traveled a whole lot as a systems analyst and let's just say that being a double platinum frequent flier is nothing to brag about." Alex paused. "After the dot com bust, I decided to look for something different."

He looked out of the window at a jet racing by. Jake sensed that there was more to the story, but he decided to let it go for now. He reached across the table and flipped open the complimentary Wall Street Journal.

Just as he finished reading the first page his cell phone on the table vibrated. Jake and Alex glared at the phone, and then at each other. Jake snatched the phone and instinctively stood up.

"It's her," he said seeing the phone number he had called.

"Hello, this is Jake Morgan."

"Mr. Morgan, this is Patti Tomanski returning your call." She paused to let Jake lead the conversation.

"Thanks for getting back to me so quickly." Jake nodded at Alex who was glued to Jake's expressions.

"I just needed a few minutes for some due diligence."

"Excuse me?" Jake asked.

"I checked you out on your firm's website. You have an impressive resume Mr. Morgan. I'm glad to see that SouthPoint took my comments seriously."

Caught off guard, Jake stumbled a bit. "Uh thanks. Yes, SouthPoint does take them seriously. And that's why I'd like to talk to you. We want to get a better understanding about some of the things you said in your exit questionnaire."

"Is ICon included in the term 'we'?"

Sensing her precondition, Jake spoke bluntly. "No, ICon doesn't know about your questionnaire. I was hired by SouthPoint Bank and I report only to the General Counsel and the Board of Directors. No one at ICon knows that I flew down to Miami to talk with you . . . hopefully to meet with you."

The line was quiet for a few seconds. Jake looked over at Alex, who was dripping to know what she was saying on the other line.

Patti broke the silence. "Look. You're smart enough to know that I'm smart enough to know what would happen if I submitted that questionnaire. It took a week for me to send it in. I just stared at it each day sitting on my kitchen table. I knew that if I sent it, someone just like you would be calling any day. But if I didn't send it, my conscience would be calling *everyday.* So, I finally decided that I'd rather take just one call and get it over with if you know what I mean."

"I understand. You just tell me where and when." Jake leaned over the table and readied his pen. He hung on the silence for what seemed to be minutes.

"Okay. I'll meet you at a restaurant called Shells on Biscayne Boulevard at 35th. Can you be there at 11:30?"

Jake exhaled, scribbling down the location. "Sure thing, see you then."

Before he moved the phone from his ear, Patti finished. "One more thing Mr. Morgan. Don't look for a blonde with glasses like the picture on my security badge, which I'm sure you've seen by now. I've changed things up a little."

"How so?" Jake asked.

After a short pause, she said "why don't I just look for you. That is, as long as your picture on you firm's website is still current."

"Just add a touch of grey hair on the sides, and you'll find me."

Jake slowly put the phone down on the table. Alex could barely restrain himself. "What'd she say? Is she going to talk to us?" he finally blurted out.

"Yup, she's going to talk to us. And I have feeling she's got a lot to say."

Jake reached into his briefcase that was lying on the table. He pulled out Patti's security badge and took a good long look at her picture. Then he tossed it across the table to Alex.

"Here, we won't need this for now. C'mon, let's get a car and I'll fill you in on the way."

Jake adjusted the mirrors of the white Mercedes sedan that was provided with a smile by the executive airport, and he turned the air conditioner on to full blast. He wiped his brow, already glistening from the sun, and looked back over his shoulder to pull out of the parking space.

"Geez, no wonder no one wears a suit and tie down here," he said to Alex who also was tugging at his collar.

"We're going to a restaurant called Shells at Biscayne and 35th. Can you put the address into that GPS thing? And apparently she's now changed her appearance from the way she looks on her security badge."

"Isn't that kind of cloak and dagger?" Alex asked.

"Well, some people are paranoid. Get used to it. You gotta understand that it's not easy being a whistleblower. It takes guts for the *real* ones. The ones who can't sleep at night knowing that someone is cooking the books or getting away with something. Knowing that they're up against a million dollar machine that can make life for them pretty damn miserable if they try to fight it. It takes a lot for someone to put their ass on the line and risk their paycheck. I've seen divorces, bankruptcies, nervous break downs. You gotta treat them with kid gloves . . . unless, that is, you think they're lying to you."

A female voice interrupted them. "In point two miles, make a left turn on Northwest 135th Street."

"And most of them *are* lying to you. It's amazing how many people don't understand what happens when they claim to be whistleblowers. I think they just assume that they'll stir up the pot and walk away with a big settlement. But a company can't just pay them off and sweep it under the rug. If there's any credibility to the allegations, a public company has to investigate."

"What happens if they're telling the truth? I mean a real whistleblower. Do they get a reward?"

"Not a reward. But they can get back wages and damages. They can get their job back if they were fired, but most don't want to go back to the same job. I can't blame them. I bet that the money never fully compensates for the aggravation."

"What do you think about Patti?" Alex probed.

"Well, it's hard to tell, but my gut tells me that she's telling us what she thinks is the truth. To be protected under the law, a person only has to *reasonably* think that there is something illegal going on. They don't have to be right. And I've seen huge gaps between what may be reasonable to think and what actually happened. Believe it or not, a lot of times there is just a misunderstanding or poor communication. From what Patti wrote, it sounds like there is almost no communication in ICon's accounting department, which is a red flag in and of itself. But she doesn't seem to me like she's being vengeful, or that she's really upset for that matter. I can tell you that she does know exactly what she's got herself into. You heard Thomas say that she used to be at a Big Four accounting firm and that she used to work in internal audit. My guess is that she's pretty certain there's something wrong going on at ICon, or else we wouldn't be here in a hundred degrees looking for some tacky seafood restaurant."

Alex chuckled as he watched the endless urban sprawl of North Miami pass by. "So I assume I'll take notes, right?"

"Yeah, takes notes. But don't try to write down the interview verbatim. We want to make sure that the notes are privileged, and a straight witness statement would not be. To be privileged, the notes have to be work product. I assume that they still teach that stuff at law school?"

Alex smirked. "Yeah, I know, work product is our thoughts and conclusions about what she says."

"An A for you Mr. Perry. Also, make sure that you get all the names, accounts, and dates, whatever she says. This may be the only time we get to talk with her. And, don't be shy to ask her if you have a question or don't understand something. This is a team effort."

"Will do," Alex said with nod.

The emotionless female voice spoke out from the GPS unit straddling the dashboard. "In one mile, turn right on Northwest 6th Ave."

"And," Jake continued, "I need you to be my second set of eyes. Do you know what it means to calibrate a witness?"

Alex turned away from the window and glanced over at Jake. "Uh, no."

Jake swung right into the adjacent lane to avoid a late model Cadillac that was barely chugging along in the left lane. It looked as if there was no one driving other than two frail hands gripping the steering wheel. As they passed, they saw a small wrinkled woman wearing blue pearled eyeglasses with a silver beaded chain looping down the side of her face. A common obstacle on South Florida roads. Jake watched in his rear view mirror as the cars following him similarly had to avoid the sluggish senior.

"Calibrating a witness means watching their mannerisms and listening to their speech patterns at the beginning of an interview when we're asking easy questions, like about their background. Where did you go to school? When did you start at XYZ company? What do you do on a day-to-day basis at work? Pay close attention to how they answer those kinds of questions because that should gauge their normal behavior. Or at least as normal as can be when they're being interviewed by a couple of lawyers. Then when we start to ask the hard, probing questions, look for changes in their normal behavior. That's called calibrating a witness."

"Do you know what kinetics is?" Jake said glancing over at Alex.

"Uh, something to do with motion? It's been a long time since I took physics."

"Well, this is more like psychology. Kinetics is watching a witness's body language to try to pick up clues about whether he or she is being deceptive. Is she wringing her hands? Is she crossing her arms? Is she fidgeting her feet? Look for the things that have changed from her earlier behavior. The biggest thing to watch is her facial expressions. The eyes speak volumes. Does she make good eye contact? Is she blinking more often? Does she look down or away when answering tough questions? You can't really tell if a witness is lying, but if you see these changes it usually means the witness is uncomfortable with the question for some reason and it's a good idea to dig further."

"Gotcha," Alex responded feeling the excitement grow.

"Since we're having a vocabulary lesson, what do you think paralinguistic is?" Jake said wryly.

"Uh, some kind of Olympic event?" Alex answered grinning.

Jake glanced over at Alex and smirked. "Nice try. It's listening to how someone talks. Their volume, pitch, and tone. Have you ever noticed that when someone becomes uncomfortable talking about something they'll unconsciously drop their voice and talk softer? That doesn't necessarily mean that they're lying, but just like body language it might mean that there's something they are nervous about."

"A witness's speech patterns are almost as important as what they say. Chronemics is listening to the rate of speech and the length of pauses. If someone starts to talk quicker it could mean that they are nervous. Or, if they pause for what seems to be a long time, it could mean that they are trying to come up with a story."

"Even little things a witness says can clue you in that they may be lying. Someone who is guilty of something is more likely to recount a story in a straight chronological order. That can tell you that they've spent time thinking it through, planning out the story. An innocent person usually tells a story in more of a scatter-shot way."

The GPS lady spoke up again. "Continue on Northwest 6th Avenue until it intersects with Biscayne Boulevard. Destination in five miles."

Jake politely let her finish before continuing. "Also, a guilty person usually only tells you the essential details of a story. It's easier to remember. Rarely will you hear a guilty person just go on rambling. They have a more controlled version. But you'll hear all kinds of irrelevant things from an innocent person because they're not thinking about concealing anything."

"My favorite trick is called neurolinguistics."

Alex looked over at him with a curious glance. "Hold on, let me guess." He sounded it out slowly. "N-e-u-r-o-l-i-n-g-u-i-s-t-i-c-s. Um, that must have something to do with the brain and language. Is it the study of thoughts?"

"Close but no cigar my young apprentice. Neurolinguistics is watching the way the eyes move when someone is thinking. Not everyone subscribes to it, but as the theory goes, when someone is asked a question their eyes unconsciously move when they are thinking about the answer. The direction the eyes move can indicate what the person is thinking."

"If the person looks up to the left, it means that they are trying to remember a fact. Like a wedding anniversary, or your college dorm room number. It's a true fact that the person is trying to recall."

"If they look down to the left, the person is thought to be having an internal discussion about whether to disclose the fact. Again, a true fact but the person is thinking about whether he should answer. Picture a kid being asked by his parents if he broke the window. He looks down and to the left, right?"

"I don't know, I always told the truth as a kid."

Jake sneered over at Alex who was grinning.

"If a person is asked a question that hits some sensitive or emotional issue, like 'Do you believe in abortion?' the person is supposed to look down and to the right."

"And lastly, if a person looks up to the right when asked a question, the theory is that he is creating or imagining something. So, if I asked you to think about what the offspring of an elephant and a zebra would look like, you'd have to try to imagine or visualize it, and you'd instinctively look up to the right."

"Or when they are lying, right?"

"You're catching on. A lie is nothing more than a creation. So if you believe in neurolinguistics, a witness will unconsciously look up to the right when he is lying."

Alex glanced out of the window at the high stratus clouds passing by as he considered the theory.

"Obviously," Jake added, "you have to take everything into consideration. Body movement, eyes, speech, grammar. No one thing is definitive. But the more interviews you do, the better you get at spotting these kinds of signals. An interview is half fact gathering and half psychological profiling."

Alex looked down and caught himself fiddling with his tie, thinking that is exactly the kind of behavior he was supposed to be looking for. But his *kinetics* were from the anticipation of his first investigation interview. His first interview of a possible whistleblower. His first fraud investigation. He was brimming inside. This was the reason he applied for a job at Levi & Everett.

L&E had investigated some of the biggest corporate frauds, and the firm was renowned for its team of lawyers, investigators, and forensic accountants. During law school, he wasn't interested in civil procedure or real property. It was corporations, securities, and white collar crime that kept him up late studying energetically. He had been glued to the television when the Enron story broke, and afterwards he read every book about corporate fraud that he could get his hands on.

He looked over at Jake, who was lost in his thoughts. Alex envied him. Jake was the head of L&E's Investigations Practice Group, and had worked on some of the firm's most high-profile investigations. He was on first name basis with several U.S. Attorneys and the Chairman of the SEC. Jake had war stories that could fill a book, and Alex hoped that he would reach that pinnacle someday. And as he stared out the window, he hoped that Patti Tomanski was telling the truth.

"Destination on the right in point five miles."

Alex glanced forward looking for the Shells sign.

"There it is, up on the right." Alex pointed towards the fading sign. Jake eased the car into the right lane and slowed as they approached the restaurant.

The seafood restaurant was almost empty inside, except for a few senior citizens catching the early bird specials. Kitschy sea-faring mementos decorated the walls and a huge plastic Marlin hung above the dining room. They did not see anyone who possibly could be their witness.

"I guess we got here first. We'll have three in our party," Jake said to the teenage hostess dressed in an unflattering uniform and clearly not thrilled to be working. She motioned to them to follow her.

They were seated at a table near the back of the restaurant. From their vantage point they had an unobstructed view of the front door. They unpacked their legal pads and waited on their guest of honor.

Jake glanced down at his watch. "We're a few minutes early, but we shouldn't have a problem spotting her."

After a few moments, a thin waitress with dark cropped hair approached them.

"What can I get you gentlemen?" She said placing two menus next to them.

"Uh, I'll take a Coke," Alex said.

"Same for me," Jake added.

"Is Pepsi okay," the waitress said automatically, almost apologetically.

"We're not in Kansas anymore," Jake joked to Alex about the restaurant not having Atlanta's world famous soft drink. The waitress did not seem amused.

"Sure, that's fine. We're expecting one more, so we'll wait to order," Jake told the waitress.

She jotted down the order and thanked them."So what do you think Patti looks like now?" Alex asked, glancing over the menu.

"Well, I'm sure that she doesn't have blonde hair and glasses anymore," Jake quipped remembering Patti's security badge.

Alex peered towards the front of the restaurant as a group of casually-dressed people walked in.

"She'll find us. We're the only ones in the place with suits on."

Alex continued to gaze towards the front door, waiting to see a woman who might be Patti. They both sat patiently in front of their blank legal pads. Each time the faux wood paneled door swung open, they both impulsively looked to see who was entering.

"Here ya go," the waitress said as she put the soft drinks on the table. Have you decided?"

Jake fidgeted with the menu that was tucked under his legal pad. "Um, we're still waiting for another person to join us. Can we have a few more minutes?"

The waitress looked around as if to see if anyone was watching. "She's already here Mr. Morgan," she said looking down at him.

Jake and Alex looked up at her with a momentary confusion. Then they realized that they were looking at the woman who they had seen on the security badge.

"I have a break in five minutes. Get your questions ready," she said nodding towards the pads, "because I only get thirty minutes."

Patti Tomanski shuffled away, leaving Jake and Alex a bit stunned.

"Expect the unexpected, huh?" Alex said looking over at Jake, who was still watching the waitress walk towards the kitchen.

Exactly five minutes later, Patti came around the corner and sat down in the chair next to Alex. She leaned towards Jake hindering Alex's view of most of the kinetic signs he was supposed to observe.

"Don't be surprised Mr. Morgan," she said glancing down at her uniform, "not many places are hiring out of work accountants these days. At least it pays the bills or some of them anyway."

She looked at Alex and then back at Jake. "Okay, so tell me how this goes."

Jake cleared his throat. "This is my associate Alex Perry. He's going to take notes of what we talk about. I don't have any recording devices, do you?"

Patti shifted back in her seat, a little surprised by the question. "No, I don't."

"Ok. As I told you, we represent SouthPoint and we're investigating the allegations you made in your exit questionnaire. I want to ask you some background questions about your job there and then I'd like to know what you know about these alleged transactions."

"Not *alleged* transaction," she said slightly pursing her lips, "actual transactions."

Her shoulder length sandy hair was now dark and crept smartly just below her ears, matching her chestnut eyebrows. Contact lenses replaced her wireless rim glasses, and her skin had more color than in the pale grainy picture on her security badge. She was more attractive than Jake expected, and he thought that she would turn heads if she dressed in anything other than the unflattering teal Shells outfit.

"That's what I meant. Sorry, lawyer speak." Jake shifted on the hard wooden chair. "Why don't you start Ms. Tomanski by telling us what you were doing before ICon? I know some from your employment application."

"Ok. Call me Patti, please. Before I went to ICon I was in internal audit at Technyx Electronics in Illinois. Technyx was a public company, so we did quarterly internal control assessments, surprise audits, inventory confirmations, and things like that. After about two years, my Mom got sick. She lives in Hialeah about fifteen minutes from here. So, I came down to Miami to live with her and started looking for a job. I saw the ICon job on Craig's List for an accounting manager, and sent my resume. I interviewed with Cain Arnold, which was kind of weird since he's the in-house lawyer. I would've expected someone in HR or in the accounting department. I guess in hindsight that should've tipped me off that something was up."

Alex was scanning her movements trying to calibrate her as Jake had explained. It was much harder than he expected.

"What did you do before Technyx?"

"I was at KPMG in audit. I mostly audited tech companies. Lots of revenue recognition issues. Percentage of completion accounting, that kind of stuff."

"How did you get to Technyx?"

"When I was at KPMG, I worked on the Technyx account. They offered me a job in internal audit and I was ready to get out of the Big Four lifestyle."

"And college? Where did you go and what degree did you get?"

Patti stared at Jake for a moment. There was no doubt about the resolve of her eye contact. "Look, Mr. Morgan. You know all of this. Can we do away with the pleasantries and talk about ICon?"

"Uh, sure," Jake blushed imperceptibly. He realized that was not dealing with the typical whistleblower. So much for calibration.

"Before we get too far," Jake shifted in his chair, "I've got a couple of preliminary questions."

"Are you represented by a lawyer regarding your termination from ICon?"

"No."

"You're not under oath, but will you agree to tell me the truth?" Jake looked at Patti intently.

He purposefully asked all witnesses for their commitment to be honest, as he studied their faces for any reaction. It's an unexpected question that sometimes causes dishonest witnesses to inadvertently show a sign of hesitancy.

"You're an officer of the court, Mr. Morgan. You can put me under oath. Go ahead, swear me in as they say," Patti snapped back politely.

"That's alright, no need." Jake said slightly grinning at her wit. "Who was your supervisor at ICon?"

"On the org chart, it was Jane Weaver, the CFO. But I had very little interaction with her. I would just get emails telling me what she needed. Supposedly, she was always very busy. Remember that I was only there for three months or so. The only time I actually saw her is when I went to her office to ask about Zapplication."

"Zapplication? Does that relate to the international transactions?" Jake asked.

"Yes. Zapplication is the client that sent the transactions."

"Can you tell me what your job was and what you worked on while you were at ICon?"

"I was initially hired as an accounting manager to run trial balances and reconciliations on ICon's financial statements. Balance sheets, income statements, and cash flows. Then I was transferred to accounts payable."

"You were transferred? Within only three months? Why?"

"ICon's financial statements were a mess. I couldn't reconcile some of the items, and some of the accounts didn't roll forward each quarter. There were tons of previous period adjustments. Anyway, I tried to ask Jane about it. I even offered to try to fix some of the problems, but Jane had her secretary send me a pithy email that just said that *thanks and have a nice day.* I never heard anything back from her. Then one morning I came in and all of a sudden ICon needed help in payables and, lo and behold, I was the one who got transferred."

"Did you make any kind of complaint or tell anyone?" Jake asked.

"No," Patti answered without any explanation. She looked away momentarily as if she regretted her previous silence.

"Are you aware if anyone ever addressed the problems with the financial statements?"

"No," she answered again.

Jake jotted a note down on his pad *what fin st'ments were given to SouthPoint in the deal? Were numbers misstated?*

"Okay," he said looking back across the table at her. She may have been nervous, but she hid it well. "What did you do in accounts payables?"

"You know the usual. Reviewing invoices from vendors, matching documents, processing checks. I posted journal entries and kept ledgers. Nothing out of the ordinary. Other than normal operating expenses, ICon really didn't have many payables. It was not the kind of work that I was looking for. But it was work, and I thought that if I did a good job, I'd move up eventually, especially because the accounting talent there was lacking. I mean some of the people really didn't understand accounting the way that I would expect in a several hundred million dollar company."

Alex tried to study her face, at least the side he could see. For the most part, she was calm and collected. Her fingers were interlocked loosely, and her hands rested on the table. She wore a small opal ring on her right ring finger. He could not detect any audible difference in the tone of her voice. Only the faint clenching of her jaw revealed any sign of anxiety.

"What interaction did you have with Jane Weaver or other executives when you were in accounts payable?" Jake asked.

"Again, very little. Even when I tried to talk to Jane about Zapplication, she barely gave me the time of day. She supposedly was very busy with the SouthPoint deal. Actually, she seemed to be very busy all the time. The only other time I dealt with anyone from management was the meeting I had with Glen Baker, the head of HR, when I was terminated." Jake glanced at his watch. He had twenty minutes left of Patti's time.

"Okay. Tell me about Zapplication. That relates to the international transactions you mentioned?"

Alex flipped the page of his pad and continued scribbling. He hoped that he would be able to read his disjointed notes later on.

"Yes. About a week or so after I was transferred, I was doing some reconciliations. I was going through a pile of pay requests for invoices that ICon needed to pay. About half way through, there were two different pay requests that for some reason had been stapled together. When I pulled them apart, the one attached in the back was for Zapplication. I noticed that the balance owed on the Zapplication pay request was zero. Like it had already been paid. I thought that was kind of strange since

I was the only one who was supposed to be processing the checks and wires." She paused seeing that Alex was frantically trying to catch up.

"So, who was it paid by?" Jake asked.

"I don't know. I don't even think that it was a pay request."

"What do you mean? I thought you said it was in a pile of pay requests for ICon's expenses."

"I did. That's where it gets weird. The pay request to Zapplication was pretty big, about $250,000. That seemed way out of proportion with ICon's other expenses, which are relatively small and are mostly for just normal operating costs. So I did a little research to try to find the actual invoices that Zapplication sent to ICon so that I could see what they were for. But the invoices weren't really invoices."

"Huh?" Jake was getting confused. He leaning forward and stared intently at Patti. Alex also looked up from his pad. She noticed their focused attention, and she looked around the sparse restaurant pausing for dramatic effect.

"The supporting documentation for the pay request was not an invoice like you would expect, but instead it was a report of credit card transactions that ICon had processed for Zapplication. That's what ICon sends to its *clients* every month, not to its *vendors*. The report is a list of all of the credit card transactions processed each day for the particular client, with the number of approvals and declines."

"So then it looked to me like Zapplication was really a client, not a vendor. But that was strange because, as a client, Zapplication should owe money to ICon, not the other way around. There were about six months of these 'pay requests' to Zapplication, and they varied each month. One month was $150,000 that Zapplication was owed, one was $85,000, and in one month there were no transactions so nothing was owed. It was up and down. "

Alex continued writing and at the same time he was trying to understand what Patti was telling them. He glanced over at Jake who looked like he did not have any better grasp on her story. They looked at her intently as she continued.

"Zapplication had an ICon client code. Every client has a seven digit number with a dash followed by a two digit number. I didn't know what all the numbers meant, that's something that ICon always kept secret for some reason. But I knew that it was a *client* code and not a vendor code because a vendor code does not have the extra two digits. The extra two digits I found out are the number of the sales rep who gets commissions on the account. So, I shouldn't be processing anything with the two digits at the end."

"Did someone miscode a payable that should've been a receivable?" Jake guessed.

"That's what I initially thought. So I sent an email to Jane asking her about it. I thought that I had found something that had fallen through the cracks. You know, maybe something had gotten screwed up in the system and the company should've been billing Zapplication instead of paying it. I had no idea. But, I thought that Jane would be happy that I caught it."

"Anyway, I didn't hear back from her for a couple of days, so I went to her office to talk to her about it. I still had this pay request, or whatever it was, sitting on my desk and I didn't just want to leave it hanging out there. I remember waiting for about thirty minutes before she had time to see me. Finally, when I went into her office I told her what I found and showed her the pay request for Zapplication. She said that she didn't know anything about it, and that she'd look into it. She has a way of looking right through you like you're not even there."

Patti paused and visibly suppressed the lingering resentment. "About a day or so later, I got a voice mail from her. It was late, like 8:30 at night. She said that she just remembered what it was. Yeah, right. All of a sudden she remembered." Patti's sarcasm dripped across the table. "Jane said that Zapplication was a *special* kind of client. Something about a secret corporate project that Alan was working on. Very hush hush, so don't worry about it."

Patti paused as Alex again flipped the page on his pad. She looked up at the clock on the wall, which had various kinds of fish around the dial instead of numbers.

"What did you do?" Jake asked.

"I guess it's the auditor in me, but I poked around some more. It just didn't sit right with me, you know. So, I was having lunch with one of the sales managers. Rob somebody, I can't remember his last name. I told him that Jane was on my case because I couldn't reconcile an account, and if I could figure out who the sales rep was, I could resolve it without bothering Jane again. Everyone knows how Jane can be, so Rob gave me the key to the client codes. I have no idea why ICon keeps that secret. I could go on for hours about ICon's internal control weaknesses."

"Anyway, I saw that the sales rep was Troy Vickerson. His two digit number is 50. So I called him and asked him about Zapplication. He screamed at me so loud over the phone that Tamara who was the cubicle next to me heard it. He said that I didn't need to worry about it and I should quit asking questions and just cut the damn check. Blah, blah, blah."

Patti cocked her head back and stiffened her back. "I never met Troy face to face, but no one talks to me that way. I might have let it go if he hadn't been such a prick."

Jake didn't doubt her tenacity, and he sensed a bitterness that Patti had kept hidden up until then.

"So what did you do?"

"Well first I looked again at the key to the client codes that Rob had given me to see what the first seven numbers mean. The first five numbers are a unique client ID number and the last two are a country code. All domestic clients end in a 00, which is the country code for the US. Any other number means that the client is located in a foreign country. Zapplication's client number has an international country code for Spain and all of the credit card transactions that ICon processed for Zapplication were international transactions."

Jake nodded to show that he understood what she was saying, and he prodding for her to continue. Alex looked up at the fish clock. The big hand was just touching the grouper's tail. Patti's thirty minute break was about to expire.

"That also was weird because Troy doesn't handle international clients. And the address listed on the client contact screen for Zapplication is not in Spain, but it's right here in Coral Gables, south of downtown Miami."

Jake took a deep breath and thought for a minute. "Well maybe Zapplication has a domestic office here."

"I'm one step ahead of you Mr. Morgan." Patti reached in her pocket underneath the worn-laced apron of her uniform. She pulled out a small cell phone and flipped it open. Jake looked at Alex with an inquisitive glance as she fiddled with the phone.

"Here, take a look at this."

Patti handed the cell phone across the table to Jake. He saw a photograph of an airport runway behind a chain link fence decorated with razor wire. Alex edged forward, but couldn't see the phone.

"What's this?" Jake asked handing the phone to Alex.

"I went to the address that ICon has for Zapplication's *office*," Patti said motioning quotations with her fingers. "That's where it is – in the middle of Runway 5B at Miami International Airport." She sat back to let it sink in.

Alex handed the phone back to her and jotted down some notes. Jake realized that Patti had been waiting for this moment for some time. The photo showed that the address ICon had for Zapplication was fictitious. Even if there really was some legitimate reason for Zapplication's international transactions, a fictitious address of a vendor is a not just a red flag, it is a flashing beacon. Patti's shoulders relaxed and Jake sensed some relief in her eyes to have finally told her story – at least part of it.

"Have you shown this to anyone?"

"No. I didn't get a chance to. I wanted to get more information about the transactions and payments before I told anyone. When I worked at Technyx, we'd always have employees alleging fraud without any real proof. It made our job in internal audit much harder, and, to be honest, we focused our time on the complaints we got that were backed up with evidence. Most of the time, the other complaints never amounted to anything, and we didn't have a huge staff to respond to everything."

"So, I wanted to be sure that I had all the support I needed. About a day or so after I took that picture, I got a call out of the blue from Jane. She said that there was an accounting seminar in Orlando that she wanted me to go to. Something about accounting for web-based businesses. She said that she heard good things about me and that she wanted me to get more practical knowledge of the business, or something like that. I needed the professional education credit anyway so I went."

"When I got back the next day, I could tell that someone had been at my cubicle. I sat down and my chair was lower that I usually keep it. That was my first clue. Also, my mouse was on the right side of my keyboard, but I'm left handed so it's always on the left side. I don't know what they did, but someone had been there, no question."

"Was anything on your computer missing?"

"I couldn't tell. Later that same day I got a call from HR. I went down there and met with Glen Baker. He said that it wasn't working out, that my superiors weren't happy with my job performance, and since I was still in the ninety day probationary period, I was being let go. I was speechless. I mean, Jane had just told me that I was doing a good job. I never got any kind of warning, or negative criticism. Nothing."

"So I took my stuff and left. I thought about telling them about Zapplication and what I found, but by then I didn't trust anyone at ICon and I knew my termination was full of crap. I probably would've just put the whole thing behind me, but about a week later, I got the exit questionnaire from SouthPoint in the mail with my final paycheck. Like I told you on the phone, it took me a while before I decided to send it in. The more I thought about it, the more I knew what I had to do. There's something going on there Mr. Morgan, but now my conscience is clear."

Patti glanced up at the clock and started to stand. The big hand was now pointing squarely at the tuna. Her thirty minutes were up.

"I hope you two get to the bottom of it. I gotta get back to work. I'll be back with your check for the drinks."

With that, she turned and disappeared into the kitchen. Alex finished his scribbling and looked over at Jake.

"Wow," Alex said not finding any better words to describe the interview. "I'm not sure that I caught all of that, but I didn't see any body language to suggest that she was lying. She didn't fidget, she looked you right in the eye. She seemed calm. I believe her. What do you think?"

Jake thought for a moment. "There could be any number of explanations for the payable to Zapplication, but if it's legit ICon definitely did not handle it in the right way. We need to talk with Jane Weaver. One thing that troubles me a little is that Patti didn't give us anything tangible, other than showing us the picture of where Zapplication's office supposedly is located. She said that she had invoices and transactions. You heard her say that at her previous job she was skeptical about complaints that were not supported with evidence. Well, where is the evidence? She darted off before I could ask her."

Alex sat back, slightly embarrassed that his inexperience may have caused him to prematurely jump to conclusions.

"Here ya go, this should be everything you need," Patti said playing the role again of a disinterested waitress. She placed the tab on the table in a plastic fold-over, which was propped opened partially by a pen. "Thanks for coming."

She quickly moved on to a nearby table to take an order. Jake picked up the fold-over and simultaneously reached in his pocket for his wallet. As he opened the fold-over to grab the pen, a small thumbnail computer drive fell onto the table. Jake and Alex glanced up at each other, and then Jake briskly snatched up the thumbnail drive. He scanned the restaurant, and buried it into his pocket.

Jake put a ten dollar bill in the fold-over and they stood collecting their briefcases without saying a word. They walked to the front of the restaurant and Jake reached into his pocket to make sure that the thumbnail drive Patti gave him was still there. He had his evidence.

"Thanks for coming," the teen hostess said in a bland obligatory fashion.

Alex looked back to see if Patti was watching them leave. He saw her glance towards the front door and their eyes met for an instant. She turned quickly towards the kitchen and disappeared. He wondered if they would ever see her again . . . and if she was telling the truth.

CHAPTER SEVEN

"It ain't good," Jake said standing and scratching his head as Thomas burst into the conference room at the Opa-Locka airport. Thomas tossed his jacket on the back of one of the leather chairs and plopped down across from Jake and Alex.

"What did she say?" Thomas moaned not really wanting to know the answer.

"Well, there's a lot we don't know yet, but it could be some sort of fictitious client or vendor scheme. She found a fake address for what looks like a client of ICon called Zapplication. We went on Zapplication's website a little while ago. It's a site that categorizes and sorts other websites that sell cell phone applications. The customer pays $1.00 a month to get a list every month of other websites selling applications for cell phones. It's a pretty basic set up and the graphics are bare bones. I'm not sure how a site like that makes any money. Even ICon can't be making hardly any money from Zapplication."

"Apparently, Zapplication's business was sporadic. Some months, there were a lot of transactions, some months there were hardly any. I think there was even one month without any transactions. Seems kind of strange for a website not to have a single credit card transaction. Also, get this. During most of the time, the transactions from Zapplication came through ICon near the end of the month. What kind of website does business only at the end of the month?"

Jake paused to let Thomas absorb the report thus far.

"The thing that set her off is that she found some ICon pay requests to Zapplication, meaning that it looked to her like ICon was paying Zapplication as if it were a vendor or some other payable. She saw that over the past six months, there was about half a million dollars in these pay requests, but the balance on each of them was zero as if it had already been paid before the pay request got to her. So, she dug a little further and found that Zapplication was set up as a client of ICon, an international client. It had a client code for Spain, but the address is domestic, here in Miami. And, apparently all of the credit card transactions that were being processed through ICon were coming from over seas."

"When she tried to ask questions about all this, she got the run around from the CFO and she got a tongue lashing about it from the VP of Sales, whose name is, uh, Alex did you get it?"

"Troy Vickerson," Alex said flipping a page on his pad.

Thomas exhaled deeply upon hearing Troy's name. "Shit. I had a bad feeling about that guy." He had a flashback from the closing dinner of Troy parading in with his big-busted stripper girlfriend. Cain's advice about taking care of Troy's clients suddenly had new meaning.

Jake continued after taking a sip from a sweating bottle of water. "She started to do her own investigation without telling anyone. Jane Weaver, the CFO, finally told her that Zapplication was some kind of secret corporate project. But according to Patti, when she started pressing, she was sent out of town to a seminar and then fired as soon as she got back. She also thinks that someone tampered with her computer while she was gone."

"So why were there pay requests to Zapplication?" Thomas asked.

"She doesn't know. But, she even had the gumption to look up the address for Zapplication and drive by."

"And?"

"The address was the middle of a runway at Miami International Airport. She showed us a picture she took on her camera phone."

"Shit," Thomas said for the second time in thirty seconds. "If ICon was processing the transactions, presumably it was generating revenue from them, right?"

"We don't know yet because we haven't seen the receivable side of it. But I image that's right. Troy apparently was getting commissions on it."

Thomas leaned back in the chair, and put his arms behind his head. He stared out of the conference room window at the runway of the executive airport. Being the General Counsel of any company is like the old fashioned one-man band. Some poor sucker wrapped up with instruments and playing them all at the same time, all the while marching around in circles. Top lawyers in companies can handle contract problems, intellectual property issues, employment disputes, and tax matters - all before lunchtime. To be successful, in-house lawyers have to wear many hats and keep everything in tune.

"Do you believe her?" Thomas asked Jake breaking the tension.

"I believe that she thinks there's something going on," Jake said in the most judicial manner possible. "I don't see why she would make all of this up and subject herself to the scrutiny. There may be a valid explanation, but ICon didn't handle it right if there is. To me, that usually is a fairly good sign that there's some fire behind the smoke."

"What proof did she have?"

Jake glanced over at Alex at the head of the table. He turned his laptop around towards Thomas and slid it closer. The thumbnail drive that Patti had given them was protruding from the side of the laptop. There were several files listed on the index of the drive.

"I haven't had a chance yet to review all this, but it looks like she gave us the pay requests, the transaction data for Zapplication, a historical roll forward of the account, some emails, and, you'll love this, a .jpeg file of the picture she took of Zapplication's alleged Miami office." Jake reached over to the mouse pad of the laptop and double-clicked the file. The picture of the empty runway at Miami International Airport appeared.

"Nice," Thomas commented facetiously.

"She also told us that ICon's financial statements are a mess. Accounts don't roll forward or balance, they're not reconciled, and there is no hard close. Who knows whether they're accurate. When she offered to revise them, she was promptly transferred to accounts payable. I don't know what ICon gave the Bank during due diligence, but from what we heard, you may have gotten bad financials."

Jake shied back into his chair, knowing that his last comment would cause consternation with his client. To suspect some kind of minor scheme was one thing, but to suggest that SouthPoint spent $750 million for ICon based on fraudulent financials was calamitous.

Thomas leaned back and rocked in the chair. He closed his eyes and rubbed his forehead. The lines on his face had deepened from the responsibility of handling the legal affairs of a five billion dollar bank. His hair was succumbing to shades of gray, and his once athletic frame was starting to bulge from inactivity. Surprises were part of the job of being a General Counsel, but they did not get any easier. Those who survive and prosper learn to develop a cool head and a rational response. Thomas was no exception. He had a sign in his office on his credenza that said *Act, Don't React.* It was a General Counsel's credo.

"Okay, what's next?" he said with a sigh.

"I think we need to go in immediately," Jake said letting his advice simmer before explaining further.

"At this point, we have to assume what Patti says is true. She seems credible and she's the farthest thing from a disgruntled employee. If she's telling the truth, there are enough red flags to cause concern. The CFO and the VP of Sales acted suspiciously, which could signal that they may be involved somehow. The entire financial reporting process is suspect, and it's possible that SouthPoint's acquisition of ICon was based on faulty numbers." Jake figured that it was best just to rip off the band aid and get it all out.

"My recommendation is that over the next few days we secure and collect the data we need, copy servers, and set up electronic tracking processes, like the dumpster Alex mentioned on the flight this morning."

Alex reveled in the recognition that he added some value to the investigation.

"Once that's done, I think we need to start with surprise interviews of ICon's executives, certainly Alan, Jane, Troy, and anyone else involved in payables. I don't think we have the luxury of spending a long time looking at documents and emails first, and I don't think that this is something that we can keep under wraps. I think it's better that we come out with guns blazing, so they won't have time to get their stories straight."

Thomas scratched some notes in his portfolio as Jake and Alex sat patiently. The shrill of a jet taking off momentarily filled the room.

"How long do you think it will take?" The question every lawyer dreads, and every lawyer invariably answers incorrectly, usually through no fault of their own.

"It depends on what we find. The first round of interviews should take a couple of days. Once we get back to Atlanta tonight, I'll put together a team to do document and email review. We can start at the beginning of next week. I'm sure we'll need to re-interview some people based on the documents we find, so I think a fair estimate for the initial phase is two weeks."

"You don't have two weeks," Thomas said bluntly. "SouthPoint's 10-Q is due next week on Monday, and we have shareholder meeting in Atlanta that same day. That's less than a week away and there's no way that it can be changed. The Bank put out a press release yesterday confirming the date of the meeting. If we cancel, there will be all kinds of questions by analysts and the stock will get clobbered. It'll be my ass. I need you two to get to the bottom of this by Friday at the latest. God forbid this has a material impact on the consolidated numbers."

Jake swallowed the harsh pill without a grimace, at least an external one. "Understood. We'll stay down here and get right on it."

He nodded confidently at Thomas to give him comfort that it would be handled expeditiously. "I'll get my firm to send down a document review team in the morning, and I'll talk to the Bank's head of IT today about locking down the data at ICon. Alex, let's find out if that can be done remotely over night."

"Once we start the interviews, we'll need an IT team to come in behind us and copy hard drives. We're also going to need some forensic accounting help, but I don't think this is the right job for one of the Big Four."

He paused and grinned as an idea struck him. "I know just the guy who can help. He's on his own and I think he's still in South Florida."

"Okay," Thomas reacted coolly. "I'll get in touch with the Bank's Audit Committee Chairman tonight to let him know what's going on and to get his sign off." Thomas stood and started packing up his portfolio. "Why don't you call my cell every night to update me. And if you get any push back from anyone at ICon, let me know immediately."

The men walked together out of the conference room and through the lobby of the executive airport. The tinted glass doors to the single gate slid open. SouthPoint's sleek Gulfstream stood ready on the tarmac. Roy was chatting with one of the maintenance crew who was finishing fueling the jet. He looked over in his aviator sunglasses and waived at them. The late Florida sun was beginning to set behind the swaying palm trees.

"Thanks gentlemen," Thomas said as he shook their hands and walked towards the plane. "And Jake," Thomas added as he glanced back, "you can tell Jenny it's my fault you're not coming home."

"Just like old times," Jake snapped back with a grin.

They watched as the plane screamed down the runway and gently climbed into the sky. Thin clouds hovered high above the coast and glowed orange from the setting sun. The lights of the cars below crawled slowly away from downtown Miami.

As the plane grew smaller, they fully expecting that morning that they would be on it and heading back in Atlanta that night. They had come armed only their briefcases, and now they were in Miami for the foreseeable future.

Jake turned to Alex, patting him on the shoulder. "Welcome to the big time. I hope you didn't have plans for the next week."

"There's nothing that I'd rather be doing," Alex said enthusiastically.

Jake chuckled as they turned to walk back into the concourse. "I know exactly what you mean. C'mon let's go shopping, I need some new clothes anyway."

* * *

They walked slowly through the glitzy Mall of the Americas on the outskirts of Miami, gazing in both directions at the ritzy stores. Above them loomed two more floors of shops topped by a ceiling of sun lights. Mostly female shoppers whisked around them, leaving behind a mixed whiff of thick perfume. As they explored for a store selling men's clothing, they felt like Lewis & Clark in a strange land.

"How about that one?" Alex said pointing up ahead at a red neon sign reading *MENZ*. As they approached, the glass storefront was blocked momentarily by a parade of women lugging swollen shopping bags. When they passed, Jake and Alex were looking at three male mannequins contorted as if they were dancing and someone yelled "freeze." The mannequins were wearing a patchwork of leather and metal held together by shiny black straps. Silver rings pierced their ears.

They both looked at each other and laughed. It was unlikely that either would need dance club wear on this investigation. As they turned to continue their quest, Alex gestured at the sign in the window and joked "the store is having a pretty good sale though."

They walked into another endless corridor of the expansive mall. "Ah, there we go. Civilization." Jake pointed to the neat script lettering of *H. Stockton* up ahead. The clothing store greeted them with chiseled-faced mannequins dressed in smart suits. No leather and no piercings. The mannequins posed as if they were conducting a very important silent business meeting. Jake and Alex walked in the store together, and paused looking around.

"Go forth and conquer."

Alex looked over at Jake, but Jake answered the question before Alex asked it.

"Don't worry, I'll talk with Jim back at the office about the firm paying for our new wardrobe. This is the kind of unexpected expense that L&E will cover for a good client . . . and SouthPoint is a *real* good client."

Alex turned to face the immaculate stacks of polo shirts and regiments of jackets standing in formation. He slowly grinned as if he had just picked the winning door on *Let's Make a Deal.*

A half an hour later, Alex met Jake at the register. He was draped with hangers of clothes.

"Looks like you plan on being here a while?" Jake joked as Alex plopped down his catch.

"Well, I . . . uh. I really have no idea. Expect the unexpected - isn't that what you say?" He shot a cocky grin at Jake.

Jake rolled his eyes and smirked to the cashier at the register. She obviously was a mother a few times over because she nodded back as if she understood Jake's gesture.

"I tell you dis," she said in a heavy Spanish accent, "sometime dose kids don't know how good dey got it." She squinted her eyes at Jake as if trying to beam the message to him.

"Oh . . . no, he's not my son," Jake chuckled motioning towards Alex behind him.

"Don worry," she said with a resentful snarl, "he somebody's son."

Jake glanced back Alex pretending to be afraid. Alex took an exaggerated step back away from the register and pointed to Jake signaling that he was on his own.

The cashier swiped his credit card and grunted her way through folding Jake's clothes.

"Thirty minutes on the dot," Jake said as he took two red starched shopping bags off of the counter. "I wish my wife could shop that fast."

"I'm sure she can. But she views it as a hobby. Try adding some sport to it and I'll be she'll get it done a whole lot quicker."

"Well first of all it's obvious that you've never been married." Jake chided him. "If it's a sport, someone wins and someone loses. And in a marriage, regardless of the outcome, it's the guy who always loses in some way. It may be years later, but believe me, he'll wind up losing. But maybe I just have to incentivize her differently. I should tell her that the faster she shops the more she can spend. I may go broke, but think of how much time I'll save. It could add years to my life."

The laughed and Jake pointed to the last hangar that Alex was holding. "Here, let *me* pay for the suit," Jake said handing his gold card to the cashier.

"No, I can't let you do that Jake. I thought the firm was paying for it?"

"This is different. I want to pay for this one. I'll tell you why in a minute."

Alex surrendered his objection. It really didn't matter to him anyway, he wasn't paying for it. Jake signed the credit card receipt and they walked out of the store.

"When I was a young associate," Jake began as they merged back into the flow of shoppers cruising the mall, "there was a partner at the firm. Mike Hammond. Mike had been a federal prosecutor in the Southern District of New York before coming to L&E. He had prosecuted some of the biggest corporate fraud cases, and by the time he came to the firm he was an icon in the investigation community. He was a real mentor to me - way back before every law firm had mandatory mentoring programs. He taught me most of what I know."

Jake paused thinking back to the beginning of his career when he was as wide-eyed as Alex.

"He ultimately retired and passed away a few years ago. But before he left the firm, he gave me his over coat. You know, one of those long gray wool coats that never go out of style. Something Cary Grant would wear in any of his movies. You really need a fedora to make it look right."

"But to him - and to me - this was a special coat. Do you remember . . . you may be too young to remember . . . but do you remember the Randall Weiss case?"

Alex looked over at Jake as they walked. "Yeah, I think. Wasn't he the guy who got inside information from printers or something like that? It was the largest ever insider trading ring on Wall Street - at least at the time, right?"

"It still is the biggest," Jake said. "Weiss had paid informants, spies really, in some of the biggest printing shops that published corporate documents, like prospectuses, proxies and SEC filings. He would get advanced notice of what companies were planning mergers, takeovers, stock offerings. I think he personally had to disgorge over two hundred million. He's still holed up in federal pen somewhere."

"Hammond was the lead prosecutor on the case. There's a famous photo of him on the steps of the federal courthouse in downtown New York right after the verdict came in. He's stoic, standing there on a cold afternoon under the pillars of the courthouse having just administered justice on a bad guy. The picture was splashed on the front pages of all the papers that day, and they called him the Corporate Cop. It was one of those great photos you see sometimes that need no explaining. Just his expression told the entire story."

Jake stopped and turned to Alex. "In that picture, he's wearing the over coat that he gave me."

"Really?! Wow, that's pretty cool."

"I've wondered what must've been going through his head. Standing there on the steps of the courthouse in frigid lower Manhattan. Looking out over the cameras and reporters having just put away the biggest swindler on Wall Street. He must've felt a sense of power . . . of justice."

They walked again silently in the mall for a minute or so, before Jake continued his story.

"I don't wear the coat that much anymore. There's not a whole lot of opportunity to wear over coats in Atlanta. But I've got it hanging in my office at home along with that photograph mounted next to it. It may sound kind of cliché, but to me that old coat represents the reasons why I got into investigating fraud. I have to admit, I look at it from time to time and it keeps me focused."

"I can see why," Alex said.

"You gotta keep in mind that an investigation is very different from any kind of case that you might work on. We're not advocates. We're not trying to develop a legal theory for our clients. We are fact finders. We're searching for the truth, no matter where it leads. We always need to be impartial because in our line of business credibility is our most valuable asset."

Alex nodded, quietly absorbing the lesson.

"I remember growing up my father used to say that life can be hard but the truth will make it a lot easier. I didn't understand exactly what he meant until years later, but it stuck with me and still it's one of the truest things I know. I think if half of the people we investigate had gotten that kind of advice from a parent we'd be out of a job."

They walked together out of the shopping mall into the humid Miami evening. Jake stopped and turned to Alex.

"I don't have any momentous garments to pass on to you, nor do I think that you could fit into any of them." Jake winked at Alex referring to his bigger frame. "But maybe that suit I bought you somehow will remind you of Hammond's old coat."

"Thanks Jake - that means a lot," Alex said sincerely to his new mentor.

"My pleasure. Let's grab some dinner and we can talk about the game plan for ICon."

* * *

"Okay, we've got a team on the way. They'll be here in tomorrow afternoon."

Jake slid his cell phone into his jacket pocket and sat down joining Alex at the dinner table. The wooden table was covered with long brown paper and the forks and knives were replaced with stainless steel tools to crack the famous crab legs at Joe's Crab Shack. A round hole cut out of the middle of the table fit a metal bucket for shells, those that made it in the bucket anyway. They were going to have to work for their dinner, but it would be well worth it.

"I spoke with Jim. He's sending down five staff lawyers to help review documents and three computer technicians to image hard drives and handle the IT. We've got hotel rooms at the Intercontinental, and they've lined up a secured conference room at the hotel that we can use as a war room. We have a call with the SouthPoint's Chief Information Officer tomorrow to talk about the computers at ICon and securing the data. I want you on the call since you're the resident expert." Jake nodded with a grin at Alex.

"Sure thing. I'll put together a list tonight of all the things we need to ask about the electronic data. Servers, applications, back ups. Don't worry, I'll interpret for you."

"Funny. You just earned yourself the job being in charge of all the documents and managing the email review. It's a thankless job, but believe me, it's the most important. Given our time frame, we'll need to do the interviews at the same time we're reviewing documents. Not the ideal situation, but those are the cards we've been dealt."

"Gotcha," Alex said making notes. "Who do you think we should interview first?"

"Well, in most investigations I like to start at the bottom of the org chart with someone who we don't think is involved in any wrongdoing and then work our way up. The lower level people in accounting who actually book the entries and record the transactions usually know the system the best and how the internal controls work. Plus, if there is something screwy going on, they typically are the ones who know."

"Can I get you guys something to drink?" A waiter asked placing plastic laminated menus in front of them.

"Yes you can," Jake said. "I'll take a Bud Light."

"Make that two."

After the waiter got out of earshot, Jake continued. "I think Patti gave us a pretty good idea of the basic accounting, so I'm inclined to start with Troy, especially because of what she told us about his reaction to her questions. Since we're going in unannounced, I don't want to give him any time to come up with a story or to talk with anyone else who may be involved. We obviously need to talk to Jane as soon as we can, and anyone else who may have worked on the Zapplication account before Patti was transferred."

"Lower on the list is the guy in HR who terminated Patti. And, at some point, we'll need to interview ICon's President, Alan Arnold. If this was just someone skimming from the bottom of the company, he may not know anything, but I'd like to size him up."

"What about the international component? Patti said that the transactions were coming from out of the country. Maybe we should talk with someone in the international sales department," Alex asked gaining confidence.

"You're right, that's a good idea."

"I hate to be naïve," Alex started, "but what's the process? I mean, do we just call these people and set up times for the interviews?"

"Not in this situation. I think that it's best if go in without any warnings. The element of surprise here is key, and we can use it to our advantage. We'll have Thomas call ICon on some pretext to make sure that the players are in the office, but then it's shock and awe."

Alex imagined bursting without warning into ICon. What's going to happen? What are they going to say? He had no idea what to expect, but he couldn't wait.

"Who is the guy that you mentioned to Thomas? The forensic accountant."

"Chuck Bradley. You'll love him. He's old school. He's like a cross between a bloodhound and a Doberman. He used to be in the FBI's financial crimes division. I think he was the only CPA they had at the time. After the FBI, he did few tours of duty in the forensic group of Blackmun Wright, the private security firm. Then he went out on his own. We've worked together on a bunch of cases. I had heard that he was supposed to be retired, but I spoke with him while we were shopping and we're going out to see him tomorrow morning."

"Where's his office? In Miami?" Alex asked.

"He doesn't work out of an office anymore. He's got a ranch in the

Everglades, about an hour or so from here. I hope you bought some hiking gear."

"I should've expected that." Alex smiled.

The waiter placed two bottles of beer on the table.

"I hope you like snow crab legs," Jake said. "This place has the best."

"Bring them on," Alex said as he rolled up his sleeves.

As Jake reached for his beer, his Blackberry vibrated in his pocket. He pulled it out and read the email that had just come in. He looked up at Alex and grinned.

"What is it?" Alex asked.

"It's from Thomas. He says 'I spoke with the audit committee chairman – you have a green light for the investigation.'"

Jake raised his beer and clinked it with Alex's bottle.

"Hold on tight."

CHAPTER EIGHT

Laws control the lesser man . . .
right conduct controls the greater one.
-- Mark Twain

The Tamiami Trail heads due west out of Miami towards the Everglades, stretching as straight as it appears on a road map. The two lanes of asphalt pierce the largest preserve of wet lands in the world, and bridge Miami's metropolis with the Everglades' sanctuary.

The white Mercedes sedan sped along the highway alone for much of the time. The vast landscape resembled the African Serengeti with expansive fields of short grass dotted with islands of shade trees. The Florida saw grass, however, concealed a stark difference in the terrains. Instead of Africa's hard dusty ground beneath, the foliage in South Florida sprouted from a hidden bed of water.

"Where did you grow up?" Jake asked as they watched the endless scenery pass by.

"I lived with my Mom in Marietta after my parents split when I was in high school. I'm the youngest of three boys. Both my brothers dropped out of school, and believe it or not, I was the first in my family to graduate from college."

"That's quite an accomplishment."

"Yeah, but it also carries quite a burden. I wasn't allowed to fail. My grandmother lived with us while my mom worked two jobs. I still remember my grandmother sitting me down when I was about sixteen or so. My grades were okay, but we didn't have a lot of money so I didn't think that college was an option. She told me that she had been stashing money away since my grandfather died. A little here, a little there, and after a while, it added up. She told me that she would pay for college but if I didn't graduate I'd have to pay it all back to her – with interest."

Alex chuckled to himself remembering his grandmother's wrinkly finger waiving at him as she offered him the deal.

"She sounds like a real matriarch."

"She is an amazing woman, especially for her time. She worked as an office manager before most women even worked outside the home. She set up investment accounts and traded in the market when people were scared of Wall Street. All with no formal education. You'll love this. She and my grandfather met before World War Two and she was three years older than him. Back in the day, it was frowned upon for a man to date an older woman. So she lied about her age and told him she was a year younger than him. For the next sixty two years while they were married, she told my grandfather and everyone else in the family that she was younger than she really was."

"You're kidding," Jake said with a smile.

"A week after my grandfather died, we were all at dinner together and she just nonchalantly blurted out that she really was eighty four. Can you imagine? My mother was even planning her eightieth birthday party, and she had turned eighty four years before."

They laughed as the car continued along the agonizingly straight highway. After forty five minutes, the car slowed and turned off the highway onto a thin dirt road that had been baked hard by years of pounding sunlight. The road led from the open highway into groves of mango trees with grey Spanish moss hanging low on the limbs.

"We're officially off the map," Alex said pointing to the GPS. The screen was completely blank except for the lost arrow pointing upwards.

"And we're officially out of touch," Jake said holding up his Blackberry with no coverage.

"Scary, huh?!"

After several miles, Jake turned slowly onto a gravel driveway. Two columns of stacked shale stone straddled the driveway. A worn wooden sign hanging on the right column read *Bradley Ranch*. A small metal sign underneath warned *Trespassers will be shot . . . repeatedly.*

"Southern hospitality, I guess?" Alex joked as the Mercedes now dusted from the trip passed through the gate and drove deeper into the

Everglades. The broken tree cover cast jagged stripes of sunlight on the windy drive.

After several bumpy minutes, the dense over brush halted and the drive opened to large clearing. A grand two-story ranch sat behind a circular turnaround drive with an adjacent four car garage to the left and an airboat dock to the right. The house overlooked a breathtaking view of dark lagoons snaking through the grassy wet lands as far as the eye could see.

The tired brakes on the car sighed as it stopped in front of the house. Jake and Alex stepped out of the car slowly and were covered in a blanket of humidity. The high pitched buzz of cicadas played background to the guttural sound of frog calls.

They began to walk towards the front door when suddenly a loud gun shot rang out, causing both to shudder instinctively. A group of birds flapped away frantically. Another shot followed. Jake and Alex looked at each other frozen in their tracks not sure whether to run or hide.

"He's out back shooting clays. Big competition next month." They looked up on the porch of the house and saw a woman in her mid fifties wearing a khaki green outfit and a welcoming smile. Jake and Alex propped up quickly trying to cover their startled reaction to the shots.

"I'm Nancy Bradley, nice to meet you. Chuck's expecting you. Just follow the path over there. It'll take you around back to the blinds." She gave them a friendly wave and pointed towards the side of the house.

"Thanks," Jake said.

They composed themselves and headed towards the path. The worn gravel path led away from the house into the underbrush. Again, shots rang out but this time they did not flinch. A long white crane leapt from its perch nearby and glided away.

After a short hike, they saw a small wooden deck rising several feet off of the ground. Chuck was standing near the far rail of the deck, turned sideways and facing out over the swamp. His right arm was cocked high as he cradled the butt of a shotgun against his shoulder. His right cheek barely touching the polished wood. He was wearing a fluorescent orange cap and green polarized shooting glasses. The thin cord of his earplugs dangled behind him.

As Jake and Alex approached the trapshooting stand, Chuck tapped a switch on the ground with his left foot. A circular clay pigeon flung out in front of him from a hidden trap on the right side, and an instant later another clay shot out from a trap on the left. The clays flew towards each other at different angles. Chuck's shoulders pivoted and he fired two shots almost simultaneously. The sound of the shotgun rang out as it recoiled in his tight grip. The higher clay shattered into dust and the lower clay broke into several pieces that fell aimlessly from the sky. He lowered the smoking gun and cracked open the barrel. Two empty shells ejected out onto the wooden stand.

"Nice shot," Jake yelled.

Chuck turned and pulled out his earplugs, the shotgun bent at a right angle over his left arm.

"Hey there," he said placing the shotgun in a stand next to another gun. "C'mon up."

Jake and Alex stepped onto the trapshooting stand as Chuck extended his hand.

"Looking good old man," Jake said affectionately. "This is my associate Alex Perry."

"Nice to know you," Chuck said shaking hands firmly with Alex.

"My pleasure, sir."

Chuck was in his late fifties and rugged from a lifetime of hunting and fishing. His six feet four frame still stood strong, honed by daily exercise and hard work on the ranch. He had a charcoal mustache that didn't show the same signs of thinning as did his hair line. He was a man's man, the kind pictured in a *Field & Stream* magazine kneeling next to a fallen deer. But beneath his rough exterior was a man of uncommon intelligence. He had a Masters of Accounting from the University of Virginia and had the highest score on his CPA test in the state. He quickly got bored with the monotony of public accounting, and instead devoted his talents to the FBI's financial crime division. For the rest of his career, in one way or another, Chuck hunted white collar criminals with the same determination as a rare twelve point buck.

"It's been a while, good to see you," Chuck said turning Jake. He removed his shooting glasses and shook Jake's hand. "Your call yesterday brought back some memories. Some of them even were good."

Jake laughed. "Well, I figured that you were getting rusty out here in the swamp, missing all the lying, cheating, and stealing in the big city."

"I guess you're talking about your clients, huh?" Chuck cackled at his own joke. "As I recall, the times you hired me were when one of your clients was knee-deep in some kind of trouble."

Chuck turned to Alex, who was gazing down at the two gleaming shotguns standing erect against the side of the deck.

"You gotta watch out for this guy," Chuck said to him motioning towards Jake, "you never know who to trust when you're working on a case for him."

Alex chuckled politely not really knowing what Chuck meant.

"Well, some things don't change," Jake said winking to Chuck.

"Before we talk business, you wanna shoot some targets?" Chuck said to Alex sensing the young man's interest. "I know better than to give a gun to Jake here."

"Yeah, sure," Alex said glancing at Jake as if he needed approval.

"Here, you'll need these." Chuck reached in a pocket of his cargo pants and pulled out an extra set of earplugs. "You can use my glasses. Have you ever shot before?"

"When I was a kid. My grandfather had a farm and he taught my brothers and me how to shoot. He had an old Remington shotgun, an 870 I think. I never hit anything except for some defenseless trees."

"The Wingmaster," Chuck said nodding.

"Huh?" Jake asked.

"The Wingmaster. It was Remington's most successful pump shotgun. Some consider, including yours truly, that it is the finest shotgun ever made. They're still making 870's today."

"Here," Chuck said to Alex, "why don't you try this one. It's a Browning Citori Gold Trap. She's my pride and joy."

Chuck slid the loading lever open and inserted two shells in the over-under ported barrels. He handed the imposing shotgun to Alex. The polished grain of the stock felt smooth in his hands, and the sunlight glimmered off of the silver receiver plate engraved with pheasants flying in opposite directions.

"Wow," Alex said feeling the weight of the shotgun. "This is a beautiful gun."

Jake inched back to the steps of the trapshooting stand as Alex readied himself at the front rail with the gun facing down.

Chuck stood next to Alex positioning him. "Make sure that you mount the gun tight against your shoulder, and keep your knees bent a little. Keep your arms firm and as you follow the clay swing your upper body at your trunk without moving your legs. Your arms, shoulder, and the gun should move together."

Alex raised the gun and mounted it against his shoulder muscle. He leaned his head towards the gun feeling the glasses rest lightly on the stock. He closed his left eye focusing on the sight mark at the end of the long sleek barrels.

"That's good," Chuck said, "and hold the forearm still. When you call for it, the clay will come from your left across the view. Try to follow the line of its path and then fire in front of it. Trap shooting is all about geometry. You have to see the angles. And don't forget to follow through after you fire. It's just like golf. Keep your eyes on the clay, swing the gun, and follow through."

"Gotcha," Alex said with anticipation.

Chuck released the safety and put his earplugs back in as he stepped a few paces backwards. Jake quickly jammed his fingers to his ears.

"Whenever you're ready," Chuck said loudly.

Alex took a deep breath, waited a moment, and then yelled "pull!"

Chuck tapped the switch on the deck with his foot, and a red clay whizzed out from behind the left brush racing across their view. Alex swung the gun trying to catch up with the clay and he squeezed the trigger. The recoil was stronger than he expected, and he bounced back a step or two. The untouched clay continued flying on its trajectory and landed safely out of sight in the tall grass.

"Try again," Chuck said. "This time it's coming from the right so you'll be able to pick it up sooner. The most important thing is don't try to hit the clay with the shot, lead the clay into the shot. When a shot is fired, the pellets come out together and then spread apart depending on the size of the choke. So, think of shot as a string of pellets. You want to throw out the string in front of the clay and let the clay fly into it. Make sure that the string is on the same plane as the clay. That's the science behind trap shooting."

"Alright," Alex said getting back into position, thinking that understanding the science was much easier than implementing the technique. After a moment, he yelled "pull!"

The clay shot out from the right side on a higher trajectory than the first. Alex swung the gun in front of the clay's angle and fired. A small piece of the clay burst off, and the remaining section wobbled as it flew injured into the brush.

"That's the way to do it kid," Chuck exclaimed like a proud teacher to his pupil.

Alex turned and beamed towards them. "That's a blast," he said loudly above the ringing in his ears and he handed the shot gun back to Chuck.

Chuck placed the shotguns in a soft case and gathered his gear. As the three walked back along the path to the house, Chuck patted Alex on the shoulder and said "shooting clays is just like catching bad guys . . . sometimes you need to throw out a string and let 'em run right into it."

* * *

"So, I assume you didn't drive out all this way just to learn how to shoot," Chuck chided Jake sarcastically. They were sitting on the back porch of the expansive ranch overlooking a dark motionless lagoon. It was quiet other than the constant hum of cicadas and the squeaking of the rocking chairs. The sun was just beginning to inch downward in the sky.

"One of my clients, SouthPoint Bank out of Atlanta recently bought a company down here in Miami called ICon. The full name is Internet Connections. Before I get in too deep, do you think you have any conflicts with ICon? Here is a list of the officers and directors."

Jake handed a printout to Chuck of ICon's website listing its executives. Chuck glanced it over.

"Nope. Never heard of it or any of these folks."

"Okay, good." Jake leaned forward in his rocking chair. "ICon is an internet payment processor. It's the conduit between a consumer using his credit card to buy something on the internet and the credit card company. The consumer puts his credit card information into the pay page, hits go, the transaction is sent to ICon, it has software that scrubs it for fraud, and then it sends it to the credit card company for approval. The transaction bounces back through ICon to the consumer and he sees in a few seconds if his card has been approved or declined. ICon makes about ten cents or so per transaction. If you have the right technology, it's like printing money."

Chuck's wife swung open the screen door carrying three large glasses of sweet iced tea on a platter.

"Thanks Mrs. Bradley," Jake said as she placed the platter on a small wicker table.

"Don't let him fool you guys, he hates retirement. He's itching to get out of the swamp for a while."

"That's enough, dear," Chuck said with his deep voice emphasizing *dear.*

Sarah Bradley winked to Jake and smiled as she strode back into the house. Jake waited until the screen door shut behind her, and he continued.

"Six months ago, SouthPoint wanted to get into the e-commerce game. But most of these internet payment processors had already been gobbled up by other banks. So when the opportunity arose SouthPoint jumped on ICon. They negotiated for an early exclusivity to keep other bidders away, and they wrapped up the deal in about two weeks. $750 million in cash. There are some small deferred earn outs, but essentially SouthPoint went all in."

Jake took a gulp of the iced tea. It was the syrupy Southern style that drew an 'ahh' after each sip.

"Yesterday, Alex and I interviewed a former employee of ICon. She was in the accounting department for about three months and then was fired for some 'personality conflict' with the CFO. She's a CPA and former internal audit. She seems credible as far as we can tell. If she's right, she found some kind of scheme, maybe a fictitious vendor or client, to the tune of about $500,000, along with a host of internal control weaknesses and tone at the top issues." Jake paused to study Chuck's reaction to what he was hearing so far.

Chuck rocked forward in his chair and put down his glass. "So, if my math is right . . ." which he knew that it was, "$500,000 is roughly, uh, .06% of the $750 million purchase price. That's not even close to being material, nor would I think enough to justify the hourly rates of an esteemed L&E partner such as yourself."

"I see that you haven't lost your sarcasm," Jake joked. "Look, I don't have a good feeling about this one. The ink is barely dry on the deal, and the red flags are everywhere. SouthPoint paid three quarters of a billion dollars for ICon just a month ago and assured everyone, including the SEC and the banking commission, that this was a good deal for shareholders and that it wouldn't change the Bank's conservative risk structure. The stock price bumped up twenty percent and has stayed at that level ever since."

"You can imagine that questions have been raised about whether SouthPoint rushed due diligence and did the deal too fast. Who knows what could've been missed? If there is something that the Bank should've found, it could ruin more than just the next couple of fiscal years, it could destroy the Bank's reputation. SouthPoint is a 150 year-old bank. The former Governor of Georgia is on the board. If this thing blows up, there could be shareholder class actions, derivative actions, government investigations." Jake paused to let the gravity of the situation sink in.

"Chuck, there's going to be a lot of eyes on this one, and I need someone really good and someone who I can really trust. That's a very short list, and you're at the top."

Chuck leaned back on the rocking chair and gazed out over the wetlands. Alex sat quietly holding his sweating iced tea and listening intently.

After a few moments, Chuck cleared his throat. "You know, I'm supposed to be retired?"

"Yeah, your wife told us how that's going," Jake snickered back.

"Well, let me talk with the misses. What's your timeframe?"

Jake shifted and sat back in the rocking chair as if retreating far enough away to be safe from Chuck's reaction.

"We're going in unannounced tomorrow morning to lock the place down and to start interviews. We have less than a week to finish because SouthPoint has an annual shareholders meeting on Monday and the ICon deal will be at the top of the agenda."

"Christ Jake, that's not much of a heads up. Does he do this to you often?" Chuck said lightheartedly turning to Alex.

Alex glanced over at Jake before answering Chuck. "Yes sir. In fact, he did it to me yesterday morning. I just showed up at the airport and didn't even know what state I was going to. I even had to buy these clothes."

All of them laughed.

"I would've called you earlier, but this all has gone down pretty fast. The General Counsel of the Bank is a friend of mine and he needed someone right away. It's part of the job."

"I'm beginning to remember why I retired," Chuck snorted.

They rocked for several minutes as Chuck deliberated silently. With a deep growl, he finally said "Aw right. I'm in. I guess Sarah will be glad to get me out of the ranch for a few days. Tell me where I need to be tomorrow morning."

Jake popped up to the front of his chair and he reached into his briefcase pulling out a manila folder. He handed it to Chuck.

"We're staying at the Hotel Intercontinental in downtown Miami. I already made reservations for you."

"That's fairly presumptuous of you," Chuck quipped.

"Not presumptuous . . . persuasive," Jake winked back. "We have a secured conference room at the hotel that we're setting up as a war room. We're meeting there tomorrow at 8:30 for me to brief the team, and then we'll go to ICon around ten o'clock. All of the executives should be in by then. ICon is just a few miles away from the hotel on West Flagler. The plan is first to interview the VP of sales, a guy named Troy Vickerson, and then to talk to the CFO. Alex, do have the disk for Chuck?"

"Yup," Alex said reaching into his briefcase. He gave Chuck a single disk in an unmarked case.

"On the disk, you'll find Alex's interview memo of our conversation yesterday with Patti Tomanski, the former employee. There also is some information that she gave us about the client at issue, which is called Zapplication. There are pay requests, transaction reports, some other data, and a nice photo of Zapplication's office in the middle of a runway."

"Huh?" Chuck said reaching for the disk.

"This Patti woman traced the address where Zapplication supposedly was located and it turned out to be at the Miami Airport."

"Goodness" Chuck said. "By the way, how will I know which conference room you'll be in at the Intercontinental? I don't suppose it'll say ICon Investigation Room."

"Just look at the information placard. You'll know it when you see it."

Jake closed his briefcase and stood, followed by Chuck and Alex who gulped down the rest of his tea.

Jake extended his hand to Chuck. "It's good to work together again."

Chuck stood on the front porch and waived at the car as it pulled away down the dirt driveway leaving a dusty cloud trailing behind.

"So when are you leaving?" Sarah asked as she opened the screen door and walked onto the porch.

"Tomorrow morning. But I'm sure it's nothing."

CHAPTER NINE

*The first and worst of all frauds is to cheat
one's self. All sin is easy after that.*
-- Pearl Bailey

Nine Months Before the Deal

Fisher Island is a tiny slice of land just a third of a square mile of pure wealth floating in Biscayne Bay below South Beach where the ultra rich and celebrities call home. It once was the private island home of the Vanderbilts and was named for automotive parts pioneer and developer Carl Fisher. The luxuriant island is so exclusive that it is only accessible by private ferry or helicopter. Not surprisingly, the U.S. Census Bureau reported in 2000 that Fisher Island had the highest per capita income of any place in the country. It was here that Troy Vickerson came to meet a prospective client – his biggest ever.

The engines of the car ferry rumbled as it eased slowly towards the unloading dock on the island. Several crewmembers jumped onto the dock to guide the ferry. After it was secured, a crewman signaled to the cars waiting on the ferry and they began to slowly drive off of the swaying platform onto shore. Troy's red Mustang hummed as it accelerated slowly onto the island passing overhanging palm trees and bright orange hibiscus.

Visitors to Fisher Island have to pass by a guard house on Dock Road, which is adorned with an ornate iron gate. As Troy's car approached, an armed guard leaned out of the structure.

"Evening sir, where are you headed?"

Troy leaned over in his tinted Ray Ban sunglasses. His dark hair was slicked back matching his bulging black shirt and sport coat.

"I'm a guest of Ivan Dvorak at 5151 Fisher Island Drive. My name is Troy Vickerson. He's expecting me."

"Can I see your ID please?"

Troy handed his driver's license to the guard, who disappeared into a small guard house. Several minutes later he returned handing it back to Troy.

"Thank you sir. Follow Dock Road until it ends and make a right on Fisher Island Drive. It will curve to the right and Mr. Dvorak's is the second house on the left."

"Thanks," Troy said and pulled through the gate and onto the exclusive island. The massive homes gazed at him from behind lush landscaping as Troy drove slowly past the monuments of wealth. Foreboding gates embraced the mansions intended more for prestige than for protection.

It only took a few minutes to drive across the tiny enclave, and he slowed peeking at a neighborhood few will ever see. As the road curved to the right, Troy saw the gold engraved mailbox for 5151 Fisher Island Drive. He pulled into the crushed shell driveway and stopped at a security call box in front of a closed wooden gate. After being confirmed as a guest, the gates glided open revealing a glass and stucco mansion with Spanish roof tiles nestled at the end of a tropical drive. The contrast between the crimson tiles, the emerald foliage, and the pink setting sun was breathtaking.

Troy parked in the motor court next to a sleek black Ferrari and a gold Bentley. He gazed at the array of luxury automobiles as he approached the huge arched doorway to the house. Faint melodies played in the warm breeze, which was scented by the aroma of the overhanging flora.

An oscillating chime sounded and Troy stepped back from the plated doorbell. After a few minutes, the huge crystal-engraved doors of Ivan Dvorak's mansion opened and a stunning brunette in a skin tight short dress appeared. Her long tanned legs draped all the way down to the marble floor of the foyer. In the background, Troy could hear the faint thumping of dance music.

"Uh, hello," Troy stammered out almost speechless at the unexpected beauty standing in front of him. "I'm Troy Vickerson. Ivan is expecting me."

"Come on in," she said turning around and flashing her perfect body. "He's out by the pool."

He followed her through the luxurious mansion, which was splashed with flowing gold draperies and vivid contemporary artwork. Ivan's collection of art rivaled any gallery and boasted two original Monets. The entire back of the house was a wall of windows looking out over a tropical oasis that was centered around a sparkling blue pool. Beyond the pool, Biscayne Bay shimmered in the setting sun, and the infinity edge of the pool made it appear as if the water spilled right over into the bay. Dusk cast a soft glow over the scene.

The music was coming from a cabana on the far side of the pool. Several groups of people were mingling around the pool area, while scantily-clad hostesses delivered fluorescent color drinks. The lagoon-style pool was lit with velvety lights and several of the more audacious guests were frolicking in the pool.

They walked out of the back doors and down wide stone carved steps leading to the pool. At the bottom of the steps, a busty blonde hostess offered Troy a drink off of a silver tray, which he graciously accepted.

His escort pointed towards the cabana. "Ivan is there."

Troy saw Ivan sitting in a lounge chair next to the cabana with two young women hanging on him – but their attention was not because of his looks. He was a stout balding Cossack with thin eyes and a squished nose. A crescent of thin brown hair wrapped around his head. His linen shirt was draped open and a thick gold necklace hung loosely resting on a plump of chest hair. Ivan's stubby hands stroked the women's smooth thighs as he chewed on an unlit Cuban cigar. In any other setting, he would be an exemplar of mediocrity. But in this tropical paradise, he was the king.

Troy thanked his guide and made his way along the pool to the cabana. As he approached the cabana, Ivan turned and saw him. He smiled at Troy with a toothy grin and tried to shoo the young women off of his knees.

"Welcome, my friend," Ivan said in a polished Russian accent.

He stood and reached his meaty hand out towards Troy. They shook hands and for an instant they resembled before and after pictures in an advertisement for body building supplements.

"Girls, can you give us a few minutes?" Ivan said taking the chewed cigar out of his mouth.

The two women walked towards the pool and, for a moment, the two men admired their exit.

"My sisters," Ivan said winking to Troy and then bellowing loudly.

"Nice family," Troy joked back.

In that instant, both men knew that they were going to get along.

"Have a seat, please." Ivan motioned to a chair. "Thanks for coming to see me."

"My pleasure. This is really a beautiful place Mr. Dvorak."

"Please, call me Ivan. All my friends call me Ivan. When I came to the U.S., I looked for a home with security, you know. I am a very private person. I couldn't find a castle with a moat, so what better place than an island?" Ivan laughed from his round belly, and Troy chuckled politely along with his host.

He had met Ivan two weeks earlier at a swanky party in Boca Raton. Ivan's date for the evening was an aspiring Brazilian model who moonlighted at The Crescent Room with Troy's girlfriend. While the two girls chatted feverously, the two men sipped Mojitos and nodded politely to one another. When Troy's verbose girlfriend mentioned that Troy was in the internet business, Ivan promptly took interest.

The two men quickly delved into an absorbed discussion of e-commerce. Little did Troy know that he happened upon an international tycoon who owned a vast array of websites. When Troy mentioned ICon and described its business, Ivan grew more interested and the men took over the conversation.

The girls soon became bored and wandered off to mingle. But Ivan and Troy spent the next two hours talking about web technology and, in particular, problems that Ivan was having with some of his international websites. The girls eventually returned to pull them away, but not before Ivan invited Troy to a party that he was having at his house in two weeks.

Ivan handed him his card. It was gold and embossed in silk fabric. The card read only *Ivan Dvorak, 5151 Fisher Island, FL.*

When he saw the address on Florida's most exclusive island, Troy instantly realized that he was dealing with a big time player.

"When we met a couple of weeks ago," Ivan began stuffing the cigar back into his mouth, "I told you that some of my franchises in Russia, the Ukraine and such were having, let's just say, difficulties in processing internet transactions."

"Yeah, the internet payment company you're using is blocking some international credit card transactions, right?"

"That is true, and it is causing a problem. A big problem. My friends are unhappy, and when they are unhappy, I am unhappy. I hope you can help."

"Well it may be the way your current internet payment company is setting up your merchant account, or it's because their system just can't handle the load."

Troy kicked in his sales pitch. "ICon has the cutting edge technology, and we just put five million dollars into our Velocity platform. It's state-of-the-art. You'll have visibility into everything. You can see real-time all of the transactions, approvals, denials, or bounce backs so you know instantly if there is any reduction in processing efficiency. We have clients in thirty two countries and our system can easily handle all of your international traffic."

Troy paused as a cocktail waitress walked by the cabana knowing not to interrupt Ivan unless he asked for her to come over.

"We can set up each of your websites on a trial basis with our platinum merchant account, and I can waive the fees for the first ten thousand transactions. Do you know the average monthly T-count of your sites?"

"Collectively it is around a hundred million."

Troy blinked several times reflexively, trying unsuccessfully to hide any reaction. The transaction count for most of his clients hovered around a few hundred thousand per month, maybe a million or so for the larger sites. A hundred million per month would not only be ICon's largest single client by far, it was more than all of the transactions of all of ICon's clients combined. The commissions alone could make Troy unbelievably rich.

"Uh . . . a hundred million, okay. Okay. How many different sites do you operate?"

"Before we get too far, I like to know who I'm dealing with. I am told that a couple of years ago you had run in, shall we say, with the government. Is this true?"

Troy was caught off guard and he could feel his face flushing under his tan skin. He shifted on the chair as his mind raced for a response. Ivan's small eyes did not give Troy any room to wander. He had no idea how Ivan had found out about his past, but it didn't matter.

"Uh, yeah that's right," Troy said as the pitch of his voice lowered and he glanced down to the left for an instant. "It was the Federal Trade Commission." Troy began to stammer out an explanation not knowing how much he should reveal, or how much Ivan already knew.

"I was working for a tele-based company that offered audio text services. It was a 1-900 number. We were accused of cramming charges on phone bills. But we settled the case and there were no criminal charges brought."

"What kind of product was this audio text service?"

"Um, it was a dating service."

"A *dating* service, you say?" Ivan's thin eyebrows rose up towards his forehead and a wry grin etched across his round face.

Troy fidgeted, uncomfortable with where the conversation was going. He finally answered truthfully figuring that his host already knew. "It was phone sex."

"Did you do it? The cramming, I mean."

"With all due respect, do I have to answer the question?" Troy asked carefully as if stepping over a land mine.

"If you want my business, I demand honesty from all my friends." Ivan's accent added a tone of graveness.

Troy glanced out over the pool area surrounded by Ivan's *friends* who were relishing in the mix of erotica and affluence. He could smell the fragrance of wealth floating among the palmettos. He did not want to leave so soon.

"Yes," Troy finally said still looking away from Ivan.

A long moment of silence hung in the air.

"Thank you for your honesty," Ivan said. "There are five hundred, give or take."

"Huh," Troy asked turning back towards Ivan.

"There are about five hundred websites operated by a holding company that is called Modos Operations. Most of the sites are in Eastern Europe, but I'd like to expand into Asia. I have some conditions that have to be met first."

He glared over at Troy and his eyes narrowed. "I will not sign any contract or provide any information about Modos other than wiring instructions to its offshore bank account. The client account at ICon has to be in Modos' name only with no sub accounts listing the names of the websites. You will deal only with me, and I will deal only with you. Also, no one at ICon can have access to Modos' transactions except you and one IT person who I will approve. As I said, privacy is important to me. Will any of these conditions cause a problem?"

"Um, well, the agreements we have with the credit card companies require that all sites related to a merchant account be identified by owner." Troy paused. "But I'm sure that I can find a way around that."

"Very good. Then we shall do business." Ivan stood up and motioned for the two waiting women to return. "Set it up and call me on Monday."

Troy stood, shaking Ivan's hand. "By the way, what kind of websites are we talking about?" He knew the answer, but had to ask the question.

Ivan smiled at him with a sly grin. "Dating services."

He cackled loudly and wrapped his thick arm around the tight waist of one of women. She sat down next to him and giggled as he whispered into her ear.

Ivan turned to the other woman and muttered something to her in Russian. Troy didn't know what he said, but he heard him call her Sasha.

Sasha nodded obediently and motioned to Troy to follow her. The Latin music rippled in the warm breeze as they walked off together towards the sprawling house.

Troy glanced back over his shoulder at Ivan. His other "sister" was perched on his stumpy thigh and his cigar bobbled in his lips as he was laughing at something.

"What did he say," Troy asked his attractive chaperone. Her soft blonde hair played around her dark eyes and reached down her smooth back. She had on a sheer ivory dress with a low-cut back held on by spaghetti straps over her tanned shoulders.

"He wants me to show you a special piece in his collection," Sasha answered with a smile in a thick Russian accent as she motioned towards the house. "He likes to show it off for his new friends."

Troy was not an art connoisseur but he was more than happy to peruse some paintings with her. He was sure that whatever Ivan wanted to show him was going to be impressive.

The chilled air of the house greeted them in tandem with a hostess handing out flutes of champagne. The atrium of the house opened to huge skylights that fed two fanned palm trees in the center. Lining the walls were colorful paintings hugged by thick frames. Guests mingled throughout the house admiring the residential museum that Ivan had created.

"Pretty nice place," Troy said as they crossed the atrium. "It must've cost a fortune to collect all of this artwork."

"He is a very - how do you say - influentious person. Many of these are gifts from Ivan's friends."

Troy decided not to correct her English. "Man I wish I had friends like that!"

She grinned at him and their eyes held each other for a moment.

"His friends are his family. If you are Ivan's friend, you are in his family. And family is forever where he comes from. You don't leave the family."

Troy was about to ask her what she meant, but he decided to leave her comment alone not wanting to spoil the mood.

"Where is he from?"

"Russia. From a town not far where I grew up. That's how I got to America. Ivan paid for me to come here. He's very generous. Many of the girls are here because of his generosity."

They started up an open curved staircase that wrapped around the atrium and led to the second floor. As they climbed the stairs next to each other, Troy looked over to her.

"Are you one of his friends . . . I mean his family?"

She smiled at his question. "No. I just work for Ivan."

"Well what does he do for his 'friends' that compel them to send him these seven figure thank yous?"

She paused as if trying to phrase her answer properly. "He makes them money. Much money."

"I'd say so. Does all of this come from his websites?"

"You ask a lot of questions, no?" She winked at him and continued up the staircase conspicuously not answering his question.

At the top, they were greeted by a magnificent floor to ceiling canvas with brightly colored geometric shapes pieced together in an abstract design. Troy stopped to admire the original Kadinsky. According to some, Kadinsky gave birth to abstract art, stirring up controversy when his work was shown across Europe in the late 1800s. The sporadic arrangement of curves and colors seemed to jump off of the background – a disturbing visual to some in the nineteenth century.

"Wow, this is amazing." Troy appreciated the grandeur of the painting even though he had never heard of its creator. "Is this what Ivan wanted me to see?"

She smiled again at Troy. "No, it's over here." She motioned to a set of mahogany doors at the end of a short alcove.

They placed their empty champagne flutes on a marble table in the hallway. Troy opened the doors and walked into the room. At first the room was dark. As his eyes began to adjust from the bright hallway, tiny lights emerged in front of him. Then like an illusion before his eyes, downtown Miami suddenly appeared. He blinked away the shadows and realized that the entire back wall of the room was a semicircle of glass. The view looked over the twinkling bay at the gleaming skyscrapers of the city on the other side. The dark sky added contrast making the office buildings appear to shimmer.

"Whoa," Troy muttered as he gazed out at the breathtaking sight. "Now that's a million dollar view."

The circular room was wrapped in plush auburn couches flanked by low glass tables. Swollen gold satin pillows were resting at the arms of the curved couches, and a cream shaggy fur rug encircled the room. The moon cast a dim glow into the room.

Troy glanced around and didn't see any artwork on the walls to his left or right.

"So where's the piece Ivan wanted me to see?" he asked Sasha who was still behind him.

"It's right here," she said closing the doors to the room.

Troy turned around and saw her gently push the thin straps of her dress off of her shoulders. The dress tumbled daintily over her naked body to floor. She gently stepped out of her shoes and over her fallen dress towards him. Her rounded breasts hung firmly over her sculpted stomach, and a small chain dangled from her pierced belly button ending in a diamond that glittered like a star.

"Compliments of Ivan," she whispered as she approached him.

They kissed passionately as Troy glided his right hand down her bare back. He traced the curves of her tight butt and lightly held the back of her head with his left hand. As they kissed, she ran her hands slowly over his chiseled chest towards his waist. She grasped his tight shirt with her French-tipped fingernails and pulled his shirt out of the tuck. Troy slipped off his sport coat and reached down to pull his shirt over his head. The room was quiet other than the faint music below from the pool and their passionate moans.

Sasha licked down his neck and kissed his chest as he worked on his belt. He pulled off his slacks and she gently pushed him towards the couch. He eased down into the couch in a sitting position, and she slowly straddled him. She pressed her full breasts against his chest and they kissed deeply.

As she began to grind on his lap, she arched her back and the shadows played over her smooth stomach. Troy clutched her waist and she groaned as she rocked on top of him. Their light caressing amplified into fervent stroking. Through the wall of windows behind her, the downtown buildings of Miami silently watched them from afar.

He now understood why Ivan's friends had been so grateful. It was not just about money, it was about power. Money breeds influence, and influence creates power. Not the kind of power relegated to individual politicians, but the kind of power amassed by governments.

Troy was flirting with an intoxicating world of unimaginable wealth and insatiable sex. He had craved to bask in the riches and pleasures of internet erotica, and now it was in his grasp. Ivan had called him his friend, and his mind raced with the fringe benefits of being Ivan's friend – his family. He had arrived.

As Troy watched Sasha's swaying silhouette against the city lights, his head whirled with carnal ambitions.

CHAPTER TEN

Rather fail with honor than succeed by fraud.
-- Sophocles

One Month After The Deal

Chuck Bradley stepped out of his late-model GMC Yukon, and handed the worn keys to the valet at the Intercontinental Hotel. The young valet gave him an annoyed glance as he climbed up into the dingy truck, trying not to stain his immaculate uniform. Palm trees lining the motor court waved in the salt air blowing in from Biscayne Bay.

Chuck walked into the vast marble lobby, which already was buzzing with business people and tourists milling about. In the center of the atrium, a huge stone sculpture rose out of a water fountain and the sound of falling water drowned out the chatter.

"Can I help you?" An attractive dark-skinned concierge approached him.

"Uh, sure. I'm looking for the conference rooms."

"Certainly. Just take the elevators to the third floor. Can I help you find a particular room?"

"No thanks. I'm told I'll know it when I see it."

He shared an elevator with a giggling newlywed couple who couldn't keep their hands off of each other, and he thought to himself that the third floor could not come quick enough. Stepping off the elevator, Chuck saw an electronic board with a listing of the thirty conference rooms and the groups occupying them. He scanned down the names of the groups looking for anything familiar. As his eyes approached the end of the list, he was just about to start from the beginning again when the last one caught his eye. He grinned. The group meeting in the Trinity room was Wingmaster, the name of the classic shotgun that he had told Jake and Alex about.

The conference room was at the far end of the hallway in a quiet alcove. Outside the room was a placard reading *Wingmaster – Private.* He took a deep breath and pushed the door open.

Two long tables divided the room in half. On one of the tables, there were five flat screen computer monitors standing at attention with printers behind each of them. A swarm of wires and cables ran under the table and connected to several blinking electrical boxes. Three female and two male associates of L&E sat facing the monitors focused on the screen. They were dressed in casual clothes, a sure sign that they would be in front of the computers for the foreseeable future.

The attire of those at the other table was quite different. Jake was at the head of the table in a dark blue suit with a red tie piercing a starched white shirt. The red, white, and blue color motif was no accident. It was the uniform that he wore at the start of all of his investigations. In Jake's mind he was pursuing truth and justice – as if he were standing on the cold steps outside the Manhattan courthouse in Mike Hammond's wool overcoat.

Panned out on either side of the table were attentive lawyers and consultants listening eagerly to Jake. It was a like a small battalion of navy blue soldiers in pinstripes.

The door behind Chuck shut loudly and everyone in the room looked over at him. His gray suit was a couple of years behind his body and it hugged him too tightly in certain places. But otherwise, he cleaned up well and had a presence in any room he entered.

"Hey Chuck," Jake called out to him. Jake stood and walked over to greet him.

"Folks, please meet Chuck Bradley. Forensic accountant extraordinaire."

"Nice to know you," Chuck said in his deep voice.

Jake motioned Chuck towards the document reviewers. "Come here, let me show you something neat."

Jake and Chuck walked behind the associates stationed at the computer screens. The screens displayed an array of concentric circles connected by straight axis lines. Each circle surrounded small dots, which were in a spiral pattern within the circle. It looked like the atomic structure of an element from a high school chemistry textbook.

"Last night, we had an IT team take a snapshot of ICon's servers. We extracted the emails of ICon's President, the CFO, the VP of Sales, and a few others. We filtered the emails by a list of key words, including Zapplication and its client number. Then all of the emails that contained any of the key terms were loaded into this sophisticated document review software."

Chuck gazed at the circles and dots on the screen having no idea what he was looking at.

"The software uses algorithms to group the emails into clusters, which are those circles that you see there on the screen, based on the concepts or ideas in the emails. One cluster might contain emails discussing revenues, another might be discussing expenses, or whatever the subject is. Each of those dots in the clusters is an email."

"So a reviewer can click on the cluster to see what the subject is and if it's something they want to review, then they click on each dot and look at the emails. If the subject is something irrelevant, the reviewer can discard the entire cluster and move on the next one. With this software, they can go through over a thousand emails a day, as opposed to a few hundred using the old software."

"Impressive," Chuck said watching the reviewers scan furiously through emails.

"We've also shadowed the email mailboxes for the key people at ICon so that we can watch what they're doing on a real-time basis and see what they try to delete, especially after we surprise them this morning."

"Sneaky," Chuck said approvingly.

They walked to the other conference table and Chuck put his worn leather bag on a chair.

"So what's your initial take about the info on the disk that Patti gave us?" Jake asked.

"Well, at a minimum, it seems fairly clear that the address for Zapplication was not right, but who knows, that could've been just a street number that was transposed. It's less clear to me why ICon seems to be paying the client – if, in fact, it was a client. That would seem to decrease revenues and increase expenses, which is not something that most businesses want to do, at least if they want to stay in business."

"I also looked at the journal entries for the credit card transactions that ICon processed for Zapplication. It looks like ICon was recording revenue on them, which you would expect if Zapplication was a client. But these were all *manual* journal entries, meaning that were not done automatically by the system like other clients. Instead, someone at ICon had to specifically approve them. Here, look at these."

Chuck opened his floppy bag and pulled out some documents. He flipped through them and separated those with yellow flags stuck to the side.

"See, these have someone's initials indicating that they manually approved." He pointed to illegible markings on the top right of the journal entries. "I don't know whose initial these are, but whoever it is specifically approved the revenue from Zapplication. This was no mistake or accident."

"What's the worst case scenario?"

"On the surface, it looks to me like an embezzlement or kickback scheme. It's fairly easy to do using a fake vendor or a fake client, but it's odd that you'd make it look like both a vendor and a client. My gut reaction is that it could be the tip of a larger financial statement fraud. Look here."

Chuck fiddled through the documents and pulled out the transaction reports for Zapplication.

"If you look at the dates that these credit card transactions were processed by ICon, they mostly came in the latter part of each month. If you're embezzling and making all this up, why would you do that? Seems to me that you'd want it to look as much as possible like a normal website client. I don't know much yet about ICon's overall business, but I would guess that internet users buying something on a website wouldn't just buy near the end of the month. They would be fairly consistent throughout the month. That kind of activity is a red flag. It could mean that ICon is trying to pump up its revenue at the end of the period to make its numbers. From what we can see here, there don't appear to be a huge number of these transactions, but it may only take a relatively small bump to get the numbers where they want them to be. If that's the case, then I'd bet all the money in my pocket that this isn't the only suspicious client out there."

"So your expert opinion at this point is that this could be bad or very bad?" Jake asked with a crack.

"You know that I've always been an optimist."

Jake snickered at him and walked around to front the table to bring the meeting to order. The others took their seats anxiously waiting for the briefing. He paused to take in the moment.

A grant of corporate authority from SouthPoint's Board of Directors empowered them to do whatever was in their means to investigate ICon. Internal investigations are *ex judicio*, or outside of the law. They are a creature of corporate resolution, not of any legal decree. Unlike litigating a case through the judicial system, there are no rules of procedure for investigations. No regulations governing the process. No judges and no juries. Aside from the rare judicial opinion on a legal issue, there is no body of law governing how an investigation should be conducted. After practicing for twenty five years, that freedom to be professionally creative stirred Jake's passion. As he looked around the table at his team, he could think of no place that he'd rather be.

"You are about to embark on one of the most challenging engagements in the legal profession. Contrary to all of your legal training, you are not going to be an advocate for a client. You are not going to try to resolve any legal dispute. You're not going to develop claims or defenses, and you're not going to write any briefs. Instead, you're going to help solve a puzzle, a financial puzzle. But this puzzle does not have a cardboard box with a nice glossy picture of what it looks like when all the pieces are together. We don't know what the puzzle looks like, and we don't know where the pieces are hidden. In fact, at this point, we're not even sure if there is a puzzle. That's the challenge."

Jake scanned the eyes around the table, which were all transfixed on him.

"I want each of you to forget what you learned in law school about legal standards and fair procedure. Forget what you've learned about constitutional rights. In an investigation, everyone is guilty until proven innocent, not the other way around. We have been deputized by the company, and we are the judge and the jury. Everyone has to be scrutinized until we prove that they are innocent. Assume that every email you review is in furtherance of a fraud, until you are satisfied that the email is clean. Assume that every spreadsheet and document you see contains some clue to a fraud, until you prove otherwise. Our job is to come up with theories about what kinds of fraud may be occurring, and then to try to disprove the theories. If we can't disprove a theory, it could very well mean that it is right."

"You are the eyes and ears of this investigation, and your most important tool is your common sense. You have to think like a fraudster. There are three things that have to exist for a fraud to occur: pressure, opportunity, and rationalization. That's called the fraud triangle."

Jake sketched out a triangle on the white board. At the top point, he wrote *Pressure*. "First, a person has to be under some kind of pressure. It could be stress to meet financial targets, budgets, or sales goals. It could be from personal problems, like debt, substance abuse, or gambling. There are any number of things that can cause the kind of pressure to drive someone to commit fraud, and many times the pressure is not visible."

"Second, the person has to have the opportunity to commit the fraud." Jake wrote *Opportunity* on one side of the triangle. "In other words, they have to be in a position or have access to be able to pull it off. A cashier might have the opportunity to skim from the cash register, but not to falsify the financial statements. So focus on the people who could commit the fraud."

"And lastly, people need to rationalize their fraudulent conduct." Jake wrote *Rationalize* on the other point of the triangle. "An employee who thinks he's underpaid might rationalize stealing money from his employer because he thinks he deserves it. An executive might rationalize cooking the books in order to move up the corporate ladder. Whatever it is, most people have to create some reason to justify their conduct."

Jake tapped his marker on the top point of the triangle. "But, it all starts with pressure. To solve a fraud, you have to start at the top and look for the pressure. Where's the stress? What strain might force someone at ICon to commit a fraud? Next, narrow down those people at ICon to those who would have the opportunity or be in the position to engage in the fraud. If you connect those dots, you can start to unlock the puzzle and see the fraud."

"Any questions?" Not seeing any hands, Jake continued. "Now, let's run through what's going to happen this morning."

He took a sip of his coffee as the room fell to a hush. Jake passed out a small pack of documents stapled together containing the floor plan of ICon, the organization chart, an ICon telephone directory, and a list of contact information for everyone in the room. Each document was labeled in bold *Privileged and Confidential.*

"We're going to have two teams go into ICon simultaneously. An interview team and a computer team. The interview team is me, Chuck, and Alex. We'll go in my car. The computer team is Kelly, Jason, and Kyle, and you guys follow us in your car."

"Our cover for the raid has already been laid. SouthPoint's CEO called ICon this morning and told ICon's President, Alan Arnold, to expect a team of regulators from the banking commission doing a routine follow up after the merger. He kept everything low key, so no one other than Alan should know that we're on our way. We have access to two conference rooms at ICon. The computer team will go to this room in the far corner, set up shop, and wait to hear from me. Alex, you go to the boardroom and wait for Chuck and me. We'll go see Alan first to tell him what's really happening, and then meet you there."

"Kyle, I want you to sweep for bugs in both rooms. Do the boardroom first and then the other room. No one say a word until you get the all clear from Kyle. After we tell Alan about the investigation, we'll have him get all of ICon's execs to go to the boardroom for some kind of meeting. When they're in there, I'll call you guys in the other room and you can start grabbing their laptops and PCs. You'll see the location of their offices on this map."

"Any questions so far?" Jake took another sip of his coffee. No one had a question.

"Don't engage with anyone. If someone asks you any questions or what we're doing there, just politely refer them to me. It's important that we have only one point of contact and that we speak through only one voice. As soon as the word spreads that we're there, the people at ICon are going to be anxious and stressed out, and that breeds misinformation and rumors. So let me be the mouth piece. Okay?"

He waited until he saw everyone nodding.

"When you're here at the hotel, or anywhere in the city for that matter, you have to be discreet at all times. Don't talk about the investigation in restaurants, in the elevators, in the gym, in the restroom, or wherever. You don't know who may be working for ICon or who knows someone working there. Remember also that ICon is now part of SouthPoint, which is a publicly traded bank. By virtue of being in this room, all of you now are in possession of material, non-public information, and it is against the law for you to buy or sell SouthPoint stock. Don't tell anyone about the investigation, including family members, because if they happen to buy or sell SouthPoint stock, you could be liable for insider trading. Everyone understand?"

Again, Jake made sure that everyone was in agreement.

"We'll meet in this room every morning at nine o'clock to discuss the plan for the day and to talk about what our diligent document review team over there has found. This room will be locked at all times, and each of you has an electronic key card. Don't lose it. Lastly, I don't want ya'll to send any emails to me or to each other containing anything substantive about the investigation. If you have a question or need to share something, then do what Chuck and I used to do back in the old days and use your phone. And, no texting, tweeting, twittering, flittering, or whatever you kids are calling it these days." There were a few snickers from the table.

"Okay, let's do it."

The six suited investigators rose and gathered up their bags leaving the document reviewers churning away in the room.

The door to the secluded conference room burst open and Jake led the silent march as they strode down the hotel corridor in unison. They were armed with the element of surprise, but before they knew it they would be the ones on the run.

* * *

The receptionist at ICon adjusted her thin wire headset as she looked at her computer screen. She took a sip of her coffee and glanced nonchalantly up from her computer. Her eyes suddenly widened as she saw through the front glass doors a group of people in dark suits parading towards the building.

"I gotta call you back," she blurted into the microphone.

As Jake approached the door of ICon, he felt a surge of excited energy. Not a single person in the building knew what was coming. For many of them, the day would end very differently than it began. The moment he and his teams barged through the door, he was in control. His assignment was to find the truth wherever it might lead and whoever it might involve. Within the walls of ICon, Jake was the corporate cop.

The tinted doors swung open and Jake led the team into the lobby. The group stopped and gathered in the foyer and Jake approached the receptionist who was waiting for him.

"Good morning. We're with the banking commission. Alan Arnold is expecting us if you can let him know we're here."

"Thank you," she said as she pecked the keyboard in front of her. After a few seconds, she said "Mr. Arnold, there are some people here from the banking commission. They said you are expecting them."

She kept her gaze at the computer screen and nodded to whatever she was hearing on the other end.

"Yes sir, thanks." She looked up at Jake. "Mr. Arnold's assistant will be out in a couple of minutes." Her tone was short, sensing that the group in the lobby was not friendly to ICon.

Jake thanked her and quickly sent an email to Thomas who was waiting for the signal. Five minutes later, the door next to the receptionist opened and a woman walked briskly towards the group.

"Hello, I'm Val, Mr. Arnold's assistant. If you follow me, I'll show you to the rooms."

They picked up their briefcases and walked into the executive suite of ICon. Val held the door as the group passed by. She began to point in the direction of the conference rooms that had been reserved for them, but it became evident to her that they already knew exactly where they were going. She glanced over at the receptionist with a curious look as the two groups walked in separate directions. Something was not right.

Jake and Chuck waited outside Alan's office door as Val caught up to them. She glanced down the hallway and saw the doors of the conference room and the boardroom shutting behind the teams. These were not banking regulators she thought to herself as she knocked on Alan's door.

"Come in."

Val opened the door. "Sir, it's the gentlemen from the, uh, banking commission."

Jake and Chuck walked past her into Alan's office, and Val slowly shut the door behind them trying to get a last glimpse of the strangers.

"Hello guys. I'm Alan Arnold." Alan stood and they shook hands.

"Have a seat. We didn't expect an audit from the commission, but we'll try to get you whatever you need."

"Mr. Arnold, we're not from the banking commission," Jake said abruptly. Alan flinched and fidgeted in his worn leather chair.

"My name is Jake Morgan. I'm a lawyer at Levi & Everett in Atlanta. This is Chuck Bradley who is working with me. We were hired by SouthPoint's Board to investigate allegations made by a former employee about some accounting matters at ICon. If you look at your in-box, you should see that Thomas Nelson just sent an email to you explaining why we're here."

Jake paused to watch the impact. He detected Alan's forehead constrict and his jaw clench slightly. Alan crossed his arms and remained silent in defiance. He turned around slowly to face his computer screen, and sure enough he saw a new unread message that had been sent two minutes ago from SouthPoint's General Counsel titled "Internal Investigation."

"I'm sorry to have had to come in under false pretenses, but this is not the kind of thing that we could've announced. We don't know that anything improper has been done and we're not jumping to any conclusions. But the allegations have enough credibility that the Bank has to investigate them."

"Who's the employee? What are the accusations?" Alan stammered for information.

"Here's what I can tell you at this stage. A former employee has raised an issue about the accounting for one of ICon's vendors . . . or one of its clients. It's a little unclear, but as we learn more, we'll share what we can with you. At this point, there may have been as much as $500,000 in fraudulent transfers to the entity. I'm not at liberty now to tell you the name of the former employee. I know that this is disruptive to your business and I understand any frustration you have at being in the dark. But I can assure that we will do everything we can to be as quick and discrete as possible. We'll need to talk to a few people and look over some information. Based on what we learn, we'll go from there."

"For God's sake, this is a terrible time for this. Can't it wait a week or two? I mean we're trying to close the quarter and get our numbers up to SouthPoint."

"Well that's precisely why we're here," Jake responded. "We need to make sure that the numbers are right. ICon is now a big part of the Bank's overall numbers."

"I thought you said it was one vendor or client? For what, $500,000? That's not material to the consolidated numbers. We'll just set aside a reserve and you can come back after the quarter has been closed." Alan pushed back raising his voice.

"There has been mention of one entity so far, but in my experience, if internal controls have been overridden, it's unlikely that it only happened once and it's unlikely that only $500,000 is involved."

"SouthPoint just finished due diligence on the deal last month," Alan barked, "and now you're telling me that there some kind of fraud going on that the Bank didn't catch? There was a team of bankers and lawyers in here looking up our shorts for days. Sounds to me like the Bank sent you down here to investigate its own fuck up!" Alan was nearly yelling.

Jake tensed at the conflict, but he chilled the urge to lash back. He had been in this situation countless times, and the message he had to deliver was never welcomed. In an internal investigation, this was the first slice of pain in what often times is a long operation to save the patient.

"Mr. Arnold," Chuck intervened in a slow Southern tone. "If there is a problem and I stress 'if,' and if there is any fraud associated with it, no matter how big the dollars are, then SouthPoint's outside auditors will not sign off on the financials. If that happens, then the Bank will not be able to file its 10-Q on time. If that happens, the stock price will plummet, the stock exchange could start delisting proceedings, the SEC could investigate, and there could be shareholder class actions filed. Now I'm sure that you don't want any of that to happen and I know that the Bank will greatly appreciate all your cooperation so that we can do our job."

Alan sat back and took a deep breath, his jaws still clenching. He exhaled slowly staring at Jake.

"It doesn't sound like I have a choice in the matter?" Alan said with a sharp sarcastic barb.

"I'm afraid you don't," Jake said staring right back at Alan. "We'd like you to gather your management team in the boardroom in ten minutes, and I'll explain to everyone what's going on. We'll start the interviews right away and we'll do our best to accommodate everyone's schedules."

Alan muttered something under his breath as he leaned forward and punched a key on his phone.

"Yes sir?" Val said on the other end of the line. She had been staring impatiently at her phone for any sign about what was happening in the President's office.

Alan shot an annoyed glance at Jake and Chuck before responding to her. "Can you ask all of the executives to come to the boardroom in ten minutes for a meeting? Just tell them that I have some news to pass on." He sat back in his chair and it squeaked as he rocked.

"You do what you have to Mr. Morgan, but I'm not going to allow a witch hunt based on what some disgruntled former employee allegedly said. I stand behind all of my people. I have a business to run, a very profitable business, and your so-called 'investigation' better not interfere with that. If this gets out, our competitors will kill us with it."

"Understood," Jake said as he stood up. "But I think your gripe is with Congress not with me. See you in ten minutes."

Jake and Chuck walked out of the office leaving Alan simmering behind his desk.

After the door closed behind them, Jake turned to Chuck. "Notice that he was angrier at the investigation than the possibility that a fraud exists?"

"Uh huh," Chuck nodded. "Not the best first impression." They walked down the hallway and opened the door to the boardroom. Rich cherry wood lined the walls behind several large paintings in thick gold frames. The centerpiece of the room was an oblong Parian marble table that had been imported from Greece. The white-veined table was surrounded by crimson leather chairs, and each corner of the room was hidden by silk Fichus trees in brass pots.

As soon as Jake and Chuck walked in, Alex raised his finger to his lips and he motioned under the table. Jake bent down to see what was there, and he saw Kyle laying on his back under the table with an earpiece and a sensor sweeping for electronic listening devices. After several minutes, he popped his head out and said "All clear."

"Good," Jake said as he placed his briefcase at the head of the table. "Let's get ready for them."

Jake unpacked a few legal pads and readied for the briefing. He didn't know what to expect from the executives, but he felt fairly confident that someone would know about the Zapplication account. Although he doubted he would get much cooperation from ICon's management team, he was certain he could detect which ones of them knew something from their reactions.

The anticipation in the room grew as they waited. Alex began tapping his fingers rhythmically on his pad. He dreamed of moments like this and could hardly contain his nerves. Chuck leaned over and he gently covered Alex's bouncing fingers with his large hand.

"Oh, sorry," Alex said sheepishly. Chuck winked at him and took a seat across the table next to Jake.

For several long minutes, the three of them sat silently, waiting. Then suddenly the door to the boardroom opened and several ICon executives walked in chatting together. Jake and his team rose and shook hands with them, introducing themselves without hinting as to who they were. The executives filtered around the table expecting some kind of sales or marketing presentation from their guests. Some moseyed to the coffee set up as the remaining executives meandered into the room. Light banter filled the room as the executives gathered around the table.

Lastly, Alan walked in the boardroom with Cain by his side. Cain had a stern look and he didn't make eye contact with the L&E team. His father clearly had given him the heads up about the real purpose for the meeting.

"Excuse me everyone," Alan began, "I appreciate you all coming on short notice."

The executives quieted down and each took a seat. Alan was standing next to Jake who was sitting at the head of the table unaware that he was in the President's chair.

"I've called you in here because a former employee of ICon has made allegations to SouthPoint that we have some kind of accounting problem. These folks are lawyers from Atlanta who have come to do an internal investigation. I want you to cooperate with them so we can get past this as soon as possible. This is Jake Morgan and he'll explain what's going to happen."

The jovial tone in the room vanished instantly. Some executives appeared stunned and others gazed back and forth at Alan and at the L&E team. Cain kept his head down scribbling something in a notebook. Troy looked somewhat confused, not knowing the implications of an investigation. Jane remained stoic. She was at the top of the accounting food chain and ultimately any accounting problems fell under her domain. If there was a problem, she had the most to lose. And, unlike the others, Jane knew exactly what an internal investigation meant.

The room was silent and the air was thick as Jake stood. He had addressed rooms of nervous executives like this before, but it never got any easier. They were not his clients, nor would they be his friends. This was not a judicial proceeding. Everyone at the table was guilty, until proven innocent.

"As Alan said, I am a lawyer and a partner with the law firm of Levi & Everett in Atlanta. The Board of Directors of SouthPoint hired us to look into allegations relating to an accounting matter. They are just allegations at this point and we don't know that anything improper has occurred. But the Bank has a legal obligation to look into it, and we hope that we can count on you to help us do our job as quickly as possible. My colleagues here are Chuck Bradley and Alex Perry."

Jake purposefully did not introduce Chuck as a forensic accountant. It wouldn't be long before Chuck's cover was known, but Jake wanted to wait until after he interviewed Jane and the other accountants at ICon. Sometimes having a hidden expert attend the interviews of accounting personnel revealed flaws in their stories that an attorney would not be able to detect.

"Over the course of the next few days, we'd like to talk to some of you. A lot of what we need is background information about ICon's operations and so forth, so don't read anything into it if you're one of the people we interview."

Jake readied himself for the news he was about to deliver. It would likely rattle many of them, most for no other reason than feeling as if their privacy was invaded. But, for others, it could mean that dark secrets might be exposed.

"Also, as we speak, the hard drives of your laptops and PCs are being copied. They'll be returned to you as soon as possible."

A grumble spread around the table as the realization sunk in. Almost every employee these days knows that their employer has the right to review their work emails. However, almost every employee these days also disregards that fact and uses work email to discuss private and purely personal matters. In an internal investigation, nothing is private.

Troy was the first to speak up. "I've got a huge sales presentation tomorrow afternoon and I have to have my computer today. Can't you copy mine first thing tomorrow morning?"

He turned towards Alan for help. "Alan, I'm meeting with the McKenna Group tomorrow and I've already put them off once. You know how important the meeting is."

Alan turned to Jake and made a feeble effort to support Troy's protest, but Jake was already responding.

"I'm sorry, I didn't catch your name?"

"Troy Vickerson, Vice President of Sales." Troy said confidently emphasizing his title.

"I'm happy to triage the hard drives of those who need them back first. It should only take a couple of hours before we start turning them. Given your situation Mr. Vickerson, we'll interview you first after this meeting so that by the time we're done you should have your computer back."

Troy slinked back in his chair annoyed that he unwittingly volunteered himself to be first in line. Jake was waiting to spring that trap for whoever gave him the most grief about the hard drives, and he was glad that Troy took the bait. Jake had planned to interview Troy first anyway, but this gave him the perfect reason to do so without raising questions among the others about why he was first.

"Any other emergencies we should know about?" Jake prodded.

No one else at the table spoke up having learned from Troy's lesson.

"Great. My associates are passing out a document preservation memo that describes certain documents that must be retained and not destroyed or deleted until further notice. Please look it over and let me know if you have any questions. As you'll see, it's fairly broad and includes electronic information and emails. If you have any doubt about whether a document is covered, err on the side of saving it. After you leave here, please distribute this memo in hard copy to all of the employees who work in your departments."

Cain raised his hand. "I'm Cain Arnold, the in-house counsel for ICon. Does anyone outside the company know about this? Does the SEC know?"

"As far as we know, no one is aware of the allegations, and we don't think that the former employee has told the SEC."

"But you don't know for sure, right?" Cain pressed.

"That's right," Jake answered.

"Is there anything stopping this person from talking to the SEC, or for that matter, our competitors?"

Jake paused. "Technically no. But from what we can tell we don't think that there is a motivation by the former employee to damage the company." Jake sensed that Cain was pushing for information, or perhaps for Jake to slip up about the identity of the informant.

"I'm just concerned that this investigation could have collateral damage and it's my job to look after the best interests of ICon."

"I understand and I appreciate your concern. Believe me, SouthPoint does not want this to be any more painful than it has to be. Why don't you and I get together later today and we can talk about the process."

Cain thanked Jake, and he shuffled together the papers in front of him as if he'd just completed negotiating a deal.

"Are there any other questions at this point?" Jake asked the group.

The bewildered executives looked around the table, but no one spoke up.

"Okay. Before you leave, it's important that you keep this investigation confidential. You all are the only people that know about it so far. If anyone asks, the safest thing is just to say is that SouthPoint is doing a normal internal review. If anything comes up or if you have any questions, my cell number and my email address are on the document preservation memo."

The management team of ICon stood and began leaving the boardroom. Unlike their arrival, their departure was silent. Troy remained at the table fiddling with his gold Cross pen and anxiously awaiting his lead-off interview.

As he watched them leave, Jake leaned over to Chuck and whispered. "Alright. We shot our string out there. Let's see which one flies into it." Chuck winked back at him.

Jake rose from his seat. "Mr. Vickerson, I'll be with you in just a moment. I need to make a quick call." Jake stepped into the empty hallway and tapped a number into his cell phone.

"Hello, this Preston." Preston Patton looked up from his computer monitor in the war room at the Intercontinental Hotel.

"Preston, hi it's Jake. We just finished the meeting with the executives, so note the time and start monitoring their emails. I want to know whether any of them send emails about the investigation and if anyone tries to delete anything."

"Will do."

Jake slipped his Blackberry into his pocket and looked both ways down the empty hallway of the executive suite. He straightened his tie and took a deep breath. Then he opened the door to the boardroom to start the internal investigation of ICon.

* * *

Jason Wie crawled under Troy's desk following the cords to unplug his computer. After receiving the green light from Jake, he and the computer team spread out to collect the executives' hard drives and then they would be taken back to the conference room for imaging.

"Hey, what's going on?" A voice billowed above him.

Jason peered out from under the desk to see a thin guy with wiry black hair.

"Just doing some upgrades," Jason said to Mick Sertoff as he disappeared back under the desk.

Mick looked around nervously. He knew that ICon's computers were not being upgraded. He was in charge of computer security in ICon's IT department, and no one told him about any upgrade. He would've had to have known as the administrator of the Velocity platform.

Mick darted around the corner and saw another technician in a dark suit leaving another office with a laptop. He followed the technician and saw him going into the conference room at the end of the executive suite. Mick looked in both directions and put his ear up to the conference room door. He gently opened the door and peeked inside. Through the sliver of the door crack, he caught a glimpse of several people opening the cases of computers. On a far table, he saw several monitors blinking with hard drives hooked up. He knew that something was happening. And it couldn't be good.

Mick looked behind him to make sure that no one had seen him peek into the room. He quietly closed the conference room door and walked briskly to his office. Once his office door shut, he quickly snatched his laptop and a pile of disks. He shoved them into a computer bag and glanced out of his office in both directions. He swung the bag over his shoulder and snaked down the back hallway of ICon.

At the end of the hallway was an emergency exit door with bright red signs warning that an alarm would sound if opened. Mick burst through the door knowing that that alarm had been disengaged long ago to allow employees to take smoke breaks in back of the building. It was the same door that his friend Bill Dixon used to escape ICon four months ago before he was murdered.

* * *

Jake sat down at the marble table and opened his notebook. Across the table, Troy tapped his foot anxiously. His mind was spinning as he watched the three people who were watching him. What was this really about? How much do they know?

Jake purposefully took an extra minute to get ready letting the still delay thicken the tension. Chuck and Alex flanked him and sat studiously waiting for his lead.

"Mr. Vickerson, thanks for giving us your time this morning. I know all of this is rather sudden and it's not something that you're accustomed to. So I want to make sure at the outset that you understand exactly who we are, who we represent, and what our objective is today. Feel free to ask whatever questions you want. And I'll do my best to answer them to the extent I can. Okay?"

Jake's technique was designed to disarm the witness as best as possible. Countless research studies have concluded that a strategy of understanding and befriending a witness has a far superior success rate than intimidation and threats. He preferred tactics designed to calmly prod as opposed to those bent on aggressively plying.

"Okay," Troy replied guardedly.

Jake then gave Troy what is referred to as an "Upjohn warning," or more colloquially as a "corporate Miranda warning." The script followed religiously by lawyers was designed to inform the witness of the United States Supreme Court's ruling in *Upjohn v. United States.* In *Upjohn*, the Supreme Court held that a company has the right to claim that discussions between its lawyers and its employees during an internal investigation are protected by the attorney-client privilege. A critical distinction has to be clear to the witness, however, that the lawyer does not represent the witness personally. Otherwise, the lawyer could find himself in a conflict of interest nightmare if the employee admits to wrongful conduct and then claims that the lawyer has to keep it confidential.

Jake knew the warning from memory, and he peered at Troy to make sure he was listening. To his left, Alex would memorialize the warning in his handwritten notes, which would soon form the basis of an interview memorandum that would be direct evidence of what was about to take place.

"Mr. Vickerson, we have been retained by the Board of Directors of SouthPoint. That's who our client is. We're not your personal lawyers, we're the company's lawyers. That means that what we talk about today is not confidential to those in this room. We will share what we learn with the Board. But this conversation is privileged, meaning that only the Board has the right to disclose what happens here to anybody outside the company. You don't have the right to do so. Understand?"

Jake waited until Troy nodded before he finished.

"And, the Board may choose to disclose this conversation to government regulators, like the SEC, if any become involved. So I want you to understand who may ultimately know about what we talk about. Lastly, you're not under oath, but I'd like you to agree to tell the truth, okay?"

Troy stared back at Jake without cutting his eyes away.

"Sure," Troy said blinking several times unconsciously.

"Do you have any questions before we start?"

Troy paused and took a gulp from his bottle of water. "Nope."

"Okay. To start off, can you to describe your educational and work background."

Troy sat up straight. "I went to high school at Crestwood Academy outside of Jackson, Mississippi. I went to two years of college at Ole Miss, and then left to start my own business. It was called Telesell and we provided telephone sales support and connectability solutions."

Troy skipped seamlessly over the six years of his more checkered past, including his run in with the Federal Trade Commission. Unlike with Ivan, he felt no compunction to tell the whole truth.

"It was tough being a small start up in the telecommunications space. You know, always in the shadows of Big Telecom. So I saw an ad for a sales job at ICon and thought that internet processing was the wave of the future. I started as a sales manager and then became the VP of Sales. That's my story." Troy sat back confidently.

"What was it that led to your promotion to VP of Sales?"

Troy did not expect the question, and Jake sensed his pause to think.

"Uh, I was the top salesman for two straight years and set a company record for yearly revenue contribution. I was making more in commissions than the former VP's entire salary and I guess that he couldn't handle it. He also was short sighted in terms of growth potentials. Alan finally decided that I had a better vision for the future."

Jake learned more about Troy in that single answer than in all the questions so far combined. He certainly was pretentious, but more important, his rise to the executive suite had been rapid. There had to be a reason other than Troy's business acumen.

"What is the commission structure for the sales team?"

"For everyone or for me?" Troy's tone had a hint of impatience.

"Well, tell me your deal and then the one for the others."

"Since I'm the VP of Sales, I have a higher commission rate to compensate for the added responsibilities and time of managing the department. I'd probably make more if I was back on the street, but I did my time. Anyway, my rate is twenty five percent and the normal rate is fifteen to eighteen percent. Plus, I get house accounts, which are accounts that come in unsolicited like through word of mouth or advertising."

Troy did not reveal the side agreement that he forced Alan into after his memorable evening on Fisher Island. For his new client, Modos Operations, Troy demanded forty percent commissions plus $250,000 in cash for every two million dollars in gross revenue that ICon made from Modos. Take it, or Troy would jump ship to ICon's closest competitor. Alan seethed at first, and then he accepted it. Greed can have a calming effect when it is shared.

"Once you bring in a client, are you able to monitor their run rate? Whether they're up or down, or whatever?"

"We can do that on Velocity. Ya'll don't know what that is?" Troy asked, frustrated that he had to explain it. The L&E team had been fully briefed on the computer platform, but Jake wanted to keep Troy talking. The longer he spoke, the more they learned.

"Velocity is our operating system that lets us see every transaction being processed through our platform. We can watch a client's active usage, or run historical analysis on almost anything you want."

Jake spent the next hour probing various aspects of Velocity and the structure of the sales department. He could see that Troy's remaining patience was waning. His answers were terse and delivered with an annoyed tenor, and his increasingly frequent glances down at his thick gold watch were conspicuous maneuvers. Troy was reaching his boiling point, which was exactly what Jake wanted. He unsuspectingly was allowing his frustration to cloud his defenses. It was about time to hone in.

"Mr. Vickerson, what can you tell me about Zapplication?" After an hour of generalities, the specificity of Jake's question stunned Troy.

"Um, what do you mean 'what can I tell you?'" He stammered back.

"Well, have you heard the name Zapplication?"

"I, I, don't remember, I may have?" Troy's mind raced as he watched Alex taking notes. Chuck was sitting back peering at Troy through thin reading glasses he donned to look over documents. Troy felt his face flush.

"Are you aware that Zapplication does business with ICon?" Jake asked vaguely.

"I'm sure that I've heard the name somewhere, but I don't remember. A lot of e-commerce companies sound the same."

"I'm sure they do. Maybe I can help you. As I understand it, Zapplication is in Miami and they appear to be a client. Here, let me show you."

Jake handed Troy a few of the transaction reports for Zapplication that Patti had provided them on the disk. "Take a look at those and see if they help."

Troy looked over the documents trying to think quickly as he reviewed the lists of transactions.

"I don't recognize this client. Should I?" Troy said looking up at Jake.

"Well, my information might be wrong, but I understood that this may be one of your clients."

Troy looked back at the documents. "Oh, I see the client code here. And it does have my rep number on the end. 50. I bet this is a house account, or maybe an old account from a sales rep who left. Sometimes my staff will just assign these to me. I have quite a few of these accounts. Anyway, I don't know anything about this client."

"Did you earn commissions on this client?"

"I'm sure I did since it's under my name. But, this doesn't look like it is a high volume producer, at least for the months on these documents. I probably didn't even notice them on my commission report. A few thousand dollars or so doesn't mean anything to me."

"I understand. Can we get copies of your commission reports for the last twelve months?"

"Why do you need those? They're confidential." Troy resisted, tensing his posture.

"We just need to make sure that the accounting for Zapplication was done right and the amount of commissions paid will validate the revenue recognized." Jake didn't miss a beat as he bluffed effortlessly.

"Um, well, okay. I'll see what I can find."

"Thanks. Also, is there anything else you can tell me about the client or the transactions by looking at these?" Jake asked flipping through his copy of the reports.

Troy glanced over them again briefly. "Uh, no. Just the dates of the transactions and whether they were approved or declined."

Jake whispered something to Chuck, who nodded slowly. Alex took the opportunity to stretch his aching writing arm.

"Mr. Vickerson, thanks for your time. That's all we have for now."

Alex looked up surprised at the ending. Troy popped up from his chair as Jake finished. His large frame loomed over the table and he looked down at Jake.

"We probably will have some follow up questions for you as we get a little farther down the road. In the meantime, it is very important that you keep this conversation confidential. Please don't tell anyone about what we talked about. That's for your protection and theirs. Okay?"

Troy mumbled an agreement and stormed towards the door.

"And if you could gather those commission reports, I'd appreciate it," Jake added as Troy barged out of the room.

"Cheery fellow," Chuck said sarcastically as he stood and finished his coffee.

"He knows a lot more than he led on," Jake said stating the obvious.

"Can I ask a question?" Alex said as he straightened his notes. "Why didn't you push him? I mean you could've pressed him about why the transactions only came near the end of the month. And didn't Patti tell us that she could tell from the transaction codes that they were international transactions? He didn't say anything about that."

"You're right about all of that. But this wasn't the time. There are different kinds of interviews and different kinds of questions. We'll talk to him again. This time I wanted to calibrate him and to read his reactions. You saw his frustration with having to talk to us, which is not unusual for busy people, but it can also tell you something about his mindset. Did you see his eyes when I asked about Zapplication the first time? He tried to hide it, but I could see his reaction. Did you see it, Chuck?"

"Uh huh. It was barely perceptible, but his eyes widened just a tad. Normally, you would expect someone to narrow their eyes or squint a bit if they don't know what you're talking about. But when your eyes widen, it's an indication of surprise."

Jake continued. "At this point, we want to stick to asking informational questions, which are non-threatening and designed to gather information. Let him get locked into a position. He says he doesn't know anything about Zapplication. We'll see about that, but we don't know enough now to challenge it and we don't want him learning what we do know. We also don't want to piss him off so much that he'll refuse to talk to us again."

"And Jake here has a track record of doing that," Chuck joked. "A couple of years ago we were investigating a grocery store chain for some kind of kickbacks. I can't remember exactly what it was, but I won't forget a woman that Jake interviewed. She was in the frozen foods department, and suffice to say that she was not a dainty individual. Jake got her feathers so ruffled that she let out a barrage of cursing that would make a sailor blush." He laughed at the memory. "After that, she wouldn't sit in the same room as Jake. From then on, I had to shuffle questions back and forth."

Jake chuckled. "I was reviewing her background with her and all I said was that it looked like she had been around food for a long time."

After a few laughs, Jake turned back to Alex. "When the time is right with Troy, we'll ask him what are called assessment questions and admission seeking questions. Assessment questions are the kind that push back on a witness. They're confrontational, accusatory. Most of the time we'll have documents or emails that might contradict the story they're telling. That's when you measure the calibration from the first interview and look for changes in their voice or behavior. Then, if we get a pretty good feeling that the witness has done something wrong, we'll ask admission seeking questions to see if they'll confess. They're not really questions at all but more like statements to see if they fess up. Kind of like 'Mr. Perry, we know that you billed SouthPoint for time that you spent shopping at the Mall of the Americas."

Jake winked at Alex who laughed at Jake's feigned inquisitory tone.

"I get the picture," Alex said smiling.

Just then, the phone in the center of the conference table rang. Jake leaned over and saw the display read "4058 – C. Arnold."

"Hello, this is Jake Morgan."

"Hi Jake, it's Cain. I'm sorry to interrupt, but can you swing by after you're done with Troy?"

"Sure thing. We finished up a few minutes ago. Is now good?"

"Yup."

Jake hung up and turned back towards the others. "That was Cain. He wants to see me. Alex, why don't you come with me and Chuck hold down the fort here. I want to interview Jane next, so be ready to cover the accounting issues."

"Will do."

As Jake and Alex approached Cain's office, they could hear him down the hallway talking loudly on his phone. His door was half open and his voice bellowed past his secretary, who was sitting at her desk next to his office.

"Good morning," Jake said with a smile to Cain's secretary. "I'm Jake Morgan and this is Alex Perry. We're here to see Cain when he's off the phone."

"Are you sure you want to do that?" She said rolling her eyes and shrugging apologetically for her yelling boss.

"We'll take our chances."

She grinned back at the two lawyers, not having any idea who they were. "Suit yourself. You can have a seat over there and I'll let him know you're here when he's off, which I'm sure you'll know." She pointed to two leather chairs straddling a small coffee table in an alcove across the hallway from Cain's office.

Cain's office was quiet momentarily, and then there was an eruption of argument.

"Look, I don't give a shit about your investors. I told you. When you clean up the site, we'll get your funds out of escrow. Until then, it's out of my hands. You can threaten to sue all you like, but it's in your damn contract. You should've taken the time to read it instead of wasting my time."

After a brief pause, Cain finished by saying "same to you," which he followed by banging his phone onto the base. He turned quickly to his keyboard and pounded out an email to a clerk in ICon's accounting department, that read:

> *escrow $122,513 from payments to #1894375-50. Wire to our account @ Nat'l Escrow. Cain.*

He scanned it and hit the Send button, watching the email vanish. A few seconds later, the blind copy of the email he sent to himself appeared bolded in his in-box. Cain dragged the email to a folder called *National Escrow Services.*

"Mr. Arnold." Cain looked up startled and saw his plump secretary standing at his door. "There are two gentlemen here to see you."

"Thanks. You can send them in," he grumbled back to her.

As Jake and Alex went into Cain's office, he quickly rose and extended his hand. "Sorry about that guys. These clients drive me crazy sometimes. Here, have a seat."

Cain's window-less office was surprisingly bare for an in-house lawyer. He had one metal bookshelf that had old law school books on the top two shelves and half dozen red well folders on the bottom two. On the top of the bookshelf, were two framed pictures of three children at different ages. His desk was adjacent to a wall decorated with yellow note tabs. A few stacks of paper sat on the desk next to a flat screen monitor and a phone. On the side wall was a framed diploma from Stetson Law School and a picture of a much younger Cain standing next to former President Bush at the Presidential Convention.

"I just got a call form Jane," Cain began. "She can meet with you for a few minutes today, but then she has a meeting downtown this afternoon."

"Well I'd like to talk to her today and then we can finish up when she gets back."

Jake did not want to give Jane extra time to learn from other witnesses about what Jake and his team were investigating. He knew that as soon as the interviews begin it is impossible to conceal what is at issue, even despite the promises of witnesses to keep the interview confidential. The reality is that people keep promises for one reason, which is to protect themselves. If someone does not feel the jeopardy of a broken promise, then there is little hope that it will remain intact. And Jake was well aware that allegiances among co-workers and friends were much stronger than the hollow peril he threatened if the promise was broken. Even though it had been just ten minutes since Troy left the boardroom, Jake assumed that Jane and others already knew that at least Zapplication was in play. He didn't want her to know anything else this early in the game.

"That's fine, I'll let her know. If you can tell me who else you want to interview, I can line those up for you," Cain asked.

"Sure, I can tell you who we'd like to talk to today. Then I'll regroup with my team and we should be able to pin down the people we're interested in talking to tomorrow. There are also some documents that we'd like to get, and I'm sure there will be more as we start to get into things. Is there someone who we can coordinate that through?"

"Uh, yeah. We just hired a new lawyer to help me out and this might be a good thing for her to get started on since she's new. Donna, can you ask Jackie to come in here please?" Cain called out loudly to his secretary.

He turned back to Jake and Alex. "Look, I don't want to step on your toes, and I understand you have a job to do. But as ICon's lawyer, I also have a job to do and being in the dark about all this makes it tough. So whatever you can tell me about this former employee or what things are under investigation will make it easier for me to help you and the company. I can assure you that if there is something going on the company will do everything to correct it."

"I appreciate your position and we'll certainly do our best to make this as easy as possible. I want to talk to a couple of more people and get a handle on things before I'm comfortable having a conversation about the specific allegations. No offense, but I'm sure that you understand we need to do some preliminary work before we know whether there is anything out there and, if so, who might be involved. But at this stage I can discuss the process so you'll know what's happening."

Jake had recited that mantra to countless executives and in-house lawyers throughout the years. It is a precarious position for management to have no control over the situation or the impact on the business, and Jake had never met a single executive who was not distressed by the prospect of an internal investigation. Not knowing what was under scrutiny certainly caused anxiety, but not knowing what might be uncovered caused sleepless nights.

There was a light knock on the door and a tall blonde woman poked her head into the office. She was in her late twenties, but looked ten years older than that.

"Excuse me. Cain you wanted to see me?"

"Yeah, come in. Jackie, this is Jake Morgan and Alex ... I didn't catch your last name?"

"Perry, Alex Perry," he said standing to shake her hand.

"This is Jackie Warner, she started with us a couple of weeks ago."

Cain turned to Jackie. "They're lawyers from Atlanta and they're investigating ... um, can I tell her?" Cain stopped himself.

"Sure. Jackie, I'm Jake," he said extending his hand. "We're representing SouthPoint's Board of Directors and we're looking into accounting-related allegations. We'll be interviewing employees, looking at documents, that sort of thing. Cain can fill you in on the details. Since you're new here, you might be a good person to help us gather documents and be our point of contact. Is that okay?"

Jake sensed that she was a tad overwhelmed by the situation that she just peeked in on. Jackie shot a curious glance over at Cain for help, but he couldn't offer her anything.

"Uh . . . yes. Whatever you need." She was unsure of the response that Cain wanted, and she glanced back at him for any clue. He kept a poker face, but at least he wasn't yelling.

"Alex, can you give Jackie the document list and the names of employees we need to talk to."

Alex flipped open his briefcase and shuffled through some papers. He pulled out two sets of clipped sheets and gave one to Jackie and one to Cain. Every glimmer of information that Jake provided to the company enlightened them about the investigation. The lists, therefore, were intentionally broad to provide a cover for the real information they wanted. But it would not be long until the sunlight shone in.

Cain sat back down and scanned the lists. If he gleaned anything from them, he didn't show it.

"We'll get on this right away. In the meantime, I'll call, let's see . . . ," Cain glanced down at the witness list, "Tamara James and have her meet you in the boardroom."

"Thanks."

Jake and Alex stood and made their way out of Cain's office. Jackie stayed and closed the door lightly behind them.

Chuck was skimming a newspaper as Jake and Alex came back into the boardroom.

"How'd it go," Chuck asked folding up the paper and looking over his reading glasses.

"Well, looks like the CFO all of a sudden has a meeting downtown, so we'll only have a few minutes with her this afternoon."

"Hmm, that's rather convenient, isn't it?" Chuck grumbled.

"Too convenient," Jake muttered back clearly frustrated by the change in schedule.

The room was silent as Jake quickly prepared for the next interview. After a few minutes, there was a faint knock at the door.

"Come on in," Jake called.

"Hi, I'm Tamara. You have some questions for me?" she said poking her head in the room.

"Yes, come in. Thanks. I'm Jake Morgan. This is Chuck Bradley and Alex Perry. We represent SouthPoint Bank's Board of Directors. Please, have a seat." Jake pointed to chair on the opposite side of the table.

Tamara's eyes were fixed on Jake as he explained who they were and what they were doing. After he gave her the *Upjohn* warning, she squinted her eyes slightly and asked, "Do I need a lawyer?"

Jake fielded that question in almost every investigation. It is a thorny question, and the answer is always the same.

"You certainly have a right to a have a lawyer present if you think that you need legal advice to answer my questions. But I'm only interested in facts and learning the truth."

More often than not after Jake's response, the interview continued unabated. If a witness still refused to be interviewed without their lawyer present, however, Jake smelled blood. In his experience, rarely does a completely innocent person insist on legal representation before answering questions about work.

"Okay, we'll let's get on with it," Tamara said in a booming voice. "I suppose this is about my overtime. I should've expected that this was coming. I worked those hours and you can ask anyone. The Lord as my witness, I've never padded any of my time." She bucked up in the seat expecting a clash.

Jake leaned back and grinned. "No, no, no. This isn't about your overtime. I just want to ask you some questions about Patti Tomanski. She worked next to you for a while, right?"

The fight instantly retreated from her face and her shoulders dropped. "Oh mercy, I thought that this was about my paycheck last month. I never had so much overtime and I figured someone would be asking me some questions. Gracious, you had my heart beating something else." She patted her chest mimicking the beating. "Well, now what do you want to know about Patti?"

"We just want to know your impression about Ms. Tomanski. Did she fit in? Did she do a good job?"

"Yeah, my cubicle was right next to Patti. Nice girl. A little soft spoken, at least compared to me, you know," Tamara chuckled deeply. "I used to eat lunch with her sometimes. You know she moved down her to be with her mamma. I think she was divorced. She never mentioned any man. I was kinda surprised when she was let go. It hadn't been a while and she seemed to be getting along."

"Ms. James, did she complain to you about anything? Problems that she was having?"

"Nah, she mostly kept to herself and what she was doing. She was in payables, so we did different things. I think she had issues with Jane Weaver, but Lord who doesn't? We all do. That woman can be a real . . . well you know . . . she can be difficult to work for, 'specially for someone new."

"Do you remember anything specific about her issues with Ms. Weaver?"

"Nah, I don't know about the particulars. She just told me that she had a few questions about an account that Jane wouldn't answer. But as I said, that's nothing new for her highness. I guess whatever she was asking Jane about got her fired."

"Why do you say that?" Jake asked.

"A few days before she left, Patti canceled lunch with me because she said that she was going to go down to Jane's office to have a word with her. Next thing I knew they were doing something to her computer."

"Who was? Who was on her computer?"

"Mick Sertoff in IT. I came in real early one morning to finish my reconciliations and Mick was sitting at her computer. I said 'hi' to him, and I think I scared the bejesus out of him. He's a strange bird. You know, one of those computer types. Anyway, after that, she was gone."

"Ms. James, have you ever heard of a client called Zapplication?"

"No, uh uh. A client you say? Do you know the client number?"

"Yes, I do. One minute." Jake searched the stack of documents that he printed from the disk that Patti had given them, and he handed one of the transaction reports to her.

"Okay, hold on." Tamara grabbed the phone in the middle of the table and punched an extension.

"Linda, yes it's Tamara. Can you pull up a client file for me. Number, uh, . . . 97840519-50."

She nodded her head as her assistant gave her the information.

"Thanks." She hung up the phone, and paused for effect. "Zapplication is a house account. Not sure who brought it in, but Troy Vickerson is the rep. He ought to know about it. We don't have any aged receivables for the client. It looks like the client has never paid any of its fees late, not even a day late, which is unusual for our class of clients, you know." She chuckled but they didn't follow her joke.

"If you want to know more, you'll need somebody to get on Velocity."

"Who has access to Velocity? You don't?"

"Nah, we don't have access in the accounting department. Only Alan and Jane. Oh, and I'm sure Mick has access since he's the IT guy."

Chuck cleared his throat to signal that he had a question. "Ms. James, can I show you some journal entries?"

He handed her a few documents. As she glanced over them, Chuck continued.   "Do you see that those are manual journal entries and appear to relate to this Zapplication account?"

Tamara flipped the pages. "Yeah. I see the client number and, uh, let's see what's happening here. It looks like the customer is paying our fees by a wire from the customer's account. See the BIN, the bank identification number, there. That tells you the bank that the wire came from. So you have a credit to this revenue account and a debit to the account receivable. And then this second transaction, here. It looks like you have a credit to cash in the same amount and a debit to an expense account. I think this is for professional services. Not sure exactly what that is."

"So if I follow you, Zapplication is paying ICon to process its credit card transactions, and then ICon is turning around and paying Zapplication the same amount for some kind of professional services. Is that right?"

"That's what it looks like to me," Tamara said cocking her neck and rolling her eyes. "That looks kooky to me. Why would ICon be paying a client? Don't make any sense."

"Okay. Can you tell who approved this journal entry?" Chuck pointed to the squiggly hand written initials at the top right corner of the form.

"Yup. Those are Jane Weaver's initials."

Chuck leaned back in his chair and glanced towards Jake signaling that his inquiry was over.

"Ms. James, thank you very much. Here's my card. If you remember anything else about Patti, or anything that seemed unusual to you, please let me know."

"I will. I hope you find what you're looking for, you know."

"So do I." Jake shook her hand and she nodded at Chuck and Alex.

After she left, Chuck looked over at Jake. "Now we're getting somewhere. Why would ICon be paying Zapplication in the exact same amount that Zapplication pays it for processing? We need to find out where the money is going."

"And where it's coming from," Alex added. "Remember Patti told us that she saw pay requests for Zapplication."

"Good point," Jake said. "Who's next?"

"Glen Baker, Head of HR. He's the one who terminated Patti."

"Okay, can you call Cain and have him come in five minutes. I'm going to the restroom."

Jake walked down the hushed executive hallway. He felt as if he were behind enemy lines probing for secrets emanating from the walls. He was an outsider in the corridors of ICon, and he felt as if all eyes were on him as he passed. There was an untouchable aspect to leading an investigation. It imbued authority and it demanded respect. Jake relished in the spotlight, even if it shone from unfriendly lights.

He was standing at the sparkling white urinal when he heard the door open. He kept his stare straight ahead as heard heavy footsteps behind him. Troy stepped up to the urinal right next to him despite the line of open urinals. Troy's imposing frame filled the urinal space, and he spread his feet purposefully wide. The tension dripped from the tiled walls as the two men stood side-by-side in silence. Jake tried to will his bladder to finish, but it had the opposite effect.

"Find what you're looking for yet?" Troy said suddenly with a biting tone.

"Uh, we're working on it," Jake stammered out apprehensively.

Troy exaggerated a groan as he started to urinate trying to make Jake feel uncomfortable. "Sometimes if you look hard enough you find things that you don't want to find. You follow me?"

Jake zipped up his pants quickly and backed away from the stall. He was flustered by Troy's brazenness.

"No I don't," Jake barked at Troy, confident now that his pants were secure and Troy was still facing the stall with his zipper down. "What does *that* mean?"

Troy didn't respond, but instead shook his crotch a few extra times and zipped up his pants. He turned and walked directly towards Jake as the echoes of his shoes on the tiled floor danced around the restroom. Jake stood his ground as Troy approached, but his nerves were screaming. Troy sauntered right up to Jake as if he was going to walk over him, and then he turned abruptly to the sinks. He bent over and wringed his hands under the faucet as Jake tried to calm his rushing breath.

"It means . . . ," Troy began still washing his hands, "that SouthPoint has the most to lose from your little investigation." He turned to face Jake. "If you think that this could be contained, you're dead wrong. News in this industry travels as fast as an email. Our competitors will find out before you finish your lunch, and they'll be using it to steal our clients before dinner. It takes a lot work to bring in a client, and in one second with the flip of a switch, the client can change internet processors. All the revenue is gone just like that."

Troy snapped his fingers in Jake's face, causing him to flinch. Jake stumbled backwards. Troy smirked and turned his back to Jake and faced the mirror again to groom himself.

"If we lose any clients because of this investigation, it's going to be your ass. I'll personally make sure of that. You might be some hot shot lawyer in Atlanta, but down there that means nothing. You just better watch your back."

Troy looked at himself in the mirror and patted his hair with his hand. He didn't look at Jake again as he walked out of the restroom.

After the door shut, the quiet echoed. Jake glanced towards the mirror and saw himself standing alone in the middle of the men's restroom. He relaxed his taut shoulders and released the breath that he had unconsciously been holding in his chest.

Troy's rant had more to do with the risk to his personal compensation than any altruistic motive towards ICon, but Jake took his threat seriously. There is no telling what someone might do when their back is up against the wall.

"I just had a rather unpleasant run in with Troy in the restroom,." Jake said as he shut the door to the boardroom behind him. "He outright threatened me that if ICon loses business from this it'll be my ass."

"You're kidding? He said that?" Alex stood as he asked feeling suddenly defensive of his boss.

"Yeah, I think the steroids are beginning to cloud his head. In any event, he's an idiot to try to intimidate me."

"Sounds like the first clay flew right into the string we shot," Chuck said winking at Alex.

There was a knock on the door and Jake said "Come in."

Glen Baker flounced into the boardroom and introduced himself, shaking each of their hands vigorously. He quickly sat across the table and folded his hands neatly in anticipation. The three men on the other side of the table looked at one another amused at Glen's dramatic entry, and they slowly took their places.

After Jake covered the preliminary items, he focused on the matter at hand. "Mr. Baker, thanks for that background. I want to ask you about an employee who was recently let go. Her name is Patti Tomanski. What can you tell me about her?"

It came as no surprise to the Vice President of Human Resources that a lawyer might someday ask about an employee who was fired. He prepared for these kinds of interviews even before the pink slip was delivered. Patti's case was no different, but at the same time, it was very different.

"Well, Mr. Morgan, as you know, I was the one who spoke with Ms. Tomanski." Glen stressed "I" in a firm, yet effeminate, tone. He then rattled off in HR lingo without taking a breath, "The individual was relieved of her duties within the ninety day probationary period applied to all new hires. Although there is no requirement to provide a reason for the decision, Ms. Tomanski's probationary period ended prematurely because of a severe violation of company policy."

Glen took a breath, this time to add drama to what he was about to tell them. He leaned in over the boardroom table towards Jake, which rang comical given that there were only four people in the expansive room all huddled at one end of the long table. Instinctively, Chuck and Alex also leaned closer to the table.

"The only reason that I can disclose the specifics to you is because you are lawyers for our parent corporation. You understand that this is strictly confidential and there are rules about what we can tell outsiders." Glen paused for the delivery. "ICon's policy prohibits any narcotics, alcohol, or non-prescribed pharmaceuticals on the premises. The cleaning crew found an unmarked bottle of pills in Ms. Tomanski's work station. They turned out to be Zanex."

"How did you know that they were hers?" Jake asked visibly surprised by Glen's report.

"I asked her about it when we met on her last day. She said that they were hers, but she couldn't produce a prescription for them. It's all in the statement that she signed."

"What? She signed a statement?" Jake glanced over at Alex, who was taking notes in disbelief. "Can I get a copy?"

"Sure." Glen punched an extension on the phone in the middle of the table. "Amy, can you bring the Tomanski file to the boardroom. Thanks."

"What else did she say about it?" Jake pressed.

"All she said is that they were hers and that she didn't have prescription for them. It really wouldn't have mattered since we were going to end her probationary period anyway. She apparently had some personality conflicts with the CFO and it just wasn't working out. Ms. Tomanski actually seemed more interested in getting her final paycheck than the fact that she was being terminated."

Jake leaned back stunned by what he was hearing. He stared down at his empty pad thinking about his next question.

"What happened to the bottle?"

"The policy is that we have to destroy any illegal substances we find. So that's what we did. It's all in the report," Glen replied with a prepared response.

"Mr. Baker," Chuck started as he removed his reading glasses, "exactly who found this bottle and where was it found?"

"One of the personnel on the overnight cleaning crew. A woman named, uh, Maria something. She was vacuuming and found the bottle under Ms. Tomanski's desk. She took it to her supervisor, who brought it to my attention the next morning."

"And I'm sure that all of this is documented in the report," Chuck asked with a hint of cynicism.

"Yes."

There was a knock on the door, and a young woman peeked her head inside. "Mr. Baker, here's the file you asked for."

"Thanks Amy," Glen said as she handed the file to him and quickly retreated.

Glen opened up the manila folder, flipped through some pages, and then gave Jake a few documents clipped together. "Here is a complete copy of her file."

"Thanks. Let me take a minute or two to look this over."

"Do you mind if I make a call outside?" Glen asked.

"No, that's fine. I'll let you know when I'm ready again."

Glen pranced out of the boardroom. As soon as the door clicked shut, Alex blurted "That sounds like bullshit to me. Patti didn't mention anything about them finding drugs."

"Well, let's see," Jake said turning the pages. "Here's her employment application, some tax forms, and . . . here it is, Report of Violation." Chuck and Alex leaned over Jake's shoulders to get a view.

The report was a one page document with four numbered paragraphs. The first two paragraphs set forth the date of her employment and her position. The third and fourth paragraph read as follows:

1. *On this date, at 9:34 a.m., Glen Baker was presented with an unmarked bottle of pills by Carlos Martinez, floor supervisor of Corporate Clean. Mr. Martinez reported that the bottle was found by Maria Sanchez the prior evening at 11:37 p.m. at the work station #L7.*

2. *On this date, at 1:46 p.m., the undersigned met with Ms. Tomanski and provided her with this information. Ms. Tomanski did not deny that the bottle belonged to her and that Zanax tablets were contained in the bottle. She represented that she did not have a medical prescription for the pharmaceuticals.*

At the bottom of the page were two signature lines. One line contained the signature of Glen Baker as the Vice President of Human Resources, and on the second line, a swirling signature appeared above the typed name Patricia L. Tomanski.

Jake flipped to the last page of her employment application to compare the signatures. The signature on the Report of Violation looked like the one on the application, but Jake was not a handwriting expert. Chuck and Alex then took turns looking through the documents as Jake considered the report.

"Mr. Baker, you can come back in," Alex said leaning out into the hallway.

Glen walked in briskly and sat back down poised to answer more anticipated questions.

"Is this the complete file?" Jake asked.

"Yes. She was only here for a couple of months."

"I'll need you to get me the contact information for the supervisor at Corporate Clean, okay?" Jake prodded to see if Glen would blink.

"Sure thing."

"Is there anything else you can remember from your meeting with Patti?"

Glen paused as if he were thinking. "There is one thing I remember. When we finished, Ms. Tomanski asked me whether a whistleblower is entitled to money damages. I thought that was fairly odd. I mean, asking me, ICon's VP of HR, whether she could sue the company. I just told her that I couldn't answer the question."

"And that was all?"

"That was it," Glen replied sharply.

"Okay. Chuck or Alex, do you have any more questions?" Jake asked his colleagues, who both shook their heads.

As Glen stood to leave, Alex spoke up. "Mr. Baker, excuse me. I do have a question. Did Ms. Tomanski ask for the pills back?"

Glen stopped abruptly and glanced at Alex with a blank look. "Um, uh, I don't recall whether she asked for them," Glen stammered, his pitch dropping an octave.

"Okay, thanks," Alex said slowly gazing at Glen to give him the chance to add anything else. Glen looked back at Jake and Chuck, and then slid out of the room.

"What do you think?" Jake asked them.

"I think it's bogus," Alex said quickly.

Chuck answered more deliberately. "I think you had better have another conversation with Patti. If this is true, then it casts a shadow on what she's told us so far, especially if she was looking for money. I don't think it changes the scope of the investigation because there still seems to be something screwy going on with the Zapplication account, but if it ends up being her word against theirs, this isn't going to be helpful."

"You're right. Damn," Jake said running his fingers through his hair. He sat back down and thought for a moment. He finally reached into his jacket pocket and pulled out his Blackberry. "I should have her cell number in my phone," he said as he scrolled through his telephone log.

"Okay, here it is. Let's see if she's there." Jake held the phone to his ear and looked over at Chuck and Alex. He shook his head as her voice mail greeting started.

"Patti, this is Jake Morgan. I have a follow up question or two if you can get back in touch with me I'd appreciate it. My number is 404-888-9546." He buried the phone back into his jacket pocket.

"Who's next on the line up?" He asked Alex.

"Jane, but remember she's only got a few minutes today."

Jake turned to Chuck. "Okay, what's our plan for her today? We won't have time to get too deep."

"I think that you should skip entirely over the pleasantries and the background. This investigation shouldn't come as a surprise to her given Patti's questions. She is either going to be helpful or not, and we should be able to figure that out pretty quickly. I think we just need to accomplish two things. Try to pin her down about what happened with Patti, and commit her to a follow up interview."

Jake thought for a moment about Chuck's advice. There are no rules of how to conduct an investigation. It's a fluid practice, guided mostly by hardened experience. Internal investigations are as much about theory and guesswork as they are about calculation and logic.

"Yeah, I agree with you. I'll cut right to the chase and see how she responds."

After a few minutes, there was a firm knock at the door.

"Come in," Jake said.

Jane entered the boardroom, this time more defiantly than she had done earlier that morning. She wore a navy pinstriped Ann Taylor suit that hugged her shapely body. Her soft brown hair reached just below her shoulders and matched her eyes, which beamed behind thin glasses.

"Thanks for coming Ms. Weaver. As you know from this morning, I'm Jake Morgan, this is Chuck Bradley and Alex Perry."

Each took his turn shaking her hand as a slight whiff of her perfume lingered behind. She sat down across the table and adjusted her skirt.

"I know you're pressed for time so we'll make this preliminary interview as quick as possible."

"Preliminary?" Jane asked. "I trust that you're aware that SouthPoint is insisting we close our books next week. So I'm pretty busy now." Her tone was respectful, but insistent.

"I understand. We're both under the same time pressures. SouthPoint can't close its books until ICon reports up, and ICon can't do that until we're finished with this investigation. Given your schedule today, we won't be able to cover everything, so we'll need to follow up tomorrow."

Jake was equally respectful to her, but with an added firmness. He wanted to set the tone that he was in charge because he sensed that she was accustomed to getting what she wanted, particularly from men.

Jake continued before she had a chance to respond. "Before we start, I need to make sure you understand who we are and what our roles are." He recited the prefatory instructions mandated by *U.S. v. Upjohn*, and made sure that she understood they were not her lawyers. As she listened, her lips were pursed and her stare was rigid.

Jake asked several questions about ICon's reporting structure and her oversight of the accounting department just to measure her temperament. Jane responded to each question with a terse reply giving him as little information as possible. She dodged Jake's open ended questions and it became clear to him that she had been coached about how to respond.

"Ms. Weaver, I'll come right to the point. I hope that you can clear some things up for us. You're aware that ICon recently fired an employee who worked for you named Patti Tomanski. And you're aware that she had raised some issues about a client called Zapplication right before she was fired. I'm interested in knowing three things. What you understood those issues to be, what you told her about them, and what support there is for your explanation."

Jake did not reveal anything more than she probably already knew about what was going on, but he fired the net to snag any escape for her. The question not only told her what he already knew, but it also put her on notice about what he already knew that she knew. It was not the kind of informational softball question that usually is tossed at the beginning of investigation interviews. Instead, it was a fastball assessment question thrown chin high on the inside corner.

But Jane didn't flinch. She took a breath and calmly eased her full lips. It was as if she took the first blow from an opponent and realized that the punch didn't hurt.

"Mr. Morgan. ICon has over five hundred active clients. We process over a million transactions every day, and the client reports I get every month are over a hundred pages long. There is a half of a billion dollars flowing through ICon's general ledger every month. I have to spend my time on the macro level. I have little visibility about any single client unless they pay us a lot of money, or unless they owe us a lot of money. So please don't assume I do or can know everything that happens here."

"Now, to answer your question. I do remember we had an employee a little while ago who didn't work out. As I recall, we were unhappy with her performance and she was still in her ninety day probationary period. And yes, she asked me questions about a number of clients, one of which may well have been the Zapplication account that you're interested in. If she did, then I'm sure I told her what I'm going to tell you. The account was some kind of IT initiative that a client was helping us with. If you want to know more, you can ask Alan about it. He's the one that told me. In the meantime, I'll be back in the office later tomorrow and if you still need to talk to me, then perhaps we can plan on meeting then."

She didn't blink the entire time as she smoothly dodged Jake's first pitch. He realized that she had keenly avoided answering the question, but also that she had learned at least part of what was under investigation at no cost. He readied himself for his next wind up.

"Yes, plan on it," Jake shot back.

She started to rise, but Jake wasn't finished. "It's just that I would've thought you'd have a distinct memory of the situation, given your previous experience with these kinds of matters from the *Corline* case you were involved in."

This time Jane did flinch as if she was surprised by a quick jab to the chin. How did he know about that case? But more importantly, what did he know about her past? She swallowed and eyed him hard as she slowly sat back down.

"That case has nothing to do with this situation and the fact that you felt it was necessary to bring it up here demonstrates how little you know about what happened. The *Corline* case was settled and it was supposed to be confidential. Now, I have to be downtown in fifteen minutes and I assume that we're done for today, right?"

The adage that anger bestows beauty was true to form. Her sharp features bristled, but she kept her cool. Jane stood and professionally extended her hand to Jake signaling that the interview was over. He stood and conceded the match, but did not cut his stare as they shook hands. There was slight grin in his eyes from the enjoyment of a worthy adversary.

The three men looked at each other as the door shut abruptly behind her.

"Well, I can't wait for the sequel," Chuck said with a snort. "You certainly went right at her. And what's the deal with that case you mentioned? What was the name of it?"

"Corline," Jake said.

"Yeah, where did you pull that out from?" Chuck asked.

Jake grinned wryly as if he just performed a perfect card trick. "I Googled her last night. There was a hit to the list of archived cases on the SEC's website. *SEC v. Corline Corporation*. Seems that about five years ago, she and a few others entered into a settlement with the SEC without admitting or denying any of the charges. But they were accused of running a Ponzi scheme, something about real estate investment trusts. There was also a short news story about it in the Florida Business Times, but I couldn't get any more details about the case."

"I was bluffing because I don't know what role she played. But the SEC would not have settled until after it did an investigation, so she had to have some experience with the process. I only brought it out because she was giving me totally evasive answers. I wanted her to know that this is just as serious and we're not going to play games."

Chuck shook his head in agreement. "I'll give you my two cents. If an accounting employee asks over and over about potential accounting problems, a CFO, a normal CFO, wouldn't forget the details, especially when it involves revenue. Even if the employee is wrong about it, you take those things seriously as a CFO. We're only talking about a few months ago. And don't forget, this is the first full quarter that ICon has to report as a sub of a publicly traded company. She knows that she has to personally certify that the financials are accurate. I think that Ms. Weaver is well aware of exactly what we're asking about. And if she did really forget about the details, then she shouldn't be the CFO."

"Agreed. Before we talk to her again we'll need to be up to speed about how Zapplication was accounted for and the impact on the financials, so see if you can get access to ICon's general ledger today. There's a new in-house lawyer who Alex and I met in Cain's office. Jackie Warner. You can work through her."

"And we also need to see how we can get into the Velocity computer platform and review the data for Zapplication. If what we're hearing is right, Velocity should tell us everything we want to know about Zapplication's transactions."

Jake flipped the pages on his legal pad closed and dropped his pen ceremoniously. He glanced back and forth at both of them.

"Okay troops, time to retreat."

* * *

Jane glanced in both directions through her dark sunglasses, and then revved her red BMW coupe out of ICon's parking lot. She raced past an elderly couple in a pale Cadillac inching its way in the left lane and she darted through a traffic light that had already turned red. As she sped along, she reached in her purse on the passenger's seat and felt for her phone.

"Good afternoon. Stein, Thomas, and Holland."

"Neal Stein, please. This is Jane Weaver."

Jane wrapped a Blue Tooth receiver around her ear and tossed the cell phone into the console. She squeezed the polished wooden steering wheel with both hands and breathed in deeply waiting for her lawyer to answer.

"This is Neal."

"It's Jane. I'm on my way. I did exactly what you said to do. I didn't answer anything definitively, and I put them off until later tomorrow. They're investigating the Zapplication account. That's the one I told you about. I'm sure they know as much as Patti knew, but I doubt that they know anything more than that."

"Okay good. What exactly did you tell them?"

"I just said that I remembered her and that we had issues with her performance. The lawyer asked about the account and all I said was that I think it had something to do with IT. I told them to ask Alan about it. He can deal with this crap. It was his idea."

"I understand. But you also need to consider what's best for you. I'll see you soon and we can figure it out."

CHAPTER ELEVEN

With a gentlemen I am always a gentlemen and a half,
and with a fraud I try to be a fraud and a half.
-- Otto von Bismarck

One Week Before the Deal

The warm Caribbean air greeted Raul Ramon as he walked out of the VC Bird International Airport in Antigua. The small island is one of the Leeward Islands in the West Indies where the Caribbean Sea meets the western Atlantic Ocean. Its once thriving sugar industry yielded long ago to the onslaught of tourism. But its most lucrative import has been offshore banks that arrived because of the island's notoriety as the center for the internet gaming industry. The cloudless sapphire sky of Antigua welcomed all types, some for pleasure and some for business.

Outside the airport, the smell of sweet papaya from the nearby hills played on the breeze and mixed with of scent of petroleum from the bustling traffic circle. Flocks of taxi drivers accosted lingering travelers for a fare as a fleet of small busses whisked tourists away to tropical resorts. Car horns barked sporadically over two young Antiguans who were playing rhythmic steel drums for coins.

Raul reached inside his beige linen sport coat and flicked on dark sunglasses that covered the scar above his right eye. He shooed away several nagging taxi drivers as he lit a tight-rolled cigarette and exhaled a plume of tobacco smoke. He watched the drifting smoke rise into the crystal air until it dissipated. A leather bag hung loosely over his shoulder, and a concealed money belt hugged him tightly under his shirt. If he was caught by the authorities, its contents would surely earn him a bruising interrogation – at the least.

As he gazed out over the bustling street, the sun shimmered off of a small metallic object across the traffic circle. He couldn't make out the source of the reflection but he could tell it was getting closer to him. His eyes narrowed to focus and then widened abruptly when he saw that the sun was bouncing off a badge. An Antiguan police officer dressed in tan Bermuda shorts and a white crimped hat was walking right towards him. Raul felt a surge race through his veins as his eyes darted in either direction for an escape route. A group of tourists blocked the entrance back into the airport behind him, and the swirling traffic kept him on the sidewalk. He was trapped. As the officer approached, Raul took a long drag off of the cigarette and braced for a confrontation.

"Excuse me sir," the police officer said in broken English with a thick native dialect.

Raul initially acted as if he hadn't heard anything until the officer stepped onto the sidewalk next to Raul.

"Yes," Raul said guardedly behind his sunglasses.

"You can't smoke here so close to the entrance. You can move over there."

Raul unclenched his grip on the cigarette and nodded to the officer, who quickly turned and walked away yelling something unintelligible to a taxi parked at the curb. Raul exhaled, but his nerves were still jumping.

He flipped the squashed cigarette onto the street and motioned towards one of the begging taxi drivers who scampered over and took his bag. Raul glanced in either direction and then walked nonchalantly to the waiting taxi with a half a million dollars in U.S. money orders strapped to his waist.

"I'm going to St. John's. Downtown. The Caribbean Overseas International Bank on Market Street," Raul said as he shut the car door.

St. John's is the capital of Antigua located on its northwest edge and tucked inland at the end of St. John's Harbour. Colorful marketplaces line the sandy streets waiting each day for the populated cruise ships to unload their boatloads of buyers. But what the tourists don't notice is that right behind any one of the tattered kiosks selling carved driftwood could be the anonymous office of a multi-million dollar offshore bank.

After the dingy taxi cab pulled away from the airport, Raul removed his cell phone from his pocket and made a call. He eyed the Antiguan taxi driver to make sure he wasn't prying, and he dabbed the perspiration on his forehead. The small car winded along the rocky coast of the island with its feeble air conditioner at full blast. Worn wooden shacks with brightly colored tarps dotted the foothills alongside the road. Their inhabitants were hopelessly poor in possessions, but rich with priceless vistas of the aqua blue Caribbean.

After several rings, the call was answered. "This is Troy."

"Hey it's me. I'm on my way to make the deposit."

"Good. Listen, we've got an issue," Troy said. "We blew the month again and Alan is all over my ass about the ratios. He says it's affecting the other business, but he's so short sighted. Modos did over ten million in gross last month. I keep telling him to relax, but he's threatening to terminate Modos. Can you believe that?"

"Terminate? He can't do that. What do you want me to do?"

"We need more credit card numbers," Troy insisted.

"Jesus Troy. I told you, I've tapped out my contacts. No one is willing to risk it with all the shit from the Patriot Act."

Raul glanced up at the rear view window again, but the driver was not paying attention. He dropped his voice anyway.

"Look, after Antigua, I can't do anymore. I've been everywhere."

"Goddamit Raul, this is a goldmine." Troy's voice rose as his anger started to boil. "We just need one more load before the deal with SouthPoint. The program is working fine but we can't keep up with the volume."

There was silence on the line. Raul wiped his brow again. The risks were growing and he was getting in deeper and deeper. It takes more than just a wink and a smile to get a bank to issue thousands of sequential credit cards numbers to a shell company for an unstated purpose – *and* to violate a cluster of laws by not reporting it. It takes money. It takes bribes.

His jaunts to Madrid and Andorra had been one thing. He knew the bank officials there and had traded them currency for credit many times before when he was working for the DEA. The transactions had always been closer to a finder's fee than a bribe. And in any event, he had the United States Government to come and rescue him.

But he didn't know anyone in Antigua, nor did he have an exit plan if things didn't go well. The brush with the police officer at the airport had him spooked enough. The scar above his eye twitched as his anxiety festered.

"There's no fucking end. You're always going to need more credit card numbers. The program is not going to stop. Can't you see that?"

"Don't worry, I'll handle things here. You just need to get some more goddamn numbers and we'll be fine."

Raul covered the microphone on his cell phone and grumbled "shit." This time the driver glanced up to his rear view mirror and met eyes with Raul. Raul scowled in the mirror and the curious driver quickly looked back at the road and turned up the scratchy Reggae on the radio.

Raul slowly raised the phone back to his ear. "I'll see what I can do, but I'm going to need another administrative fee. Double. And this is the last time. I mean it Troy."

"Good. Email me when it's done." A far away click signaled that the call was over. Raul slipped the phone into his pocket and glared out at the passing waves crashing endlessly along the jagged coast. The view was spectacular, but paradise is all about perspective.

The taxi slowed as it navigated the tight streets of St. John's. Teal and yellow buildings with crimson roofs illuminated the culture of the city under the watchful steeples of the stoic St. John's Cathedral that peered down towards the harbor. Two colossal ivory cruise ships hovered alongside the Nevis Street Pier. They towered over the tallest structure in the city as a constant reminder of what fueled Antigua's tourism economy. The taxi turned on Market Street and stopped in front of a three story modern building that was seemingly out of place among the small decorative shops. The placard next to the nondescript front door listed the sole tenant only as *COIB*.

Raul sat in the small lobby of Caribbean Overseas International Bank fiddling through the peach hued Financial Times but not really reading anything. Four metal chairs and a wooden magazine table were the only comforts for customers, but the chilled air conditioning was a luxury in itself. This wasn't anything like the plush lounge of the Banca d'Andorra.

Making a deposit into a numbered bank account in the Caribbean was one thing, but bribing a bank official was a crime. He knew that his previous conspirators would at least confidentially entertain a financial proposal with dubious purposes. In minutes, however, Raul would have to look a complete stranger in the eye and propose a business transaction that violated countless international banking regulations. A pure risk with no hedge.

He would be alone and vulnerable, a proposition gravely warned against by DEA rules of engagement. His frustration about the unexpected assignment mixed with the adrenaline of the impending crime. The surge felt like he was back in the Agency. Moving funds across the globe. Managing tens of millions of dollars in secret U.S. accounts that never existed. He remembered how a dangerous risk felt like octane fueling a euphoric high that lasted for weeks. There was no way to explain the sensation of escaping unscathed from a brush with danger.

This would be the last time, however. He was done with the stress and his nerves were frayed. One last time would set him right. One last time would be all that he needed.

"Mr. Sanchez, this way please." A dark skinned woman with a headset sitting behind an empty desk motioned Raul towards the locked door to her left. He stood up quickly and wrapped the leather strap of his bag around his shoulder. Instinctively, he tapped his waist to feel the money belt secure against his mid-frame.

As soon as he opened the door, a thin suited man and a hulking bodyguard on the other side greeted him.

"Good day. We understand you have a deposit to make. Please follow me." They led Raul down a picture-less hallway lined with thin doors. Tiny cameras in all of the corners spied down to film any movements. He instantly assessed that he had no way out.

"Right in here," said the thin man pointing to an innocuous door on the right.

Raul nodded and entered the room. In the room, was a small wooden desk with a plump middle-aged man on the phone. He motioned for Raul to have a seat on the wicker chairs facing the desk.

"And good day to you." The bank official eased down the phone and smiled broadly at Raul.

"What can I do for you today?"

The banker had a welcoming grin worn in by years of greeting travelers who had come a long way with a lot of money. His dark native skin tone matched his deep indigenous accent. But his eyes suggested that his jolly island veneer could tarnish quickly into anger.

Raul zipped open his money belt and carefully placed $500,000 in U.S. money orders on the knotted desk.

"I would like to make a deposit into account number XR69347."

"Very well. Can I see your papers and I'll need the pass code?"

Raul reached into the outer pocket of his bag and removed a small envelope. He opened it and handed the folded documents to the heavy Antiguan banker.

"The pass code is Alchemy."

The dark skinned man eyed the documents carefully. He slowly folded them up and placed them back into the envelope. He handed them back to Raul, who put them in the inside of his jacket.

"Very well, how much will the deposit be?"

"Five hundred Thousand U.S." The banker studied the money orders and then punched at the keys on a scratched calculator.

"You will get a confirmation on your way out. Will that be all?"

Raul examined the sparse office. He knew that he wouldn't be able to any detect any concealed listening devices, but he was trained to spot hidden video cameras. Feeling secure that he wasn't being watched, Raul chanced the proposition.

"Yes, I have a proposal that my client would like you to consider." Raul stopped to safely gauge the interest.

The banker paused from counting the deposit and cautiously looked up at Raul. He narrowed his round eyes and leaned back in the aching chair.

"What did your client have in mind?"

"One thousand sequential credit card numbers issued from the Caribbean Overseas International Bank to surrogate names. My client would provide you with a list of the names, but it would hold and use all of the numbers. My client requires certain confidentialities, so certain reporting requirements would need to be overlooked. I *trust* that we can agree to something acceptable."

The banker slowly began to chuckle and then laughed deeply.

"My friend, this business is not a trusting business. Your client has a numbered account here because your client does not *trust* the bank, and the bank does not give unsecured loans because it does not *trust* your client. We have what you would call a mutually beneficial *lack* of trust. I'm sorry, trust is not the currency of this bank. What your client proposes cannot be accomplished under countless anti-money laundering regulations of Antiguan and international law. Even an attempt to breach the law can be punished in this country as harshly as the breach itself."

The banker lost his grin and began to reach for an old rotary phone on the desk. Raul's mind raced as to who might be on the other end of the call. He had been escorted through a locked door by an armed bodyguard. There was no place to run and he was not carrying the proper equipment to force his way out. Troy was the only person in the world who knew that Raul was in the middle of the Caribbean Sea, and the fake passport that Raul was carrying would ensure a long stay in an Antiguan jail. Raul decided that it was time to put all the cards on the table.

"Perhaps there's a way to procure your trust. Your personal trust that is, with adequate financial security." Raul emphasized 'personal' both verbally and nonverbally.

The bank officer stared with dark eyes at Raul. A bead of sweat inched down over his fleshy temple as he considered whether to entertain Raul's overture. For an agonizing long minute, the two men stared at each other. Raul tried to hide his anxiety, and the banker tried to hide his interest. Finally, he slowly returned the phone to its base without cutting his gaze at Raul.

"You have *procured* yourself five minutes."

Raul swallowed hard realizing that the next few minutes could determine whether he was going to leave Antigua anytime soon. This would not be the first time that he bribed an unknown bank official, but it would be the first time he did so without the secreted protection of the United States Government. If he faltered now, no one would come under the cover of night and negotiate his freedom through a clandestine agreement.

"As you say, you have no reason to trust me or my client. But trust is not necessary in business if the risk is outweighed by the benefit conferred. My client is in a position to provide a benefit of $25,000 U.S. in cash to compensate for the risk of its proposal to the bank. Of course, how you decide to allocate that benefit is up to you."

The room was silent except for the ceiling fan that was squeaking as it rotated through the think air. The bank official opened the desk drawer still looking straight at Raul. He removed a small cassette tape recorder, which was winding slowly, and he placed it on the desk. Raul's eyes widened and his chest pounded as the adrenaline pumped. The bank official pressed the stop button with his thick finger and removed the tiny cassette. He placed the tape in his shirt pocket. A smile meandered across his heavy lips.

"This is my security," he said grinning as he tapped his pocket. "I've got your voice and your picture from the security cameras in the lobby. With one call, you will spend a very long time in one of our jail cells."

He paused to relish his control of the situation. "I weigh the risks you talk about a little different than you do, my friend. In order to adequately compensate for the trust you seek, I will need $50,000 or you do not leave our little island paradise."

The bank official leaned back in his chair and weaved his meaty fingers together.

"Let me explain to you how this will work. You have twenty four hours to have a wire sent to your client's account here at the bank. You will withdraw $50,000 in cash and you will deposit into this account," the banker said as he scribbled a number onto a slip of paper and slid it across the table. Once I get confirmation of the deposit, you'll get your credit card numbers. And one other thing. My cousin is the head of customs. No wire, no way home." He chuckled from his round belly.

"I'll get the wire." Raul stood to leave, angry about being cornered by the slobbering bank official, and angry that his job wasn't finished. As he turned to leave, the banker cackled at him.

"You know that there hundreds of banks on this island. How is it that you came to me?"

Raul stopped and turned towards the gloating official. "My former employer used to have an account here a few years ago." Raul toyed with adding an implied threat that he was once backed by the U.S. Government, but that association was not always welcome.

"Then I'm so glad, my friend, to have a repeat customer." The banker laughed again enjoying his unexpected windfall.

Raul closed the door behind him and skirted down the narrow hallway. He burst through the metal door of the empty lobby. At the exit, he glanced up behind him and saw a tiny camera peering down from the corner recording his frustration.

As soon as he was out on the dusty curb he cursed loudly not realizing that he was in the middle of a busy sidewalk. A few startled tourists huddled away from him, but several native Antiguans just strolled past unbothered.

Raul looked both ways down the dusty island street, and then headed towards the harbor.

"It's me. We need to talk."

He lowered his voice as he spoke into the cell phone. He was sitting on the patio outside a pink café overlooking St. John's Harbor. White sailboats dotted the blue water in the shadow of a twenty story cruise ship.

"Dammit, I told you to email me. I'm in a meeting. What's the matter?" Troy snapped back at him in a hushed frustrated tone from a cooled conference room in Miami.

"The price went up on the supply side. I need $50,000 wired to the account by tomorrow or else it's my ass." Raul looked around the café suspicious of every eye that he met.

"What? Shit. Hold on," Troy muttered and then there were muffled sounds on the phone.

"Okay, I stepped out of the meeting. What happened?"

"Look, I told you I don't have any connections here. I'm fucking lucky not to be in jail right now."

Troy paused on the other end. "A wire can be traced. Do you know how hard it is to send an international wire without tripping every goddamn federal agency?"

"That's the deal Troy. I didn't exactly have any bargaining power. Just get the damn wire sent and email me when it's confirmed. Otherwise,

I'll be stuck on this fucking island and you can explain to your sister why her husband hasn't come home."

"Alright. Shit. Just sit tight." Troy tried to calm his brother-in-law. "I'll take care of it. In the meantime, just chill out and enjoy some of that native ass."

Raul could hear Troy snicker.

"Fuck you Troy."

CHAPTER TWELVE

Very few of us are what we seem.
-- Agatha Christie

One Month After The Deal

Jake slid his key card over the small black panel next to the conference room door. A small red light turned green and he entered the war room reserved for Wingmaster at the Hotel Intercontinental. The room was buzzing with printers spewing out emails that the document reviewers were tagging as they continued their endless march through the electronic communications. At the table, Alex and two associates were rifling through stacks of documents and were engrossed in speculating about what a particular email meant. On the far end of the table, Kyle was sitting behind a monitor that was hooked up to several blinking computers. A webbing of cords from the equipment snaked underneath the table and joined at of couple multi-jack strips. Next to Kyle was a stack of hard drives, each labeled with the name of one of ICon's management team.

On the wall behind the table was a white board with a sketched organization chart of ICon. An array of handwritten lines and boxes all flowed out of a box at the top encircling *Alan Arnold, President.* Slash marks were drawn over each employee's box who had already been interviewed by the team. Notably, there was no mark yet over the top box.

"There's our fearless leader," Chuck said from across the room as he saw Jake enter the room.

"Alright folks, gather round," Jake said. "I have a call with the Board in the morning, so I need to hear status reports from everyone."

Jake put his briefcase on the table and headed towards the coffee station in the corner to choke down the thick hotel brew. As he loaded up the cup with sugar and creamer, he continued.

"Let's start with the computer guys. I want to hear about how the collection of the hard drives went. Then I want to hear what the email reviewers found, especially what happened after we surprised ICon. Next, Alex, let's talk about Patti. We need to find her as soon as possible and ask her about what the HR guy told us. Right now, this whole thing hinges on her credibility. And, last but not least, Chuck, I'm interested in what you think about the Zapplication transactions now that you've had some time to analyze them." Jake took a swill of the coffee, grimaced, and plopped down in the chair at the head of the table.

Kyle looked up behind his flashing monitor at the far end of the table. "We obtained forensic images of all of the PCs and laptops of the management team that were on the premises. I got an inventory schedule from IT with all of the assigned computers, and cross-checked it with the one's that we harvested. It looks like we got everything except for a laptop from Mick Sertoff who apparently left the office after we came in. We've filtered the drives for user-created file types and de-duped across custodian. We're now finishing up the key word search terms and we'll batch them to the reviewers first thing in the morning."

"Good. Did the forensic images capture the slack space on the drives?" Jake asked.

"Yup. And we've included it in the review population. Any hits probably will be to document fragments, but we might find something."

"Maybe an old dog can't learn new tricks, but what's slack space?" Chuck asked.

Kyle took the lead, thrilled that anyone, let alone an accountant, would want to understand the finer points of computer fragmentation.

"A file system on a computer drive is made up of clusters. Picture a record album with groves going around it."

"Do you all know what a record album is? It's an old fashion way to play music," Jake joked the younger associates who smirked back at him.

Kyle continued unabated. "You can think of a computer drive like a record album with rings going around it from the outside to the center. Clusters are like pieces of those rings, and when you save a file the system puts the file into these clusters. The bigger the file, the more clusters it takes. But each file always starts at the beginning of a cluster. So you might have a file that takes four and a half clusters. The next file you save is going to start at the fifth cluster, so there would be some space left over in the last half of the fourth cluster between the last byte of the first file and the first byte of the second file. That's called free space or slack space. Follow me?"

Chuck nodded slowly realizing that Kyle was rapidly approaching his ceiling of comprehension. "I understand . . . kind of. But why would you care about the free space?"

"Because," Kyle's voice raised as he headed towards the punch line, "the free space is not always empty. If you delete the first file in those four and a half clusters, the file actually is still there, it doesn't go anywhere. But now the computer thinks that those clusters are available to save another file. So, let's say that another file is saved in those same clusters, but this time the new file only takes up three clusters. There are still one and a half clusters worth of the original file in the free space. Those pieces of the original file are called fragments. They might be a few paragraphs of a letter, columns on a spreadsheet, pieces of an email, who knows. If you make a full forensic copy of the hard drive – which we did - you also get all of the free space. You can search it with key words just like any other kind of files." Kyle paused to let his lesson sink in.

"And if you're lucky," Jake said, "you might be able to see portions of documents that the person deleted . . . or thought he had deleted. I had a case a few years ago where a CFO was keeping two sets of books. When we started the investigation, he tried to delete the records. We didn't find anything until we searched the slack space of his hard drive and we found a piece of one of the real income statements. The piece we found really didn't tell us much, but we knew that it differed from the part of the income statement that the company published. So I used it to bluff the CFO into thinking we extracted the whole thing. You should've seen his face when I quoted to him the real numbers on the piece we found. He confessed five minutes later and now he's in federal prison."

"Okay, good work Kyle. Sarah, can you bring me up to speed on the email review?"

Sarah Newton was a fourth year associate at Levi & Everett. She was a mousy five foot three inches tall with light red hair and a diminutive frame. But she had the stamina of a quarter horse and she billed more hours than any associate in the firm. What she lacked in physical presence, she more than made up in brain power.

For some, reviewing documents was considered bottom-feeder work that young associates had to endure as a rite of passage in large law firms. Sarah, however, had a unique ability to look past the monotony of document review and see the challenge of searching for a needle in a haystack or, as is otherwise known, the smoking gun. Being able to assimilate thousands of emails from the incessant electronic chatter of modern business was like a cognitive puzzle to her. She thrived on detecting patterns in communications and perceiving tone in lifeless emails. Although most of her peers would rather bang their heads against the table than review emails, Sarah quietly made herself an invaluable and indispensable asset of L&E. Of all the associates on the team, she was the only one that Jake specifically requested.

"Let me first explain our review protocol and then I'll go through what we found so far from the key custodians." She flipped over the first page of a perfectly neat pile of papers standing at attention in front of her.

"I've documented everything in a protocol memorandum that I'll update as we continue our review, so you can always reference that. Okay, to start, we loaded a snapshot of ICon's exchange server into the review platform. We also collected the dumpster files, which had been reset to a 180 day deletion schedule so any email these custodians tried to delete went to the dumpster file. After that, we extracted the .pst files for the key custodians. At this point, they are Alan Arnold, Jane Weaver, Troy Vickerson, Cain Arnold, Glen Baker, and Patti Tomanski. For these six custodians, we had about thirty gigabytes."

"As you may know, well maybe not you Chuck," her friendly slight was delivered so smoothly he almost didn't pick it up, "one gigabyte is equivalent of about 50,000 pages. So we had about one and a half million pages of emails. We then culled the emails by time periods that we thought were relevant to the investigation. We chose the two quarters before the merger and the quarter right after the merger. That reduced the total population down to 450,000 emails. From there, we searched the remaining emails using a set of relevant key words. For example, we included terms like 'fraud, mistake, false, misrepresent, omission, wrong.' We then used terms specific for the investigation, like 'Patti, fired, terminate, Zapplication, international, payable.' You get the picture. After all those terms were applied, we had 167,000 emails to review."

"Gracious, how did ya'll review all of those?" Chuck asked.

"They didn't," Jake responded with a grin. "Here's where the technology I showed you the other day gets really cool."

Sarah took Jake's lead and continued. "The software that we use to review the emails is not limited to a linear review, which means that we would have to look at every email. Instead, the software uses logarithmic analytics to cluster the emails based on the subjects that are being discussed in the emails. So, instead of having to look at every email that has the term 'international' in it, the software groups the emails into clusters that relate to, say, international travel, or international phone calls, or international transactions from clients. We can then quickly discard the clusters of emails that are talking about some irrelevant subject. Using this kind of fuzzy logic, we can get through about ten times as many emails as we could if we had to review every one."

There was a twinkle in her eye from the peculiar excitement that she got from explaining the state-of-the-art software. "We're just about done with them."

"Well, I'm impressed," Chuck said. "So does this fancy software also find fake international transactions?" He playfully searched for an Achilles' heel of the technology.

"No, it leaves the easy jobs to the accountants," she quipped without missing a beat causing Chuck and the others to laugh.

"Touché," he retorted.

"Okay, now do you want to hear what we found?"

"The floor is still yours," Jake said to her as he smirked at Chuck.

Everyone at the table moved in slightly to hear what they were waiting for. It goes without saying that modern communication changed profoundly with the advent of emails. And for those who investigate corporate fraud, emails are a veritable treasure trove. When the telephone was the primary means of business communication, frauds could hide in verbal sound waves that disappeared when the phone was hung up. But with emails, the record was preserved sometimes indefinitely. Despite the visibility of emails, and the countless cases in which courts established that emails at work are not private, employees still talk freely and openly assuming that their messages will never be seen. This assumption has led to the revelation of more frauds in the past decade than most all of the frauds discovered in the past fifty years.

"First, the dumpsters. It looks like the only person who deleted a lot of emails after the surprise raid was Alan. But, there does not seem to be any rhyme or reason to the deletion activity. There were big batches of emails that he tried to mass delete, but they did not cover any specific time period or topic or recipients. For example, he tried to delete emails that he sent or received from Visa and MasterCard, but at the same time, he tried to delete junk emails and purely personal emails. He also skipped over certain months. We're looking deeper at them to see if we can figure out whether he was trying to hide something, or if he just was doing a regular purge of his emails. I think that you'll need to ask him about it."

"Jane did not delete any emails, but interestingly the only email that she sent the entire day after the raid was to nstein@sthlaw.com. I assume that's her lawyer. The email only said 'call me on my cell ASAP.'"

"I bet that was the meeting she suddenly had," Jake guessed correctly.

"Shrewd lady," Chuck said.

"Troy tried to delete a couple of emails that vaguely referenced an internal corporate project that he was working on. Those raised our eyebrows and I'll tell you more about them in a minute."

"The dumpsters of the others appeared to have what we would expect. Spam emails, ministerial stuff, nothing unusual."

"Now, here's what we've found so far from the email searches. It looks like the first time Zapplication appears in any email is about six or seven months before the deal. We found an email with an attachment that was a client implementation form for Zapplication, but the form only had a mailing address for the client. No phone number, email, or even a contact person. The address was the same one that Patti gave us."

"There were only a handful of other emails that referenced Zapplication. One was an email from Alan to Jane that just had the name of the client and the client number and said 'this is the client that we discussed yesterday.' There also were a few emails from Patti to Jane where Patti was asking questions about Zapplication and trying to schedule a meeting with Jane. The only other email that mentioned the client was from an accounting clerk to Jane asking her to approve a journal entry that was attached. I'm not sure what the journal entry is for. Here, Chuck, maybe you can tell."

Sarah handed the print out to Chuck, who put on his reading glasses and studied the document.

"Hmm, this is one of the journal entries that I showed Tamara," he said after a few moments. "It shows that ICon is paying for some kind of expense, some kind of professional fee, but it's not clear what it is for. I can only assume that it somehow is related to Zapplication since that's what the cover email refers to. I bet this is why Patti saw a pay request for Zapplication."

"Maybe that's why Patti was confused about whether Zapplication was a client or a vendor," Jake said as Chuck passed him the journal entry.

"What this proves however," Chuck stressed, "is that whatever money was going to Zapplication was coming directly from ICon."

As soon as Jake heard that he quickly looked up from the document at Chuck. He knew exactly what Chuck was thinking.

"Why would ICon pay a client?" Alex asked.

"Because maybe ICon was using Zapplication to round-trip revenue." Jake answered as Chuck nodded in agreement.

"Huh?" Alex asked, still confused about what obviously was clear to Jake and Chuck.

"Round tripping is a fraudulent scheme where a company pays a third party, like a client, to use its services or to buy its product. That generates revenue. In essence, the company is paying for itself which it inflates its revenue. The money is going in a circle. That's why it's called a round trip."

"Why would a company do that? I mean it's spending money to make the same amount of money. Wouldn't it all even out?"

"It could, but it may not matter," Chuck responded. "If a management is trying to meet revenue goals, it may want to artificially increase the revenue even though it costs the company to do it. More often than not the company will capitalize the expense, meaning that it will spread the expense over a long time instead of incurring it all at once. So the company increases its revenue, but the related expense is just a fraction of the total cost, so the net income also becomes inflated. It's accounting fraud plain and simple."

"And if you remember from the transaction reports that Patti gave us, Zapplication sent transactions through ICon mostly near the end of each month," Jake added. "I bet that they would see how they were doing mid month, and when they needed more juice, they paid Zapplication to shoot through transactions."

"Holy crap," Alex muttered. "If this started right before the merger, then maybe ICon was doing it to make the company look better so that SouthPoint would pay more."

Jake leaned back and finished the remnants of his coffee. His mind was going through the possibilities and trying to connect the disparate dots of information they had found so far. The room was silent as the weight of the potential discovery bore down on the investigation team. Finally, Chuck spoke up.

"We need to see a rollforward of all of the expense and cash accounts, and analyze the revenue that was being recorded." He turned to Jake. "If there was a round-trip scheme going on, we should be able to isolate it." Chuck paused, and then added the kicker. "Unless, of course, ICon was using off-balance sheet entities like Enron. It's time to have a frank conversation with Jane, with or without her attorney."

Jake nodded. "Agreed. I'll call first thing in the morning to set it up for tomorrow. Sarah, can you put all of those emails in a binder for me? Okay, what else did you find?"

"We saw several emails between Troy and Alan around the first time that Zapplication was mentioned about a confidential project that they were working on. These are the ones I said that Troy tried to delete. The emails were fairly cryptic and we couldn't really tell what they were about, but we saw some like this one . . . ."

She showed Jake a one sentence email from Alan to Troy that read *Can you discuss the project at 3:00?* "It looks like they always met in person about the project. Cain was copied on almost all of the emails and they were labeled *Privileged and Confidential,* but he never responded to any of them." Sarah waited as Jake reviewed a few of the emails.

"We searched Cain's emails and specifically included the term 'project,' but we didn't find anything other than the emails he was cc'd on. He mostly dealt with legal matters, contracts, customer complaints, those kinds of things. We also found a bunch of times that he sent client funds to a company called National Escrow if the client was doing something that violated a copyright or Visa or MasterCard's rules. Nothing else really stood out. Right after the raid, he sent an email to the entire management team that reiterated the importance of preserving documents. He sent another email to the group telling them to cooperate with the investigation and to answer all our questions truthfully. So at least he seems to appreciate what's going on."

"What about Hulk Hogan?" Jake asked mocking Troy.

"Other than the one's I told you about, he mainly yelled at the sales reps about increasing business or meeting their goals. Every morning, he received an email with a huge Excel spreadsheet of what looked to be the prior day's transaction activity for every client. Then, we would see emails Troy sent to various sales reps asking questions about a particular client, or complaining about inactivity. Most of his internal emails referred to a specific client number so we couldn't tell exactly which clients he was talking about. He's definitely a micromanager. He also got a commission report every week. I looked at a couple of them and he was making a ton of money. He always had the most commissions of anyone. The interesting thing is that although he has a lot of clients, I'd say ninety percent or so of his commissions come from one client. Here, I wrote down the number. Maybe you can find out what client it is."

Sarah slid a sheet of paper across the table to Jake. On the sheet, she had written *2763759-50.* Little did she know that the number was for Modos Operations, ICon's secret client.

"Maybe that's why he balked when we asked him for his commission reports," Jake said. "It may have nothing to do with what we're looking at, but let's run that down. I think he was full of shit in the interview and I don't believe him for a second that he doesn't know anything about Zapplication, even if it was a house account. If he's hammering everyone to make budget, then he knows what's happening with every account. I want you to put one of the reviewers solely on Troy's emails."

"Oh, and I guess I should mention," Sarah said, "that he was sleeping with at least two women who work at ICon."

The others snickered as Sarah's face flushed. The inevitability of scouring through emails is the eventual discovery of personal indiscretions in addition to professional ones.

"And how did the magical mystery software find those emails," Chuck asked sarcastically.

Sarah answered bashfully "Let's just say that he talked about pounding more than just the pavement." They all had a much needed laugh.

"Okay, Chuck you're up. Impress us," Jake said as if coaching a veteran ball player. "Show these youngsters that it takes good ol' detective work to figure out a fraud."

Some giggles escaped from the far end of the table.

"Well, I didn't uncover anything as salacious as Sarah did, but I think I can take us a step closer to proving a round trip revenue scheme. I took a good look at the transaction reports Patti gave us for Zapplication, and I saw a few interesting things. The reports list the BIN number for the bank that issued the particular credit card for each transaction. That's the bank identification number. Every bank that issues credit cards has a unique BIN number. It brought back my time in the FBI's banking crime task force. We'd use these kinds of codes to track the cash flow. The first thing that jumped out to me is that the BIN number was the same for all of them."

"So the *same* bank issued every one of the cards? How many were there?" Jake asked.

"I don't know the total, but there looked to be at least a few hundred from what I saw. That has got to mean that the Zapplication transactions are fake. There's no way that all of the customers of a website got their credit cards from the same bank. It means that the transactions have to be coming from a single source with all of the credit card numbers."

"We also know that all of the transactions were for one dollar because the cost of subscribing to Zapplication is one dollar. So you have a lot of small transactions being processed by ICon. Remember that ICon generally makes the same percentage on a transaction regardless of whether it is one dollar or one thousand dollars. That means that if ICon wanted to boost its revenue by processing fake transactions, all it would need to do is run the minimum dollar amount per transaction because the revenue to ICon will be the same. Any more, and it's just a waste of money."

"And I bet that the numbers are sequential," Chuck added. "You can't tell by looking at them because sequential credit card numbers are not numerically sequential. There's no pattern that you can detect. The sequence is based on a logarithm, and you'd need the bank's formula. But, in my experience, if a bank issues cards in large quantities, it would do so in sequential batches. Just like if a company got a bunch purchase cards for its employees. You couple all that with the fact that most of the transactions occurred near the end of the month when ICon probably could tell whether or not it was going to need more revenue to meet its targets, and that doesn't smell right to this old nose."

The table was quiet as they considered Chuck's discovery.

Finally Sarah spoke up. "But didn't you go onto Zapplication's website?" she asked. "It was an actual website, right?"

"Yeah, but it was just a simple conduit site," Alex answered. "All it really did was list other sites that people could go to to buy cell phone apps. I could construct a site like that in a couple of hours."

"What bank issued the cards?" Jake asked.

Everyone turned to Chuck in anticipation of the answer.

"Well, the BIN schedule is not publicly available. It's a strictly confidential document that the banking regulators keep under lock and key."

There was a deflation at the table from the fleeting expectation that Chuck would identify the bank. He had the answer, however, and he grinned at his charade.

"It took a little cajoling," he began, "but I persuaded an old buddy at the Bureau to help me out. The BIN number was to a bank in Andorra called Banca d'Andorra."

His audience responded with confused looks from the foreign-sounding name.

"Andorra is a tiny country next to Spain," Chuck explained. "It's a financial haven, like the Caymans, only instead of bikinis and rum, there are snow suits and schnapps. I worked a bunch of cases where laundered funds went through Andorra."

The mention of Spain sparked Alex's memory. "Remember that Patti told us that Zapplication's client number had the country code for Spain. That's the connection! That's why the transactions were run through Andorra."

"But why would they need to go to Andorra to get the credit card numbers?" Jake asked.

"Dunno. Seems a long way from Miami when the Caribbean is just a hop away. But maybe they were looking for distance. It's not as easy to run secret funds out of the Caribbean as it used to be. You'd have to grease someone pretty well to pull that off these days."

"So, if we can prove that ICon paid for the credit card charges," Jake said, "then it will be clear that ICon was paying for the transactions that it was generating revenue from. That would close the loop on a round trip scheme, right?"

"Right," Chuck said disheartened, "but searching through all of ICon's disbursements in cash, checks, and wires over the last year would take months, even if we had a team of accountants. We only have a few days left before the shareholder meeting, and you only have me."

"Then we'll just have to get lucky, huh?" Jake said with a wink. "Okay, good work folks. If there is nothing else tonight, I'm calling it a day. Chuck and Alex, let's meet down here at 7:30 in the morning for the Board call."

As the door to the conference room shut behind them, the team split up along generational lines. Jake and Chuck went upstairs to unwind in their rooms, while Alex, Sarah, and the other associates headed downstairs to unwind at the lobby bar.

* * *

Jake dialed a telephone number and hung on each ring for an answer. After four rings, a small voice answered.

"Hi Daddy." Jake pictured his son's blonde hair, which given the time of day was likely a curly mess of cuteness.

"Hey buddy, whatcha doing?"

"Reading stories with Mommy." The image of Zack and Jenny wrapped up together reading bed time stories pulled at his heart.

"I wish I was there with you guys. Are you being a good boy?"

"Yeah, I even helped set the table." Zack was as excited about doing the chore as he was that he remembered doing the chore.

"That's great."

"Daddy, when are you going to be home?" Jake's heart strings were pulled taut by the little voice.

"I'm not sure pal. Maybe just a couple more days. But it will go real fast, I promise."

"Mommy said that you're working on a puzzle. It must be a big one."

Jake laughed. "Yeah, it's like a puzzle. My client heard a story and we're trying to find out whether or not it's true."

"What was the story about?" Zack asked. Jake grinned at his son's infinitely inquisitive nature.

"Well, it's a long story, but we're trying to figure out if someone lied about how much money a company made."

The phone was silent for a moment. Just as Jake was going to say something, Zack asked "Daddy, why would someone lie about that?"

Again, the phone was silent. Father and son both paused to ask the same question.

"Um, maybe the person's Daddy didn't teach them that lying is wrong. You should always tell the truth, right?"

"I know, I know."

Jake smiled at Zack's fleeting frustration because he knew it was the result of his paternal lessons.

"Okay. Well, good night buddy. I love you. Be good to Mommy."

"Love you too. Bye."

Jake heard a bang and a muffled noise, and then a click. He sighed at the thought of yet another bruise on the phone from Zack's apparent toss to the floor. It was these moments that he truly understood the difficulty of trying to put into words just how much love a parent has for a child.

* * *

"After the tone, please state your name and press the pound button."

Jake was facing the phone in the center of the table and he glanced over at Chuck and Alex, who were nursing their early morning cups of coffee.

"Levi & Everett." He pressed the pound button and they were connected to the boardroom in Atlanta where SouthPoint's Board of Directors was meeting.

"Good morning, this is Jake Morgan, Chuck Bradley, and Alex Perry."

"Hey Jake, this is Thomas. I'm here with the Board. Thanks for calling in. I've told them about what the former employee of ICon is claiming, and generally what you're doing. Can you give us an update about what you've found so far and a sense of the timing."

The Board of Directors of SouthPoint resembled many corporate boards. Seven graying male titans of business who dabbled in corporate governance as a hobby. The fees that directors earn are usually nominal in relation to the gravity of the decisions they make and the liability they could face. These seven men are the stewards of the shareholders and are charged with one singular objective – to maximize the value of the shareholders' interests.

Jake imagined them sitting around the elongated table in SouthPoint's lavish boardroom on the fortieth floor of its midtown Atlanta headquarters. Hunter McMillan would be perched at the head of the table, and the others would be flanked based on their seniority. It was in that room that the decision was made to acquire ICon, and it would be in that room that the consequences of the deal would be deliberated.

"Sure Thomas," Jake answered. "Hello Gentlemen. Well, we arrived on the scene yesterday and we've interviewed several people so far, including the former employee. We've reviewed thousands of emails and other documents. At this point, our suspicion is that there may have been an effort at ICon to boost its revenue by paying for credit card transactions. We've still got a lot work to do, but that's what things seem to be pointing towards."

He paused before getting into the specifics. There was silence on the other end of the phone, so he continued. "We have a concern about a pattern of low dollar transactions that are being run through ICon near the end of each month for the past six months or so. The credit card numbers were all issued from the same bank in Andorra, a small country in Europe. That could indicate that there may be some kind of fraud going on."

"Uh, Jake. This is Hunter." The silver-haired and silver-tongued Chairman of the Board interrupted slowly with a Southern accent. "I'm sure you know that we've got a shareholder meeting this coming Monday. This is the first quarter that we're reporting earnings after the ICon deal and Wall Street will be watching us. If we miss our earnings, the stock price will get hammered. We simply can't have that, you understand? So, I assume that this matter you're working on down there will not impact the very favorable report we are planning on giving on Monday."

Six hundred miles south, Jake looked over at Chuck and hunched his shoulders. He knew that he could not give the Chairman an unqualified response. There was no way to tell at this point whether any shenanigans at ICon could materially impact the Bank's financial report. Jake also knew from Thomas that the Chairman was not happy to learn about the investigation and that he wanted it wrapped up before the weekend.

McMillan had been at the helm of SouthPoint for almost five years, but he was a longtime director of the Bank. Now in his early seventies, he still was a force to be reckoned with in the Atlanta banking community. Over the previous forty-five years, he stepped on just about every rung in the ladder, and on just about everyone standing in his way. Corporate leaders from his generation rarely reached the pinnacle of power through a benevolent reign. Instead, especially in the South, business tended to follow Darwinian principles. Only the fittest survived, and the rest became prey.

After starting and selling two community banks before he was fifty, McMillan quickly became a predator. Over the next two and a half decades, McMillan made a fortune in the banking industry. His arsenal of friends included a fishing buddy who was on the Federal Reserve's Board of Governors, and classmates at the highest levels in the Office of Comptroller of Currency and the Federal Deposit Insurance Corporation. McMillan was sought after as a director for dozens of public companies, and he had been an advisor to two U.S. Treasury Secretaries. He was not someone who Jake wanted to disappoint.

"Well, Mr. McMillan, that's really hard say because we still need to confirm our theory and, if we're right, we need to quantify the amount at issue. However, we are working night and day, and I can assure you that we will get answers as soon as possible." Jake clenched his jaw as he gave the Chairman an overt, but necessary, hedge.

Just as McMillan began to grumble, Gary Cassell interceded. Gary was sitting at the other end of the boardroom table directly opposite of McMillan.

"Hunter, no one wants to deal with something like this now. But the lawyers think that we gotta look into it to satisfy our fiduciary duties, and I'm sure that Jake and his team will get to the bottom of whatever is going on."

Gary was covering for Jake as much as he was signaling to him that he had an ally on the Board. Gary's maneuver, however, was not purely pacifist. Although the ICon deal had been unanimously approved by SouthPoint's Board, it was Gary and his management team who identified ICon as a target and who blessed the due diligence. If there was something going on in Miami, Gary would likely field the brunt of the blame.

Jake felt the tension on the other end of the phone. Gary was the newest director on the Board as a result of SouthPoint's acquisition of Central Bank of Georgia, which Gary had founded. The professional friction that existed between Gary and McMillan emanated strangely enough from their similarities. Gary's trajectory so far was much like McMillan's. Both had similar pedigrees, both were banking prodigies from the South, and both had created successful financial institutions. Through circuitous paths, the two men who were twenty-two years apart in age sat facing each other on SouthPoint's Board. For whatever reason, however, these parallels repelled McMillan. Seeing oneself in another does not always engender gratification. Instead, the mirror oftentimes reflects flaws.

"I just don't want this Board to lose sight of the big picture," McMillan drew out his comment for effect. "If there is some kind of gerrymandering going on down there, I can't see how it would be material to the consolidated results of the Bank. If we go spatting off to investors about every time some disgruntled employee claims to be a whistleblower, then how are we doing what's right for the Bank's shareholders? With all due respect to the lawyers, I don't want to turn a mole hill into a mountain."

As General Counsel, Thomas spoke up for the record although the details of the Board's conversation would not be memorialized in the minutes. There would only be an innocuous reference in the minutes that a discussion was had about ICon.

"Hold on, Hunter. No one said anything about publicly disclosing the investigation. We're not anywhere near that decision yet. As I said, we think the former employee is credible, and we're just engaging in a reasoned response, which is required under Sarbanes-Oxley. The last thing we want is for her to go to the banking regulators or the SEC and claim that we didn't properly follow up on her allegations. Then we *would* have a mountain of trouble."

Jake, Chuck, and Alex sat quietly staring at the small dimpled speaker phone between them.

Finally, McMillan grunted something inaudible and then barked "Alright, just get it done with . . . and quickly. Let's move onto other business. The next item on the agenda is to hear from Lisa Harrison on the loan review committee."

"Thanks Gentlemen, we'll sign off." Jake happily hit the red button on the phone and sighed. "Whew, I'm glad we didn't have to give that report in person."

"No doubt," Alex said.

"One thing is clear," Chuck started, "in a couple of days, we better be damn sure we know what's going on."

"I hear you," Jake agreed. "We should learn more today from interviewing Jane, and hopefully we'll be able to talk again with Patti. I'm still worried about her credibility."

As they stood to leave, Jake's BlackBerry vibrated in his pocket.

"Jake Morgan," he answered.

"Jake, this is Thomas. I just stepped out of the board meeting. Look, I'm sorry about McMillan. He's been riding me hard about this investigation because he thinks I jumped the gun instead of waiting to do it until after the shareholder meeting. I tried to explain to him that delaying the investigation might look like the Board intentionally put its head in the sand, especially if this thing results in some kind of litigation. I also have Gary pushing me on the other end because he and Vic have to certify that the financial results in the 10-K are accurate. It's their ass if it's wrong and they don't want to sign the certification until we know if ICon's numbers are right. I'm right in the middle. So, I'm counting on you guys to figure out what's going on down there. Fast."

Jake felt the stress heating up his body. He took a deep breath to calm the anxiety. "I know. I understand. We'll get the job done, just hang in there. I'll call you later today after we interview the CFO."

Jake slipped the cell phone back into his pocket. He glanced over at Chuck and Alex, who had heard enough of the conversation to appreciate the pressure that they all were under.

"Okay, let's go."

Jake stood and removed the keys to the courtesy car. He tossed them to Alex, who did not expect the toss, but nevertheless dexterously caught them in one hand.

"Alex, can you drop Chuck and me off at ICon and then run over to Shells to see if Patti is working. Here, take this file. If she's there, ask her about the Zanax and the whistleblower comment. Make sure to take notes, and call me if you need to."

Alex tried to hide his excited grin. "Will do," he said gathering up his briefcase.

The three strode silently out of the war room for another day of battle.

* * *

"Just one for lunch?" An older hostess asked Alex as he walked into Shells through the door adorned with artificial barnacles.

"Uh, no. I'm looking for Patti Tomanski, is she working today?"

The hostess gave him a sneer. "Hold on, I'll be right back," she snorted.

After a few minutes, a heavyset man in a striped shirt a few sizes too small approached him. "I'm Stan Moore, the manager. Can I help you?"

"Yes sir, I'm looking for Patti Tomanski, one of the waitresses. Is she here?"

"Nah, she's off. Won't be back for a week." He wiped his thick mustache, which permeated with fish smell, with the back of his meaty hand. "Something you need from her?"

"Well, yes, kind of. If you talk to her before then could you please ask her to call me. Here's my card." Alex pulled a crisp business card from his wallet and handed it to the sweaty manager. It was the first business card that he had ever given out and he felt a sense of importance in the moment.

As Alex began to leave, Stan asked "You're a lawyer, huh? Is Patti in some kind of trouble?"

Alex stopped. "No. I spoke to her a few days ago about her last job. I just have a follow up question or two."

"So you're not with the other guys?" Stan asked.

"Uh, no. What other guys?" Alex looked curiously at him.

"Two goons came in here earlier looking for her. The one that asked me about her had some kind of accent. Russian maybe, I don't know. Anyway, not the kind of guys that I think Patti would want to hang out with."

"Did they leave their names or anything?"

"Nope. I told them the same thing I told you that she'll be back in a week. One of them said something in a foreign language and they left."

Alex paused, his mind racing. "Uh, alright, I appreciate your time."

Alex turned to leave the restaurant wondering who else was looking for Patti and hoping that he found her first.

* * *

"Okay, okay, calm down," Jake said to Alex on his cell phone who was feverishly describing what he learned at Shells. Jake was standing by the window in ICon's tropical lobby looking out over the parking lot.

"We don't know if she's in trouble, but I agree with you that we need to find her."

"Do you want me to go to her house?" Alex asked. "We should have her address in the personnel file we got."

"No, I need your help here on other things. Come back to ICon."

"Will do. I'll be there in about fifteen minutes."

Jake turned back towards the lobby. Chuck was sitting in a plush chair and he looked up from a fishing magazine.

"Seems as if we're not the only ones looking for Patti. I don't have a good feeling about that."

"Nope. Especially if what the HR guy said about the pills is true," Chuck added.

The door next to the receptionist opened quickly and Cain burst through. "Gentlemen, I'm very sorry for the delay. I got stuck on a phone call. Come on back to my office and we can talk about the schedule today. Jackie also got most of the documents on your list."

Jake and Chuck followed Cain through the executive suite to his office. Jake smiled at Cain's secretary who was wearing a mid-morning scowl until she saw Jake.

"Hello again," Jake greeted her as they passed her desk and disappeared into Cain's office.

Jackie was sitting in Cain's office, and Jake and Chuck took the remaining two chairs. Cain shut the door behind them and sat behind his desk. He looked tired and the wrinkles in his shirt suggested that it was yesterday's shirt. Before he started to talk, Cain paused as if he needed the time to collect his thoughts.

"I know that you gave us a list of people that you want to talk to today, and we're fully prepared to make them available. But let me suggest something to you that might speed all of this along. Lawyer to lawyer. I'm not trying to get in your way, but I think I have an idea about what you all are investigating. If I'm right, we should be able to clear this up today."

Cain stopped to gauge Jake's reaction. Jake's curiosity was piqued, but so was his suspicion.

"Uh, sure. What's your suggestion?"

"I suggest that the next person you interview is my father. Then talk to Jane. I think that you should review the package of documents and information that Jackie has for you." He motioned towards her and she handed Chuck a three ring binder. Chuck thanked her for the binder and he glanced over at Jake with curiosity.

"I'm sure you knew," Cain continued, "that we'd put two and two together fairly quickly and figure out what this investigation is all about. A new employee asks the CFO questions about accounting issues, the

CFO provides a less than satisfactory answer, and the next thing you know the employee is fired. I can see exactly why that would cause concern, and I understand why the Bank is looking into it. In fact, I'd be disappointed if the Bank did not look into it. That's not the kind of company that my father started, and that's not the kind of company that I want to work for."

Jake eyed Cain, still not sure just where he was going.

"So after you came in the other day, I looked back through the former employee's file to review her situation. Her name is Patti Tomanski, right?" Cain asked while nodding to Jake to confirm that he was on the right track. Jake nodded back slowly, and Cain continued as he expected.

"Ms. Tomanski was terminated because of a conflict she had with Jane Weaver. I wasn't involved in that decision. But, Glen Baker did come to me after he learned that Ms. Tomanski violated a company policy by having non-prescribed pharmaceuticals in the office. Since Ms. Tomanski was still within her probationary period, I approved her termination from a legal perspective. I spoke again yesterday with Jane about the situation so that I could better understand the conflict issue. Jane said that Ms. Tomanski asked over and over about the Zapplication account, even though client accounting was outside the scope of her job. Jane apparently told her that she was aware of the account and not to worry about it, but Ms. Tomanski was fixated on it. It ultimately became a problem and created a difficult work environment. I agree that it could have, and certainly should have, been handled better by Jane. But, Jane was only doing what she was told to do by my father."

Cain reached for his coffee and sipped it, leaving the group hanging on his last word.

"If you want to interview Alan now, I'll let him explain the whole thing to you so that you get the proper background and context. One condition, however, is that I need to be present when you interview him. I'm not only ICon's lawyer, but he's my father. He's has always looked to me for advice. I also was involved to some extent with the Zapplication account, and I think that together we can explain to you what happened. After that, you can talk with whoever you want, but I think you'll want to talk to Jane."

Jake leaned back in his chair considering Cain's request to attend

Alan's interview. It was against best practices to allow anyone else to attend a witness interview, other than the witness's own lawyer. If witnesses are interviewed together, they are privy to each other's stories and can immediately corroborate their versions. Interrogators lose the ability to calibrate witnesses when there are others in the room who support, and perhaps even created, the story being told.

But there was not much Jake could do. The ticking of his short time frame to finish the investigation demanded speed over process. Now he knew that Alan, Jane, and Cain were somehow involved in the Zapplication account, and at least he would get their story quickly.

"I guess if we can get right to, that's fine," Jake answered. "But, depending on what we hear, I may need to talk with other people."

"Certainly," Cain shot back and started to stand. "He's waiting in his office for us, and Jane can talk to you after that. But she insisted on hiring a lawyer. I think she's just gun shy, given some things that she's been through. Her lawyer is Neal Stein of Stein, Thomas, and Holland. His office is downtown, we'll get you directions."

Jake was skeptical about the production that was being played out, and he was wary of the planning that appeared to have occurred over the last day at ICon. Whatever was coming, however, at least Jake would have something to report to Thomas later on. He stood and followed Cain out of his office, glancing back at Chuck who was following with a skeptical smirk.

Chuck leaned up close to Jake and whispered sarcastically "This must be what you meant last night about getting lucky, huh?"

Jake shrugged as they headed to the President of ICon's office.

Cain knocked lightly on the open door to Alan's office. "Are you ready for us?"

"Sure, come in," they heard from inside the office.

Cain entered the office, but before Jake and Chuck followed, Alex came through the door to the executive suite. He waved at Jake, who motioned for him to join them.

"What's up?" Alex said approaching Jake and Chuck outside of the office.

"Apparently, we are going to be enlightened about Zapplication. Make sure to take good notes. And also since you'll be off to the side, watch closely how Alan and Cain interact, even when they're not talking. I want to know if they're signaling each other in any way. Watch their eyes, watch for nodding, tapping a pen. Anything like that."

"Gotcha," Alex said.

As the three of them walked into the office, Alan stood and extended his hand. Cain was sitting in a chair by the side of Alan's desk, and there were two chairs facing his desk for Jake and Chuck. Alex sat at a round glass table in the back with an unobstructed view of Alan and Cain.

After they all sat, Alan rested both elbows on his spotless desk and clasped his hands together. "I appreciate you changing your schedule. I don't want to interfere with your process, but Cain tells me that you're interested in the Zapplication account and I think we can clear some things up." Alan was about to deliver a scripted dialogue when Jake interrupted him.

"Before we start, Mr. Arnold, I need to make sure that we cover some preliminary matters with both you and Cain. As I'm sure you know, we are not your personal lawyers and what you tell us will be reported to SouthPoint's Board. Our conversation is protected by the attorney-client privilege, but that privilege belongs to the Board, meaning that the Board can decide whether to disclose what we talk about to a third party if it chooses. Do you understand that?"

"Uh, yeah, sure," Alan replied guardedly and glanced over at Cain who nodded back to him.

"Okay, thanks," Jake said. "You were saying?"

Alan took a breath and began. "It might help to first give you some background. This business is all about speed. Website users want their credit card transactions approved in seconds, so the process has to take fractions of seconds. Our experience has shown us that if the average time from transmission to approval begins to exceed ten seconds, the percentage of users who cancel their transactions multiplies. Our society has been so addicted to instantaneous gratification from the Internet, that people have zero tolerance for any delay. It's not like when you and I were younger and we'd wait weeks to get something in the mail that we bought over the phone. So if the cancellation rate increases it amounts to lost business for the websites who are our customers."

"There are any number of things that can cause transmission delays. It could be the website's host server on the front end, or it could be the credit card company's server networks on the back end. Hell, even the weather can sometimes affect transmission. But, for us, in the middle of the transaction process, the most common reason for delay is if our platform experiences some kind of backlog or overload. In other words, too many transactions being processed at the same time. If we experience a delay in the speed of the transactions being processed, we call that a transaction delay drift or t-delay drift. If we get a t-delay drift of ten seconds or so, we hear about it from our customers - and loudly. Our customers are sophisticated and they watch the transmission timing very closely."

Alan paused to take a sip out of his water bottle as Jake cringed recalling the same story line that Troy had spewed at him in the restroom.

"As you probably know by now, every transaction that we process is electronically scrubbed for fraud. The merchant agreements we have with the credit card companies require us to constantly monitor the transactions for things like stolen credit cards, identity theft, money laundering. So we have software that is constantly updated that analyzes the transaction flow for these kinds of things. But that slows down the process, especially with international transactions because, among other things, there are different exchange codes and card algorithms. It also may not come as a surprise to you that there is a much greater occurrence of fraud from overseas transactions. Now, the real problem with all of that is that we have non-exclusive contracts."

Cain interrupted to explain. "A non-exclusive contract means that a client of ours can switch its processing portals to one of our competitors with just a flip of a switch. No one in the industry has been able to leverage an exclusivity provision into their contracts. It's crazy. I mean imagine if you were unhappy with your cell phone carrier and you could just switch carriers whenever you wanted to on the drop of a dime. You get dropped from a call with Sprint, so you just switch to AT&T. Think about what that competitive pressure would do to the telecom industry. They would have to engineer cell phones to be as good as land lines. But the telecom industry is in bed with Congress and there is too much lobbying money to ever let that happen. For internet payment processors, no one cares because no one sees what we do. We can't even get a state senator to call us back." Cain sat back realizing that he was departing from the script.

"Anyway," Alan continued as he shot a scowl at his son, "we have to be hyper reactive to make sure we don't lose customers. If we're not the quickest, we're out of business. And that brings me to Zapplication. About a year ago, we decided that we wanted to be proactive and head off any backlog or overload problems that might arise. So, in consultation with IT, we started a secret corporate project to routinely test ICon's operating platform. We called it stress testing. This stress testing involves sending thousands of transactions through the system at select times to see how the system reacts, and to make sure that the increased volume does not result in any t-delay drifts. Because delays happen most with international transactions, we have focused the stress testing to the international portal so the test transactions appear to be coming from overseas."

"What do you mean 'appear' to be coming from overseas?" Chuck asked.

"The test transactions actually originate through a local website, which is where Zapplication comes in. However, the credit cards numbers were issued from a foreign bank and carry a foreign BIN number. So, our system thinks that they are international transactions and they are routed through the international portal to receive enhanced fraud scrubbing."

"So how does it work?" Jake asked. "I mean, is there someone at Zapplication typing in these hundreds of thousands of credit card numbers and sending the transactions?"

"Good question. I'll let Cain explain that since he handled the legal mechanics of how this works."

"The short answer is no," Cain said. "We engaged a third party called Web Assist to do all this through Zapplication. Web Assist obtained the credit card numbers and loaded them into a computer program they created that resides on Zapplication's server. Whenever the program is activated, it batches the numbers and sends them through Zapplication's website as if they were individual transactions. Here, I have the Web Assist contract."

Cain handed Jake a two page document titled Service Testing Agreement. Jake scanned over it and handed it to Chuck.

"I'm sure you're wondering 'Why Zapplication'?" Cain continued. "Well, we needed to send the transactions using one of our client's internet provider addresses because we couldn't run the tests directly from a computer at ICon. ICon's system would've recognized our IP address and it would not have processed the transactions, which is a built-in internal control. We also needed a client with low monthly volume so that the test transactions didn't interfere with its regular business. So we ran some queries on Velocity to see which of our clients were at the bottom in terms of activity. Zapplication was near the bottom and we thought that its business model would fit the stress testing. I'm not sure if you've been on the site, but it's basically a clearinghouse for cell phone application websites. The reason we liked it was because the subscription to the site was just one dollar. For the stress testing, we needed actual credit card purchases, but the amount of the purchase didn't matter. So, the lower the better."

"The guys at Zapplication were more than happy to do it since they're a low traffic site. They don't have to do anything and we give them free processing in return. I don't think they even know when the transactions are run, except maybe if they look at their Velocity reports."

"Well then who decides when to run the test transactions?" Chuck probed.

"Web Assist has complete discretion, which is spelled out in the contract. We, of course, discussed with them the characteristics of our overall business flow and the international market so that they understood our vulnerabilities to backlogs or overloads. But, they're the ones who decide when to test the system."

"What are ICon's vulnerabilities?" Jake followed up.

Alan edged in to answer. "We see that most of the activity tends to be back ended in the month. The trajectory looks like a bell curve with the peak being around the twentieth of each month. It's hard to say what causes it, but we've always suspected that people do more on-line discretionary spending after they've paid their bills in the early to mid-month weeks."

That explanation, Jake thought, was rather convenient given that the end of the month also is typically when revenue goals and sales targets are measured.

"Ok. We'll need to get some contact information for the owners of Web Assist," Jake said.

"Sure," Cain replied fully expecting the request, "but just so you know, Web Assist is a foreign-based company so we've only communicated with them over the phone and the internet."

"Where are they based?"

"In Andorra of all places," Cain answered nonchalantly.

When he heard Andorra Jake glanced over at Chuck as both recognized the pieces starting to fit together.

"How were the credit card numbers obtained?" Jake asked.

"I'm not sure, that was all handled by Web Assist. We just paid a deposit and they took care of everything on their end."

"Does Web Assist provide any reports or data substantiating the stress testing?" Jake asked.

"We've got the transaction reports showing the dates and amounts of test transaction being run through Zapplication, which is all there really is. Our system naturally detects the testing because, as I said, they are low dollar transactions sent in batches. I'm sure the numbers are sequential as well, which is one of the triggers for our fraud detection software. Anyway, we know real time when they are being processed, and we can measure the t-delays to see if there is any drift."

"In terms of the accounting," Chuck began, "how was the revenue treated that was generated on the test transactions? I'm assuming that there was revenue to ICon."

Alan quickly interceded and deferred the question. "Jane will be able to discuss how the accounting works, but from a disclosure standpoint there was no material impact."

Jake and Chuck paused their questioning to absorb the impact of the stress testing story. There were questions that still nagged at them, but the testing seemed to explain a lot about the transactions that Patti had identified. Cain looked over at his father, as they both quietly awaited further inquiry. The room was silent except for Alex frantically scribbling notes to catch up.

Finally, Jake broke the tension. "If this was really just legitimate stress testing, then why didn't you or Jane tell Ms. Tomanski when she asked about it? Seems to me that all this could have been avoided."

"That's my fault," Alan responded quickly. "I didn't want this stress testing to be something that was known outside a small control group. For one thing, I was concerned that if got out it might raise questions about the capability of our platform. The fact that we're testing it for peak loads could be seen as being reactive to some kind of problem, as opposed to being a purely proactive measure. I wanted it to be kept confidential. Another thing, quite honestly, is that I didn't trust the employee, this Tomanski woman. She was brand new and for all I know she was feeding information to our competitors. Jane came to me and asked what she should do about it. She thought that it was unusual that the employee kept pushing about the Zapplication account, especially because I understand she was in a different department or had different duties. So I told Jane to blow her off."

Alan paused to reflect. "In retrospect, maybe that wasn't the best decision. I guess I should've listened to Cain," Alan said looking over at his son. "He thought that we should explain it to her and have her sign a confidentiality agreement. But those agreements sometimes are only worth the paper they're written on. I've been in business a long time Mr. Morgan and I know that if a confidentiality agreement is breached, you can't put the toothpaste back into the tube. And what are we going to do, sue her? She couldn't hope to pay the damages it might cause us."

He studied Jake and Chuck for any sign of understanding. "Look, I realize that there was a misunderstanding and that we didn't handle it right. I'm even willing to reinstate her if it'll help. But that's all it was and I hope that you won't blow this out of proportion." Alan finished contritely.

"What involvement did Troy have in this project?" Jake asked with a vendetta obvious to only two of the others in the room.

Alan and Cain struggled to not look at each other, but Cain knew to defer to his father in these instances.

"Troy had a limited role," Alan answered. "As VP of Sales, he knew a little about the project, but he didn't know any of the specifics. He has enough on his plate."

Jake and Chuck similarly struggled not to look at each other, this time in skepticism. Alan's delivery of what was certainly a scripted answer did not persuade either of them. If there was anything going on at ICon, Jake thought, Troy knew about it. Not only was he a senior executive, but the commission reports showed that he was the company's breadwinner. Alan's protection of Troy may have been out of loyalty, but to Jake it also tainted the credibility of his story.

Cain interjected sensing that all the questions he expected had been asked. "The binder that Jackie gave you has all of the supporting information relating to the stress testing project. Once you look over that, you may have more questions, and we're happy to answer them. It may make sense that you talk with Jane now so that you can understand the accounting."

"I have just one more question before we go," Chuck responded. "Did it work? The stress testing, did it work?"

Alan blinked a few times. He had not expected that question and glanced upwards before he answered. "Uh, yeah, it has worked. So far anyway. We haven't had any significant drifts in the transaction times even with the test loads."

Chuck paused and looked hard at Alan over his reading glasses. He hesitated but continued his gaze to see if Alan had anything else to add.

"Okay, thanks," he finally said in his deep voice.

As Jake and Chuck looked at each other to see if either had any more questions, Alex noticed that Alan glanced over at Cain who nodded almost imperceptibly.

"I think that's all for now," Jake said.

Cain stood up quickly as if the mere act officially ended the interview.

"Uh, I have one more thing that I need to talk to Alan about," Jake said. "And this does need to be alone," he added when he saw Cain start to sit back down. "It does not deal with the stress testing."

"Uh, well," Cain stammered, "anything that you discuss with him you can share with me." Cain turned to his father, who tried to hide any reaction to Jake's request.

"Sorry Cain, I'm going to have to insist this time. Mr. Arnold, it'll just take a moment."

"It's okay," Alan said gesturing to his son.

Cain reluctantly agreed, having no viable argument or alternative. He left the others sitting in the room, and he glanced back at his father as he slowly shut the office door.

Alan leaned back and crossed his arms, unconsciously guarding against the unexpected.

"Mr. Arnold, I need to ask you some questions about your emails."

Alan fidgeted before responding. "Sure, sure. What do you want to know?"

"A couple of days ago when we first arrived we gave everyone a document preservation memo, including you. It is my understanding, however, that on the same day, you deleted a couple of hundred emails. Or attempted to delete, I should say."

Alan felt his chest start to pound. He started to rock slightly in his chair. "Uh, yeah, I guess I did . . . I assume that I did if you say so." His mind raced as to how Jake would know what emails he deleted.

"I clean out my in-box from time to time. That's normal because I get all kinds of junk, and IT is always on me to purge it. I do know, however, that I didn't delete anything after you passed out the memo. As I recall, we got that memo during the meeting yesterday morning with all of the execs. I'm sure that if I cleaned out my emails it was before that. I never would've deleted anything after I got the memo."

Jake looked carefully at Alan to detect any signs of deception, but Alan seemed positive about his account.

"Hold on, I bet we can tell," Alan said. "Do you know the time that the emails were deleted?"

Jake knew the exact time from Sarah's report, but he was reluctant to disclose it. Knowing the time would reveal that ICon's deleted emails were being captured by the dumpster, and it might tip off Alan as to how the emails were captured. But Alan had to be confronted about the deletions, and the time might prove that Alan tried to intentionally delete critical emails. Jake figured that it was better to get to the bottom of it, but he nevertheless cringed at revealing the information.

"Our records indicate that the deleting activity started at 9:53 a.m."

Alan quickly swiveled in his chair to face his computer, and Jake looked over at Chuck and Alex with an anticipatory glance.

"Okay, let's see. That was Wednesday morning . . . ." Alan glided the mouse so that the cursor highlighted emails in his Sent box. "I know that I sent an email to Val on my way to the meeting telling her that I'd be tied up for a while. Uh . . . oh, here it is."

Alan slid his chair to the side so that Jake could see the monitor. The email to Val read *I'll be in the boardroom. Don't know how long. Hold all calls*. Jake could see that the time sent was 10:02 a.m.

"So, it looks like I did purge those emails before I got the memo," Alan argued with a slight grin as if facing twelve jurors.

Jake was instantly unimpressed with Alan's attempt to split hairs. Alan may have fortuitously deleted the emails before he was told expressly not to, but the fact remained that he did so seven minutes before he left for the meeting. Jake and Chuck had been in his office at least fifteen minutes before the meeting. When Alan tried to mass delete the emails, he already knew that SouthPoint's Board had sent them to investigate ICon. The deletion time was irrelevant as far as Jake was concerned.

The more important question was what was Alan trying to hide? Jake had not yet told Alan what they were investigating, so he had deleted all the emails *before* he even knew what they were looking into. That's the sign of a guilty conscience Jake thought. But there was no need to argue with Alan because he had enough of his technicalities. Jake was not advocating a position, he was trying to prove one, and Alan's response was all the evidence he needed that there was something in his emails that Alan didn't want them seeing. The art of interviewing is not only in asking a question, but in knowing when you got the answer.

"Okay, I see. Thanks," Jake said. "We appreciate your time and I'll let you know if we have any follow up questions."

Jake stood to leave, this time officially signaling the end of the interview. Alan stood, seemingly relieved, and shook Jake's and Chuck's hands. Alex quickly gathered his notes and followed behind them out of the expansive President's office. The three didn't say a word as they walked down the executive hallway towards the lobby. They walked out of the main entrance of ICon into the already-smoldering Miami sun.

Jake started into the parking lot until he realized that he didn't know where Alex had parked the car upon returning from Shells. Alex winked at him and took the lead towards the car. As they approached the sedan, Alex tossed the keys back to Jake, who reached for them, but he missed the catch.

"The throw was there," Alex chided Jake.

Jake sneered in jest as he bent over to pick up the keys from the simmering pavement. Before they got into the car, Jake turned to Alex.

"Alex, you've been in IT. Does this stress testing sound like something you would need to do to a computer system?"

Alex shrugged. "Well, after we used to build computer networks, we would test them by mimicking additional users to see how the additional number would affect the speed and functionality of the network. So in a way, that was stress testing the system. I just don't know enough about this particular kind of platform to know if that's customary or not. I think we need to interview ICon's IT person. His name is in my notes somewhere."

"It all seems a bit too convenient if you ask me," Chuck said. "A supposedly unrelated third party in Andorra of all places is deciding when to test ICon's system, and it just so happens the tests fall at the end of the month. I may be an old dog, but that smells to me."

"Yeah, I agree," Jake said, "especially given everything else that we know."

"It should all come out in how they accounted for the stress testing," Chuck added. "We should be able to see exactly what revenue ICon recorded from the transactions, and whether they gave proper treatment to the expense. If it's not perfectly clear, or if we can't follow the cash flow, then we'll know there's a problem."

Jake paused in thought, standing next to the car. "Well, I'll be very interested to hear Jane's explanation of the accounting and why she dodged us yesterday. I bet that she lawyered up because she's worried about something."

"It could've been because of the warm reception you gave her yesterday," Chuck chided him facetiously.

"I just don't trust her. She seemed a little too cool and collected if you know what I mean. I'd think that a CFO would be wound up pretty tight if someone came in and started questing the accounting. And she emailed her lawyer immediately after the meeting with management. That's a red flag to me."

"Chuck, when we interview her, push hard on the details of the accounting. We need to trace every penny relating to this stress testing. I'll handle her lawyer if he tries to get in the way. And Alex, we also need to talk with Patti to see if this testing makes sense to her. We've got her address in her personnel file, so can you drop Chuck and me off downtown at the lawyer's office and swing by her house to see if she's there."

Jake tossed the keys to the car back to Alex, who snatched them out of the air adroitly with one hand.

"Nice catch," Chuck remarked.

Alex shot a grin over to Jake as if taunting him for his earlier miss.

"What? The sun was in my eyes," Jake said reaching into his pocket and slipping on his sunglasses.

As the white Mercedes turned out of ICon's parking lot, Alan watched them from his office window. He didn't know whether he convinced the investigators, but he knew that it was now out of his hands. If this deal imploded, he had a lot more to worry about than SouthPoint.

Alan picked up the phone next to him and punched his son's four digit extension.

"They're gone. We need to talk."

*　*　*

The shiny skyscrapers of downtown Miami stood with their toes at the edge of the Atlantic Ocean and reached up towards the sun. The South's biggest city is alive with a vastly different culture than its American geography might suggest. Swaths of Latin American influence blanket the city and have transformed Miami from the southernmost American big city to an international mecca of ethnicities.

"That's it up on the left."

Jake pointed to the Bank of America Tower, a curved three-tier tower with horizontal pinstripes of windows. It housed the financial elite. Bankers, brokers, and lawyers. The iconic downtown landmark was designed by famed architect I.M. Pei, and it appropriately glows green neon when the sun rests.

Alex pulled off of International Place and guided the car under the glass canopy of the building's motor lobby.

"We'll meet you back here after you talk with Patti," Jake said to Alex. "Email me when you're on you're way back."

Jake shut the car door and followed Chuck into the expansive lobby of the Bank of America tower.

Stein, Thomas and Holland was perched on the 37th floor and enjoyed a commanding view of Biscayne Bay. Its namesake, Neal Stein, cut his teeth defending middle management drug professionals. He soon had a taste for real money and honed his reputation by defending white collar criminals. He preferred being paid in sanitary wires as opposed to tainted cash, and he slept much better having clients whose only weapon was a pen or computer. Hiring Neal Stein signaled to others that you were in trouble, but it also meant that you would most likely sleep in your own bed and not in a jail cell.

The respectful chime of the elevator announced their ascent to the 37th floor. Jake and Chuck walked into the vanilla wood lobby, which was adorned with gold leaf lettering of the firm's name. Floor to ceiling windows displayed an aerial view of the bay and the surrounding islands.

Jake approached the receptionist waiting for him behind a mahogany desk.

"Hi, I'm Jake Morgan. I'm here to see Neal Stein."

"Thank you sir, please have a seat and I'll call him."

Jake walked over to Chuck who was gazing out of the window. Their eyes met and Chuck's raised his eyebrows impressed with the decor.

"I bet it takes a lot of billable hours to pay this rent," he quipped.

After a few moments, Jane's lawyer approached them.

"Gentlemen, thanks for coming."

Neal greeted them as he walked across the lobby. He dressed as smoothly as his shaved head, with a pastel colored dress shirt and shiny gold cuff links. His flowered tie guaranteed that he would not go unnoticed in any courtroom.

They introduced themselves and shook hands. Neal skipped the pleasantries and got right down to business.

"I understand that you're conducting an internal investigation of certain accounting issues at ICon. Ms. Weaver would like to cooperate and I'll let you interview her in a moment. However, if you plan on showing her any documents or emails, I'd ask that you give us the opportunity to look at them first. She also has not had a chance to go back and review all her emails about the issues, so there may be things she'll need to get back to you about. And, as you may know, her employment contract contains an indemnification agreement, so I want to confirm that ICon will be paying my fees."

Neal knew the drill when representing corporate executives during investigations. He was savvy enough not to overly interfere with the process, and wise enough to promptly secure his collections. Although an executive typically has the right to seek repayment of legal fees, these funds dry up quickly if any indicia of guilt is discovered during the investigation.

"You'll need to speak directly with SouthPoint's General Counsel, Thomas Nelson, about the indemnification, that's outside our authority," Jake answered. "But at this point I don't think there will be a problem covering reasonable fees." He gently emphasized *reasonable* because he likewise was savvy enough to know that defense counsel needed to be controlled. Especially those wearing flowered ties and gold cuff links.

"As for the documents, I'll be happy to show you the ones that I'd like to ask Ms. Weaver about today. But, I expect and hope that *she* will be the one to identify key documents to us," Jake said politely, but firmly.

"I understand, thanks. Okay, well come right this way and we can start."

Jake and Chuck followed Neal across the lobby towards two smoked glass doors. He opened a door and gestured for them to enter. Jake took the lead and walked into the large conference room. Perched at the head of a long table with just a bottle of water in front of her was Jane Weaver. She sat stoic as if waiting for the jury to return to the courtroom.

"Hello Ms. Weaver," Jake said extending his hand.

"Hello again, Mr. Morgan."

The thickness between them was palpable as they shook hands. Both were used to being in charge of the situation, and both were set to vie for control of the present one.

* * *

"Turn right onto Bay Street. Destination is on the left."

Alex turned the volume down on the GPS, and he looked ahead down the thin street lined with townhomes. Mangrove trees shaded the searing Miami sun and bright orange flowers lighted the street. As he approached No. 180, he slowed the car and took a long look at the unit. The garage door was shut and the plantation blinds in the first floor windows were turned down half way. He could not tell if Patti was home or not. He eased the car past the house and pulled behind several parked cars a few units away.

There were a few people on the sidewalk walking their dogs as Alex approached Patti's unit. Just as he was about to walk up the steps, he froze. He caught a glimpse of two men sitting in a black sedan parked across the street. The car windows were open and both of them were staring in his direction. They looked out of place, just sitting there with dark sunglasses on a quiet neighborhood street. He had seen enough Law & Order episodes to know that something was wrong with that picture.

While his head spun about what to do, his legs instinctively continued their pace and he walked past her unit down the sidewalk. He did not look back until he passed a thick hydrangea with big blue flower balls and he ducked behind the bush. He slowly peeked around towards the men in the car. They were still focused towards Patti's townhome. He didn't know if he was just being paranoid. After all, this was his first investigation and maybe he was dramatizing his solo assignment. At that point, however, his instincts were more persuasive than his reason.

As he huddled in the bushes in his brand new slacks, it struck him that there was one way to tell if these were the same men that were looking for Patti. Alex hopped out of the bushes and glanced in both directions. He crossed the street and walked back towards Patti's house on the opposite side of the street. The sedan with the two men was just ahead, and he could see the driver's elbow leaning out of the window. As Alex approached the car, his chest pounded. He tried to forget that he was just a first year lawyer, not a private detective.

"Excuse me, do you know where Lincoln Avenue is?"

The driver turned to see the junior lawyer on the sidewalk. He had thin dark hair and his face was pitted from a bad case of pubescent acne. Alex saw his own image reflected in the driver's sunglasses and he hoped that he didn't really look that scared. He tried to get a glimpse of the passenger, but he shifted as if trying to conceal something by his side. He kept his head facing the other direction so that Alex could not see him.

"Uh, I don't know. I'm not from here." The driver's Eastern European accent sent a shock wave through Alex, and it confirmed what the Shell's manager had told him about the Russian visitors.

Alex stuttered to thank the driver and he continued down the sidewalk amped with nervous energy. He crossed the street and quickly got into the car. The sudden silence inside the car as the door shut revealed his heavy breathing, and he ran his fingers through his hair trying to calm his nerves. Whoever those guys are, Alex thought, they were not going away until they found Patti.

Alex pulled the car away from the side of the street and he glanced up in the rear view mirror. The sedan was still lurking across from her house. As he drove away, he silently prayed that he found her before they did.

* * *

"Okay, Ms. Weaver," Jake started, "let's now talk about the Zapplication account and the stress testing. Tell me when you first became involved."

Jane glanced to her left at Neal, who was sitting next to her at the conference room table built for twenty. The polished wood surface reflected long fluorescent lights that spanned the table and lit the lavish room. Neal nodded slowly giving her permission to answer. They had spent the better part of the night before rehearsing the interview and scripting her performance. Not only was she prepared on the substance, she was ready for the show.

"Well, I'm not sure exactly what you mean by being involved," Jane said with a sharpened tongue, "but the first time I recall knowing about the account was about nine months or so ago. Alan informed that there was an IT project they were doing that entailed testing the computer system. He told me that one of our clients would be processing transactions and he gave me the supporting contract with the vendor that would be doing the testing."

"I asked him a few questions about our payment agreement and when our liability for the fees accrued. Then I set up an accrual on the P&L under Professional Fees just like any other vendor."

"Why did *you* set up the account?" Chuck asked. "I wouldn't think that a CFO would handle that kind of ministerial task."

Jane turned towards Chuck in a slow deliberate way to buy more time.

"Alan told me that this was a confidential project so he wanted me to personally handle all of the accounting for it. That was what caused the issue with Patti. She came to me a couple of times asking about the account and Alan told me to ignore her."

"Did he say why it was confidential?"

"He said that he didn't want the fact that ICon was testing its system to get outside of the company. Alan tends to be a bit paranoid about our competitors."

Chuck continued his line of inquiry. "Can you run me through the journal entries that were made to set up the accrual and those that relieved the accrual? I'm also interested in seeing what, if any, revenue was recognized from the transactions. I'd like to see the complete impact on the P&L."

"Sure, Mr. Bradley," she said as if she had been waiting to explain that since the interview began.

She took a sip from the almost empty bottle of water as Neal interceded before her answer.

"We made copies of the entries for you. It might help if you follow along."

He opened up a cabinet and removed two sets of bound documents, giving one to Jake and one to Chuck. Jake bristled realizing that Neal had asked them to see any documents that they were planning on showing Jane, but Neal conveniently did not similarly tell them that he also had documents he was planning on using. That was an underhanded move that Jake would not forget.

"Ms. Weaver, other than the contract, what documentation do you have to prove that the expense for the stress testing was actually incurred?" Chuck asked.

"Since this was a rather unusual account because we were incurring an expense through a revenue-generating client, I decided that the simplest thing was to support it by the client transaction reports off of Velocity. The reports show all of the monthly transactions for the client, and we coded the test transactions to start with a nine so that I could easily go through the reports and substantiate that the testing was taking place."

"We understand that these reports for Zapplication were made to look like payables." Jake premised his question from what Patti had found. "Why was that?"

Jane turned back towards Jake, who had been letting Chuck ask most of the questions. "Because otherwise it might appear to an untrained eye that there was some kind of fraud going on."

She slowed as she said *untrained eye* as if easing over a speed bump for emphasis. She clearly had not gotten over Jake's initial attempt to intimidate her by dredging up the *Corline* case, and her answer dripped with an annoyed tone. Neal had warned her not to lose her cool, but she was beginning to get a little warm.

"Had we reflected the testing as a receivable instead of a payable," she continued, "it might have appeared that we were generating revenue through our own funds. That would be round tripping, wouldn't it be Mr. Morgan?" she asked acidly without expecting an answer. "And, quite frankly, a pretty novice one at that. It would also be securities fraud, bank fraud, a violation of accounting principles and of my professional ethics."

She paused to finish her water, and the three men watched her lips glisten. "If that's what you think happened, then SouthPoint could've just sent Mr. Bradley here to find out in a civil way instead of having you barge in with a battalion of lawyers. I'm afraid that your mission is in vain because I can assure that ICon's books are accurate."

Neal could not restrain a slight grin watching his client spar with Jake. He was confident that Jane was telling the truth about the accounting, which was a sentiment that he didn't always feel with other clients. The night before Jane explained all of the debits and credits relating to Zapplication. Everything added up. Everything made sense. In another case, Neal might have refused to allow his client to be interviewed until he saw every last document. With Jane, however, he thought that it was best for her to be available immediately to obviate any appearance of hiding.

Jake peered at Jane with a hard look, but did not react in any way to her bark. He was playing a role as the bad cop that he had cast for himself yesterday. Pushing her was part of the script, and watching her performance was part of the act.

"Look Ms. Weaver, we are not a witch hunt," Jake said firmly.

"We are following up on allegations that are based in large part on your admitted mistreatment of Ms. Tomanski. Had you been more transparent to her about the Zapplication account, we might not have had to embark on this mission as you so colorfully call it."

She pursed her full lips and Neal gently put his hand on her shoulder to calm her.

"Ms. Weaver," Chuck said interceding, "we've covered a lot today and I appreciate your time. I have just a few more questions for you."

Chuck put on his thin glasses and shuffled the paper in front of him. "Can you take me through the revenue impact of the stress testing and the accounting?"

Jane had regained her composure. "At the end of each month and each quarter, I ran a query on Velocity that showed the fee revenue generated for Zapplication. I wrote off that amount by treating it as contra revenue, a reduction of gross revenue just like a rebate. So, it was a wash. There was no revenue recorded for the stress testing, and it had no P&L impact whatsoever on net income."

Chuck nodded slowly as he looked over the journal entries that Neal had given them. "Okay, and I'll be able to confirm all of this on the GL?" he asked her in a decidedly good cop tone.

"Yes, you can," she answered him.

"And I presume that there are no other accounts similar to Zapplication, right? This stress testing was only run through that one client?"

"Yes, that's right."

Chuck leaned over to Jake and they whispered to each other.

"Neal, can we take a short break," Jake said. "That may be all we have but I want to talk it over with Chuck."

"Sure, that's fine," Neal said quickly. "If you would like some privacy, you're free to use the patio. You'll see it at the end of the hall."

"Thanks."

Jake looked at his BlackBerry and saw an email from Alex to call him as soon as possible. He and Chuck grabbed their notes and walked towards the patio door.

The warm air enveloped them as they stepped out onto the law firm's patio towering high above Biscayne Bay. Ivory yachts churned tiny white lines across the bay that dissipated slowly like jet trails in the sky. Countless deals had been struck in this serene patio setting, which at times lent the proper perspective to a dispute.

As soon as the patio door shut, Jake turned to Chuck. "So if she really did back out all of the revenue from the stress testing, there shouldn't be any revenue increasing effect, right?"

"That's right," Chuck replied. "Gross revenue would be inflated, but not net revenue, which is what SouthPoint would've relied on when valuing ICon. We ought to see the line item for the write-off on ICon's financial statements."

"Then why in the hell are they acting so suspicious?" Jake asked still looking outward. "I mean, it seems odd to me to keep the stress testing a secret project, and to have the CFO handle the minutia of doing the journal entries, just to make sure that no one finds out that ICon is testing its damn computer system. That doesn't make a lot of sense to me."

"I agree."

"She was prepped well by Stein," Jake said as he turned and looked off into the distance, "but I sense that there's something more to the story. I can't put my finger on it. She didn't show any signs of deception, but I just have this feeling about it."

"Well, whatever there may be going on, she's covered herself on the numbers. She clearly has made sure that the accounting for Zapplication was done right."

Jake paused as he stared out to sea. "I'd like to go back in there and turn up the heat on her, but I'm not sure it will be that productive – at least before we get some real evidence that there's more to it."

"And I suspect that Mr. Clean in there is not going to let you intimidate her."

"Damn," Jake blurted as he hit the railing in front of him. The time was growing short and he felt like a pawn being played. With each small space that he was moving, ICon was zigzagging like a bishop. The stress testing story that he heard from Alan and Cain that morning was convenient, maybe too convenient. But the fact that Jane had dodged them the day before to meet with Neal seemed like a purely defensive move.

"Okay then, we're done here. Let's get back to the war room."

Jake's BlackBerry began to vibrate and he saw Alex's cell phone number on the screen.

"Hey Alex, what's up?"

Alex's voice was jittery and excited. "The guys were there, the same guys!"

"Who? What guys?"

"The guys that went to Shells to look for Patti were outside her house. They were just in a car watching her place."

"How do you know that they were the same guys?"

"Because I talked to them."

"You what? You talked to them?"

"Yeah. I just asked for directions and one of the guys had an accent just like the manager at Shells said. There's something going on, Jake. I mean these were mean looking guys and they clearly were waiting for her. What if she comes home?"

Jake tried to calm his anxious associate. "Well, she hasn't returned the voicemails I left, so maybe she took the week off and is on vacation somewhere. Or maybe she's visiting her mother. Remember she moved down here to be close to her."

"That's right," Alex said. "But, we don't know her mother's name, only that she lives in Hialeah. I'll get online to see if I find if there are any Tomanskis in South Florida. It's a long shot, but it's worth a try."

"Good thinking. Okay, come pick up Chuck and I. I'll fill you in about what Jane said. We're going to drop Chuck off back at the hotel so he can confirm what Jane told us, and you and I need to get back to ICon to talk to the IT guy. What was his name?"

"Uh, Mick Sertoff," Alex remembered.

"Yeah, that's right. He should know about the stress testing. Since you're our resident computer expert, do you want to take the lead on the interview?"

Alex could barely contain his excitement. "Absolutely," he said quickly, "I'll be there in a few minutes."

* * *

"Hello, Thomas Nelson."

"Thomas, it's Jake. Do you have a moment?" Jake asked as Alex drove back to the Hotel Intercontinental. They passed over the Brickell

Avenue Bridge as a sailboat patiently waited below for the draw bridge to open.

Thomas put his cell phone on speaker mode and put it on the dashboard of his Porsche Cayenne as he inched along in the Atlanta gridlock. "Yeah I've got time. I'm just sitting in traffic on I-75. I dropped an arm and a leg for this car and I can't even get the damn thing out of second gear in this traffic. What's up?"

"We've had an interesting day so far. The story we're hearing is that the international transactions that Patti found were part of a secret IT project to test ICon's computer platform. Apparently, they were stress testing the system to make sure that it could handle increased loads of transactions to process. I'll spare you the details, but we just interviewed the CFO and, if it checks out, she wrote off all of the incidental revenue that would've been generated from the tests."

"So ICon's financials are good?" Thomas' voice rang with a positive note. With the shareholder meeting only a few days away, he had enough on his plate without having to deal with a financial scandal in Miami.

"Chuck will confirm that today, but as far as we can tell the financials look alright. But I gotta tell you," Jake hedged, "I really think that there may be something else going on down here. A lot of things don't make sense."

"I hear you Jake, and I trust your instincts. But if you confirm that ICon's numbers are good, the Board is going to want you to close down the investigation. The last thing they want is this to be open when they have to sign the 10-K and release the earnings on Monday."

"I know, I know. But the Board needs to see this all the way through. The investigation is not a financial audit. I understand that they're focused on the numbers right now, but there may be more to it. We're dealing with international transactions, credit card numbers, and bank wires. There could be a host of things that could be material to the Bank."

"Look Jake. I'm just telling you as a friend that time is running out. McMillan is not the only one on the Board who is giving me heat about this."

Jake sighed feeling the pressure all the way from Atlanta. "I know that McMillan wants this finished before the weekend, but can you buy me another day? We're finishing up the email review and we're trying to get in touch with Patti to see what she knows about the stress testing."

"Trying to get in touch with her? Where is she?" Thomas asked.

"Uh, we're not exactly sure." Jake grimaced at having to admit that he lost contact with the person whose allegations started the whole investigation.

There was a long pause before Thomas continued with a sigh. "I'll hold them off as long as I can, but we gotta know before Monday. There's no more time. No excuses."

"Okay. Thanks Thomas. I mean it."

"And call me if you find anything. I don't want to be surprised."

"I hear you."

Jake slid the BlackBerry into his pocket and looked over at Chuck who had heard enough of the call to know that time was running out.

* * *

After dropping off Chuck, Alex pulled out of the Hotel Intercontinental motor lobby and he and Jake headed back to ICon. He was now well familiar with the route to the company, and he turned down the volume of the female navigation narrator.

"Before you start interviewing Mick, give him the *Upjohn* warning. Do you remember how to do that?" Jake asked his pupil.

"Yup."

"Okay, good. Then ask him about his educational background, and then his work experience. Get him talking so we can calibrate him."

Alex nodded politely as Jake was schooling him unnecessarily. Alex had been the scrivener at every interview except for Jane's, and he had prepared detailed memoranda of all of the interviews. He knew the questions and the process cold.

"So once you get to the substantive issues, ask him about the stress testing in a non-confrontation way. Don't accuse him. Just ask as if you're following up on what Alan told us. And be sure to listen to his answers."

"I know, I've got it," Alex answered like a son to his overbearing father.

Jake smiled to himself realizing that his student already knew the material for the test.

As the endless strip malls passed by, he had a flashback sitting at the kitchen table. He was eleven and struggling with his math homework. As he was trying to get his head around fractions, his father came to the rescue. Before he was through, his father had not only taught him fractions, but geometry as well. That same scene played itself out countless times through grade school. All Jake wanted was help to finish that night's assignment so that he could watch TV before bed, but his father always pushed him to achieve more. He learned algebra a year before it appeared on the curriculum, and calculus before anyone in his class had even heard of it. While other fathers were shacked out on a La-Z-Boy recliner, Jake's father was propped up on a hard wooden kitchen chair going over his homework. Although Jake's interest in math finally gave way to liberal arts, his father's lessons extended far beyond school work.

"Alright, sorry to micromanage," Jake said with a grin.

Alex chuckled. "You just make sure to take good notes," he said turning the tables on his mentor.

* * *

Mick Sertoff entered the boardroom and looked around meticulously as if he was trying to find someone hidden in the artificial fichus trees. He was thin with wiry dark hair and pale skin, which had been exposed to far more fluorescent lights from ICon's computer room than to the Florida sunshine. From the moment that he spied Gary and Alan touring ICon's facility a month before the deal, he suspected that there might be something going on. But when he saw L&E's computer team yanking computers from ICon's executive's offices, he knew there was going to be trouble.

He shook hands feebly with Jake and Alex as his eyes darted around them.

"You can have a seat Mr. Sertoff," Alex said pointing to the chair on the other side of the table. Mick cautiously walked around the table and sat down.

"Mr. Sertoff, before we begin I'd like to explain a few things about who we are and who we represent."

Mick interrupted Alex. "Can I see your business cards first?"

Alex looked over at Jake, who shrugged curiously and nodded. They both reached into their wallets and handed their cards to Mick. Mick flipped out his iPhone and began tapping the screen.

"So as I was saying, we represent . . . ."

"Hold on," Mick said to Alex not looking up from his phone. Jake and Alex glanced at each other, and waited patiently watching the nervous witness manipulate his phone.

After a few minutes, Mick looked up at Jake. "Okay, the bios on your firm's website check out, although you might want to change your picture Mr. Morgan. It's a little out dated." Jake sneered back at him as Mick continued. "I just needed to know that you guys are not from . . . well, I mean that you are who you say you are."

Jake and Mick looked at each other again, puzzled by the extent of Mick's skepticism. "As I was saying," Alex began, "we were hired by SouthPoint's Board of Directors to . . . ."

Again, Mick interrupted as he fidgeted in his chair. "Is this being recorded? Are you wearing wires?"

"No, no," Jake said. "We're not taping this interview, we're just taking notes."

"Who are you going to tell about this interview? Is this a criminal investigation?"

Alex glanced at Jake for help to field Mick's nervous questioning.

"Mick, we're just lawyers. We were hired by SouthPoint's Board to follow up on a few matters."

Mick eased back in his chair starring intently at Jake and Alex as if to detect any sign that they were masquerading. He then slowly leaned forward towards Alex who was directly in front of him and lowered his voice.

"I know what you came down here to investigate." Mick glanced to his left and right as if someone had somehow snuck into the boardroom. "I can tell you everything you want to know, but not here. They're watching. I can't be in this room for more than a few minutes. Give me your cell phone number."

"Look, Mick," Alex said trying to gain some semblance of control over the interview. "We just want to ask you a few questions about . . . ."

"I told you, I'll answer your questions, but not here. Give me your phone number and I'll let you know where to meet." Mick wiped away a bead of sweat and glanced at Jake to override his young associate.

Jake paused and exhaled at the unorthodox request. "Okay, okay. But it has to be today."

"Fine," Mick said looking back at Alex for the number. Mick was wringing his hands as if he was washing away a stubborn stain.

Alex reached for the business card he had given to Mick, and he wrote his cell number on the back. As soon as he handed it back, Mick snatched it, stood up, and started for the door. He stopped before he opened the door and turned back towards Jake and Alex.

"If anything happens to me before we meet . . . it was Modos."

And then Mick vanished through the boardroom door.

Jake and Alex sat silently for a moment trying to comprehend what had just happened.

"Modos," Alex finally said. "What the hell is that?"

"I have no idea. I think maybe he's spent too much time starring at a computer screen. Anyway, nice first interview," Jake said jokingly. "You cracked the case wide open."

He smiled and patted his protégé on the shoulder not realizing yet how true his joke actually was.

CHAPTER THIRTEEN

The cheaper the crook, the gaudier the patter.
-- Dashiell Hammett, The Maltese Falcon

Troy's eyes slowly adjusted from the bright sunshine outside to the dark aura of the Gold Room. The grinding music inside the strip club played for the women dancing on narrow stages as men slinked below in lounge chairs visually lapping up the dancers dressed only in high heels. Scantily-clad waitresses feathered between the tables delivering overpriced cocktails to the patrons who didn't come in for the drinks.

"Hey Isaac," Troy said to the massive African American bouncer standing guard near the bar. He was one of the few people who made Troy look average built.

"Troy, my man. How's it hanging?"

"A little to the left today," he answered as they bumped fists. "Is Ivan around?"

"Yeah, he's in his office. He's not looking happy so I sent Carmen back there to entertain him. I wouldn't bring him any bad news today."

"Great," Troy said facetiously. He groaned under his breath knowing that he could not follow the bouncer's sage advice. He did not have good news to deliver. "Thanks for the heads up."

He snaked through the velvety club passing by a stage decorated with a stunning blonde with soft curves and smooth legs. She watched him walk past hoping to lure him into paying for a look. On any other day, Troy would have dropped a few hundred dollars for the visual entertainment, but today he was at the club on business.

He parted the shimmering black curtains in the back of the club and came face to face with the second massive bouncer that Troy had become friends with over the last fifteen months. After that unforgettable evening on Fisher Island with Ivan, the ultra-luxury strip club that he used to visit on occasion became his second office. Even his secretary at ICon knew where to reach him if Alan, and only Alan, requested. Not only did the change in venue have far better views, it meant that he was close to ICon's secret client.

Troy shook hands with the huge bouncer who was wearing a headset with a tiny microphone hugging his cheek. The bouncer pressed a button on the headset and motioned for Troy to stay put.

"Sir, Troy's here to see you." The bouncer nodded and said "Yes sir."

He led Troy down a purple neon-lighted hallway and stopped at a shiny wooden door. The bouncer tapped it twice and opened it for Troy.

"Thanks man, catch ya later," Troy said and entered the dimly lit room.

Ivan's office was part business and part pleasure. On the business side of the office was a glass desk in front of a sleek stainless steel credenza. An oversized Lucite computer monitor on the desk displayed a wavy screen saver that seemed to drip off of the computer. The other side of the office was for pleasure. There was a semi-circle leather couch sitting on a thick fluffy rug. A short round platform faced the couch and was accentuated by a shiny brass stripper's pole. It was the ultimate mixture of business and pleasure.

Ivan was on the pleasure side buried in the plush couch with a think cigar perched between his lips. A smooth Brazilian dancer was slowly writhing on the pole in front of him as a thin wisp of smoke rose from the cigar and dissipated into the background music.

When Troy entered the room, Ivan stood and approached him.

"Troy, thanks for coming." They shook hands, both squeezing firmly.

"Carmen, thank you dear."

The stripper slipped off the pole and slinked over to Ivan. He gave her five one hundred dollar bills and she kissed him lightly on his plump cheek. She eased by him towards the door as Troy could not help starring at her sumptuous body.

"Please," Ivan said motioning Troy towards the desk on the business side of the office.

Troy sat in a black leather chair facing the desk, and Ivan eased into his throne-like desk chair. He tapped the chewed cigar over a marble ash tray and slid it back into the corner of his mouth. Ivan was physically unimpressive, but the power he possessed was formidable. From his lair in the Gold Room, Ivan held the purse strings of a multi-billion dollar adult entertainment enterprise.

He took a long pull from the cigar as he rocked in his chair, and then he released the smoke upwards in a billowing cloud. He watched the smoke rise and then focused his narrow eyes on his guest.

"Tell me, what's going on at ICon?"

His accent was as thick as the tension in the room. Ivan did not need to clarify his question. Troy knew that he had ways of knowing what was happening within the company and there was no use beating around the bush.

"SouthPoint is doing an internal investigation. There are lawyers from Atlanta asking about the Zapplication account."

Ivan seethed for a moment before bursting out. "Goddamn it!" His round face suddenly reddened. "I was told that the merger would not impact our operations. I had assurances from Alan, *directly* from Alan!"

Troy skulked down in the chair feeling the brunt of being the messenger. Alan had finessed Ivan about why ICon was merging with SouthPoint. The story was that ICon needed a bigger platform to operate and Modos would be the undisclosed benefactor because the combined company would be able to generate triple the revenue. Modos was hidden so deep in ICon's system that SouthPoint's due diligence would never uncover its anonymous client accounts. ICon's management team would remain in place and the only thing that would change, according to Alan, was the name on the door.

"I don't think this has to do with the merger," Troy said trying to calm his angered client. "I think this has to do with an employee who Jane fired last month. She was asking Jane a lot of questions that Jane didn't want to answer, so she canned her. She must've told SouthPoint."

Ivan glared with his beady eyes at Troy unconvinced. "But if there was no merger, there would be no SouthPoint, *no?*"

Troy knew better than to respond to the question. After a moment and another puff of the dwindling cigar, Ivan continued.

"I chose to run my network through ICon because Alan – *and you* – promised to operate under *my* terms. *I* was the one who chose ICon, you understand . . . ," Ivan's voice was one octave under a yell, "and *I* can bring it all down in a second! If I say the word, Modos is gone. I flip the switch, do you hear me? ICon would be over, done. Alan might think that he's in charge, but I own the fucking company. Me! Alan should fucking thank me. He wouldn't be sitting on a $750 million pot of gold without the business that I give him every month. I don't know what was going through his head with this deal."

Ivan's forehead was starting to shimmer with perspiration and his face began to swell. He waved his pudgy finger at Troy as he raged.

"I have hundreds of websites running through ICon and nobody knows. Not the FBI, not Interpol, no one. If I pull them all out now and ICon blows up it would be like turning on the lights and saying 'Here I am!' Do you have any idea how hard the authorities have been trying to find the link between all the websites? Modos has succeeded because it is a network connected by the unconnected. Modos is invisible. If Alan fucks this up I swear I'll . . . ."

Ivan caught a hold of himself and slowly regained his composure as he gnarled through the remaining nub of the cigar. He wiped his brow with a silk handkerchief and buried it back into his pocket. Troy sat motionless but he wanted to flee with every fiber of his body.

Ivan got eerily calm. "Modos is a shadow. It's a silhouette of society, you understand. The dark side, perhaps, but the side that *every* society has in common. Sex links all people *everywhere*. I can see it. My sites have customers from *every* country in the world that has access to the Internet. Do you hear me? *Everywhere* in the world, Troy. All races, all nationalities, and all religions. No one wants to know me, but *everyone* wants me here."

He paused to light another cigar before he continued.

"But the Internet didn't create a global demand for sex . . . it has *always* been here. From the beginning of mankind. Sex is biggest market in the world, other than *maybe* for food and water, and it had been untapped for thousands of years. Until the Internet. The Internet finally connected the hundreds of millions of buyers with the sellers and almost instantaneously created a marketplace that's just a click away. The Internet was *made* for this business, and Modos is the biggest seller on Earth. So you understand, I'm sure, that I will take *any* measure to ensure that it stays that way."

The office fell silent, only the muted beating of the music in the club seeped into the room. After a long minute, Ivan finally asked "What does she know, this employee?"

Troy exhaled the breath that he had been holding for too long.

"I don't know, but I don't think she knows anything about Modos because the lawyers only asked me about the Zapplication account. I told them that I didn't know anything. They didn't get a thing from me," Troy said defiantly as if trying to exonerate himself.

"It's not you that I'm concerned about, it's our, how do you say, *weak link* at ICon." Troy knew exactly who Ivan meant. "Have the lawyers spoken with him?"

"No . . . at least not yet. And if they do, I've put the fear of God into him. He's controllable. Trust me, Mick will not cross us."

Ivan shifted in his chair as his narrow eyes stared through Troy. "I hope you are right . . . but I don't want to take any chances. This Mick holds the key to the network. We need to keep an eye on him, and silence him if it looks like he is giving the lawyers too much information. You understand that, don't you?" The question was not a question at all.

Troy shook his head having no idea how to accomplish Ivan's wish. "Don't worry Ivan, I'll take care of it."

Ivan glared at him unconvinced. "We also need to find this former employee and find out what she knows before the lawyers do. I presume the company has her address."

"Yes, it's in her personnel file. We also know where she works now."

Ivan thought for several moments as Troy waited patiently.

"I mean no disrespect to you, you understand, but this job should be done by someone who might see the objective a bit more clearly. A professional, if you will."

Ivan reached for the phone on the desk and punched a button. In less than a minute the door to the office opened and a large man with a pitted face and thin dark hair entered. He glanced at Troy without an expression and then focused on Ivan.

"Yah?" Even with just one word his Russian accent was noticeable.

"Taras, we have a situation that I'd like you to handle," Ivan said.

The man's hollow eyes waited for his assignment as his jaw clenched in anticipation.

CHAPTER FOURTEEN

For the most part, fraud in the end secures for
its companions repentance and shame.
-- Charles Simmons

The sun was setting outside as Jake walked down the long hotel hallway, which was silent other than the clamoring in his head. Stress was part of his job. Most times, hundreds of millions of dollars were at play and professional lives were at stake. He'd seen entire companies implode under the weight of a crushing accounting fraud, and he'd seen the ripples wash up victims far down river. Shareholders, employees, customers, suppliers, lenders, vendors. The reach of a devastating financial blow can knock out many more than just the company in the center of the ring.

For Jake, there was no room for error. He could not afford to be wrong, nor could he miss the unseen. But the one resource necessary to ensure success was the one he had the least of – time. That was nothing new. He'd never had a client hire him to investigate a possible fraud and then tell him to take as much time as he needed. By the time Jake was hired, it was already too late. He was there to stop the bleeding, not to prevent the cut.

He turned down the corridor and approached the innocuous room at the end of the hall. Inside the conference room were not only the clues, but also the answers. Somewhere in that room was an email, a document, or a fragment that holds the key to the puzzle. There were dots that first needed to be found – and then connected. But Jake was sure that they were in the room.

The hotel conference room had served hundreds of purposes over the years, but for the last three days it was Levi & Everett's secret war room. The command center for the investigation. Jake read the block letter placard reserving the room for the fictitious Wingmaster. He remembered what Chuck had told him. He needed to think like a shooter. Don't aim directly at the target. Follow its path and look at where the target has been to see where it's going. A shot contains thousands of pellets, but he only needed a few to break the target.

"Everyone," Jake called out over the buzz of the war room. "Can you all gather around?" The entire team made their way to the table and sat down. "I know that everyone has been working hard, and I really appreciate all the effort. But now we're back at square one." Looks of confusion spread around the table.

"It looks like we have disproven our theory that the Zapplication account was used to inflate revenue through a round trip scheme. We have confirmed that the stress testing did not have an impact on revenue and was not done to boost ICon's earnings. All of the income that was incidentally derived from the testing was written off as a reduction of revenue, and not reported to SouthPoint. Also, the commissions that were paid on the Zapplication account appear to be too small to be a driving factor in any scheme."

There was a murmur around the table as Jake delivered the news, but he raised his hand to quiet the team.

"With that said, however, every instinct I have tells me that there is something there. Something we're missing. There are just too many red flags and too much suspicious conduct."

"So, we need to go back to the drawing board and look at everything with a fresh perspective. Remember the fraud triangle. Look for the pressure points. Why would ICon need to boost the number of transactions by using Zapplication? If it's not for revenue, then what are the other key performance metrics? This is the time when we have to dig down deep and not lose our focus. We have only two days to give the Board our final report. On Monday, as you know, SouthPoint is holding its annual shareholders meeting in Atlanta. The Bank will be releasing its earnings results and giving guidance on what it expects to earn next quarter. Wall Street will be watching very closely, especially because this is the first quarter after the merger with ICon. This will be the first time that SouthPoint talks publicly about how merger impacted its business and how ICon has performed."

"I need not remind you that ICon is a major component of the Bank's revenues. If there is any material fraud going on down here, it could have a significant impact on the consolidated performance. Our client is counting on us. We cannot, and I repeat cannot, allow SouthPoint to paint a rosy picture of ICon only to later have to disclose a problem. If that happens, there could be a parade of horribles, from a stock drop, to regulatory investigations, to class actions. So folks, we have forty eight hours to solve the puzzle before tens of thousands of people rely on what SouthPoint says on Monday. There literally could be millions of dollars in market capitalization in our hands."

Jake could see their faces tightening under the weight of the strain.

"The first thing I want everyone to do is to take a break." Their faces seemed to relax a bit. "You need to clear your heads and get a fresh perspective. I want you all to talk to each other about what you've found so far — even if it seems completely irrelevant. Brainstorm, theorize, and guess. Remember, everyone is guilty until proven innocent."

Jake glanced down at his watch and saw that it was nearing 6:30 p.m.

"So I've reserved a private room for you to have dinner downstairs at Indigo."

There was an excited chatter at the prospect of dining in the upscale steak and seafood restaurant, which would be a nice change from pizza and room service that had so far sustained the overworked team.

"And remember, you can't trust anyone . . . *especially* the waitresses." Jake winked at Alex, who nodded back with an understanding smile. "Okay, your reservation awaits."

The group got up from the table and shuffled out of the war room. Jake, Alex, and Chuck remained.

"Have you heard anything from Mick since this morning?" Jake asked Alex.

"Nope, nothing yet."

"Shit," Jake said. "We told him that it had to be today."

"What do you think he's going to tell us?" Chuck asked.

"I have no idea. He seemed pretty wound up. His warning about

Modos, whatever that is, was a bit overly dramatic. I don't know, he may have a screw loose. I've run across these types in investigations before. Sometimes they just crave the attention. Sometimes their imagination gets the better of them. But we gotta follow up on it." Jake was clearly not excited about having to miss the first good meal since he left home.

"If it's all the same to you," Chuck said, "I'll chaperone the kids at dinner and then take another run through ICon's financials."

"That's fine. Save the leftovers for us. I can only imagine where we'll have to meet this guy. Probably some dark alley on the south side."

"That's pretty close," Alex said staring down at his BlackBerry. Jake and Chuck quickly looked over at him.

"Mick just sent me a text. He wants to meet us in thirty minutes in South Beach. A place called the Dark Side on Collins Avenue."

* * *

The night air was sticky as Jake and Alex walked down Collins Avenue. The legendary street parallels the beach and is adorned with art deco hotels and nuevo eateries. South Beach is a playground for everyone from sultry international models to tattooed street bikers. It is alive day and night with a constant flow of people splashed with color and culture.

And that night was no different. Jake and Alex walked passed cafes that were swollen with tables on the sidewalk. Latin music played on the breeze along with the sweet smell of grilled papayas. Beautifully bronzed women decorated the thoroughfare as flashy suitors cruised by in imported convertibles.

"There it is up at the corner."

Alex pointed towards the red neon sign. The Dark Side was a trendy bar inhabited by sharp dressed singles and those trying to look like sharp dressed singles. Jake and Alex walked into the outside patio of the bar, which sat alongside Collins Avenue and across from the beach. Above them, the clear sky twinkled in the lights of South Beach and the palm trees lining the street swayed in the breeze.

They tried to look like they came for pleasure as they scanned the busy patio for Mick. Alex did his best to play the part, but it was difficult to hide the briefcase he was shrugging over his shoulder. They scanned the crowd but didn't see Mick, so they sat at a table on the patio with a clear view of the entrance.

After a moment, a waitress appeared. "Can I get you guys something from the bar?"

They looked at each other and resisted the urge to order a real drink. Unfortunately, they were still on the clock.

"I'll take a Diet Coke," Jake said taking the lead.

"Me too," Alex added. The waitress nodded and disappeared in the throng of customers.

They could hear the waves crashing on the beach over the music from inside. Mick was nowhere. Jake checked his Blackberry for the third time and Alex instinctively reached for his. It had been forty five minutes since Mick's text, and they were beginning to get the feeling that their host was a no-show.

The waitress reappeared several minutes later and brought them two Diet Cokes in tall glasses with a maraschino cherry impaled by a plastic sword. The fruit and skinny glasses gave away their decidedly un-adult beverages.

Jake checked the time again impatiently. "So, where's our guy?"

Alex shrugged. He was transfixed on the eclectic crowd and was enjoying people watching. At one end, a group of businessmen in rolled up dress shirts and loosened ties were chatting with two tattooed female bikers in leather vests. At the other end, a couple of clearly inebriated college guys sporting jerseys with Greek letters were clumsily putting the make on three obviously uninterested models who each towered over the sophomores by at least a foot.

Alex chuckled and pointed the latter group out to Jake. "Now that's ambitious."

"Isn't that what college is all about?"

As they chuckled, two large guys in skin tight t-shirts parted the crowd and walked towards the table where Jake and Alex were sitting. Alex watched as they approached, thinking momentarily that they were going to stop at the table. Instead, they passed the table. But as soon as they did, Mick - who was using the two guys for cover - sat down quickly between Alex and Jake to their surprise.

"Sorry, I'm late. I thought I was being followed."

Mick's eyes darted around the patio searching for a stalker. He was dressed in a baggy shirt, jeans, and running shoes. He was painfully out of place in the bar, which made his choice of venues all the more strange. Jake and Alex glanced at each other dubious of Mick's paranoia.

"Look Mick," Jake began, "We want to understand why you didn't want to talk to us at ICon, but first Alex has few things to go over."

Just as Alex was about to explain the *Upjohn* warning, the waitress returned and asked Mick for his order.

"Long Island iced tea, top shelf please."

Alex glanced over at Jake. They would have preferred that their witness remain sober during the interview, but Alex nevertheless pressed on. Mick barely listened to Alex's prefatory speech as he continued to nervously study the crowd.

"Before we get to whoever or whatever Modos is, let me ask you about what we've been told. We understand that ICon has been conducting stress testing of its computer system. Do know about that?"

Mick smirked. "Yeah, I know about the stress testing. It's bullshit if you ask me. I designed the Velocity system. It's got plenty of capacity – there's no need to test it. The system can churn out over a million transactions in an hour. ICon doesn't do half that amount. I told them that it's a waste of time to stress test."

"Who did you tell?"

"Alan and Cain. They came to me about nine months ago and told me that they had been to some industry conference and someone there was pitching this kind of stress testing. They said that we had to do it to make sure we didn't lose customers. Cain went on and on about regulations and requirements. I don't remember exactly what they said, but I didn't want to do it at first."

"Why not?" Alex asked.

"Because it meant that I had to turn off the fraud scrubber." Mick saw a look of confusion on Jake's face. "We run sophisticated software that analyzes every transaction potential fraud. It looks for all kinds of things, from stolen cards to fake accounts to suspicious patterns. In order to run the stress testing transactions, I had to turn off the software because they were all run from sequentially issued credit card numbers. The software would've flagged them immediately and knocked them out."

"But you ultimately did turn off the software?"

Mick paused, unsure of whether he was implicating himself. "I did, but it was after Alan insisted and Troy, that prick, threatened me."

"How did he threaten you?"

"He cornered me one day in the hallway and said that if I didn't do the testing, in his words, it would be a *painful* decision for me. He's a 'roid head, but what am I going to do?" Mick gestured towards his thin frame.

"I know what you mean," Jake said referring to his altercation with Troy in the restroom.

"Why was Troy involved in the testing?" Alex asked realizing that Troy had lied to them about being unaware of the Zapplication account.

"I don't really know. He's too dumb to understand that the testing was unnecessary. But Alan should know better."

"Had ICon ever experienced problems with the volume of transactions?"

"Nope. I've been in IT since the inception, and we've never needed to test it."

"So, you turned off the software. What happened?"

"Well, all I care about in my job is to make sure that there are no fraudulent transactions. Under the agreements we have with the credit card companies, ICon has to have controls and software in place to prevent fraud. The stress test transactions that they ran were all paid for, meaning that the charges were approved by the credit card companies and there were no charge backs. So as far as I was concerned, they were not fraudulent. I didn't see the need for the testing, but it wasn't worth my job - or my physical wellbeing - to make a big deal about it. I don't get paid enough to deal with that crap."

"What are charge backs?" Alex asked.

"It's when someone complains to their credit card company that there is a charge on their bill that they didn't make. If the credit card company reverses the charge, usually because the card number was stolen, it's called a charge back. They don't like doing that, and from what I understand, they can penalize the internet payment processor pretty heavily if they don't stay under a certain ratio."

Alex sat back, considering his next line of question. Sensing the pause, Mick leaned forward. "I think what you guys really should know about is Modos."

Mick reached for his drink and raised it to his lips. Just as finished taking a sip, the glass suddenly shattered in his hands. He jumped back and looked down at his hands, which were dripping with his cocktail but otherwise were unscathed. Alex and Jake looked stunned, and a few other people looked curiously towards their table.

"I've asked some hard questions, but I've never seen that happen before," Jake said laughing as he glanced over at Alex.

Alex, however, was not laughing and was still looking at Mick. Seeing Alex's tension, Jake immediately turned towards Mick. Mick's face turned cold as he glared out of the patio towards the dark beach. Across the narrow street, Mick saw a man emerge from behind a palm tree and put something in his jacket pocket. Taras stared straight at Mick and began rushing towards the bar.

Mick frantically got to his feet. "Shit! C'mon we have to go!"

He yanked at Alex who was pulled to his feet and almost to the ground. Jake stood and looked backwards to see what scared Mick. He saw a large man with thin dark hair crossing the sidewalk quickly, pushing people aside on his way towards the entrance to the Dark Side. Jake turned and met eyes with Alex. In an instant, their flight instincts kicked in and they scampered behind Mick who was heading off the patio and into the bar.

"Follow me," Mick yelled as they dodged bar patrons. Jake was following right behind Alex. He tried to look back to see how close they were being pursued, but his sight was blocked by the crowd. Mick was moving swiftly as if he had mapped out his escape. He had picked the Dark Side because he knew the layout – and the way out. The back of the bar was closing in as they raced towards it, and Jake had no idea where they were going to go.

Alex shot a look back to make sure that Jake was close, and then he almost ran into a waitress with a tray of dangerously balanced martinis. He ducked under the tray, barely missing her arm, and she just closed her eyes and prayed. She opened her eyes just in time to see Jake easing by her in a more orderly fashion as the cocktails rocked back and forth.

Taras crossed the patio and forced his way into the bar. He saw the back of Jake's head for a second as Jake disappeared into the bar. He pushed forward, determined to finish his assignment.

"Through here," Mick said to Alex pointing to an almost hidden nondescript door at the back of the bar. Alex paused for an instant to question Mick's direction, but he had no alternative. He followed Mick as they burst through the door with Jake close behind. They found themselves in a thin alley between the bar and the back of a condo building.

Mick continued running down the alley. "This way, hurry!"

Jake and Alex caught their balance and followed him. In what seemed like just a second later, the bar's back door banged open. Taras looked left, and then quickly right. He saw Jake and Alex as they glanced back at the sound of the door.

Taras' eyes locked on Alex and he instantly recognized him from earlier that day outside Patti's townhouse. Alex's eyes widened, and in that frozen moment, Jake saw the recognition between them. Taras reached for the gun in his jacket pocket, but the three of them ran out of the alley and back onto the sidewalk alongside Collins Avenue.

The sidewalk was now thick with nightlife, and they had to slow to a quick walk. Mick darted quickly ahead, snaking through tourists walking in front of them. Jake and Alex did their best to keep up, but the wake of people that Mick was leaving obstructed them. Behind them, Taras was closing.

After another block, Jake caught up to Alex who was stopped at an intersection.

"Where'd he go!?" Jake said trying to catch his breath.

"I don't know. I thought he turned left, but I lost him."

They frantically scanned all four corners, but to no avail. Sensing Taras gaining, they ran across the street in front of a passing car. The car stopped abruptly, almost knocking Jake down, and they heard something yelled in Spanish that didn't sound very friendly. Taras had to stop and run around the stopped car, slamming the hood of the car with his fist as he passed.

Jake and Alex covered another block. At the intersection of Collins and 16th Street, Alex took a hard left. Jake followed him sliding on the smooth concrete before regaining his balance. The side street was less populated, which made their flight easier, but it also made their visibility clearer to their pursuer.

They ran past closed storefronts as their reflections kept astride of them in the windows. Up ahead, on the corner of 16th and Washington Avenue was a parking lot on the left. Just as they were about to pass it, a small red Honda screeched out of the exit and bounced onto the street. The car skidded to a stop and white reverse lights flashed on. It screeched violently backwards towards Jake and Alex. They stopped running and braced to change directions. Behind them at the corner Taras looked left and spotted them. He started to run towards them reaching in his pocket. They were caught in the middle.

The red car approached them too quickly to flee. Jake and Alex had no where to run. In an instant, the car skidded next to them and jerked to a stop.

"Get in!" Mick yelled from behind the wheel.

Jake and Alex fumbled with the door handle and jumped into the worn Honda. Mick rammed the car into first gear, and just as he was about to accelerate, a bullet ripped through the back window. It lodged into the head rest of the passenger's seat, barely missing the three in the car. Jake and Alex ducked to avoid a second shot, and they were thrown down on the floor board as Mick slammed down the pedal. The car lurched forward and sped down the thin side street leaving Taras alone in the dark watching his prey escape.

"Are you alright?" Jake asked Alex, who nodded as he pulled himself up from the floor of the car.

"Who the hell was that!?" Jake exclaimed at Mick angry at being shot at.

Mick was glaring up at the rear view mirror to make sure that they were safe. "Someone from Modos. They don't want me talking to you. That's why I didn't want to meet at ICon."

"Enough of the goddamn intrigue, Mick. What in the hell is Modos?"

"It's part of Bratva, the Russian mafia. It's run by a guy named Ivan Dvorak. He runs Bratva's entire sex trade. From what I could dig up on the Internet, he is the largest owner of strip clubs, brothels, and porn websites across Eastern Europe. He worked out of Moscow until the Russian Ministry of Internal Affairs finally caught up to him. He escaped on his way to Siberia and somehow he ended up in Miami. The guy is worth billions."

Mick paused to catch his breath as he continued to check the rear view mirror.

"Modos is a network of hundreds of porn websites. Everything you can imagine. From mainstream to hard core. The content is filmed over seas somewhere, and then it's distributed on their sites all over the world. The money Bratva makes from Modos is sick – tens of millions of dollars every day. About a year ago, Troy met Ivan and convinced Alan to allow ICon to process a few of the websites. The rumor is that Alan didn't want any part of it, at least initially. That is until he saw the revenues start to flood in. ICon was a bit player in the industry before Modos, and I think Alan saw this as his way to put ICon on top. Almost overnight, we went from around $50 million in income to $250 million."

"But I don't think that Alan had any idea of what he was getting into until it was too late. My guess is that Troy worked him pretty good. After the first few websites were implemented, ICon started to add more sites pretty quickly. Alan may not have even known about the ramp up. We now have nearly the entire Modos network, at least I think so. The thing is that the Modos accounts at ICon all have anonymous client numbers and are hidden in ICon's system. You could never link them together. So if the police shut down one of the websites for fraud or illegal content, it just vanishes and a new one pops up. It's like playing whack-a-mole."

Jake sat back in the faded cloth seat of the car and rubbed his forehead as he stared out at the passing lights. He tried to comprehend what Mick was telling him. ICon had intentionally concealed the adult entertainment business from SouthPoint during the due diligence for the merger. SouthPoint never would've bought ICon had it known that ICon was so deeply involved with porn, let alone the Russian mafia. The bank that prided itself on eschewing *southern conservatism* just spent $750 million dollars to buy the pornography conduit of an international criminal enterprise. The revelation would be disastrous.

"Holy shit," was all Jake could say for several minutes. The car was silent other than a sporadic knocking in the Honda's drive train.

"You're telling me that ICon lied about this entire line of business?" Jake asked out loud to no one.

"I figured that's why you guys came down here to investigate." Mick turned sharply onto Dade Boulevard and he pushed the little red Honda to accelerate over the bridge leaving South Beach behind.

"So that goon tried to kill you – us – to keep it covered up?"

Jake still had not calmed down from the chase. Alex instinctively kept looking back watching for any suspicious head lights following them. The passing street lights reflected awkwardly in two large cracks in the rear wind shield that were beginning to spider away from the bullet hole.

"That's part of it. But I know the key – the link between them. I can expose the entire network."

Jake turned away from the window and glared at Mick.

"I don't understand. What are you talking about?"

"The websites in the Modos network are constantly changing so that they can't be detected. Their web addresses are fluid and the URLs are constantly scrambled using an algorithm. I've heard that they are hosted on servers that are housed in underground silos somewhere in the Caucasus Mountains in Southern Russia."

"All of Modos' websites that run through Velocity have fictitious customer accounts. The site names and owners are all fake. There's no way to tell them apart from ICon's traditional business, and they are spread randomly among the thousands of current and former clients on the system. I'm the only one who knows where the sites are hidden, and I know the algorithm to unscramble them."

"So what happens if the sites are identified?" Alex asked.

"If the network is unencrypted, it would mean that Modos and, more importantly, its bank accounts around the world, would be exposed to the FBI, Interpol, Homeland Security, the Russian Ministry of Internal Affairs, you name it. Not to mention rival factions of Bratva."

"Worth killing for," Jake muttered understanding Mick's dilemma.

"Why do you know the link?" Alex asked Mick trying to come to grips with the situation.

"Because someone at ICon had to know or else we couldn't initiate the accounts and process the transactions. We wouldn't be able to track the revenues, fees, or commissions if no one knew which were the Modos sites. I'm the Administrator of Velocity, so there was no one else who could do it. Believe me, I didn't want any part of it. I tried to resign twice, but Alan begged me. He said that the sites were legal and complied with the credit card companies' adult entertainment policies. He made all kinds of promises to me. He said the entire company was counting on me. That I'd get a promotion and bonuses, blah blah blah. It was all bullshit. I was as naïve as he was."

Mick paused as if to reflect on his mistakes. "I know too much now. I'm constantly being watched. I see them all the time. Lingering outside my apartment, following me in traffic. Even my girlfriend was being followed before she finally dumped me because of it. I haven't gotten a good night's sleep in nine months. My hair is falling out, I'm a mess."

Mick sped through a red light, causing a truck to brake hard as Jake and Alex held their breath. He continued unnerved.

"I was hoping that the merger with SouthPoint would somehow expose Modos, and that ICon would be forced to drop the business. I'd finally be able to get out. I was sure that SouthPoint's bankers would find something, anything. I tried to talk with the due diligence team but Troy told me that if I made any contact with them, I'd live to regret it. I mean you have to understand, these guys know where I live – where I park my car. Every time I turn my car on I hold my breath."

Mick paused and took a deep breath. "Then when you guys came down, I thought that this is my last chance. I can't take it anymore. You guys have to expose this or I'm going to disappear - forever."

The car fell quiet as Mick continued to drive. Jake was oblivious to where they were heading and unclear about what to do next. His mind was racing about the implications. How would the Board react? Who was at fault? What would the Bank tell its shareholders? How did the stress testing fit in? The shareholder meeting was less than two days away. His stomach began to tighten and he breathed deeply to try to fend off the debilitating pressure.

The one thing he was certain of was that he needed to know all the facts before the Board was told anything. There was sure to be an eruption of anger within SouthPoint's boardroom, followed by a cataclysm of blame. Without a full assessment of the damage, the Board would be paralyzed. Jake had to get his arms around the situation, and fast.

Jake turned to Alex, who looked bewildered. "At a minimum," Jake began, "SouthPoint is going to have to write down the value of ICon and restate its earnings. If there is any hope to save SouthPoint, it's going to have to terminate Modos, disclose all of this immediately, and throw itself on the mercy of the government and its shareholders. Jesus, this is going to be ugly."

"Mick, we're going to need to know ASAP the entire financial impact that Modos has had on ICon. All the revenues that flowed through the network, the expenses, the margins, and the income the ICon made. Can you access Velocity and download that information?"

"That's where we're going now," Mick said eerily calm.

"Where?"

"ICon," he answered.

"Can't you access Velocity remotely?" Alex asked. "I thought that ICon's customers can do that to monitor their activity."

"Not for Modos. They made us create a special firewall for external and internal access. Only two computers in the whole world are hard wired to see Modos' activity. Ivan's personal computer is the only one that can access it remotely, and the desktop in my office is the only one that can access it from within ICon."

"How in the hell are we going to get into your office now? Won't they be watching the building for us tonight?"

"Yup," Mick said glancing in the rear view mirror at his nervous passengers. "But we're not going to use the front door."

CHAPTER FIFTEEN

*The man who is admired for the ingenuity of his larceny is
almost always rediscovering some earlier form of fraud.*
-- Freda Adler

Two Months Before The Deal

The glistening pearl hull of the Faeton cruiser fishing boat gleamed as it cut through the choppy waters of Biscayne Bay. Two 500 cc Volvo diesel engines thrust the boat through the water and left a carbonated wake that slowly dissipated washing away the trail. Several thin antennas reached for the sky atop the sleek triangular cruiser, and a flat radar dish rotated in a circular fashion. The cabin was flanked on each side with long trawling poles extending high above the bridge.

At the stern on an elevated platform, Cain sat alone on a teal striped couch watching the white caps pass by. It had been a while since he had been on his father's pride and joy. Partly because of the friction with his father, and partly because he hated fishing. The latter reason had been his excuse to decline the last few invitations, but at his father's insistence, he reluctantly agreed to take a ride that day.

High above Cain on the bridge, Alan was piloting the fifty foot cruiser. The red foam Croakies holding onto his wayfarer sunglasses flapped behind his head and his flowered shirt waved in the wind. He stood in the open-air cockpit gazing far out over the horizon as the boat slid across the dark blue bay. The warm salty breeze always lifted his spirits and distanced him from the stresses on shore.

After a half hour, the hum of the engines died down and the waves slapped loudly against the hull. As the boat floated to a stop, it rocked lightly on the chop. The inlaid anchor at the bow splashed down into the water and the chain made a metallic clicking as it followed the anchor to the bottom. When the anchor reached its destination, the only sound was the clanking of the trawler poles waving in their supports. The quiet of the open water was almost startling.

Alan's leather topsiders gripped the rungs of the wooden ladder as he descended from the bridge. He reached the platform outside of the rear of the cabin and glanced over at Cain who was still sitting in the built in couch behind his dark sunglasses.

"Ah, there's nothing better, huh?" Alan said taking a deep breath of the untainted breeze.

Cain nodded, but didn't say anything. There had been a time when he and his father were closer, but that was before the divorce, before Alan started ICon, and before the insistent drive for money. His father had been a victim of marital strife, not the instigator. But there was a part of Cain that couldn't forgive his father for not saving their family, even though he knew as he grew older that there was nothing left to rescue. Deep down, Cain loved his father and envied his success. On the surface, however, they drifted apart as adults despite being together almost every day.

Alan went inside the cabin and returned with two bottles of beer. The cold brown glass bottles beaded with perspiration in the warm sun. He handed one to Cain, who thanked him and took a long sip.

"C'mon, let's see what's biting."

They walked down a flight of stairs from the platform to the polished wooden deck at the stern of the cruiser where two seats equipped with harnesses waited for the big catch.

After several hours of fishing, they had each reeled in a handful of bonito and kingfish. The fish box gave off a pungent whiff, which hung on the thick air each time that the breeze let up. Alan and Cain dripped with sweat from battling with their watery prey under the late afternoon sun. With their poles propped up in the holders, they relaxed and finished off the rest of the beer. The camaraderie of fishing together lightened the tension that had been apparent earlier in the day, and the beer smoothed the rough edges of their relationship.

"I've decided to sell ICon," Alan said bluntly like ripping off a band aid. He had repeated the line many times in his head over the last several months, but this was the first time he said it out loud.

"What!?" Cain blurted.

"Just hear me out, okay?" Alan said as Cain reluctantly stood down.

"Troy and Ivan are bullying their way into controlling ICon. They've intimidated the board and threatened management. Jane is screaming at me about the accounting, especially for the secret program, and they've scared the living shit out of Mick. He's tried to quit two times, but I've begged him to stay. I'm telling our management and employees that everything is going well, but I can't sleep at night because I'm waiting for the FBI to bust down the door any minute. It's a time bomb Cain, and I feel like it's going to explode anytime."

"Well, what is Troy saying about it? Modos is his client, it should be his problem."

"He's in so deep with them that I can't even talk to him. I clearly don't have his loyalties anymore. All he cares about are his commission reports because he doesn't have to deal with the operations. " Alan paused to sip his beer. "The money's not worth it to me anymore."

Cain stood up quickly and started pacing the deck. "Why don't we just terminate Modos? Tell them to go somewhere else." Cain felt his anger brewing.

"How the hell are we going to do that? You know who these people are. They're not just going to accept a termination letter from us and move on. They won't let us walk away."

Cain looked over the side of the boat and gripped the railing tightly. "I told you not to hire Troy after that phone sex thing. He's a scumbag. He's the reason we're in this mess."

"Goddamit Cain, how many times did I save *you* from the trouble you got in over the years?" Alan was standing facing Cain who still had his back to him glaring out over the water.

"If it wasn't for me, you'd be in jail somewhere. I make the decisions and you live with them. You at least owe me that."

Alan barked defensively and then turned away. The two of them stood on opposite sides of the deck facing away from each and staring across the Atlantic Ocean. They were different in many ways, but they both shared a quick fuse.

Finally after a few minutes, Alan turned towards his only son. "Look Cain, yelling at each other is not going to solve anything. I didn't come out here to fight again."

Cain's head was speeding through the implications. Selling ICon would mean that teams of investment bankers, accountants, and lawyers would sift through ICon's books and records. Thousands of pages of documents. The financials would be scrubbed, and every corner of the income statement searched. Management would be interviewed. Countless representations would have to be made by ICon to the buyer, each of which could be used to nullify the deal if they are false or misleading. There were a hundred different ways that the deal could go bad, and only one way it could go right.

"Christ, do you know what selling the company will involve. It'll be like a corporate enema, who knows what they'll find. Someone's going to find out about Modos."

"I doubt it. Those sites are hidden so deep that there's no way they'll find them in due diligence."

"At some point, it's going to come out. What if Troy leaves? What if Mick talks? The buyer is just going to come back and sue us for fraud and breach of contract. How are we going to defend that?"

"You think so?" Alan asked rhetorically obviously having thought through the likelihood. "You think whoever buys ICon is going to admit in a public lawsuit that it missed the fact most of ICon's business is from porn? Everyone would point fingers at each other. The business people would blame the lawyers, the lawyers would blame the bankers, and the bankers would blame the business people. It would be a goddamn nightmare."

"Yeah, but we'd be right in the middle of it. A buyer is not going to walk away from hundreds of millions of dollars because it might be embarrassed about fucking up."

"But that's the thing, the buyer won't be losing money. ICon is making a killing. So where are the damages? How will a buyer have been harmed? Maybe it will have gotten something that it didn't bargain for, but ICon is a gold mine – as long as Modos stays. I think that whoever buys ICon will either keep it or sell it for a boatload."

"That's a pretty big guess and a huge risk to take."

"Maybe, but it's not a bigger risk than being a pawn of the Russian mafia."

"But, we control the process," Cain pressed. "Modos needs us to process its credit card transactions. The other internet payment processors have already been bought up by bigger companies, so Modos can't go anywhere else now. *We* have the leverage."

"Are you kidding me? What leverage? They won't blink an eye at taking us out if it suits them. Even if you're right, what's the end game? Ivan is not going to just let us walk away. We can either take our piece now or he's going to take it later. And I'll be damned if I'm going to let that happen. So, what's the worst case scenario? We get sued by whoever buys ICon. That'll be tied up in litigation for years and you know it'll ultimately get settled. That's why we have insurance. Cain, I've thought this through and it's time to get out."

Alan unilaterally ended the conversation by climbing the ladder back up to the bridge of the cruiser. He turned on the blower and primed the engines. Then the loud grumbling of the two diesel engines broke the silence of the tide and the anchor motor churned as it pulled the anchor from the depths.

Below on the deck, Cain sat back down in the seat next to his still fishing pole and he gazed out over the rippling water. The late afternoon sun had begun its slow descent into the ocean, and the sky was dotted by seagulls returning to shore. He knew he was not going to change his father's mind, and he simmered at the idea of losing his future. ICon was supposed to be his inheritance, his nest egg.

Alan held the equity in ICon, but Cain was counting on ascending to the throne of ICon when his father retired. Only a few years away, he thought. So he had been living life large, especially after his wife left him. Cars, clubs, girls. He blew through his salary like it was an unending stream of water because once he took over ICon, he would realize real wealth, the kind his father had achieved, the kind he deserved. Now, that dream was floating away like the swells on the horizon and there was little that he could do to rescue it.

"Dammit, I hate fishing," he said to himself as the boat turned and accelerated back towards the mainland.

The name across the back of his father's boat was a fitting double entendre: *IConic.*

CHAPTER SIXTEEN

There is nothing as deceptive as an obvious fact.
-- Arthur Conan Doyle, Sr.

One Month After The Deal

Mick turned into an apartment complex and drove past the lighted front gate. The moon shone brightly and lit the narrow driveway. He followed the drive around several two story apartment buildings separated by low hanging palm trees. As the car approached the last building, he eased it into a parking space facing a thick batch of tall juniper trees that formed a privacy fence between the apartment complex and the commercial development behind it. The lights of the car illuminated only the first row of the darkened trees. Mick turned the ignition off and looked back at Jake and Alex. Their confused faces were vivid in the moonlight.

"Where are we?" Jake asked.

Mick pointed through the front wind shield. "The back emergency exit of ICon is through those trees. The emergency alarm has been dismantled. Thank God for smokers, huh? I programmed a dummy key card that doesn't record on the access log so I can come and go without anybody knowing."

"Well maybe we can wait for you here and you can just go get the data," Jake suggested.

"If you guys want to see Velocity the way I can see it, this is your only chance because I'm certainly not going to be coming to work on Monday morning. There's no way that I can show my face around here again. And you can bet that after tonight's festivities in South Beach, they are going to be in here bright and early trying to delete everything they can get their hands on. If you want the answers you're looking for, now's the time."

Jake was not excited about the prospect of sneaking into SouthPoint's subsidiary. Sometimes clandestine activities are necessary in an investigation, but breaking and entering had never been part of his arsenal. However, he also had never been shot at or bumped up against organized crime in any of his investigations. A part of him relished the danger - the part of him that considered a career in the FBI so long ago. That smart ass kid in high school who took on the bully with his acerbic tongue and who barely escaped without a black eye. The adrenaline from being chased through South Beach felt familiar - and oddly satisfying. Whatever risk might await them, he knew that extreme circumstances called for extreme measures. He needed the answers and he could not escape the weight of his looming deadline. He didn't have the liberty to ponder the issue or to wait until morning.

"Ok, let's go," he said opening the car door.

They followed Mick past a huge juniper and disappeared into the darkness behind the parking lot. Only shards of moonlight stole through the thick branches and streaked on the path in front of them. Mick was moving quickly while Jake and Alex rushed to keep up. They caught up with him as he was hunched down at the edge of the tree line. In front of them was the nondescript back wall of ICon. A ten foot clearing separated the trees from the wall and circled the back of the building like a grass moat. The back wall was barren except for a small concrete landing in front of a door marked *Authorized Personnel Only*. On the landing stood an overfilled ash tray and a shower of cigarette butts littered the grass around the landing.

"Wait for me to open the door, and I'll signal you if we're clear," Mick whispered to them.

He looked both ways and shuffled out of the safety of the thick trees. Just as he was almost totally exposed, a stream of light suddenly shone from the side of the building. Mick leapt back into the cover as a security guard with a flashlight rounded the corner. He shined the light down the back of the building and stopped on a tree that was still rustling from Mick's retreat. The three of them froze as the light ricocheted around them.

The guard took a few steps around the corner of ICon and began to walk along the trees lining the back of the building. He stopped near the back door and studied it with the flashlight's beam. The man was only fifteen feet away and they had a clear view of him from the darkness. He was not a regular ICon security guard and he was not wearing a uniform. Instead, he had on a black shirt and black cargo pants. In his left hand was the flashlight, and in his right hand he was holding a nine millimeter pistol.

Alex fidgeted at the sight of the gun, but Jake grabbed his arm and held it firmly. He raised his finger to his lips, and Alex nodded silently regaining his composure. The man looked around, and then continued walking past the back door. He turned the far corner of the building and the light from the flashlight dissipated. For several long minutes, the three of them remained hunched over and motionless, staring at the now dark corner of the building. Finally, Mick exhaled and glanced back at Jake and Alex who both sighed with relief.

Mick inched back up to the tree line and looked hard in both directions. He gripped the key card tightly and took a deep breath. Then he scampered out of the trees and onto the concrete landing. He passed the key card quickly in front of a pad on the wall near the door handle. A red light flashed on and the door did not unlock. Mick looked around nervously. He again passed the card in front of the pad, this time slower. A green light flashed on and he heard an impermissible click indicating that the door unlocked. Mick exhaled, and Jake and Alex watched him slide inside ICon keeping the door barely ajar.

A few seconds later, they saw Mick's hand reach from behind the door to motion them in. They hesitated, peering in either direction. Jake silently counted with his fingers to three, and they both ran across the grass clearing towards the door. As soon as they reached the concrete landing, Mick opened the door and they darted inside. The door closed quietly behind them, and the back of the building was silent again.

The hallway inside ICon was dimmed by nighttime spotlights as they slinked in the shadows. Mick led them past several closed doors and a bay of cubicles. He motioned to a single door on the left. He looked around as he punched a code into a small pad on the wall next to the door. The door clicked open and they quietly slipped inside Mick's office.

For a moment, it was pitch dark in the office. Then a haze of gray fluorescent lights began to flicker on, and then the room instantly burst into brightness. Mick quickly brushed Jake and Alex away from the door and jammed a tattered sport coat on the floor at the base of the door to block the light from escaping underneath. He stood and walked past them to his desk.

The windowless office looked more like a showroom of a computer store. The side wall of the office was lined with silver computer servers that were blinking sporadically. Half a dozen hard drives in various states of disrepair littered the floor, and a short bookcase in the back was crammed with old computers, a web of computer cords, and worn software guides. But the main attraction was the wall behind Mick's desk. Nine flat screen computer monitors were hung together in a tight square pattern forming a huge video screen.

Mick swiveled on his chair to face the monitors, and he typed swiftly on a double keyboard. Only the middle screen of the nine monitors was lit and it displayed Mick's desktop. Jake and Alex watched over his shoulder as he manipulated the operating system. After a few clicks, a large window appeared that had four open spaces for passwords. The hyper-secure system not only required his current password, but also his previous three passwords. He quickly typed in his four passwords and hit the Enter key.

Suddenly, the outer eight monitors surrounding the middle screen lit up in unison and their liquid crystal screens displayed a massive graphic of *Velocity*. Jake and Alex instinctively backed up as the entire wall looked like it came alive. The graphic seemed to be breathing as it radiated across the monitors. It then vanished and the Velocity operating background appeared on the entire wall of monitors.

"This is the Velocity platform. It tracks the real time transaction activity of every customer twenty four hours a day, 365 days a year. Let me show you."

Mick clicked down through a folder structure labeled with only nondescript nine-digit client numbers. He highlighted one of them, and double clicked the folder. A series of files appeared under the client folder, and Mick scrolled to "T Graph."

Instantly, all nine monitors changed to display a complex graph with an array of tiny colored numbers on three axes. From the left of the graph, four colored lines matching the colored numbers on each axis moved slowly against the background grid towards the right of the graph. The entire graph was moving, inching along the bottom axis as the lines snaked forward. A blue line was the highest on the graph and it moved in a curved upward direction, followed closely underneath by a green line tracking the same pattern. Near the bottom of the graph were black and red lines following a horizontal linear path. Across the top of the screen were various counters increasing at different speeds, and a menu bar framed the entire display with numerous drop down options.

Jake and Alex were speechless, not knowing where to start. Mick turned to see their expressionless glares.

"Pretty impressive, huh?" he boasted. "What you're seeing is the current credit card transaction activity for this one client that I opened up, which is American Auto Parts. There are four different metrics of activity that are being shown here simultaneously and it's all color coordinated. These colored lines correspond to the same colored numbers on the side axis and to the grid. The bottom axes are time periods broken down into minutes and seconds."

"See the blue line on top? That's measuring the volume of credit card transactions that this client is sending through ICon for processing on a real time basis. The blue numbers on the left axis measure that volume in tens of thousands. So, right now, around 9:00 p.m., this client is sending about five hundred transactions every ten minutes." Mick pointed to the line and the axis to show them.

"The green line right below it tracks the gross revenue that ICon is earning from those transactions and the green numbers on the left axis show dollars in thousands. You follow, so far?"

Jake and Alex both nodded, still looking wide-eyed at the display.

"The black line nearer to the bottom of the grid is showing the percentage of the credit card transactions that are being successfully processed through ICon. The best obviously is successfully processing 100% of the transactions we receive, but the normal range is around 95%. There are things that can bring it down. The customer may enter a wrong credit card number or transpose a digit. Sometimes the billing address they enter is not the right address. If any of that happens the transaction does not get approved by the credit card company and it gets bounced back. The line should remain flat like this one. We know if there is a problem on our end if that line starts to dip below 90%. Then it may be some system or connectivity issue."

"And the red line under that is the percentage of charge backs, which I told you earlier are when a customer calls the credit card company to dispute a charge on the bill. If the credit card company takes it off the bill, it's a charge back. They hate doing that, especially for the small websites who tend to be our clients. It costs them time and money. So they make us police our clients and in the contract that ICon has with them, there's a limit of charge backs per month that we have to stay under. I'm not sure what it is, but if we exceed it there's a hefty penalty. That red line tracks the chargeback ratio, which is number of charge backs over the total number of the client's transactions. That ratio should stay fairly constant. For mainstream websites, it varies between 2%-5%. The pink sites, of course, have much higher charge back ratios."

"Pink sites? What are those?" Alex asked.

Mick looked back at them surprised that they were not familiar with the lingo.

"Pink means porn. The pink sites are Modos' websites. Let me show you the graph for one of them. Wait 'till you this."

Mick began clicking through a drop down folder to pull up a menu of options. He scrolled down to *Clients*, and opened a large list of nine digit numbers running down the screen in three columns. Mick directed the cursor to a button called *Reveal* and instantly the list of numbers changed into client names. He then scrolled to the middle of the list.

"There they are," he said as he highlighted a large block of innocuous looking client names. "Those are the porn sites that we process for Modos."

"How can you tell?" Alex asked. "The names look like regular websites."

Mick grinned. "There's a hidden letter 'm' for Modos in front of each of the names. You can't see it and you'd have to have run the algorithm to show the hidden code."

Mick double clicked on a website called JewelryDepo.com.

A large hourglass icon appeared in the middle screen, and it rotated slowly as the computer system generated the client graphic. After a few seconds, the nine computer screens displayed the Velocity background grid and axis for JewelryDepo.com. The four colored lines recording the site's real-time activity formed a completely different pattern than the online auto parts site that they had just seen.

The blue line showing the volume of transactions running through the secret Modos website hovered steady near the top of the graph showing that the website was sending a consistently high number of transactions to ICon. As a result, the green revenue line also hugged the top of the grid. The black line showing the approvals, however, was not flat like it had been for the auto parts client. Instead, it looked like a wave, indicating that ICon couldn't successfully process the porn site's transactions in a consistent way. And the red line showing the charge back ratio had jumped from the bottom of the grid to the middle of the grid and carved a jagged path across the screen. At the top of the grid was the real name of the website: amateurrawsex.com.

"See the charge back line on this one? It's at about ten percent."

"Why is it so high?" Alex asked.

"Think about it. This is porn. What do you think a guy says when his wife sees something like amateurrawsex.com on their Visa bill? 'It wasn't me honey.' 'Someone must've stolen my credit card number.' Then he calls Visa as fast as he can to get it taken off the bill, and that's a charge back. There's also a ton of fraud with these sites which increases the number of charge backs. As you can imagine, they're not operated by the most reputable people, and a pretty big percentage of the transactions come from stolen credit card numbers. Compared to mainstream websites, the porn sites have triple the number of charge backs. Here, let me show you something else."

Mick clicked out of the graph for the fictitiously-named JewleryDepo. com, and went back to the client list with all of the Modos sites highlighted. He quickly clicked through several drop down menus and options, too fast for Jake and Alex to pick up what he was doing. After a moment, Mick sat back and looked up at the screens. He clicked a button called *View* and the nine screens lit up again.

Each screen was split into four segments, and a different Modos website's graph appeared in each segment. In all, thirty six of the hundreds of Modos sites were being displayed at once. The amount of data on all the screens was almost too much to comprehend, with tiny counters racing away and all of the grids inching forward. Mick manipulated the menu on the bottom of the middle screen, and the four colored lines on each of the thirty six graphs suddenly were highlighted prominently and the background data was changed to a muted grey tone. The effect was that they could clearly see that each of the thirty six graphs for the thirty six different Modos websites had the same patterns of activity - mirroring what they had just seen for the site concealed as JewerlyDepo.com. Mick clicked and dragged the graphs from each of the eight surrounding screens to the middle computer screen, and he overlaid them. The patterns were nearly identical.

"Damn," Alex said not finding any better word to describe the impressive three-dimensional display.

"And these are only a fraction of the porn sites. You can see how much revenue ICon is making every minute from these sites. Like I said, it's sick."

"Why does this group of sites down here have a lower volume coming in?" Jake asked pointing to the bottom three screens. The activity patterns were the same, but they were creeping along at a lower volume and revenue than the sites on the top three screens.

"*Time zones*," Mick said. "Those particular sites are run out of the Pacific Rim. Porn sites tend to dip in volume during the daytime, and then rise sharply during the night for obvious reasons. Some people surf porn at work, but it's mainly a hobby that most do at home after work. So, it's the middle of the day in Japan, that's why the activity is lower. If I mapped all these sites based on geography, you'd see the volume of transactions increasing in a direct relationship with the time of day. You can almost see the activity increase as the Earth turns. It's unbelievable. I've never seen anything like it on the web."

Jake and Alex were transfixed on the Velocity display of the Modos sites. It was mesmerizing to watch real-time internet activity, but also disturbing and oddly voyeuristic to know what these millions of people were viewing — and how much they were paying for it. Sex is the largest industry on the planet, and they witnessing it first hand.

"You said that the credit card companies make you police these sites. How do you do that?" Jake asked.

Mick chuckled to himself. "I surf these sites and look for violations of the credit card companies' policies. Some companies will not approve a charge from a site that contains under age actors, bondage, celebrity images. That kind of stuff. If I find anything like that, I report it to Cain and he's got the authority under our access agreements to escrow whatever money we might owe the client until they clean up the website. So, I literally get paid to look at porn," Mick said with a proud grin like a five year old who just found hidden candy. His smile disappeared slowly when he remembered why they were sitting in his office after hours. "Or at least I did before tonight."

"That's what I call fringe benefits," Alex quipped and winked at Jake, who smirked back.

"Can you show us the data for Zapplication?" Jake asked.

"Sure." Mick turned and clicked his way back to the client list. He scrolled to the bottom and the last client on the list was Zapplication. Mick double-clicked on the Zapplication icon and the nine screens on the wall flashed to display Zapplication's transaction activity.

The background grid and axis were the same as they had just seen for the other sites; however, Zapplication's graph was completely blank. There were no colored lines moving across Zapplication's graph, and the numerical counters at the top of the screen all displayed a zero.

"Why isn't there any data?" Alex asked.

"Because there is no activity for this client. No credit card transactions are being sent to us to process."

"Can you look back to prior time periods?"

"Yup, I can go back a year from the current date. Anything before that is backed up on tapes that are stored off-site. Let me change the time period axis to the last twelve months."

Mick manipulated the axis to show the last year of activity for Zapplication. The graph didn't look anything like the others. Instead of the activity lines running horizontal over the time period, Zapplication's graph looked more like a bar graph with vertical columns near the end of each month. Between the peaks, there was no transaction activity.

"Why does it look like that?" Alex asked.

"Because the only activity this client has had in the past year are these brief, high-volume periods at the end of each month. All of these credit card transactions are being sent over the course of just a day or so during these months. Every single transaction was approved and there were zero charge backs."

"Those have to be the stress testing transactions," Alex said.

"Exactly," Mick responded.

Jake was still studying the graph. "If that is true, then there were no other credit card's run between these periods of activity. That means that Zapplication wasn't doing *any* other business. But Alan and Cain told us that Zapplication was a real client, it just had low activity and that's why it was chosen to do the stress testing."

Jake turned to Alex. "They're full of crap. This shows that Zapplication was set up *just* to do the testing."

He paused and then motioned to the left axis. "And the volume of these transactions is much higher than we were led to believe occurred for the testing. Look at April, for instance. If I'm reading this right," he said pointing to one of the peaks of the blue line, "there were roughly 500,000 transactions sent that month. That's about the same peak volumes for May, June, and July." Jake traced his finger in the air across the peaks of the graph. "If you add all of those together, there must be about five million test transactions sent over the nine months or so. Jesus, that's – what -- almost five times as many transactions as we thought took place."

"But if ICon backed out the revenue, why would they under-report the volume to us?" Alex asked. "I mean, there wouldn't be any impact on the financials regardless of the number of test transactions."

Jake thought for a moment about Alex's observation. "I don't know. They're hiding something. Mick, can you download this data for us? I want to cross-check this with the other information we got."

"I can copy the raw data into an Excel spreadsheet. But, the only way to display it in this form is through Velocity."

As Mick began downloading the transaction data, Jake asked "Do you know, or can you tell, if someone at ICon is actually behind Zapplication?"

Mick paused. "Um, you might be able to tell by tracing Zapplication's IP address to see who owns it. But the only way you can do that is through the internet provider, like Yahoo! and they're not going to just tell you. I think you'd need a subpoena or something like that."

He began again downloading the Zapplication data, but stopped abruptly. "Wait, maybe there is a way that I can tell."

Mick turned and opened a laptop computer on his desk, and the screen quickly illuminated. He accessed the Internet and typed "zapplication.com" into the search field. After a couple of seconds, the home page for Zapplication appeared. The website looked legitimate, but it had simple graphics.

"First, let me see what happens when I try to subscribe."

He clicked on a subscription tab, which took him to a page describing the terms and conditions for a subscription to Zapplication. He scrolled to the bottom of the page and clicked that he accepted the terms. A pay page appeared with ICon's logo and format. Mick entered his address and credit card information, and then he clicked *Subscribe*. Instead of processing the transaction, another page appeared that read *Subscription Unavailable At This Time*.

"Well, that's why there's no activity other than the stress testing. They're not letting anyone subscribe, so there are no credit card transactions being processed. My guess is that they enable the subscriptions only when they're sending test transactions."

"I'm sure that's because Zapplication is just a cover," Jake murmured.

Mick clicked back to the Zapplication home page. "I may be able to get into the HTML and find something."

"What's that?" Jake asked.

"HTML means hyper text markup language. Basically, it's the programming code behind the look and function of a website. Most of the time, it's not something that a website tries to keep secret, and you can get to it by right clicking and viewing the source. Let's see, here . . . uh . . . good here it is."

A box titled *HTML[1] Notepad* appeared over Zapplication's website. The first line read *<title>HTML - Zapplication</title>*, and was followed by hundreds of lines of computer code. Mick scrolled down slowly scanning the lines of code that were indecipherable to Jake and Alex.

"Ah ha, there we go!" Mick said excitedly after a few minutes. He pointed to several lines of the code that were offset by dashes.

"See these lines? Each starts with an asterisk. That means that they are comments inserted by the programmer. Comments have no functionality in the code, meaning that they don't make the program do anything. But programmers sometimes put comments in the code to describe what's happening so that other programmers can read and understand it." Mick pointed to a section of Zapplication's HTML.

```
* ---------------------------------------
* Dynamically generated stylesheet for html4strict
* CSS class: source-html4strict, CSS id:
* (C) 2004 - 2007 Bill Dixon.
* ---------------------------------------
```

"Oh my god," Mick exclaimed when he read the last line. Jake and Alex glanced quickly over at Mick's reaction.

"What? What is it?"

"You see there, the programmer was Bill Dixon."

"Who is he?" Alex asked.

Mick hesitated and leaned back in his squeaky desk chair. "Bill used to work at ICon, he was a programmer."

"That's it!" Jake blurted. "That's the connection. ICon created Zapplication. It really is a fake client and it proves that they lied to us."

Alex suddenly realized the implications. "That means that *ICon* chose when to send the test transactions, not Web Assist. Alan and Cain told us that Web Assist was an independent third party in Andorra that had the discretion to do the tests. If ICon is really behind Zapplication, then it also is behind Web Assist."

"And if ICon controls Web Assist, we may have bigger problems," Jake said as he sat down in a hard metal chair and ran his fingers through his hair.

"Somehow, Web Assist or ICon got hundreds maybe thousands of sequential credit card numbers from the bank in Andorra issued to fictitious names. That had to be illegal in some way. They went all the way to an overseas bank in some remote financial haven. As Chuck would say, *'that don't smell right.'* It could bribery, bank fraud, foreign corrupt practices, who knows."

Jake took a deep breath and rubbed his forehead as the possible scenarios hurried uncontrollably through his head. The situation was developing into an iceberg, and he feared that he was only seeing the tip.

"But, I still don't understand the reason for the cover up," he continued. "Why not just tell us that they formed Zapplication to do the testing? We're missing something," Jake said staring into space. "Mick, are you positive that there was no legitimate need to stress test the system?"

"I can tell you that Velocity has never crashed. There were times when we had a t-drift delay, but never more than ten seconds or so. Not enough to justify testing."

"Maybe Bill Dixon knows something. Do you know where he is?"

Mick stood and began to pace behind his desk, conspicuously not answering Jake's question. He covered his face with both palms and rubbed his temples with his fingers as he walked back and forth. Alex looked over at Jake curiously and then back to Mick.

"Mick," Jake asked again, "do you know where Dixon is?"

Finally, Mick stopped and looked at both of them with solemn glare. "Yes. Bill is dead. Modos killed him."

"What? How? When?" Jake asked in rapid succession.

Mick exhaled deeply and plopped back down in his chair. "A few months ago Bill was sitting in his car outside his house around one o'clock in the morning and a pick up truck came out of no where and rammed right into him. He was killed instantly. They wrote it up as a hit-and-run."

"How do you know that it was Modos?" Alex asked.

"Because the truck was found a couple of days later down by the port. It had been torched and the plates were removed."

"But that doesn't mean it was Modos. Maybe whoever hit him just panicked and tried to get rid of the evidence."

"Not likely," Mick responded. "The police said that the vehicle identification number had been scraped off long before the collision – even the VIN that is stamped deep in the engine block had been scratched off. The airbag had been deliberately disabled so that it didn't activate, which the police said was probably so that the driver could drive away quickly. And the tires had been removed so that they couldn't be traced. That's not the work of an amateur."

"There's something else you should know," Mick added looking away. "Bill had just gotten home from ICon before he was killed. He snuck in there in the middle of the night because he suspected that someone had infected ICon's computer system with some kind of spyware program. That's why he was in his car at one a.m."

"How do you know all that?" Jake asked incredulously.

Mick turned towards his desk. "Here look at this. He sent me an email right before he was killed."

Jake and Alex watched intently as he opened a locked drawer of his desk. He pulled out an innocuous file of spreadsheets and removed a singled folded sheet of paper that had been hidden deep in the file. He unfolded it and handed the paper to Jake.

On the sheet was an email from Bill to Mick at 1:12 a.m. The subject line read *Print and purge after reading*. Alex leaned over and Jake held the email so that they could read it together.

> *Mick — I found what I was looking for. A program was imbedded in the source code at line 15,343. It hides the cross-sell box on M sites for all IPs other than internal, so you wouldn't see it. Billing also is staggered 2 months. Massive fraud. I'll disable it and then I'm going to the police. Let's meet tomorrow at DS at 6:00. Watch your back pal.*

Jake read the email again and handed it to Alex, who continued to study it.

"What does it mean?" Jake asked Mick.

Mick took a deep breath, clearly fighting back his emotion. "Bill told me last year that Alan asked him to work on a secret project. It was all very confidential, but Bill and I go back a long way and he told me a little about what was going on. Alan wanted him to design a mock portal to be able to run dummy transactions through Velocity that would not trip the fraud scrubbing software. Bill told me that some huge prospect wanted to try out Velocity before signing up. The client supposedly demanded complete secrecy, and Alan never told Bill who it was."

"Modos," Alex said confidently.

"That's right," Mick answered. "And seeing Bill's name in these programmer comments means that he was the one who designed Zapplication. That's what he was working on when he first noticed something in the code. "

"So what does he mean that he found what he was looking for?"

Mick took a long breath. "We were at the Dark Side having a beer about three months or so before the SouthPoint deal. You see in his email he says meet at DS at 6:00? We were supposed to meet there later that night."

Jake and Alex immediately understood why Mick wanted to meet them at that dive bar in South Beach.

"So Bill told me that soon after he started working on this secret project he went to the office after dinner on night to catch up on some work and he saw that the door to my office was open. As you saw, my door has an electronic lock and Alan is the only other person who is supposed to know the code. But Bill saw Troy and some guy that he didn't know at my desk. He could see that the source code for ICon's processing application was up on the monitors. They were doing something to the source code, but he couldn't tell what. That's why he went back that night – to try to find out what they were doing."

"What did he find?"

"All I have is this email – I never talked to him again. But it he says that he found a program that had been inserted into the processing software that hides the cross-sell box. Do you know what that is?"

Jake and Alex shook their heads.

"When someone subscribes to a website, primarily to a pornography website, there usually is an option at the bottom of the pay page to also subscribe at the same time to another website owned by the company. It's a cross-sell. The customer sees a box that is pre-checked, and if he doesn't want to subscribe to the second website he has to un-check the box. There's nothing illegal about it as long as the customer can easily see the pre checked box. But what the program that Bill found does is to conceal or hide the box so that the customer doesn't know he is getting hit twice or more."

"Don't you monitor the sites for that kind of fraud," Jake asked.

"*Exactly.* But, look," Mick said pointing to the email, "Bill says that box is hidden for all IP addresses *other* than internal ones. That means if the website is accessed by any computer *outside* of ICon, the box is hidden. So anyone outside of this building that goes onto the site won't see it. But if it is accessed by an ICon computer, like mine, the box is *not* hidden. Just as he says here, I never would've seen it. This is a highly complex spyware program - I've never seen anything like it. You see here where he says that it staggers billing two months? He means that the second charge, the fraudulent one, does not appear on the customer's credit card bill right away, but it is staggered by two months. Most guys who frequent these kinds of websites do it all the time and don't remember what they subscribed to months ago. So they wind up paying it. Maybe they cancel the subscription afterwards, but if you add up all of the fraudulent charges, you're talking about tens of millions of dollars."

"And if they contest the charge," Alex added, "then it becomes a charge back, right?"

"Bingo. That's one reason why I showed you that the pink sites have such a high charge backs."

They sat silently absorbing the impact. Only the hum from the array of computers echoed in the office.

"What does Bill mean by M sites?" Jake asked.

Mick turned to Jake. "Modos." He paused, and then added "That's why they killed him."

Suddenly, the door knob of the office rattled. Jake and Alex froze, and a burst of adrenaline rushed through them. Mick instinctively hit the escape button on his keyboard, and all nine screens instantly turned black. Again, the door knob shook, but the locked door held fast. Mick raised his hand silently and motioned for them to stay still. The sport coat that Mick had crammed under the door made it appear from outside in the hallway that the office inside was dark. They all held their breath.

Finally, after several minutes of silence, Mick spoke softly. "Probably just security doing their rounds, but we better get out of here."

He tapped the keyboard and the Velocity display reappeared. Mick completed the download of the Zapplication data, and he removed a thumbnail drive. He handed it to Alex, who stuffed it into his pocket.

Mick turned off the lights in the office, which remained dimly lit by the still glowing computer screens. He slid the sport coat away from the door jam and placed it on a nearby chair. Quietly, Mick turned the door knob and eased the door barely ajar. Jake and Alex stood behind him, waiting to follow his lead.

Mick slowly opened the door and glanced both ways down the hallway. He leaned back into the office and motioned for them to follow. The three slipped out of the office and Mick closed the door softly behind them. Hunched over, they made their way down the hall towards the emergency exit. The only sound they could hear was the air conditioning unit pushing air through the overhead ducts. When they got to the exit door, they paused. The door had a sign in large red letters reading *Emergency Exit – Alarm Will Sound.*

"You're sure there's not going to be an alarm?" Jake whispered.

"Not unless they fixed it yesterday," Mick answered, which did not give Jake the confidence he was looking for. Mick put both hands on the long horizontal door opener and slowly pushed it forward. Alex closed his eyes unconsciously, praying that the alarm did not sound.

As Mick expected, the emergency door opened without a sound. He peeked outside in both directions. "Okay, let's get go."

They filed out of the building and raced across the grass walkway. Mick darted into the junipers knowing exactly where the path had ended. Jake and Alex were right behind him, and they disappeared into the darkness. As soon as they were hidden, a beam from a flashlight turned the corner with the guard moseying behind it. He flashed the light down the back side of the building, but he just missed the intruders' escape.

"All clear," the man said into a small microphone clipped to his jacket, and he turned back into the night.

* * *

"Right over there," Alex said pointing to where they parked the Mercedes sedan in South Beach earlier that evening. It had seemed like an eternity since they were walking down Collins Avenue to meet Mick. Mick pulled the red Honda over to the side behind the car. South Beach was still hopping. Its thoroughfares would be packed until long after midnight. Mick looked around cautiously, but did not turn off the car.

"It was nice knowing you," Mick said still edgy from the evening.

"Is there a way we can contact you if we need to? We may have a follow up question or two," Jake asked not wanting to lose touch with his most important witness.

Mick paused and looked into the rear view window. The hole in his rear windshield was a stark reminder of how close he had gotten away this time. He was not about to take another chance. "I'll give you my cell phone number, but I'm not promising that I'll answer."

"I know the risk you took and we really appreciate it."

"I'm no hero. I just wanted a way out. If you guys hadn't come, I don't know what I would've done. If I were you, I'd get the hell out of here too. No offense, but the Russians are not going to run away from a couple of lawyers."

Mick scribbled on a torn piece of paper and handed it back to Alex.

"Take care of yourself Mick," Jake said and shook his hand.

Jake and Alex got out of the car, and watched as Mick drove the injured car away.

Alex looked down at the slip of paper that Mick gave him. "Look at this," he said surprised. He handed it to Jake.

There was no cell number on the paper. Instead, Mick had written *modosisbratva 4x. Run 4058IG.prg to unhide M sites.*

Jake looked up at Alex with a confused gaze. "What does this mean?"

After a few moments, it hit Alex. "His passwords to Velocity. Remember he had four of them to sign on. He just used *modosisbratva* over and over. And this is the name of a program. He's telling us which program to run to reveal the Modos websites. This is the key to identifying all of them!"

They looked down the street and watched the tiny taillights of the Honda turn a corner and disappear. That was the last time they would ever see Mick Sertoff.

* * *

The war room in the Intercontinental Hotel was no longer neat and organized. It looked as if its hair was on fire. Stacks of papers blanketed the room edged by empty soda cans and coffee cups. Food wrappers teetered over the tops of the two trash cans, and piles of folders and binders lined the walls. A make shift time line was taped to the wall, with emails hanging below marking notable evidence.

Jake stood at the head of the table as the entire team starred back at him. For a lingering moment, the room was silent as the story of the previous night sunk in. Finally, Sarah, the most reserved of the group, could not hold back her reaction.

"Holy shit, you guys. I can't believe it. You were shot at?"

With that, the room exploded into chatter. Every minute of the night was relived, detailed, and analyzed. Questions were posed that only guesses could answer, and theories were espoused that only time could confirm. Alex was instantly a celebrity and his account of the drama kept the younger members of the team hanging on every word. Each internal investigation has its own twists and turns, but this one had the mother load. The buzz in the war room was electric.

For Jake, however, the electricity was tempered by responsibility. They still had to complete the investigation, and time was running out. In just two days analysts, investors, bankers, lawyers, brokers, regulators and competitors would be dialed into SouthPoint's shareholder meeting, which will be broadcasted to the world on a public conference call and on the Internet. This transparency was the tenet of the Sarbanes-Oxley Act and other mandated corporate reforms, but transparency oftentimes is blurred by materiality. Not every internal corporate matter does, or should, see the light of the day. Only those that are deemed to be material become visible to the outside world. If a reasonable investor would consider the matter important in making a decision about whether to invest in the company, then the matter is material. Hardly a precise standard. It is the cause for much consternation in boardrooms, and much litigation in court rooms.

SouthPoint would have to decide whether the issues that L&E were investigating were material, at least whether enough was known at that point to deem them material. If so, they would have to be disclosed to Wall Street on Monday and a calamity was sure to follow the meeting. If not, the SouthPoint could – at least for the time being - treat the issues as confidential internal affairs of the company. As he sat back and watched his team engaged in enthusiastic debate, he realized that he already knew what the answer was.

Jake's eyes met Chuck's across the room, and Jake silently motioned him to come over.

"What's up?"

"Let's go take a walk," Jake said, and they slipped out of the conference room towards the hotel bar.

Jake swirled the caramel colored scotch in his thick crystal glass, and he watched the soft lights of the patio bar shimmer off the ice. Their table overlooked the hotel's pier, which housed several rows of sailboats. The metallic clanking of the masts in the warm night's breeze provided a background symphony. Any other time, Jake would've enjoyed the music. That night, however, Jake didn't hear anything other than the clamoring in his head.

"How's the kid doing?" Chuck said as he took a long swill of his beer.

"Alex? He's fine, great even. I think his exact word was 'awesome.' Poor guy, though. He doesn't realize yet that an investigation with this kind of drama only happens once in a career, if at all. He's got no where to go now. It's his first investigation, and all the excitement is over."

Chuck's laugh was deep and sincere. "How are you doing?"

"Well, it's not everyday that I get shot at and break and enter into a client's office. I'm not sure how I'm going to describe that on the bill," Jake said with a grin. "But, between you and me – it was the most excitement I've had in a long time."

"I know what you mean. Sometimes I miss the good old days in the Bureau. But that's a job for a younger man. These old nerves can't take that kind of rattling anymore. So did you get any sense of how much of ICon's business is adult entertainment related?"

"Not really," Jake answered. "Mick got onto Velocity and showed us the revenue charts for some of the Modos sites, but we couldn't put it into proportion with the overall business. It's a hell of a lot though. We have his passwords to Velocity and someone at the company should be able to run a report for those sites. I'm sure we can figure that out. The harder question is what SouthPoint should have known or found out about the porn business during its due diligence on the deal? It's one thing not to have detected the cross-sell scheme – no one would've ever found that. But there's going to be a lot of scrutiny over how fast the due diligence was done and whether they should've caught the porn business."

"Was the diligence done in-house or by outside counsel?"

"Both. Thomas hired a law firm in Miami to run the process, but there were SouthPoint people on the team. As I understand it, the diligence was done quickly over a couple of days. ICon was pushing for a quick deal and, in retrospect, it now seems clear why. This is going to be a nightmare. Everyone is going to be pointing fingers at everyone else."

"Let's hope they don't kill the messenger," Chuck said pointing his finger at Jake in jest. "Have you called Thomas yet?"

"Not yet. I want to think through everything before I call him because he's going to explode. Any words of wisdom?"

Chuck took another sip of his beer before answering. "Be calm. The last thing a general counsel needs in this situation is more anxiety. There's going to be enough of that going around very soon. Be prepared to tell him exactly what we're going to do to get the bottom of things, and outline the issues that he's going to need to address with SouthPoint's board. Give him something productive to focus on."

Jake marinated on the advice. "Sounds right. So how *are* we going to get to the bottom of things?" He asked only half facetiously.

"Well, I think we have all the pieces to the puzzle now, we just need to figure out how they fit together." Chuck raised a finger as he counted off three of the pieces. "First, Zapplication was a front to run the stress test transactions, but they were done for some other reason than to increase ICon's revenue or to test the system. Second, ICon concealed the porn business by hiding the Modos websites. And, third, the fraudulent cross-sell computer program. They're all connected somehow. We've got a sharp team back in there, much brighter than you and I were when we were their age, and they have better toys."

"That's partly what I'm concerned about. This is getting dangerous. Whatever is going on, it's clear that we're dealing with some pretty bad guys. I'm wondering whether we should pull the team out of Miami, at least the document reviewers. They can do that from anywhere."

"You saw their faces when you told them tonight's story. Do you really think any of them are going to go home now?" Chuck asked rhetorically. "Besides, no one knows that we're in this hotel."

"How do you know? I mean, we've driven back and forth to ICon several times. We could've easily been followed." Jake's voice rang with a tone of nervousness.

"I'm not downplaying being shot out, but it sounds to me like it was Mick who they were after tonight. They probably didn't even know who you guys were. I think we're fine at the hotel," Chuck continued, "and we'll only be down here for another day or so. We'll just make sure the kids stay in the hotel. Anyway, if it makes you feel any better, I didn't come alone on this trip."

Jake turned to Chuck curiously. Chuck glanced around the patio, and then lifted the leg of his pants. Jake peered slowly under the table and saw a black Glock handgun strapped to Chuck's leg. Jake shot a look up at Chuck. Before Jake could say anything, Chuck said sheepishly "Well, you didn't think I was going to come to Miami without being armed did you?"

"I thought you only shot clay pigeons for sport," Jake quipped.

"I do," Chuck said and paused for effect. "I just come better equipped if the pigeons can shoot back at me," he said winking at Jake.

Chuck took the last swallow of his beer and stood. "Well, I know you've got a call to make tonight. I'm going to go back upstairs and re-run the analytics on the transactions. I'll also talk to our computer guys about disabling that cross-sell program. Hang in there, we'll get this thing figured out."

Chuck patted Jake on the shoulder and strolled out of the bar. Jake sipped the last of the silky liquor and he slowly inhaled its syrupy vapor. The moon was almost full, but it was twice as bright as it shone on the water. As his mind slowed down, his other senses caught up. For the first time since he had been sitting there, he heard the knocking of the sailboats' masts and the drifting sounds of the tide. He smelled the warm ocean air, which carried a faint tangy whiff from the pier. For the first time that day, he was still.

After a long moment of peace, he slowly reached into his pocket and pulled out his cell phone. The keyboard chimed softly as he typed in the phone number that he had memorized long ago. This would be his most important call of the night, he thought to himself. A call to someone who really needed him.

On the third ring, a far away voice answered.

"Daddy?"

"Hey pal, it's me. Whatcha doing?"

"Just reading stories with Mommy. I miss you."

"I do to. Why don't you tell me all about your day?"

* * *

The thumping music boomed through the dance club as flashes from hundreds of strobe lights momentarily froze the writhing throng on the dance floor. The club was packed with Miami's hottest crowd gyrating below a DJ high above in a lofted booth. He was dressed in all white, with white sweatbands on his wrists and earphones wrapped around his neck. As he spun and scratched on two turntables, his worshipers below bowed rhythmically to his electronic hymns.

A winding bar was perched on a level above the dance floor. From behind the bar, a soft blue light glowed and lit a tower of liquor bottles on the wall. In front of the bar, a mass of people lined the trough waiting to be fed by two bartenders who were hopelessly understaffed.

Troy edged his way through the crowd towards the bar. His tight silk shirt hugged his ripped chest and a thick gold rope chain reached widely around his neck. As he moved through the club, he parted the waves of people. When he reached the second level, he posed and peered down the bar looking for somebody. After a moment, a grin slid across his face and he made his way towards her.

"Hey there," he said standing over a blonde woman's bare tanned shoulder.

Jackie Warner was sitting on a bar stool and as she turned her long hair swung around with grace.

"Troy, hi. Man it's crazy tonight, huh?"

She was wearing tight sequined shorts and a teasingly open v-neck blouse. Her fleshy chest pushed together and heaved in the stares from those trolling the bar.

"No doubt. Sorry I'm late. There was a wreck on Bayshore. You look great by the way." His eyes lapped her up from head to toe like a giant tongue.

"Thanks. I'm glad you suggested this place, I haven't been here yet. It's so cool."

"Whatcha drinking?" Troy asked over the dull roar of the club.

"Absolut martini, dirty and extra olives," Jackie grinned back.

"How do you drink from that glass? It looks like an infinity-edge pool," he said mocking the dangerously frail martini glass as Jackie giggled at him. "If that were a guy's drink, it would be in a short stocky glass that couldn't be spilled . . . like a weeble-wobble. That's why the older guys get, the smaller and fatter their glasses get."

She leaned back slightly and laughed, and Troy opportunistically and instinctively gazed down her blouse. She wasn't the best looking woman that he had ever chased, but he knew that he would enjoy the catch. The fact that his quest was not only for flesh made it all the more fun.

"Dean," he yelled to one of the bartenders, who looked over and smiled at him. The bartender winked at the girl he was talking to and walked towards Troy, ignoring a field of hands waving for his attention.

"Troy, long time no see. What's new?" Troy and the bartender bumped fists and snapped their fingers in a choreographed movement.

"Just fighting the good fight, if you know what I mean," Troy replied in a hip code that has no real meaning. "How's the old crew?"

"Same ol', same ol'," he said in a Southern accent. "Tucker has a new girl, so I don't see too much of him. Do you remember Jason? He's out in L.A. doing some kind of movie. He says it's the real thing, but my money is that he's doing a sex flick." They both laughed obviously knowing that Jason did not have the right *talents* to star in that kind of movie.

"Dean, this is Jackie. We work together at ICon. Watch out, she's a lawyer."

The bartender pretended to duck at the warning, and then he laughed and extended his hand.

"Nice to meet you. They sure don't make lawyers that look like you from where I'm from." He winked playfully at her.

"I guess that's why you're here and not there, huh?" she joked back.

"Fair point, counselor." He nodded to his worthy adversary. "Hey, can I get you guys something?"

"She'll take another one of those high octane martinis," Troy ordered presumptively, "and I'll take a double gin and tonic."

"Sure thing," he said and darted off for the drinks.

Jackie looked up at Troy impressed by his success, and aroused by his physique. It had been almost a year since she dated anyone, but it wasn't a supply problem. There were hoards of guys cruising the clubs in South Florida. At times, she felt like she needed bug repellant to keep them off. The problem, instead, was demand. She demanded that a guy had to have it all. She was long past the stages of trying to rescue a guy, or trying to train a guy, or, as is too often the case, trying to forgive a guy. So far for her, however, the supply and demand curves had not yet intersected.

After another round of drinks, and a shot of Tequila to grow on, Troy leaned in towards Jackie's ear to talk over the pounding of the dance music. He inhaled her intoxicating perfume as his lips inched close to her neck. She felt his breath and a spark radiated down her back.

"If you're into it," he said, "Dean can get us some blow." Troy pulled away to sense her reaction to his offer.

She gazed up at him with a twinkle in her eye and a smile on her face. "That would be cool," she said as the vodka soothed her inhibitions.

They danced for what seemed like hours and were both glistening with perspiration as they grinded together to the non-stop music. They were surrounded in the center of the misty dance floor by faceless bodies grooving anonymously to the mix. As the beat reached a crescendo, Jackie raised her hands in the air and felt the cool mist of dry ice being pumped from below the floor. Troy grabbed her waist and pulled her close snaking his hands over her body.

"You wanna get outta here?" he yelled into her ear.

She turned and their lips locked, followed by their tongues entangling. She grabbed his hand and pulled him off of the dance floor almost knocking over a couple next to them. As they headed for the door, Troy planned his next move to get what he was really after.

A loud car engine grumbled towards them as a valet drove Troy's new black convertible Ferrari to the front door of the dance club. Troy opened the passenger's side door for Jackie, and then handed a few bills to the valet who seemed happy enough that he got to drive the gleaming fantasy car. Troy revved the engine and pulled away from the club as the warm night breeze ran through their hair.

"Wow, great car," she said feeling the powerful gyration of the sports car underneath her as it raced down the street. The street lights blurred by her and her head swimmed in the night's inebriations.

"Thanks. It was a present to myself when I was promoted to VP of Sales." He didn't tell her that it was really his newfound cash flow that funded the extravagance, rather than his ascension to Vice President. Modos had made him rich, and he would not soon forget what Ivan had done for him.

"Well, you certainly treat yourself right," Jackie said looking up at the motionless stars.

"Yes, I do," he said quietly under his breath looking over at her long legs. He reached and laid his hand on her smooth thigh. "Hey, what's up with that investigation?" He steered her towards his main objective.

"I don't know that much about it other than what Cain has told me. He said that SouthPoint's lawyers from Atlanta are looking into some possibly fake transactions at ICon. They've got me pulling information for them."

"What kind of information?"

"Oh you know, the usual. Client reports, commission statements, contracts. Those sorts of things."

"Have they found anything?" Troy pressed her as he squeezed her leg.

"They're real interested in Zapplication, which seems like just a tiny little client from what I can tell. I'm not sure what they're looking for, but I had to deliver a bunch of stuff to them about that, some wire transfers too. And for some reason they asked a bunch of questions about an escrow company that we use."

She winked flirtatiously at him. "Wait a minute, should I be telling you this?" She giggled as the martinis clouded her judgment.

"Oh yeah, there's no problem telling me. I'm in the loop. I've been interviewed and cleared by the lawyers," he lied. "What wires transfers did they want to see?"

"Uh, I can't remember all of them. But I do remember that one was to a bank in Antigua. I thought, Antigua of all places, can you imagine? There's got to be something fishy with that one." She glanced over with a smile and Troy tried to hide his grimace when he heard *Antigua*. The lawyers were getting too close.

"Did they ask about Modos?"

"What? Modos? No, I've never heard of that. Is it a client?"

"Nope. Just something I heard, don't worry about it."

Jackie fiddled in her tiny silver purse. "Do you mind?" She asked holding up a cigarette.

"Not at all," he said still stroking her leg and inching up her thigh.

Jackie leaned forward to light the cigarette out of the wind. As she did, Troy peered over to catch a glimpse of the small of her back that was exposed. A thin red strand of her G-string panties peeked out, and he saw the muted gray etching of the top of a curved tattoo. A craving rushed through his body. He would enjoy finding the rest of that tattoo. But first things first.

"So, I guess the lawyers are staying at the Hilton near the office, huh?" he fished nonchalantly.

Jackie sat back up and exhaled a plume of smoke that was swept backwards quickly in the breeze.

"No, they're at the Intercontinental downtown. I had to go down there to deliver the stuff to them in one of the conference rooms." She took another drag off of the cigarette oblivious to her negligent leak of information.

Troy grinned as he looked in the rear view mirror. He had gotten what Ivan wanted. As they sat at a red light, he reached for his cell phone in the console. He sent a text message to his favorite client. *hotel intercontinental. they don't know about M. asking about zapp.* Troy tossed the phone back into the console and leaned over to kiss Jackie deeply. His hand squeezed the soft flesh of her inner thigh. Now it was time to get what *he* wanted.

As the light turned green, he punched the Ferrari through its gears. The raw acceleration drove Jackie back into the sculpted leather seat laughing out loud. She flung her head back in the wind as they flew in the night towards Troy's bachelor pad.

CHAPTER SEVENTEEN

Once you eliminate the impossible, whatever remains,
no matter how improbable, must be the truth.
-- Arthur Conan Doyle, Sr. (creator of Sherlock Holmes)

There was a heightened level of anxiety in the secluded war room at the Intercontinental Hotel the morning before SouthPoint's shareholder meeting. The team was scattered throughout the room, with the reviewers huddled behind their computer terminals, and Alex and Sarah were at the table with their heads deep in documents.

"Hey Chief," Chuck said looking up over his glasses as Jake strolled in. Chuck looked tired. "How'd Thomas take the news last night?"

Jake plopped down in a chair next to Chuck and exhaled.

"Not good. He is panicking over the shareholder's meeting, and rightfully so. It can't be postponed. If they call off the meeting, Wall Street will vilify SouthPoint, and the stock will get killed. So the question is whether our revelations last night of the porn business and the cross-sell scheme have to be disclosed . . . at least tomorrow. We don't have a real handle yet on the size or scope, so materiality is still unclear. We haven't been able to corroborate what Mick told us, and we still don't know what the purpose of the stress testing is. Thomas is worried that a premature disclosure would do more harm than good, especially if it was something that the due diligence team missed. If there is any litigation that stems from this, he doesn't want the issues to be public before we get our arms around every thing, which I think is smart."

"On the other hand, there definitely will be questions by shareholders about the ICon merger, and it could be a far bigger problem if SouthPoint responds in a misleading way. If any of this comes out later, which I can't see how it will not, you can count on a class action based on what they say at the shareholder meeting. It's a god awful catch-22."

"Well, we all worked pretty late last night, and the good news is that I think we may be on to something. Here, look at this."

Chuck slid a spreadsheet across the table to Jake, who propped up and caught the spreadsheet.

"In June, ICon's revenue starts to tick up fairly dramatically. There is a flurry of emails from Troy about implementing new websites, but strangely none of the clients are identified and he's cryptic about whether the required approvals were given. I'm assuming that those are the Modos sites. Then, there are a bunch of emails from Alan to various people boasting about the increased revenues. We also found several emails from Cain to one of the accounting clerks instructing her to escrow funds to a company called National Escrow Services. That seems consistent with what he told us when a client doesn't comply with the credit card company's standards, but I'm having Sarah run those down to see if she can reconcile the escrow account."

"Here is where it starts getting interesting." Chuck pulled out one of the emails and handed it to Jake.

"Alan stared getting emails like this throughout the fall." The email was from tcollins@visacreditservices.com. Jake skimmed the brief email and read it aloud. "Please be notified that during August ICon exceeded the ratio limit in Section 36(b) of the Amended Master Merchant Agreement. Please contact me to discuss. Timothy Collins."

Jake looked up at Chuck. "What is Section 36(b)?"

Chuck opened a black binder on the table.

"This is the merchant service contract between ICon and Visa." Several red flags poked out from the side of the contract. "First of all, I didn't find anything about allowing stress test transactions. The only provision that was anywhere close prohibits any transactions that the internet payment processor knows or reasonably should know are fake or fraudulent. You could argue that the stress tests are fake transactions because they weren't done to buy anything on a website. On the other hand, they were from legitimate credit cards and ICon paid for all of the transactions, so I'm not sure that they would be considered to be fake."

"Hmm," Jake murmured, "close call. But I thought that Alan told us that the contract specifically allowed for stress testing?"

"He did," Chuck said confidently, and defiantly. "A lot of what he said is not panning out."

Chuck continued. "Section 36 deals with performance metrics, and subsection (b) provides the limit for the monthly charge back ratio. It says that if ICon exceeds the ratio, the credit card company can penalized ICon in an amount based on the percentage that the ratio is exceeded. It's a pretty complicated formula, but the bottom line is that ICon would have to pay big bucks if it exceeds the charge back ratio."

"Last night, Mick showed us on Velocity that the porn sites had high levels of charge backs. I guess that's not surprising, huh?"

"Nope, but look at this email." Chuck handed a sheet of paper to Jake. "It's from Alan to Cain, Troy, and Jane about two months after the porn sites came online."

Jake read it aloud. "Can we meet ASAP? Got a call from Visa. They want to penalize us $2.1mm."

He thought for a moment. "Is this tied to the emails about Section 36?"

"We don't know for sure but the timing sure fits. I'm going to look through ICon's financials to see if I can find anywhere that would indicate that Visa did, in fact, impose that penalty. I don't remember seeing anything like that. The strange part is that after this email, they go radio silent. We didn't find any more emails that mention Section 36 or any penalties from Visa. Kyle is looking through the deleted files on the slack space of their hard drives, but that's a shot in the dark."

"Okay, keep hammering away at that. Did you find anything more about the stress testing?"

"So far, there's nothing coming up on our key word searches for 'stress testing,' but they could've been using some other term. We did get a lot of hits for 'Zapplication,' and the reviewers are looking through those now. The problem is that because it is listed as a client the name appears on all of the commission reports sent to the sales department, so there are a lot of false positives with Zapplication's name. On top of that, Troy sent emails all the time about his commissions, so the attachment with the term Zapplication keeps getting sent back and forth. But we're making good progress."

"What about Patti's emails?"

Chuck turned and called Alex over from his huddle with the document reviewers.

"Alex, tell Jake what you found from the emails about Patti."

"You'll love this," Alex said sarcastically. "As soon as Patti was terminated, ICon specifically deleted her entire mailbox from the server. So we don't have any emails that come from her in-box or sent box. The IT guys at ICon claimed that it was standard operating procedure to do that for any employee who left in the first ninety probationary period."

"How convenient," Jake said frustrated.

"But," Alex continued raising his index finger, "they couldn't, or didn't, go through everyone else's emails to delete any that Patti sent to someone else. So, for instance, we found some of the emails that she sent to Jane in Jane's deleted box and some of the ones that Jane sent to her in Jane's sent box. You follow me?"

"Yup."

"It's clear that Patti was trying to talk with Jane in the weeks before she was fired. We found several emails from Patti asking to meet that were still in Jane's deleted box. Jane brushed her off a couple of times, and then it looks like they finally met because we found this email that Patti sent to Jane three days before she was fired."

Alex handed the email to Jake and he read it silently.

> *Thanks for talking with me about Zapplication the other day. Since this expense seems to occur each month, I want to set up an accrual. So I spoke with IT (mick sertoff) to get a sense about what to expect next month. He acted really weird and told me to forget about it if I knew what was good for me. Do you have any idea what he's talking about??*

"Did Jane respond to the email?"

"Not that we could find. But, about one minute later she sent Alan an email that just said 'We need to talk now' which was followed by four or five exclamation marks."

"Huh." Jake sat back and stared into space. "She didn't tell us that she spoke to Mick did she Alex?"

"Nope. I looked back at my notes and she didn't say anything about talking with Mick or that he warned her. And I know that Mick didn't tell us last night that he spoke with her."

"We gotta talk with Patti. Any luck finding her?"

"Not yet. I looked through the online white pages and didn't find anyone else with the same last name. I also Googled the name Tomanski and didn't come up with any hits in South Florida. It's possible that her mother's last name is not Tomanski. We don't know if Tomanski is Patti's birth name or her married name. The only thing I found online was a roster for a junior soccer team that listed a kid named Aaron Tomanski. Here it is."

Alex handed a couple of pages to Jake. "The Hurricanes," he said looking over the print out. "Hmm, there's a game schedule here too. Let's see . . . the Hurricanes are playing the Storm today at ten o'clock at Pembroke Pines Elementary. Isn't Pembroke Pines just north of Miami?"

"Yup," Chuck said. "You're not suggesting we go are you?"

"What do we have to lose? It's worth a shot."

"Well then I'll come with you, you shouldn't go alone," Chuck said and gestured towards the concealed traveling companion strapped to his leg. When Jake realized what Chuck meant, he regretted his last choice of words.

"Well, I think I'll be safe from the soccer moms, but we may need some firepower to knock off the concession stand."

Chuck grinned slyly as Jake walked passed him and patted him on the back. "Come on killer, let's go hunting for a whistleblower."

* * *

Jake pulled the car slowly into the elementary school's parking lot. The lot was bloating with minivans and SUVs.

After parking in the back of the lot, Jake and Chuck looked around for the soccer field. They saw a mother on the far side of the lot trying to keep up with a uniformed boy who was dancing in his cleats around a soccer ball. His clean white shirt signaled to them that he had not yet played.

Jake pointed in their direction. "That way."

They followed her around a brick class room building and saw a wide path that led down to a large grass field divided into four smaller soccer fields. The fields were crowded with parents watching throngs of kids chasing balls around. Sporadic cheers erupted when a team scored, which was more by chance than by plan, and an occasional referee's whistle chimed along with the shouts of encouragements from the sidelines.

Chuck and Jake stood at the edge of the field, gazing out over the sea of people. "What does she look like?"

"Uh, thin. Early thirties. When we met her she had short dark hair, but she had changed that from sandy blonde hair. There's no telling what her hair style may be now."

"Ah," Chuck smirked, "that's helpful. She should really stand out in this crowd," he said as he followed Jake down onto the field.

After fifteen minutes of crisscrossing the soccer games, Jake was sure that he had looked at every woman's face, and he didn't see Patti. He was also sure that he probably appeared to be some kind of stalker, staring intently at each woman as he passed them slowly. He finally stopped back where they began and shrugged. Chuck caught up with him a moment later.

"No luck, huh?" Chuck said.

"I didn't see her. Hold on." Jake stepped towards a woman watching the games.

"Excuse me, do you know which team is the Hurricanes?"

The woman looked over. "The Hurricanes are on this field," she pointed to the game she was watching.

"Oh, okay thanks. Would you happen to know which of those little guys is Aaron Tomanski?"

The woman narrowed her eyes slightly at Jake, sizing up the stranger who was looking for the young boy. Jake saw her hesitation and continued, "I'm actually looking for his mother, who I think may be Patti Tomanski. I'm a . . . . uh, I'm a friend of Patti's," Jake quickly added realizing that the little white lie was the only way he was going to get any information from her.

Hearing that, the woman eased and pointed to a boy running with a pack of kids around a ball in the middle of the field. "There's Aaron, number 9. And his mother is on the sidelines over there with the baseball hat on."

Jake followed the line where the woman was pointing, and his eyes scanned the sidelines for anyone wearing a hat. His gaze stopped at a woman in a tan cap with a capital "I" on it for the University of Illinois, which he then remembered from Patti's resume was her alma mater. The cap was pulled down over her forehead and her short brown hair peeked barely out from the sides. She wore oversized dark designer sunglasses hiding most of her face. She clearly was trying not to be seen. As Jake focused, he realized that he had found Patti.

"Thanks," he said to the woman, who had already turned back to the game. Jake looked over at Chuck and motioned for him to follow.

"Excuse me, Patti?" Jake said gently as he approached her. She turned towards Jake and instantly recognized him. Although her sunglasses concealed her expression, her body language told her emotion. She was surprised to see him, but not in a good way.

She reached up and removed her sunglasses. Her eyes were the same and Jake could see the same shimmer of worry.

"Very impressive, Mr. Morgan. I'm not sure how you found me, but I should've known that I wasn't going to get off with just one interview."

She glanced over at Chuck, and he introduced himself.

"I'm sorry," Jake began, "but there are a few things we need to follow up with. It can't wait until tomorrow. Really. It'll just take a few minutes."

Patti looked hard at Jake and she saw his sincerity. She could tell that he was not just doing a job, he cared about the truth. She knew that the only reason that Jake was standing on that soccer field was because she had decided to speak up, to start the process that she knew would lead to this. So many times she wished that she hadn't found that payable report for Zapplication. That she hadn't had to question the account. If Jane had just responded to her, instead of ignoring her, she might have believed their story. If ICon hadn't fired her for simply doing her job, she might have looked the other way. All she wanted to do was to start a new life, to start over.

But it is rarely a convenient time when someone's character is challenged. She had to tell someone about the things that were going on at ICon, at least some of the things, even though it would mean that she couldn't start over, not yet anyway.

Patti nodded and turned to an older woman sitting down next to her. "Mom, can you keep an eye on Aaron. I need to talk to these guys. It's about ICon."

"Are you okay honey?" the aged woman asked looking for any sign of concern in her daughter's face.

"Yes, I'm fine, thanks. These are the lawyers I told you about. The one's I talked to a few days ago."

Patti led Jake and Chuck to the far side of the soccer field where they could talk in private. She looked back and got a glimpse of her distant mother's face trying to mask that she'd been watching her walk away, just to be safe.

"Ok, so what do you want to know?" she said politely, but a little defiantly.

"You didn't tell us that you spoke with Mick Sertoff about the Zapplication transactions, why not?" he asked politely, but a little disturbed.

He was well past the informational stage of interview strategy, and he was bearing down on the accusatory stage. Time was short, and she hadn't told him everything the first time.

She expected the line of inquiry, but just not so abruptly. She stood steadfast in the decision she made, and was prepared to defend it.

"I, um . . . I told you what I thought was necessary to tell you and I didn't want to get him involved. I don't know what was going on, but I have a son to protect, as I guess you've figured out now, and a mother to look after. And I know what happens to whistleblowers. I saw it over and over when I was in internal audit. We worked with lots of them."

Patti paused and looked out over the field. Jake and Chuck sensed that she was describing a personal experience, not a work assignment. They also sensed that she had more to say before she was going to answer Jake's question.

"Before I came to ICon, I was in internal audit at Technyx as you know, along with the name of my high school prom date I'm sure," she added with sarcastic flare.

"Anyway, this girl, I call her a girl, but she was probably twenty one or so. She was a clerk in shipping and receiving and she knocked on my door one day. She told me that the day before one of the truck drivers had been flirting with her. Not unusual for the drivers to do that, but when this guy left to deliver his shipment he forgot his cell phone. So she jumped in her car to catch up with his rig to give it back to him. About two miles down the road, she saw the rig turn into a hotel parking lot. She followed it around back and saw that there were four other Technyx trucks parked in the parking lot of this hotel. She thought that was strange, so she came to me about it."

"Turns out that Technyx was falsifying its sales numbers by recording those shipments as revenue even though none of the product had actually been delivered. When I started asking questions about it, the shipping manager fired *her* for leaving her post to give the guy his phone back. It was a complete sham. But that wasn't enough. Some of the truck drivers who were also fired for participating in the scheme began to harass her. Threatening calls late at night. Emails saying horrendous things about her. Strange cars following her. One time, they even threw a brick through her window. They made her life a living hell. This innocent young girl who had done exactly what she should have done was being tormented by these thugs."

Patti paused to collect herself. "I remember getting the news from our lawyer that she had killed herself because of the tormenting. I was speechless. I couldn't talk for hours. The injustice was just so painful to me, so tangible. It really took me a while to come to grips with it. My entire professional life had been centered on doing the right thing. But I have to admit, I lost something that day. It was like a flame went out. It's not easy to explain, and I don't know why she affected me that way, but she just did."

Jake and Chuck silently absorbed Patti's story. There seemed to be so much to say, but neither could come up with any words. She blinked hard a few times fighting back her tears, and she looked away towards the soccer games. The jovial sounds from the kids playing below eased her back into control.

"Ms. Tomanski," Chuck began in a deep soothing voice, "there is no forgiveness for what happened to that girl, and I cannot begin to imagine the grief. We're not here to criticize you, and we are not here to put you in a position that you don't want to be in. As far as I'm concerned, we're concerned, this conversation never happened." Chuck looked over at Jake who already started nodding in agreement. "We just want to ask a few questions and we'll be on our way."

Patti continued to stare out over the fields for a moment. She finally took a deep breath and turned towards them.

"To answer your question, Mr. Morgan, I did talk with Mick. After Jane brushed me off, I asked Mick about the Zapplication transactions thinking that he might know something. At first, he thought that I was some kind of spy or mole. He's was wound up pretty tight. Anyway, he finally warned me to stay away from Zapplication. He didn't tell me why, he just said that I should forget about it."

"Did he say what Zapplication was doing?"

"Not exactly. He said that Zapplication was somehow testing the computer system. But he said that the testing was bogus and that the transactions would've just been diluted in all of ICon's regular transaction. I do remember distinctly that he told me that one of ICon programmers who had worked on Zapplication figured out what was going on and was about to expose it when he was killed in a car accident. Mick said that he got a call a few days later threatening him that the same thing would happen if he talked to anyone. It may have all been his imagination, but like I said, he seemed pretty nervous about it. All I could think about was that girl on the shipping dock . . . and about protecting my son."

"Do you know what Modos is?" Jake asked her.

She turned towards him. "No, never heard of it."

"Did you know that ICon was processing transactions for adult entertainment websites?"

"What? No." Patti responded looking shocked. "I guess that explains all the secrecy. But Zapplication was just a cell phone app site – at least that was what I thought."

"Why do you think they were running the Zapplication transactions?" Chuck asked.

"Well, like I told you, I suspected that it was a phony vendor scheme or something. I was only there for a few months, but from what I saw, I didn't think that ICon needed to boost its bottom line. While I was there ICon never had any issue with cash flow."

She paused for a moment. "I wasn't there long enough to understand the whole operations side. Maybe ICon needed to increase the number of transactions for some reason. But I don't know how Zapplication fit in. Maybe Mick was paranoid. It doesn't make any sense."

"Unless, the mob needed to *clean* their other transactions," Chuck said thinking out loud.

"Huh? The mob? What are you talking about?" Patti asked, but Chuck was too far along in his thought process to explain.

"Patti, you said that Mick told you that the test transactions would've been *diluted* with the other credit card transactions, right? Maybe *that* was the purpose of the Zapplication transactions – for dilution."

"I'm not following you," Jake said with a questioning look.

Chuck turned towards Jake. "You said that last night Mick showed you on Velocity that the Modos business, the porn websites, had high charge backs and low approval ratios, right?"

As he asked the question, Chuck raised his left hand to mimic the high level of charge backs on the graph, and he lowered his right hand to show the low level of approvals.

"And we know that ICon paid for all of the Zapplication transactions, so they were guaranteed to be approved and none of them would be charge backs, right?" Chuck's tone hurried as he was bearing down on a theory.

"What if the Zapplication transactions were a way of diluting or reducing the high charge backs of the porn business? The charge back ratio is the number of charge backs over the total number of transactions. So if you increase the denominator with the stress test transactions without increasing the number of charge backs in the numerator you'll *reduce* the charge back ratio. The high charge backs from the porn sites would come down and the approval rate would increase." He slowly brought his right hand and left together in front of him.

Jake thought for a few seconds and then his face lit up. "That would explain why the testing was done at the end of each month."

"Exactly," Chuck said. "ICon could tell how many transactions it needed to run through Zapplication to bring the charge back level in line. I bet that they would just turn on the program and run transactions until they reached the level they needed. That would explain why the volume of the Zapplication transactions was sporadic each month."

Jake thought of the massive Velocity display in Mick's office, and he visualized the red lines for charge backs creeping forward on the graph. "I bet they could even watch the Velocity graphics for the Modos sites and see the lines start to go down as the Zapplication transactions were dumped into the system."

"But why would the level of charge backs be so high?" Patti asked. "I mean even if they were processing adult sites, that seems to be a lot."

The answer hit Jake like a ton of bricks. "The cross-sell scheme! Holy shit, that's it!" He looked excitedly to Chuck. "They had to compensate for all the charge backs from the fraudulent cross-sells, so they came up with Zapplication to counteract it. That's the connection. That's the missing piece of the puzzle!"

A roar of cheers erupted on one of the soccer fields as if tacitly applauding Jake's and Chuck's breakthrough. Patti watched intently as the pieces began falling into place for them.

"And that's why ICon wrote off the revenue that it earned from the transactions," Chuck added. "They weren't looking for cash, they were trying to game the ratios because the Modos sites were blowing them way out of whack. ICon had no way out. If ICon got rid of the porn sites, it would've lost hundreds of millions of dollars. Or if it didn't remove the sites, it would've exceeded the limit of the charge back ratio and the credit card companies would've penalized ICon millions or terminated its access. Either way, the company would've crashed."

"Do you remember the timing of those emails that you showed me this morning about the charge back levels?" Jake asked.

"Not all of them. Let me call Alex."

Chuck quickly dialed Alex's cell phone number and tapped his toe in the dirt as he waited impatiently.

"Alex, it's Chuck. We may be on to something. We think that the stress testing transactions were used to offset the high charge backs of the porn business. Can you get those emails that we showed Jake this morning from Visa to Alan, and also find the transaction data that we have for Zapplication." Chuck looked at Jake and Patti in anticipation as he waited for the information.

Chuck started nodding as Alex was reporting back. "Uh huh, yes. When were those emails sent in relation to the first Zapplication transactions? Okay. And when did the Modos sites start to come online?"

A broad smile began to reach across Chuck's face as Alex told him that the timing was perfectly consistent with their theory. "Once the Zapplication stress testing transactions started, did you all find any more of those emails to Alan about the high charge backs or low approvals?" Chuck nodded. "Good, I didn't think so. And what was the amount that ICon was fined for the violations?"

Chuck turned to Patti after getting the answer. "Patti, did you hear anything about any fine or penalty that ICon paid for $2.1 million?"

She thought for a moment. "I know for sure that there was no fine or penalty when I was there because I would've been the one to make the journal entry. The only item that high was a legal settlement that was paid by ICon right when I got there. I think it was around two million."

Her eyes widened with the memory. "I was brand new and I didn't know what the case was about. But it stood out because that was the only lawsuit that ICon was involved in. I remember that I had to get approval from Cain because the money was supposed to be wired directly to Visa, which I thought was weird because the plaintiff was a former client of ICon, so I asked Cain why we were sending the wire to Visa. He said that the client was in a lot of debt and wanted the settlement to be paid directly to his creditors, or something like that."

Jake reached for the phone. "Alex, this is Jake. Can you have Sarah look through ICon's financials to see if there is any disclosure of a $2.1 million legal settlement? It should be on the P&L under non-operating expenses, or it might be described in a footnote to the financials. I'll bet the money in my pocket that ICon masked the charge back fine so that SouthPoint wouldn't see it in due diligence and ask questions."

"Chuck and I are on the way back, and I need you to get the crew working on this theory. Have someone look at ICon's charge backs before and after the stress test transactions were run to see what the impact was on the charge back ratio. Also, see if there is any way to calculate what the penalty would've been under the contract if the stress test transactions were not run. Got all that? Good, thanks a lot."

Jake turned to Patti. "There's one more thing that I need to ask you. The HR director at ICon, Glen Baker, told us that they found unprescribed Zanex pills at your workstation, and that was the primary reason you were terminated. Is that true?"

Patti recoiled as if she had been hit in the face. "Those bastards. Yes it's true, I mean no it's not." Jake and Chuck looked confused. "The stupid pills must've dropped out of my purse, but they had nothing to do with my termination."

"Okay, okay," Jake said with a hint of reservation.

Patti saw in his eyes that he wanted a further explanation, but was hesitant to ask. She relieved him of his dilemma. "I was hoping that I wouldn't have to get into this, but so be it."

She paused to collect her thoughts. "I had a hard year last year. On top of the whistleblower's suicide at Technyx, I went through an ugly divorce and my mother got sick. I needed to be here for her, but Aaron was in school back home and I couldn't move to Florida until the divorce was finalized. I was just overwhelmed, so a friend of mine gave me some of her pills to help me cope. I obviously didn't even take them all."

Patti looked across the field at her mother, who waved up to her as Aaron's game was ending. Patti waved back with a feeble smile.

"How is your mother doing?" Chuck asked genuinely.

"She's fine now, thanks for asking. But I'm concerned about this ICon thing and whether Aaron and I are safe. I mean you two found me, so what's to say that the mob won't. No offense," she added realizing that her comment could be taken the wrong way.

"None taken," Jake said with a smile. "It might be best if you and your son could disappear for a while." Jake thought better than to tell her that Chuck was packing heat because of the previous night's events. "Is there any place here or back home that you could stay?"

"Not really. I have some friends that are still in Illinois, but I don't want to involve anyone else in my situation."

Jake thought for a moment. "Has Aaron ever been to New York City?"

Patti looked at him curiously. "No, why?"

"Well, my law firm has an apartment in Manhattan and I could pull some strings so that you two could stay there until things blow over here. I'm sure we could help you find some temporary accounting work. It might be a fun summer vacation for him."

Patti saw Aaron running towards her with a soccer ball in his arms and a huge smile on his face. His once white uniform was now accentuated with swaths of tan dirt, and his ruffled brown hair bounced with each stride. Patti's mother was following at a much slower pace behind him.

"Mommy, mommy, we won! We got five goals and they only got one." The excitement in his voice brought a smile to all three of them.

"That's great," Patti said welcoming the little athlete into her arms. "Aaron, this is Mr. Morgan and . . . ," she glanced at Chuck not remembering his last name.

"Bradley, Chuck Bradley."

". . . and Mr. Bradley," Patti finished. "They're friends of mine from work. I was watching you play and you did great."

Patti's mother finally caught up. "I'm so sorry dear, he just took off like a flash," she said catching her breath.

Patti turned towards her son and rubbed his disheveled hair. "Aaron, how would you like to go to New York City for a little while?"

"Yea!" he yelled wildly without knowing anything about New York City or where it was.

Patti's mother looked over at her with surprised apprehension.

"It's okay, Mom. It'll just be for a little while until the ICon situation blows over. Besides, Aaron and I can use a little time together away."

They all walked together across the field following Aaron who was playfully kicking the soccer ball out ahead of them. The elementary school's parking lot was filled with parents trying to corral their dusty kids as an influx of clean little soccer players readied for the next round of games.

Standing next to a black SUV in the corner of the lot watching them was Taras. Dark glasses concealed the focus of his stare, but it was clear that he was not there to watch a soccer game. His jaw tightened as he gazed at Jake opening a car door for Patti and her son. They waved at Patti's mother, and Patti got into Jake's car.

Jake stood momentarily at the driver's door and slowly scanned the parking lot. For an instant, he thought he saw someone looking at him from across the lot. As he squinted in the sunlight, a family hauling chairs and coolers trudged in front of him. When they cleared, the figure was gone. Jake looked back and forth again, but he lost whoever he thought he saw.

Taras slowly stood up from behind the SUV. He watched the Mercedes back out of the parking spot and follow a caravan of minivans out of the lot. He wiped his brow, and then flipped open his cell phone to call his boss.

"It's me," he said in his thick accent. "I followed the lawyer from the hotel. He spoke with the woman and they left together."

He listened motionless to his instructions from Ivan.

"Ya, I'll take care of it."

CHAPTER EIGHTEEN

Honesty is the best policy – when there is money in it.
-- Mark Twain

Cain pressed his folded clothes down hard into an already stuffed suitcase lying on his bed. He leaned down on the bag as he pulled the stretched zipper around its track, cursing as it hung up on the corner. Finally yanking it around, he stood up and exhaled. He was breathing heavily from the rush to pack, and he scanned the room one last time. He had everything he needed, for a while anyway.

Just as he was about to walk out of the room, he caught a glimpse of himself in a standing mirror in the corner. He had traded in his pinstripes and power tie for jeans and a t-shirt. He stood there for a moment staring into the mirror. The gruff shading of his unshaven face outlined his tense jaw. He rubbed his weary eyes with his fore fingers and slowly squeezed his hands down his face as if trying to wring out the stress. He looked tired. He took another deep breath, and then looked away from the mirror. He snatched his car keys from his night table and pulled the bulking suitcase off of the neatly made bed.

The roller wheels of the luggage clacked loudly in rhythm over the stone tile in the hallway of his condominium. The afternoon sun slid through the blinds and cast shards of light against the floor. Cain left the suitcase standing in the foyer and he went into his office. A flat screen computer monitor on his desk displayed an email that he had drafted and was ready to be sent. It had taken him almost an hour to write the one paragraph email, but it would only take an instant to send. He sat down in his desk chair and re-read the email that he had addressed to SouthPoint Bank's General Counsel Thomas Nelson, with a copy addressed to Jake Morgan.

Again, he studied the words and moved the cursor to hover over the *Send* button. He paused and lightly stroked the mouse with his index finger, staring over the message one last time. Glancing down at the clock on menu bar, he saw that time was getting short. He tapped the mouse and sent the email off on its electronic voyage through the web. It was done.

He removed his passport from the desk drawer and he turned off the computer. In the foyer, he picked up his thin wire Ray Ban sunglasses from a metal tray. As he was about to leave, he turned and stood for a moment glancing around his condo. He didn't know when he would be back, if ever. After a deep breath, he slid on the sunglasses and pulled the suitcase through the open door into the Miami heat.

* * *

Jake loaded Patti's suitcases into the truck of the Mercedes and looked up and down the tree-lined street in front of her townhome. It was a quiet Sunday afternoon and the street was empty. He thought of Alex's earlier encounter with the men watching her house, and he hoped that they had abandoned their search. The investigation had suddenly turned into a dangerous race against the clock to expose Modos and to save SouthPoint from financial ruin. He now felt like he was being watched, and he sized up every stranger who caught his eye. The guy peeking over his coffee cup in the hotel lobby. The driver of the car that seemed to follow him on the road. An image in the parking lot at the soccer fields. For the first time, he understood how thin the line is between reality and paranoia.

"Okay, let's go," Jake said as Patti and Aaron climbed into the back seat.

Jake shut Patti's door and looked over the car at Chuck. "I'll be happy when they're out of here . . . when we're *all* out of here."

"Me too partner," Chuck said.

As they were driving to the hotel, Jake's cell phone rang. "Hello, it's Jake."

"Did you get it?"

"Did I get what? Who is this?" Jake asked. Chuck looked over at him from the passenger seat intrigued by the one side of the conversation that he heard so far.

"It's Thomas. Did you get the email from Cain?" Jake instantly recognized the harried voice of SouthPoint's General Counsel.

"Uh, I don't know, let me check. I'm in the car."

Jake pulled the Blackberry away from his face and glanced down at the phone to access his email in box. Sure enough, there was an email from Cain sent thirty two minutes ago with a one word subject. *Resignation.*

"I did get it," Jake told Thomas as he looked back up to the road. "Let me read it and I'll call you right back."

Jake turned to Chuck in the passenger's seat, who was still looking at him. "Here, read this email to me while I drive." Jake handed his phone to Chuck.

Chuck frowned and pulled out his thin reading glasses in order to see the tiny font on the phone. "Are you trying to make me look old in front of our guests," he playfully motioned towards Patti and Aaron.

"No, but it sounds like that email you're about to read is going to put some years on both of us. Cain just resigned and we have less than twenty four hours to wrap this all up before the shareholder meeting tomorrow morning."

Chuck's grin evaporated. He understood the implications of ICon's lead lawyer quitting in the middle of an internal investigation. Cain had to have known that resigning would yank the spotlight into his direction and brighten any of his own shadows. Maybe he was hearing footsteps, or maybe it was part of some plan. Regardless, Cain's resignation threatened to pull apart the bow that they were just about to tie on the case.

Chuck cleared his throat, and Patti politely shushed Aaron's inquisition about New York to listen. Chuck read Cain's email aloud.

Thomas:

I regret to inform you that I am submitting my resignation as Executive Vice President of Legal Affairs of Internet Connections, Inc. I can no longer continue to serve in that position because of moral and professional reasons. For the past twelve months, I have been aware of a fraud being perpetrated at ICon to manipulate charge back levels. I was forced to conceal it from the auditors, from SouthPoint during its due diligence, and most recently, from Levi & Everett during its investigation. I discovered this scheme during my own investigative efforts, but I was prevented from disclosing it. I am a whistleblower under the Sarbanes-Oxley Act, and I am entitled to damages and protection against retribution. I trust that you will take the appropriate measures.

Cain Arnold.

The car was silent after Chuck finished the email. Jake stared down the road as he processed Cain's email, and Chuck re-read it to himself.

"I think he's full of sh--," Patti caught herself in front of Aaron, but her message was loud and clear. "There's no way he wasn't involved. He walked those halls like he ruled the place. He was part of everything that was going on there." She bristled at the notion of Cain claiming to be a whistleblower.

"When we met with them in Alan's office the other day, Cain didn't seem troubled at all with spinning the stress testing story," Jake said to Chuck about the new twist. "I didn't pick up any clues that he was being coerced into it, did you?"

Chuck took off his reading glasses and looked up from Jake's Blackberry. "Nope. But his father was right there next to him. If there is any truth in what he is saying, he could've put on a pretty good act for us. It seemed rather rehearsed when they spoon fed us the story. Just playing devil's advocate, though, Troy did try to bully you in the bathroom and he threatened Mick. I suppose it's not a stretch that he also intimidated Cain. I will say however, whatever happened, Alan and Cain have a *special* kind of father-son relationship. Son narks on his dad who allegedly forced him to lie to cover up a fraud. Quite a family there."

"I think he's just trying to deflect the blame at the eleventh hour. I don't believe him for a minute," Jake said unconvinced. "I can't wait to hear what Thomas thinks."

Jake took the cell phone from Chuck to call Thomas back. The phone rang only once before it was answered without a greeting.

"Whistleblower?!" Thomas yelled into the phone. "He thinks he's a fucking whistleblower? He waits until right before the shareholder meeting, and now he wants protection? I knew that there was something I didn't like about that little prick."

"I know, I know," Jake said trying to calm down his client. "Let's think rationally about this. We need to try to interview him again and see what he has to say about it and, more importantly, who else was involved. For better or for worse, he's been the lawyer for SouthPoint's subsidiary and the Bank is a public company. So no matter how bogus we might think his story is, SouthPoint has an obligation to determine whether there is any basis to it. We really need to talk to him."

There was silence on the other end of the line.

"Goddammit," Thomas finally conceded. "Alright, but I'm on my way down there. I have to tell Gary what to say about all this, if anything, at the shareholder meeting tomorrow and I want to look Cain right in his beady little eyes when he answers your questions. I'll take the jet down. Meet me at Opa-Locka in two and a half hours and you can brief me about everything in the car. Goddammit," Thomas repeated.

Jake heard a click on Thomas' end and turned to Chuck, who was eagerly awaiting the report.

"I guess he took it as well as I expected," Jake said with a dash of sarcasm. "He's on his way down here and in the meantime I have to somehow get Cain to meet with us."

Chuck's thick eyebrows bounced up. "How are you going to do that?"

Jake gazed down the road in thought. After a moment, he turned to Chuck and winked. "I'm going to shoot a string out there and let him fly right into it."

* * *

Jake left Patti and Aaron to check in at the registration desk of the Hotel Intercontinental, and he crossed the lobby where Chuck was watching a gleaming yacht cruise by in the channel.

"Nice boat," Jake said as he approached.

"You know, behind every boat is a story," Chuck said prophetically as he read the satirical name of the gaudy yacht passing: *Itylldo.* "When I was a kid, my father had a sailboat. Thirty-five foot, sloop rigged, single mast. It wasn't anything special, but he sure loved it and at the time I thought it was the Queen Mary."

Chuck grinned at memories that he thought were long lost. "I learned a whole lot more than how to sail on that boat. Whenever he wanted to talk, or just to get away from my mother, we'd go out and sail. He taught me more about being a man out there than how to rig a jib sail. We'd be out there for hours, just father and son battling the winds and tide together. He wasn't perfect, but he was there, which is more than I can say for a lot of fathers these days."

"Funny thing is that he never named that boat. He always said that it wasn't big enough to be named. He was a humble man, but I don't think he could ever find just the right name. My mother, on the other hand, had a few choice names for it." Chuck snickered fondly.

"Anyway, I remember the day that he took me out and told me he had cancer." His expression changed. "He wasn't scared, or sorry, or even resentful. He approached death the way he had approached everything. With honesty. You know, I may be old fashion, but I think kids need to see their father . . . ," Chuck glanced across the lobby and saw Patti with her arm around Aaron as they headed to the elevators, ". . . or their mother set a good example. If they're not honest, then their kids won't be either. Plain and simple. I don't profess to know what happened between Alan and Cain, but the apple seems to have fallen fairly close to the tree."

They watched the woman across the lobby who had come forward with the truth at great risk to herself and to her son. "She's the real hero," Chuck said with the experience to know. Jake nodded as Patti and Aaron disappeared around a corner.

"What ever happened to the boat?" Jake asked.

"Huh?" Chuck responded looking back over at him.

"The sailboat. What happened to your father's sailboat?"

"Oh, he passed it down to me in his will. And wouldn't you know it, he left me a note asking me to finally give it a name that it deserved."

"What did you name it?"

Chuck smiled. "Fatherly Advice."

* * *

"Cain, this is Jake Morgan. I got your email and I'd like to meet briefly to talk about it." Jake spoke into the speaker phone in the middle of the table in the war room. Chuck and Alex were huddled on the other side of the table listening motionless.

"Uh, no can do, sorry Jake. I'm on my way out of town. How about getting together in a week or so?"

"Well, that's a little too late. As you know, SouthPoint has a shareholder meeting tomorrow morning and I really need to talk to you about your resignation before then. It shouldn't take long." Jake glanced up at his team hoping his sales pitch would work.

"Look, I'd like to help you, but I said what I needed to say in my email."

Jake could feel the stress rising inside. He somehow had to get Cain to meet him. Thomas already was in the air on his way to Miami, and there now were too many loose ends to wrap up the investigation. He had to think of something.

"I really appreciate your email. SouthPoint appreciates it, and its stockholders will appreciate it. I know that it was not easy to send, and I can only imagine the pressure that you've been under. But, there are some questions that I need to ask you and some documents I need to show you so that we can fully understand exactly what happened. I'm sure you know about SouthPoint's obligations as a public company under Sarbanes-Oxley."

"I'm not as familiar with the law as you are, but I know that I'm a whistleblower and that I have protections. I'm in my car on my way to the airport to get away for a while. I'll call you when I get back and maybe we can meet then."

Jake cringed expecting to hear Cain hang up, but the line stayed open. He could see the tension on Chuck's face as the clay pigeon they were aiming was flying through their sights. Jake quickly refocused and fired again.

"Cain, hold on. Under Sarbanes-Oxley, if you want whistleblower protection, Section 806(b)(2)(i) requires that the claimant, being you, submit to an interview within twenty-four hours of the complaint so that the company can assess the allegations and try to remedy the fraud as soon as possible. I'm afraid that if you don't meet with me, you're not entitled to whistleblower protection and you can't get a monetary award for being a whistleblower. I'd sure hate to see that happen after all you've been through."

Alex glanced over at Jake with a puzzled look. He had studied the statute from start to finish in law school and didn't remember anything about a required meeting in twenty-four hours after a complaint. Alex shrugged his shoulders at Jake and mimicked a silent "huh?"

Jake winked at him signaling back that he was bluffing Cain. He had to take the chance that Cain didn't know the finer points of the law. The four of them held their breath and starred at the phone.

After what seemed like minutes, Cain finally responded. "Uh, well . . . I guess I could meet you."

Jake pumped his fist in silence as his team quietly cheered.

"I have a few things to do first, but, uh, I can meet you at the Marriott on Brickell Avenue. The lobby bar. Can you be there in an hour?"

"Give me an hour and a half, and I'll be there." Jake added just enough time to swoop up Thomas at the executive airport and to race downtown.

"Alright, but I'll only have a few minutes or so."

As soon as the line went dead on the speaker phone, Jake sprung into action calling the play like a quarterback in a huddle

"Okay, we have forty-five minutes before I have to meet Thomas. Alex, give me a report on what you were able to connect between Zapplication and ICon's charge backs. Where's Sarah? Did she find out anything about that legal settlement that Patti remembered?"

"Yup, she did. I can tell you about it. She's down in the business center using one of the computers because all these are tied up. She's trying to finish up the project that Chuck gave her about the escrow payments."

"Okay, good. So then Kyle, after Alex, I want to hear about what you found on the hard drives."

Alex eagerly teed up his notes and readied himself to take the first swing. His youthful energy radiated the thrill of fitting together the pieces of the puzzle.

"First, remember what I told you about Section 36(b) of the contract with Visa. ICon had to keep its monthly charge backs under two percent of the total transactions. That means that the number of charge backs in a month over the total number of total transactions in the month can't exceed two percent. If it does, Visa will impose huge penalties on ICon, and they can terminate ICon entirely if they don't get back under two percent in sixty days. According to the spreadsheets we saw attached to those emails to Alan, ICon's charge back ratio started exceeding that amount about ten months ago."

"So, right after those emails, guess what new client comes on line?" Alex paused for a second and continued before anyone could answer. "Zapplication. And right after the Zapplication transactions started, ICon's charge back ratio dropped below two percent each month. So then I calculated what ICon's charge back ratio would've been without Zapplication, and it would've blown the threshold every month. There's no doubt to me that your theory is right. Zapplication was just a front to manipulate ICon's charge back ratio."

Jake glanced over at Chuck with well-deserved deference. "Chuck deserves the credit for cracking the case. We couldn't have done it without him."

Chuck nodded humbly and there was a recognition of gratitude between them.

"Okay, what about that settlement?"

"Here's what Sarah found." Alex pulled out a short stack of documents. "There isn't any settlement noted in the income statement, but in the footnotes to the financials there's a reference to a case in Dade County, Florida that ICon apparently settled in the second quarter of last year. *Vitek.com v. Internet Connections, Inc.* It was for $2.1 million, which is the exact same amount as that initial penalty that Visa charged ICon for the first charge back violation. Sarah accessed the court's online docket and there is no case with that name or any case against ICon. There also is nothing on the Internet for a Vitek.com. We think that the settlement is just a cover up to hide the Visa penalty so that SouthPoint wouldn't find it."

Kyle could not wait any longer to announce what he found. "I think that I found the connection to the credit card numbers issued from the bank in Andorra that Zapplication used for the stress test transactions."

The others all looked over at him intrigued by his dramatic teaser.

"I forensically accessed the deleted portions of the hard drives that we copied. For the most part, there were just unintelligible fragments. But I did find an email that Troy deleted right before Zapplication came online. It was in the slack space on his hard drive, so I know that he double deleted it after he got it. I'm sure that he figured it was long gone."

Kyle pulled out a single sheet of paper and slid it across the table to Jake. Chuck leaned over and read it along with Jake. It was an email to Troy that he received at 2:37 a.m. from r.ramon@yahoo.com. The email read in its entirety: *Just left the bank, I got the card numbers.* It was the email that Raul had sent seven months ago after he left the Banca D'Andorra.

Kyle continued. "I checked, and there is no one with the last name of Ramon on ICon's employee list. So we searched all of Troy's emails for any other emails from r.ramon@yahoo.com. We found an old email that Troy sent to a group of people, including r.ramon@yahoo.com, that had directions to a wedding reception. I thought maybe I'd get lucky, so I Googled 'ramon' and 'wedding.'"

Kyle grinned trying to hold back the excitement of his discovery. "Here's what I found."

He handed Jake the print out of a wedding announcement from two years prior. A smiling couple was standing in a gazebo overlooking a sunset that was hovering just above the horizon behind them. Underneath the photograph read "Mr. and Mrs. Raul Ramon."

Jake read aloud the first part of the announcement. "Ms. Brittany Vickerson and Mr. Raul Ramon were united in marriage at Carillion Beach, Florida. The wedding ceremony was performed at sunset on the beach and was followed by a garden reception. The bridal party included maid of honor Jessica Wellington and best man Troy Vickerson, the bride's brother."

Jake looked up quickly as he realized the connection. "Jesus. This Ramon guy is Troy's brother in law. Ramon is Web Assist, he's the one who got the credit card numbers."

"But Troy got that email at 2:37 a.m.," Chuck noted. "Ramon's email says that he just left the bank, but the bank would have been closed at that time in the morning."

"Maybe the time of email was changed somehow because it was being sent internationally?" Jake guessed.

"Nah, it shouldn't unless there was a server problem," Kyle answered.

They all sat silent trying to figure out the inconsistency.

Alex suddenly remembered what Mick had shown them on Velocity. "Time zones!" he blurted out. "Remember what Mick said about the Asian websites. Troy got the email at 2:37 a.m., but Central European Time is, uh, six hours ahead of Eastern Time. It would've been 8:37 in the morning in Andorra when the email was sent. He must've just left the bank in Andorra with the card numbers."

"Damn good work," Chuck said to the excited associate.

Alex and Kyle high-fived over the table, and then Alex blushed a little at his over exuberance.

"Alex, were you able to quantify what the penalty would be if there were no Zapplication transactions?" Jake asked.

"It's pretty complicated under the agreement," he began, "but assuming that there were no offsets from Zapplication, ICon most likely would've been charged at least five million dollars each month, and then it could've been terminated by Visa after the second month."

"Goodness," Chuck said in his deep voice. "That would've been the end of ICon. The company would've been worthless."

"So instead," Jake followed the train of thought, "they concocted this scheme to cover up the charge backs from the cross-sell scam on Modos' websites, and then they turned around and sold the company to SouthPoint for $750 million. Unbelievable."

After a short pause, Alex asked the question that was on all of their minds. "Do you think SouthPoint should've found it in due diligence before the deal?"

Jake tensed at hearing the question said out loud. He knew that he would have to be able to answer it. It was his job to follow the truth no matter where it took him, even if the path led into SouthPoint's wood-paneled executive suite. If it did, he prayed that it passed right by the General Counsel's door, especially because he was about to pick up his friend at the airport. Thinking about what Cain might say made him uneasy, but thinking about Thomas being there made him worried.

"I hope not," Jake answered and exhaled with a sigh. "But we're on our way to find out."

Jake gestured to Chuck. "It's that time, let's go pick up Thomas."

Jake turned and began loading his briefcase with some documents. He didn't see the brief look of disappointment on Alex's face when Chuck was recruited to come instead of him. Chuck noticed it, however. Alex corralled his files and he and Kyle walked over to the computers.

"Uh, Jake," Chuck began, "why don't you take the kid?"

Jake looked up from his briefcase at Chuck, who continued his pitch.

"He's done a great job and I've got a feeling that this is going to be a memorable interview. I've been on my share of them. Besides, Alex takes much better notes than I do."

Jake grinned as he imagined the thrill that he would've had when he was Alex's age to be the wingman on a jet-fueled investigation. Without a doubt, Alex was an ace and he deserved being in the cockpit.

"That's a good idea," Jake said. As Chuck turned, Jake added "And that's a real nice gesture from you." Chuck nodded back and strolled over to the coffee station.

"Alex," Jake called across the room. Alex turned from his conversation. "Wanna go on a ride?"

Alex's face lit up. "Awesome," he said and scampered over with a stack of papers under his arm.

* * *

Sarah froze as she starred at the Excel spreadsheet on the computer in the hotel's business center. She had checked and re-checked the data. She ran the calculation three times, and even checked the Excel formulas. Everything was correct, except that the account did not reconcile. There was money missing, and a lot of it.

She scanned the small business center, which was lined with computer terminals. Only two other people were in the room, and both had their back to her as they busily typed away on email. She walked over to a table with a printer and a house phone. She looked around to make sure she couldn't be overheard, and she quickly dialed the number for Wingmaster's conference room.

"Hello."

"Alex, is Sarah. Has Jake left yet?"

"No, but he and I are packing up to go meet Cain. Are you done?"

She took a deep breath. "Yeah. Meet me in front of the business center on your way out. I have something for you guys." She went back to the computer terminal that she was using and printed the spreadsheet.

As she waited for Jake and Alex to pass the glass door of business center, she began tapping her pen unconsciously. Her wire rim glasses stood sturdy on her thin nose, and her lips pursed with anxiety. She couldn't believe what she had found.

"Uh, *excuse* me." A woman across the room swiveled in her chair at Sarah's insistent tapping.

"Oh, I'm sorry." Sarah put the pen in her purse, slightly embarrassed. The minutes dragged.

She finally exhaled when she saw Jake motioning towards her from the hallway. Sarah snatched up a manila folder and walked out of the business center.

"You gotta see this," she said handing the folder to Jake. "There's something else you need to know."

Jake flipped open the cover of the manila folder and quickly scanned the first document. Sarah dangled as she waited for a reaction.

He glanced up at her. "Are you sure about this?" His forehead creviced as his eyes scanned her face for any doubt.

She was confident. "Yes. I'm sure. And behind the spreadsheet are the bank account records that we got this morning. There's over four million dollars missing."

"Geez, that's all we need. Okay, thanks Sarah." He buried the evidence into his briefcase. He turned to leave hurriedly, but then he stopped and looked back at her.

"Sarah. Great job."

She nodded dutifully and watched as they marched off.

The business center was quiet after Sarah and her nervous pen walked out. She was outside talking in the hallway when the man at the other computer terminal peered around. It was Taras. He glared at the three lawyers talking outside the room. He quickly turned his face so that they would not recognize him from the night before when he was chasing them in South Beach. His jaw clenched as the anger simmered that he had not completed his assignment. Ivan told him that he couldn't touch the lawyers, but he would use them and not miss again.

Taras looked over at the empty chair in front of the computer that Sarah was using. Her documents were strewed about, but the computer screen still displayed the Excel spreadsheet that she had printed. He glanced again towards the hallway. She was still talking with the other lawyers.

He stood and peered over at the only other person in the room. The woman who had been annoyed by Sarah was now laughing at her screen as she read an email. He again checked the hallway and saw the young associate hand a folder to one of the other lawyers. Taras quickly walked over to Sarah's terminal and motioned the mouse to print the Excel spreadsheet that was still on the computer screen.

Just as the printer began to activate, Sarah burst back into the business center towards her terminal. She hastily gathered up her documents. Taras stood nonchalantly at the printer table with his back to her as she logged off of the computer.

She looked around to make sure that she had collected everything, and then she hurriedly crossed the business center towards the door. Taras rotated so that she couldn't see his face. As she rushed out with an armful of documents, she had no idea that she passed within just a few feet of a professional killer for Bratva.

As the door to the hotel business center closed behind her, a copy of the Excel spreadsheet squeezed out of the printer. Taras reached for it and as he read the spreadsheet his stone-clenched lips turned barely upwards in a grin. The information confirmed Ivan's suspicions. There would be hell to pay.

CHAPTER NINETEEN

Large puffy clouds crawled slowly across the blue sky as Jake gazed upwards and shielded the sun from his face. He was standing on the tarmac of the executive airport next to the car, and Alex sat inside preparing for the interview with Cain. A flock of tiny black birds raced across the runway like squirrels daring to cross a street. Just as the last bird passed flapping feverously to catch the others, Jake saw a glimmer of light reflect from SouthPoint's plane.

The sleek jet seemed to just barely be inching closer, but it was flying at over four hundred miles per hour. As it descended towards the runway, its landing gear extracted and reached out for the runway. In less than a minute, the plane hovered above the concrete and the tires cast off a puff of smoke as they touched the surface. The engines of the plane whirled in reverse, and it began to slow to a cruising speed as it passed on the runway. The jet turned and maneuvered back down the palm-tree lined runway and across the tarmac, stopping adjacent to Jake standing next to the car. After a few minutes the door opened and Thomas pounced down the steps with his briefcase in tow.

"Welcome back to paradise," Jake said in jest extending his hand.

"It feels more like purgatory. When are we meeting with Cain?" Thomas asked.

"In about thirty minutes. The Marriott downtown. And I've got something new to show you on the way. You're not going to like it."

"Great," he said sarcastically, "the hits keep coming."

They got into the car and raced off of the tarmac towards Miami.

Even for a quiet Sunday, the lobby bar at the Marriott was unusually slow. Just a few weary business travelers were sharing a drink and watching a baseball game drag endlessly into the twelfth inning.

"I don't see him," Jake said looking around the bar. "Let's sit over there."

He pointed to an empty corner of the bar where a low marble table was surrounded by four chairs.

As they approached the table, Jake patted Thomas on the back. "Hey Thomas, let me ask you something." Thomas turned and Jake gestured to the side for a private conversation. "Alex, I need to mention something to Thomas. If Cain comes, tell him we'll be right back."

"Sure," Alex nodded and walked over to the marble table.

Jake led Thomas to a secluded corner of the bar. "Look, you know that you're technically not my client. The Board of Directors is my client and you're really not supposed to be in these interviews. I mean, hell, you were at the table negotiating the ICon deal and it's about to blow up. It's going to get messy, Thomas, and you're likely to be a witness if any of this ends up in court. You're not supposed to be hearing what other witnesses are saying."

Thomas started to protest, but Jake interrupted. "Hold on, hold on. Let me finish. I've known you for a long time, and I don't think for a minute that you knew what was going on down here. But you didn't hire me just to do a job. You could've recommended anyone for that. You hired me to do the job *right*, and you knew that I would do it in the right way. And the right way is to doubt everyone."

Thomas looked away as Jake's words set in. "You knew that I would have to doubt you," Jake said sternly.

Jake glanced over Thomas' shoulder across the bar to see if Cain had arrived, but Alex was still sitting alone at the table. Jake turned back to him.

"So before we go over there, consider this your interview." Thomas looked at Jake realizing that his friend was giving him the chance to talk off of the record. No *Upjohn* warning. No associate taking notes. No interview memorandum. Just old colleagues talking.

Thomas looked Jake straight in the eye. "I told the Board to hire you because I *knew* that you would doubt me. I knew that because we were friends, you would have to look at me harder than anyone or else *your* credibility would be questioned. I also knew that when you cleared me, it would mean more than if anyone else was on the job. I knew that I'd have to answer your questions Jake," he said decisively, "I just thought that at least you'd have the decency to let me sit down in a comfortable chair and maybe a even giving bottle of water, instead of cornering me in a hotel bar." He smiled and winked at Jake relaxing the tension.

Jake smirked back. "Okay, fair enough. One question for now. Did anyone at SouthPoint know about or even suspect the extent of ICon's adult entertainment client base?"

"We didn't know for sure," Thomas said positively. "But Gary and I suspected that there could be a possibility of it. ICon was supposed to be different from the other payment processors. You know, the internet connection for mom and pop websites – only mainstream websites. That was Alan's pitch. I told our team to look for porn clients but they didn't find anything, at least in the diligence that they did. I wanted to conduct another week of due diligence, but the Board nixed it. McMillan said that there wasn't enough time because he wanted the deal closed before the shareholder meeting so that the stock price would peak. His two cronies on the board, Richards and Martin, are both up for re-election and they're being challenged by a faction of the Board. If the stock price is down, the directors take the blame, and if Richards and Martin got voted off the Board, McMillan would lose his majority and probably his Chairmanship. He needed SouthPoint to buy ICon – and fast. Regardless of whether it was a good deal."

Thomas looked around and then back to Jake. "I was uneasy from the very first time we came down here. And then at the dinner after the closing, Cain mentioned something to me about a big client that Troy had recently brought in, but I didn't see that anywhere in the diligence. There were just a lot of holes that we hadn't been able to fill because of the expedited schedule. Between you and me, I was close to resigning because of it. But as the general counsel of a public company, the Bank probably would have had to issue a press release about my resignation, especially if I refused to sign any certifications. And that would've drawn a lot of unnecessary attention right before the deal. So I did what any other lawyer would do in my situation. I made sure that the Board knew that I was against the deal, and I held my breath."

Jake glanced over and saw Cain walk into the bar. He was in jeans and a t-shirt, with his sunglasses straddling the top of his head. He looked like he hadn't shaved in days. Jake motioned to Thomas, who turned to see ICon's former lawyer scanning the bar. Cain saw Alex sitting in the corner and made his way through the tables towards him.

"You're going to let me handle this, right?" Jake asked Thomas, who visibly tensed at seeing Cain.

Thomas turned back towards his friend. "Well, since I'm technically not your client, you're technically not my lawyer."

Jake sneered at him. "Smart ass."

They made their way over to the table where Cain and Alex were sitting. Cain stood as they approached and they all shook hands. Alex readied his pen and pad in anticipation while they settled in. Jake began their final interview with Cain.

"Cain, as I'm sure you know, your email raises serious issues about whatever is going on at ICon. You apparently have some degree of knowledge about it, and it sounds like you also have some degree of involvement in it. I appreciate what you said in your email, but what we really need you to do is to tell us everything you know. No more hiding, no more lying."

Cain looked back defiantly at the three of them. In his jeans, he appeared younger and rougher. His thick arms stretched the sleeves of his t-shirt, and he wore black boots that looked old and bruised. He was not the polished pin-striped executive they had watched perform in Alan's office earlier that week. Instead, he seemed ragged, unprepared.

"Okay, but I'm a whistleblower, right? Since I'm meeting with you I get protection, right?"

Jake was not about to answer those questions and he did not blink in his response. "That's not my decision and I wouldn't tell you even if it was. Now, since you only have a few minutes, may I suggest that you start talking?"

Cain looked over at Alex and at Thomas, but he found no ally. He was alone and he knew it. He took a deep breath and started from the beginning.

"A couple of years ago, we were doing fine. ICon was in the middle tier of the industry and our revenue was moving the needle forward a little bit each year. We were just starting to get our legs, when the consolidation craze hit. It was like our sleepy little industry suddenly popped up on Wall Street's radar. All of the biggest financial institutions began swooping in and buying up our competitors. E-Exchange was bought for $600 million. Axis went for $925 million. I know the guys who started Axis. They were a couple of schmucks who used to work for ICon. They financed their start up with credit cards, and sold the company for $925 million. It was unreal." Cain paused to reflect. "But ICon didn't get any offers."

"Why not?" Jake asked.

Cain glanced over at Thomas. "He'll tell you. ICon's revenues were too low. About $50 million per year. It wasn't until ICon hit $250 million that I got a call from SouthPoint."

Thomas didn't like being part of Cain's story, and he peered hard at his former employee. "That's because you lied about the revenues, didn't you?" he barked at Cain, who scowled back at him.

Jake turned to Thomas. "Easy. Let me ask the questions."

Thomas clenched his jaw and eased back in the plush bar chair. His outburst was intended more as a show of frustration, than part of the inquiry. Cain could feel the heat of Thomas' glare as he continued.

"The revenues were *real* alright," he said flashing a cool stare at Thomas. "The problem was that we couldn't increase them enough to sell the company without getting into porn. And that's where Troy came in. He hooked up somehow with a huge player in the porn business. I told my father not to do it, but, well, let's just say that he doesn't always listen to me." There was a noticeable edge of a scorned son.

"But you did more than just object," Jake said, "you took part in the cover up, right? You helped conceal the adult business from SouthPoint during due diligence."

"I never lied to anyone. No one ever asked me about the client basc."

"Bullshit," Thomas blurted.

Alex looked up from his notes, surprised by the expletive. Jake kept his eyes locked on Cain, but he raised his hand up towards Thomas to signal that was enough.

"The fraud wasn't in hiding the porn," Cain snapped back. "SouthPoint could've figured that out if they took the time to look hard enough. How else did they think that ICon's revenues increased that much in just one year? The market for payment processing for mainstream websites was only increasing by about thirty percent, but the competitors for that business were doubling every six months. There were too many fish in the pond for mainstream sites to make real money. Anyone who knows the industry knows that porn was the only way to generate that kind of increase in revenue."

Cain glanced over at Alex to make sure that he was getting it all in his notes, and he continued his diatribe. "The fact is that SouthPoint didn't care *how* we made the money, they just wanted a piece of it so that they didn't get left behind. SouthPoint needed the deal just as bad as ICon did."

Thomas grunted, but held his tongue as Jake pressed on. "Okay. Tell me what fraud you were referring to in your email."

"Zapplication," Cain said. "Troy came up with the idea for the website to cover up the excessive charge backs that the porn sites were generating. There were no real transactions. No customers. No stress testing. That was the fraud. I didn't want any part of that, but they made me do it."

"Before we get to that. How did the Zapplication scheme work?"

"Alan and Troy met near the end of each month and they ran a report showing the charge back levels. They'd figure out how many transactions were needed to bring the ratio under the credit card companies' limits. It was simple math. And then they would just run a program that batched the transactions from Zapplication to ICon."

"Who wrote the program?"

"A guy named Bill Dixon. He was a senior programmer at ICon before he was . . . before he died."

"We heard that he was in a car accident."

"Well, I'm not so sure it was an accident."

"Why? What do you think happened to him?"

"I think he found out too much about what was going on. Those porn sites are not run by nice people if you know what I mean. That's why I told my father to stay away from Troy and his clients, but did he listen to me?" Cain asked rhetorically.

"So that's why I didn't, why I couldn't, come forward? I was scared. They forced me to stay quiet. That's why I finally had to resign."

"Then why are you talking now?"

Cain paused, knowing that the question was coming. "I . . . I just couldn't take lying any more." He blinked hard as if trying to hold back tears. "Not for my father, and not for myself. I've been a wreck. You have no idea how hard it is to keep something like this inside. Especially since it goes against everything they teach us in law school." He rubbed his forehead to demonstrate the stress.

Thomas exhaled loudly with skepticism and shifted in the chair. He was not buying Cain's performance for a minute. Jake's job, however, was to keep a poker face so that the witness thinks that his story is being believed, at least until the admission-seeking questions were launched and the trap was sprung. Jake was holding back for just a few more minutes. He needed to get a little more information. Just a couple more questions, and then Jake would pull out the ace up his sleeve.

"Who knows about the real purpose of Zapplication?"

Cain looked towards the floor, still acting distressed by his confession. He knew that there was no turning back now. To save himself, he had to sacrifice others. Even his own father.

With his eyes drawn down, he answered. "Alan, Troy, his brother-in-law Raul Ramon, and Mick. Like I said, Bill probably figured out what was going on too."

"Ramon was the one who got the credit card numbers?" Jake pressed.

"Yup."

"How?"

"He has connections somehow. Troy said that he used to be in the DEA. I don't know if that's true or not, but he was able to get the numbers from banks in Spain, Andorra, and in Antigua. I didn't ask how he did it 'cause I didn't want to know."

"What about Jane? Did she know?"

Jake flashed back to the chill during her interview at Stein, Thomas, & Howard. Her lawyer had been so confident as Jane coolly skated through the interview with all of her rehearsed answers. In the pampered conference room overlooking Biscayne Bay, Jake had felt like a pawn on a chessboard between two bishops whose grooves were turned slightly upwards as if grinning at him. This was now the moment of reckoning for her.

Cain looked up at Jake slowly. "Yes, she knew. She was the one who insisted that the revenue be written off, and she was the one who created the fake expense account on the income statement for the stress testing. She knew alright." He seemed to take the most pleasure in outing her.

Jake's anger seeped through his façade as his forehead cringed. He was used to being lied to, it happened in every investigation. But she had acted so pompous and so demeaning to him and the process. By fraudulently misstating ICon's financial statements, she violated much more than the civil provisions in Sarbanes-Oxley. Jake would enjoy making the phone call to tell Neal Stein that his client now needed advice about criminal liability.

"Okay Cain, I want a simple 'yes' or 'no,'" Jake said firmly. "Did anyone at SouthPoint know about the extent of the adult business?"

Thomas glared at Cain as he hedged, hesitated, and then finally answered. "No."

Did anyone at SouthPoint know that ICon was doing business with organized crime?"

"No."

"Did anyone at SouthPoint know about the real purpose of Zapplication?"

Cain looked at the three of them, and again reluctantly responded. "No."

A knot that had been tightening inside Jake began to untangle with those three answers. He didn't show it on his face, but a wave of relief washed over him. If Cain had implicated SouthPoint, whether true or not, the accusation would have escalated the entire investigation. Jake would've had to move his war room north from the hotel in Miami into the Bank's headquarters in Atlanta, and he would've had to start a second front of the investigation. Cain's story didn't exonerate SouthPoint from rushing too fast into the deal, but there was no evidence that the Bank was involved in or knew about the fraud. SouthPoint's steeped foundation might now be chipped by ICon, but hopefully it would not crumble.

Jake eased back in his chair and leaned over to Thomas to whisper in his ear. "I think that's all we need on that."

Thomas nodded and whispered back. "Ok. Time to hit him with the other thing."

Jake reached down into his briefcase and pulled out the manila folder that Sarah gave him. He opened the cover and glanced inside, shielding the contents from Cain. Cain looked cautiously at Jake and Alex not knowing what was coming.

"Cain, just one last thing."

Jake pulled out the spreadsheet and laid it on the table in front of Cain. As Cain anxiously scanned the document, Jake summarized the conclusion in one dramatic conclusion.

"We know that you embezzled over four million dollars from ICon."

The charge raced like a shock through Cain. He began to fidget and flush as Jake pointed at the spreadsheet. "This column shows every time that you instructed that client funds be wired to National Escrow Services to be escrowed purportedly because the client was violating the credit card companies' decency standards. And this column shows every time those funds were returned once the sites were cleaned up. There's a difference of \$4.23 million that never came back to ICon."

Cain bucked up and snapped back. "So what? For all I know, that money is still in National Escrow's bank account. I don't have any control over it. You can't prove that I stole anything." His head was starting to spin.

"You're lying Cain," Jake said firmly. "SouthPoint filed a lawsuit on Thursday morning and got an emergency subpoena for National Escrow's bank records. We got them this morning hand delivery."

Jake opened up the manila folder and removed the remaining documents. Alex looked on wide-eyed, too enthralled to continue taking notes. Thomas just sat back and stared at Cain, relishing in the moment. Cain turned white.

Jake placed each of the bank records in front of Cain, identifying each one as he placed them on the table.

"This is the account opening form for National Escrow's account at Florida South Bank. And this is the signature card signed by only one person, the purported President of National Escrow . . . a Mr. Cain Arnold. That's your signature, isn't it Cain?" Jake peered across the table at Cain, who sat there frozen without looking up.

"And lastly, there are these." Jake laid the documents down slowly for dramatic effect. "Four wire transfer receipts totaling \$4.23 million sent to a numbered bank account in the Caymans. And, once again, those are your signatures, right?"

For a moment, the table with the four men in the corner of the bar was eerily quiet. Time stopped. It was a moment that no one at that table will ever forget.

Then suddenly, Cain exploded. "Fuck you! You tricked me into coming here." He yelled and he stood up quickly. He swept the documents off of the table and they flittered around as he turned knocking over the chair next to him.

"You stole from your own client Cain. Did they teach you that in law school?" Jake called out to him as Cain stormed away holding up his arm and prominently displaying his middle finger.

The three of them watched ICon's former lawyer stomp out of the bar. The few other patrons turned to see what had caused the commotion, and then returned to their conversations.

Jake turned to Alex who was still a bit shell shocked at the way the interview concluded. "Now *that's* how to ask a question," he winked to his associate and began to gather the strewed documents.

Alex was gazing at the swath that Cain had left as a waiter cautiously approached the table to size up the situation. The papers were spread out on the marble table, and Cain's chair was lying on its side from his hasty departure.

"Uh . . . is everything alright? Can I get you guys something?" he asked warily.

"Yes," Jake said, "to both of your questions."

Jake and Alex ordered a drink, and the waiter turned to Thomas who was still focused far away from the table.

"Sir?" the waiter asked Thomas again.

"Yeah, I'll take a Crown on the rocks."

Just then Thomas' cell phone range. He pulled it from his jacket pocket and looked at the screen. It was McMillan.

Thomas was expecting him to call. When he had rushed out of Atlanta that morning to meet Jake, he had been in a grueling meeting with McMillan. They were arguing about what to say at the shareholder meeting about the ICon investigation. McMillan's opinion was that the investigation was still ongoing and that any public disclosure about it would be premature, but Thomas was worried that SouthPoint knew enough already and that not saying anything could amount to a fraudulent omission. To disclose or not to disclose is the daily dilemma of securities lawyers.

Just before Thomas raced down to Miami, he and McMillan had agreed on a tentative statement that they could both live with. *The integration of ICon into SouthPoint is in the process of being completed, and there is an internal review taking place to determine whether any purchase price adjustments are appropriate.* Interpreted into non-lawyer speak, the statement meant that now that SouthPoint owned and controlled ICon, it was determining whether the price it paid for ICon was appropriate. "Internal review" was a watered down term for investigation. The script was the product of a two hour long negotiation between them, but in the end, it was mostly true, and purposefully vague.

Since he touched down in Miami, however, Thomas had learned enough about the fake stress testing and the cross-sell scheme to know that SouthPoint had been misled and had grossly overpaid for ICon. There was little doubt in his mind that that information was material, and there was *no* doubt in his mind that SouthPoint could now not make the agreed upon statement that McMillan wanted. SouthPoint's shareholders would have to be told.

The phone rang again in Thomas' hand. Before he answered it, he called out to the waiter who was about to walk away.

"Excuse me, you better make mine a double." He turned to Jake and Alex. "This isn't going to be fun."

They watched as Thomas shrugged to the bar to answer the phone.

"So how did Cain think that he would get away with taking the money that he escrowed?" Alex asked Jake.

"Because he was stealing from criminals," Jake explained. "Most of the funds that he escrowed were from the Modos websites because those sites were showing things that were banned. And he had authority under the contract to do that - at least theoretically - until the websites removed the illegal content. But, he must've realized that if ICon didn't return it Modos wouldn't file a lawsuit or go to the police to get its money back because the funds were proceeds from criminal conduct. So he formed National Escrow as a dummy escrow company and then began sending escrowed money to the account."

"I don't know how he figured out which websites were run by Modos, but in all, there was nearly five million dollars that he escrowed. The bank statements that we got for the National Escrow account show that Cain treated it as his own personal expense account. On top of the money that he wired out to the Caymans, he spent tens of thousands of dollars in clothing, electronics, trips, and night clubs. He even wrote a check out of the account for a new car. He was really living the high life. Until, that is, we came down and raided ICon. Look at the date and time of these wire receipts. He sent the four million dollars to the Caymans about an hour after we first met with all of the executives and told them about the investigation. I bet that after our meeting he went right back to his office and made the transfer."

"So how come no one at ICon noticed the escrows?"

"There were almost no internal controls. Sarah found a bunch of emails from Cain to an accounting clerk instructing her to wire various amounts to National Escrow. There were no other sign offs or approvals, and there was no separation of duties. He controlled the amounts going in and he directed the amounts going out. In fact, there was one email from the accounting clerk asking Cain who she could contact at National Escrow because she had a question about some of the wires. He told her that as ICon's lawyer he was the only one allowed to communicate with National Escrow. That was an obvious red flag, but she didn't do anything because he is the President's son."

"Man, he stole from his own father's company," Alex realized. "Can you imagine?"

"And it's no wonder that he came clean about the stress testing scheme. I'm sure that once he realized that we were investigating Zapplication, he was hoping that we would focus on the stress testing and miss his embezzlement. He threw his own father under the bus to try to get away with it. It's just unreal."

"So what happens to him?"

"It's up to the Board. SouthPoint has insurance that should cover the money that Cain stole. Then the Board will have to decide whether or not to inform the authorities."

"You mean if they don't Cain could get away with the money?" Alex asked looking concerned.

"Well I have a feeling that Cain is not going to get away from everyone. But if the company calls the police, the embezzlement could turn into a public embarrassment, especially for a bank. If it were up to me, I'd be on the phone with the FBI right now. But Thomas has a bigger problem. He's got to figure out what the Bank has to tell the thousands of shareholders at tomorrow's meeting. If the stock price drops just ten cents, there will be hundreds of millions of dollars in market capitalization that will vanish just like that." Jake snapped his fingers for effect.

"I don't know what's going on down there," he said watching Thomas bark into his phone, "but it doesn't look good."

Alex saw Thomas end the call with McMillan, and then slam his hand down on the bar causing his drink to hop. He trudged over to the corner table with his shoulders slouched as if he were carrying a weight on his back.

"McMillan is refusing to authorize any disclosure of the ICon mess at the meeting tomorrow. He thinks that it's premature since we don't know the full extent of the problem and we don't know what the real value of ICon is. It's suicide." He fell down in his chair and sighed audibly.

"Can he do that?" Alex asked.

"He's the Chairman of the Board and controls the majority," Thomas grumbled. He's made fortunes for those guys. They'll do whatever he tells them to do. I can probably get my arms around holding back the story about Cain – at least for a little while - but there's no way that management can talk about ICon and not tell them that they just learned that it paid $750 million for smoke and mirrors. I don't care what the actual value is, but it's clear that it's a shitload south of a quarter of a billion dollars. It would be securities fraud if the company paints a rosy picture of the ICon deal while investors are out there buying up the stock." Just saying that out loud wrenched his stomach.

"Jake, you know me. I can't sit on the sidelines and watch that happen. I've got my own legal obligations as an officer of a public company, and I'll be damned if I'm going to put my neck or Gary's on the line for McMillan. I'll resign before that happens."

Thomas finished his drink and kept the glass tilted as he watched the last of the golden liquor slip off the ice. "I need you to come back to Atlanta with me tonight. Maybe he'll listen to you since you've seen it all first hand down here."

"Sure thing," Jake said. "I'll have Alex swing me by the hotel to get my stuff. If you want to grab a cab to the airport, I'll meet you at the plane in about an hour."

They all stood and began to gather their things. "Oh," Jake added, "do you have room for two more on the plane?"

"Sure," Thomas answered assuming that two of the Levi & Everett team were catching a lift home.

* * *

The thickening clouds glowed in an orange hue as the sun fell slowly from the sky. Tiny lights from the skyscrapers of downtown Miami started shimmering through the heavy Florida air. On the tarmac, SouthPoint's jet stood ready with its hatch open and steps extended. Alex guided the Mercedes through the gate of the executive airport and eased it onto the tarmac. He slowed to a stop next to the aircraft.

"Alex, make sure that all of the interview memos are taken care of, and have Kyle create a chain of custody for the hard drives, and Sarah needs to revise the spreadsheet so that it reflects the bank records we got today, and ask Chuck to evaluate what the reserve should be for the penalties that Visa is owed, and . . . ."

Alex interrupted his speeding mentor. "Whoa Jake, don't worry. I'll take care of everything. Look," Alex said holding up his Blackberry to Jake," you sent me three emails about all this on the way over here and you were sitting right next to me. It's all here," he said waving his phone in jest. "I got this."

Jake smirked and opened the door. "Yes, you do."

He extended his hand and they shook, no longer as a partner and an associate, but now as colleagues and friends. It was a brief moment, but it was memorable to both. Jake caught a glimmer of himself in Alex from a long time ago, and he realized he had come full circle.

From the back seat of the car, an excited young voice rang out. "Do we get to fly on that plane Mommy?" Aaron had his face plastered to the car window with excitement.

Patti was sitting with him in the back and she playfully rubbed his hair. "Yup, tiger." She had never flown on a corporate jet before, and she felt an odd mixture of anticipation and fright.

They all got out of the car and Jake led Patti and Aaron towards the plane. Thomas emerged from the open hatch and walked down the steps to greet them. The wind blew unimpeded across the runway and rushed around them.

"Cool!" Aaron yelled and broke free from his mother's grasp, charging up the steps of the plane. Thomas smiled as he watched the boy race past almost oblivious to him.

"Aaron," Patti called for him with little hope that it would stop his charge into the jet. "I'm sorry," she said to Thomas, who was pleasantly surprised that Jake's two extra travel companions were not more lawyers.

Jake made the introductions. "Thomas, this is Patti Tomanski. Patti, meet Thomas Nelson, General Counsel of SouthPoint." Patti smiled and shook Thomas' hand, but she was preoccupied at seeing Aaron disappear into the plane.

"Don't worry. I'll go make sure that he doesn't fly alone," Jake joked and walked up the steps into the plane.

Patti turned back to Thomas and chuckled. "Sometimes it's like he just doesn't even hear me."

Thomas smiled back. "Believe me, I have two girls in high school. Most times it's like they don't even *see* me."

It seemed like forever ago that Thomas was working late to finish up just one more employee exit questionnaire. He remembered the feeling of doom as he read Patti's meticulous handwriting warning of fake transactions at SouthPoint's newest acquisition. The nondescript post script at the end launched the internal investigation exposing a massive fraud at ICon, and unwittingly revealing a multi-million dollar embezzlement. As he had re-read her questionnaire over and over during that long night, he wondered who was behind the words.

Finally, standing in front of him was ICon's whistleblower. The person who had the courage to come forward to speak the truth, and to continue the progeny of Sherron Watkins at Enron and Cynthia Cooper at WorldCom, who both exposed massive frauds at great personal expense. Those are the kind of crusaders that Congress had in mind when it endowed federal protection for corporate whistleblowers. As he stood on the tarmac facing Patti, Thomas felt a sense of comfort that there are heroes among the heretics.

"I want to thank you on behalf of SouthPoint and its shareholders. Jake told me about all the help you've given us. You did the right thing, and I can imagine how hard it was."

"I'd like to think that anyone would've done what I did," she said humbly as she brushed her blowing hair out of her face.

"I'd like to think that too," he said, "but in my experience, that's usually not the case. That little guy in there sure has a good role model," Thomas added gesturing towards the airplane. "Anyway, I want you to know that SouthPoint is going to pay all your back salary from the date that you were terminated through the end of the year, and we're going to throw in a healthy thank you to make sure that you and your son land on your feet. If you're interested, we'd sure like you to come to work at SouthPoint when this is all over. We're always looking for good people."

Patti blinked hard fighting back a tear as the memory of the girl from Technyx came rushing forward. She might still be alive if someone like Thomas had been there. "Thank you Mr. Nelson. Thank you."

"Okay, then," he grinned. "After you." He extended his arm towards the plane.

As she passed him, she added, "And in my experience, I think you're setting a pretty good example yourself."

Thomas watched her climb the steps into the jet. For a moment, he gazed up at the darkening Florida sky. The palm trees were beginning to rustle in the increasing breeze. Jake had done his job. The fraud that Patti tipped off with the stroke of a pen was now revealed, and Cain's embezzlement had been discovered by a stroke of luck. Now, it was his job. He had to pilot SouthPoint through the oncoming turbulence and guide the company to fly within the law. It was going a bumpy ride.

CHAPTER TWENTY

Things gained through unjust fraud are never secure.
-- Sophocles

Cain slammed down the accelerator of his Corvette and it lurched into the oncoming lane of Highway U.S. 1. He sped past a lagging minivan that was heaving with luggage, and he swerved back into the right lane as the approaching headlights got nervously close. The 113 mile stretch of highway from Miami to Key West is known as the Overseas Highway. It hops from key to key and crosses over forty-two bridges heading south until it hits the southernmost tip of the United States. The last exit is Key West, a commune of sun drenched beach bums and waterlogged artisans. Its avenues overgrown with mangroves feel closer to a Caribbean island than to Miami's metropolis. Indeed, Key West is 154 miles from Miami, but only ninety miles from Cuba.

Cain glanced up in the rear view mirror and saw a string of headlights behind him. Ahead of him the highway vanished into darkness. Thick clouds hid the stars as they rode the winds of an oncoming storm. He flashed on his high beams and illuminated an additional fifty feet of endless pavement.

He reached for his cell phone and scrolled to send a text. *I'll be there in 1hr,* he typed with one hand. He checked his speed to confirm the timing, and sent the text. The rendezvous in Key West had been planned to take place an hour earlier, but he was running late because of the unexpected detour with Jake and Thomas. His anger over the confrontation subsided only after the painkillers he swallowed afterwards took effect. It didn't matter anyway. There was nothing that SouthPoint could do. The money was safe in an offshore account and he would be gone by morning. He eased back in the sculpted leather seat of the sports car and turned up the screaming guitars of Metallica on the compact disk.

A half mile behind Cain, a pair of headlights trailed the Corvette. Taras stared ahead at the red taillights that he had been following since Miami. The lawyers had led him to the Marriott where he waited until he saw Cain charge out of the hotel. His instructions were to find and follow Cain, and then to call Ivan for the completion of his assignment.

The sooner the better. With each mile marker that zoomed past, he was growing more and more frustrated at the distance he had to travel for this assignment. He took a long drag off of a cigarette and ashed it in the wind of his open window. Outside the storm clouds were brewing, and inside his anger was seething.

After nearly four hours of driving, Cain stood next to the car at his final destination and stretched. The winds were picking up in Key West, and the palms tress bowed in the breeze. He paid the parking lot attendant and crossed the narrow thoroughfare to Dale's Raw Bar. One of many timeless Jimmy Buffet tunes was repeating on the juke box as a nonchalant bartender leaned on the bar chatting with a couple of scruffy regulars.

Cain scanned the sparsely populated bar and saw his accomplice sitting alone at a table on the far side.

"Sorry I'm late, I had a few things to do before I could get out of Miami." He plopped down in a chair across the table. The table was still littered with a basket of empty crab shells and balled up napkins.

From beneath a faded Florida Marlins baseball cap, Mick looked up at his cohort. He was wearing baggy cargo shorts with docksiders and blended in inconspicuously with the bar's shaggy clientele.

"I was beginning to think that you spazzed on me," Mick said with an overt hint of frustration.

"Nah, I wouldn't have done that. C'mon man, we're partners."

"We *not* partners Cain," he said in an obviously annoyed tone. "I just wanted to get out."

"Yeah, get out and get rich," Cain smirked back. "You knew the risks. Now let's bask in the rewards."

Cain turned to look around the bar, and signaled to a waitress who slowly began to mosey over. He turned back to Mick with a smile.

"Don't look so worried, buddy. You're a millionaire now. And best of all, we stole it from the Russians! Now *that's* the American dream, huh?"

"Shhh!" Mick snapped back anxiously glancing around the bar. "Someone might hear you."

"Who? That beach bum over there? Or maybe that guy in the fishing hat is really an international Russian spy."

Cain was enjoying poking fun at him, and he was feeling the exuberance of the second round of painkillers he had just downed. Mick, however, was in no mood for levity.

The waitress finally sauntered over and Cain ordered a Red Stripe beer and a basket of conch fritters. She scribbled his order on a pad and started to meander back towards the bar.

"Excuse me," Cain called out loudly to the waitress so that everyone in the bar heard him. "The next round for everyone in the house is on me."

She shrugged unimpressed, but there were a few gracious hollers from the regulars at the bar. Cain was gleaming as he turned back to Mick who scowled at him.

"Are you crazy?!" Mick blurted and tried to shroud himself.

"Oh, calm down. No one knows us here. I'm just in the mood to celebrate."

"Well then wait until I'm gone. I don't trust anyone – and you shouldn't either. Do you think Modos is just going to let us walk away?"

"As far as they know, their money is still sitting in National Escrow's bank account. You and I are only one's who know about the Cayman account."

Cain didn't tell Mick about the confrontation he had with the investigators a few hours earlier, or the fact that they knew that National Escrow was a sham. Mick would've had a nervous breakdown and there was no telling what he might do. Cain continued to try to console his accomplice.

"Look, we had the right to escrow the money after you found all the bad shit on their websites. I'm sure that Modos wrote that off long ago. Believe me, they make so much money that they'll never miss a few million dollars. It was just the cost of doing business, right?"

Mick took a long swallow of his beer to calm his nerves. "I'll feel better after I get my money."

The waitress returned with Cain's beer and the tab for his round of drinks. After she left, Mick coaxed the last sip of beer from the brown bottle and wiped his hands on a frayed napkin.

"I hate to eat and run Cain, but I've got a plane to catch in a couple of hours. When are you going to Grand Cayman to get your share?"

"In a day or so. I think I'll take the leisurely route."

"Suit yourself, but I'm not sticking around. You got the account number."

Cain glanced around and reached into his pocket. He took out a folded slip of paper and tossed it across the table to Mick.

"Here ya go partner. There's four million dollars in there. Fifty fifty split."

Mick opened the slip of paper and saw a ten digit account number for an anonymous numbered account at First Cayman Financial. Below the secret account number was the password *stresstest*. Mick looked up and smirked at Cain's choice of passwords. He buried it into his front pocket and dropped a twenty dollar bill on the table.

He and Cain stood and shook hands. Behind the façade, they were never friends or really even colleagues. Circumstances had forced them together, but opportunity had created their conspiracy. Cain had the authority to escrow the money, but only Mick knew which were the Modos websites to hit. Each had their own justification for the larceny, but both were looking for a way out – and a way to cash out. While Ivan and Alan were focused on covering up Modos' charge backs, Cain and Mick quietly absconded with the escrowed funds.

As they parted ways they both knew that it would be the last time that they ever saw each other. That was the deal.

"See ya when I see ya," Mick said. And then he added omnisciently, "Watch your back Cain."

Cain watched as Mick walked out of the bar. He sat back down in the battered wooden chair and grinned to himself. If he was not going to inherit ICon, then he'd at least leave with a parting gift of a couple of million dollars.

The rain began to shower as Mick left the bar. He pulled his cap over his face and walked briskly down the empty street passing closed storefronts. He glanced behind him a couple of times to make sure that he wasn't being followed. His shoes sloshed in the puddles as he headed towards his car.

Up ahead he saw a black sedan parked on the opposite side of the road. He crossed the street and cautiously approached the car. He had one more deal to consummate – this one for his life.

The street lights reflected off of the dark windshield of the sedan and Mick couldn't tell if anyone was in the car. Just as he neared the car, the door opened and Taras stood up. He glared at Mick who froze in his tracks.

"Get in," he ordered.

Mick opened the passenger door on the sidewalk and looked both ways before reluctantly sitting down in the car. A smoky stench emanated from the bucket seats, and the floorboard was littered with empty coffee cups. Taras closed the door and looked over at Mick. The rain began to loudly smack the windshield.

"You have the information?" he said with his thick accent.

Mick nodded and reached into his back pocket. He was shaking and dripping as he handed him a folded piece of paper. Taras yanked it from Mick. He opened it up and saw that it contained the name of a bank with a ten digit account number and a password. He stuck the piece of paper in his pocket and reached into the console between them. He took out a Makarov handgun and a long cylindrical silencer. Mick's eyes widened and he began to helplessly fumble for the door handle.

"Wait, wait! I made a deal with Ivan last night. You have the account number," he stammered as he saw Taras screw a silencer into the barrel of the gun. "We had a deal - wait!"

Taras grunted and looked over at Mick, whose face was soaked with fear. He tried to cover his head in self-defense as Taras raised the menacing weapon. Mick cringed expecting the explosion any second.

"Get out!" he blurted at Mick.

Mick dropped his hands, but it took a second before he realized what Taras said.

He frantically turned and tugged open the door, tripping out of the car onto the slick sidewalk. He scrambled to his feet and backed away keeping his eyes on the black sedan. Taras got out of the car and buried the gun in the back of his jeans. He shut the car door and started walking in the rain towards Dale's Raw Bar. Mick stumbled backwards and turned to run in the opposite direction, disappearing around the corner.

After scampering four blocks, Mick stopped under a store canopy and bent over to catch his breath. He was breathing hard as he took off his drenched cap and wiped away the rain from his face. The adrenaline was still pumping through his veins and he took several deep breaths to try to calm his nerves. A few minutes and several deep breaths later, he stood up and leaned back against the store front. The dark street suddenly was illuminated with a flash and a deep clap of thunder shook the sky.

Mick glanced both ways down the tree-lined street of Key West. He reached into his front pocket and pulled out the slip of paper that Cain had given him in the bar. He slowly grinned as water from his hat dripped down his face. By the time that Ivan realized that he had given Taras a phony Swiss bank account number, Mick would be long gone. And as Bratva's assassin was bearing down on Cain, Mick would no longer have to share the wealth. With a new identity and four million dollars in his pocket, he would vanish into anonymity.

He brought the slip of paper to his lips and gently kissed his winning lottery ticket. Again, he looked both ways down the street and returned the slip to his pocket. He pulled his cap back over his face and he disappeared into the rainy night.

Cain paid his tab and stood at the doorway of the bar. The rain was starting to come down harder, and he watched several people trudge past underneath umbrellas. He wasn't ready to head to the hotel, so he glanced down the road for another to bar to visit. A couple of blocks away, he saw a flickering purple neon sign that read *The Doll House*. The perfect way he thought to spend his last night before his escape. He trotted in the rain towards the seedy strip club.

Inside the club, Cain shook off the rain and ran his fingers through his wet hair. He looked through the smoky haze and saw several men scattered at tables throughout the dingy club. On a cramped stage, an overly voluptuous dancer was circling a brass pole to an 80's re-mix. Her stretched garter belt hugged her thigh and held a few folded dollar bills. She was nothing like the perfectly-shaped strippers who graced the glimmering clubs in Miami, but beggars can't be choosers he thought to himself.

Cain sat at a table next to the stage and winked up at the dancer, who smiled back at the attention. She slowly slinked over to him and danced for her newest customer. After a few minutes, Cain stood up next to the stage with a five dollar bill in his hand. She bent over to expose herself and he slipped the folded bill into her garter belt. He sat back down and watched the dancer return to her pole.

"What can I get you sweetheart?" A middle-aged waitress in an unflattering tight outfit asked him.

"Just a beer. Whatever you have on tap. And where's the men's room?"

"In the back over there," she said pointing to a dark doorway.

Cain walked around several tables towards the back of the club. The restroom had two urinals and a battered stall. He went into the stall and closed the door behind him. He reached in his pocket and pulled out a small bag of cocaine. Sitting down on the closed toilet seat, he scooped out a small mound of white powder with his car keys. He brought it slowly up to his nose and inhaled quickly holding one nostril shut. A few white speckles fell aimlessly to the floor.

Just as he finished, he heard the door of the rest room open. He hurriedly put the small bag and keys into his pocket and stood up. As he slid the rusting metal lock open, the stall door slammed open towards him. The thrust knocked him back down onto the toilet. Taras was standing in the stall.

"Compliments of Ivan," he said.

As Cain reached up to block his face, the gun fired twice sounding like two bursts of compressed air. Cain lurched backwards, and then slid slowly down the side of the stall leaving a trail of blood behind his head on the grimy wall. Taras closed the stall door and quickly sleeked out of the rest room. Outside a roar of thunder boomed loudly over the muted music in the club, and the rain continued to beat down.

CHAPTER TWENTY-ONE

The truth of the matter is that you always know the right thing to do.
The hard part is doing it.
-- Robert H. Schuller

Jake turned his Land Rover into the driveway of the Four Seasons Hotel in midtown Atlanta, and he slowed as he approached the entrance. He took a ticket from a uniformed valet and rushed through the wide rotating doorway into the hotel. The grand lobby was walled in rose marble and richly adorned with brass railings. A tremendous crystal chandelier hovered in the air and radiated elegance throughout the reception area. Even at 7:00 a.m., the epicenter was bustling with guests.

Jake walked through the lobby and saw a placard pointing to the second floor ballroom for SouthPoint's shareholder meeting. He raced up the wide marble stairway dodging people to meet Thomas so that they could try one last time to prevent SouthPoint from concealing the fraud at ICon. McMillan was poised to risk the survival of the entire company just to ensure that he kept his grip on the majority control, and he was going to use Gary as the conduit.

Gary was the opening speaker at the meeting and he planned to greet SouthPoint's shareholders with a glowing report of the company's record profits. His presentation was going to applaud the company's employees whose hard work had generated increased margins and profitable investments. After boasting about SouthPoint's performance, McMillan made sure that Gary would brag about the merger with ICon. His PowerPoint slides showed how the transaction had been accretive to SouthPoint's bottom line, and his script attributed the rising stock price to the successful deal. Gary was planning on congratulating management for a smooth integration with ICon, and then the agenda was for him to turn it over to Vic Tomlinson, SouthPoint's CFO, to break down the Bank's financial results for the quarter.

On the second floor, Jake darted around groups of shareholders as he looked for SouthPoint's General Counsel. He burst through the ballroom doors and saw Thomas near the stage talking with several executives. The vast room was beginning to fill up and the clanking of coffee cups and dishes rung out over the background of conversation. Jake made his way towards the stage. When Thomas spotted him approaching, he excused himself from the group and led Jake through a door at the side of the room.

"I haven't seen Gary yet," Thomas said as soon as the door shut. "He was supposed to be here thirty minutes ago. He sent me an email that he was meeting with McMillan this morning, but I haven't heard anything. I don't have a good feeling about it."

"When he gets here, we'll just lay it out for him very clearly. I've got all the evidence in my briefcase and the numbers are substantial. He either has to disclose the fraud or cancel the meeting." Jake dropped his voice as several people in suits walked past them.

"But McMillan doesn't see it that way, Jake. And at least for now he's got the majority of the Board behind him." Another group of people approached, and he smiled at them as they passed.

As Thomas looked back, he saw Gary and McMillan coming down the hallway. Jake saw Thomas' gaze and turned to see the two men nearing them. McMillan's wrinkled face was jovial as he hobbled alongside Gary, who clearly looked pained. An odd couple he thought. McMillan was a thin craggy senior citizen, while Gary was a rotund sociable presence. The differences in their physiques mirrored the differences in their expressions.

"Gentlemen," McMillan said greeting them. "Gary and I have talked and we both agree that now is *not* the right time to disclose the, uh, difficulties at ICon."

McMillan sounded triumphant in his scratchy voice. Before Thomas could interrupt, McMillan added, "I trust that you understand that your fiduciary responsibilities are to SouthPoint."

Thomas grimaced at him. "My loyalties are to the law first, and no client can stand in the way of that."

Thomas turned to his boss. "Look Gary, there's no question that ICon fraudulently avoided huge penalties through the stress testing scheme. We have the proof. And the cross-sell fraud may have amounted to millions."

"Have you all been able to calculate the amounts to any degree of certainty?" Gary asked.

"Not yet," Jake said, "but we know that ICon concealed at least one of the penalties for two million dollars through a fake legal settlement."

McMillan interrupted. "But if you can't reasonably estimate what the amounts would be, they're too contingent to put on the books," he said reciting accounting rules governing when companies have to establish reserves for liabilities. "Besides, even assuming you're right about the two million, that isn't close to being material to SouthPoint's consolidated numbers. Hell, you can triple that and still it doesn't move the needle."

"We might not be able to determine the exact amount of the liability yet," Thomas interceded, "but we sure as hell know that ICon wasn't worth $750 million."

"Then how much was it worth Thomas?" McMillan barked at him. "400 million? $200 million? You have no earthly idea. You can't go out there and tell these shareholders that we overpaid for the goddamn company when you have no clue what it's worth. Do you know what kind of pandemonium that would cause? That would be plain irresponsible."

Thomas snapped back at the Chairman of the Board. "It's irresponsible to let them think that everything is rosy when SouthPoint bought a piece of shit."

The four men stood brewing in the corner of the hallway. The last groups of shareholders strolled past them towards the ballroom, and the four of them did their best to flash artificial smiles at them.

The ballroom now was packed as the late arrivals hunted for seats. Gary's introduction was minutes away.

"You can argue as much as you want," the aged director said to Thomas, "but the fact is that the Board of Directors has not had any time to discuss this and it has not approved any disclosure of this matter. No one, and I repeat no one, has authority to mention anything about this today. You hear me?" McMillan growled and marched away towards the ballroom.

Gary turned towards Thomas and Jake. "My hands are tied boys. I gotta do what I gotta do." He turned and walked into the ballroom. The door shut leaving Thomas and Jake alone in the hallway, stunned and silent.

"We did everything we could," Jake finally said to his friend. "Our job as lawyers is to give advice, but the client has to make the decision. Unfortunately, we're only as good as our clients."

They heard Gary's booming voice on the speaker through the thin wall.

"Good morning and welcome to the annual shareholder meeting of SouthPoint Bank. I'm Gary Cassell, Chief Executive Officer of SouthPoint, and it's my pleasure to welcome all of you to Atlanta and to a record year for the Bank. We're proud of our commitment to the fundamentals of the business, and that has paid off handsomely this year with increased shareholder value and revenues that exceeded our goals."

Applause boomed in the ballroom and echoed into the hallway.

Jake patted Thomas on the shoulder as they began to walk away from the ballroom. "C'mon, let me buy you a coffee." They could still hear Gary's rehearsed speech through the doors.

"All too often the value of a company is measured not by the integrity of the company but by whether the short term results exceed some artificial target set by analysts. Wall Street is more concerned with quarterly results than with long term credibility, and a stock price no longer reflects what the true value is, but instead what the whims of the market happen to be. I am here today to usher in a new era of transparency."

Thomas stopped instantly when he realized that Gary had departed from his script, which had been poured over by countless eyes. Thomas had read Gary's prepared words several times and he knew that he was hearing something different.

"Wait a minute," Thomas said and started walking back to the door of the ballroom as Jake followed.

Quietly, they slipped into the ballroom and stood against the back wall. The ornate room was packed with twenty tables of people starring intently at Gary who was standing alone on the stage behind a thin podium. A huge logo of SouthPoint was emblazed on the screen behind him. He no longer had the stressed expression that they had seen in the hallway. Although Gary was gazing out at over 2,500 shareholders, he seemed at ease and in control.

"Instead of focusing solely on price earnings ratios and trading multiples, a company should be valued by the quality of its people. Because at the end of the day, the employees are the one's who drive earnings. I hope that your decision to continue your investment in SouthPoint turns on whether you trust us as your stewards to speak openly and honestly with you about what's really going on with the business, what mistakes we have made, and what lessons we have learned."

Gary gazed at the curious expressions looking back. A murmur seeped through the ballroom as the attendees were beginning to sense that Gary's unorthodox start had not been planned.

"I tell you this because despite our record financial performance last quarter, we recently discovered some problems that you all should know about at our newest subsidiary, ICon."

The expansive room fell eerily silent. Gary caught a glimpse of Thomas and Jake standing against the back wall. He nodded to them and took a deep breath. This would be the defining moment of his career. As he looked over the room, he thought that it could be last time he stood as Chief Executive Officer of SouthPoint. But he knew that it would not be the last time he stood for the truth.

"My father always told me that a clear conscience is the softest pillow in the world. So ladies and gentlemen, there may be many reasons that I don't get much sleep tonight, but I can assure you that it will not be because of my pillow."

McMillan stormed out of the ballroom with the door echoing behind him, but he was the only one in the room who moved. Gary wiped his brow in the strong lights and slowly closed the folder on the podium that contained his presentation. He would no longer need the script. Gary looked up into the eyes of SouthPoint's shareholders, and he began to tell the sordid tale of ICon.

* * *

As Jake walked towards the school's playground, he heard jovial shouts and calls from children scampering around. He scanned the area for blonde curly hair bobbing around, and finally saw his son hanging upside down from monkey bars. A wide smile spread across Jake's face. Zack was going to be surprised to see his dad pick him up early from school, and Jake had been excited about it all the way from the shareholder meeting.

"Hey Zack," Jake called out above the adolescent chatter. The five year old looked over while hanging and saw his dad upside down. It took a second for Zack to process the image of Jake appearing to stand on his head, but as soon as he did he screamed out with joy.

"Daddy!" Zack hopped down and ran over to Jake at the gate to the playground. "Daddy!"

The curly towhead leapt into his father arms blindly confident that he'd be caught.

"Whoa!" Jake laughed as he lifted the growing boy. He rocked back with him and then plopped him down on his feet.

"I didn't know you came home," Zack said excitedly.

"I got in late last night after you went to bed, and I had to leave for a meeting early this morning before you got up. Hey, wanna go do something fun together?" Jake asked knowing the answer.

"Yeah!" Zack said enthusiastically gleaming up at his father.

Jake waved at Zack's teacher on the playground, and he reached down for his son's hand. As they walked together down the sidewalk away from the school, Jake looked at the boy holding his hand and skipping alongside him. For a moment, Jake sensed the tingling of his own father's hand holding his. He felt the strength and the security of his father's grip long ago, but most of all, the memory evoked the embrace of his father's guidance. Whichever way Jake had wandered in his youth, his father always kept him on a straight course, as if holding his hand along the way. Young boys often think of their fathers as the strongest and smartest, and for a while, they are. But even though boys sometimes learn otherwise as they grow into adults, their fathers will always be their first heroes.

CHAPTER TWENTY-TWO

If you stand for nothing, you'll fall for anything.
-- Alexander Hamilton

Three Months After The Deal

The graying anchorman looked into the camera as he began his report.

"In business news, it looks like hindsight really is twenty-twenty for SouthPoint Bank, which today announced a sale of its internet payment subsidiary Internet Connections known as ICon. SouthPoint had acquired ICon several months ago in a $750 million deal that was initially applauded by investors. Until, that is, SouthPoint's recent shareholder meeting where CEO Gary Cassell shocked Wall Street by revealing that an internal investigation of ICon had uncovered wide-ranging fraud at the subsidiary. As we previously reported, that revelation sparked a number of shareholder lawsuits against SouthPoint as well as a criminal investigation targeting the former executives of ICon."

He turned to a side camera, and a chart of SouthPoint's stock price appeared next to him as he continued the story.

"The share price of SouthPoint's stock initially took a dive after the startling revelation, but since then the price has recovered to its former levels. On Monday, our own Travis Thompson caught up with Cassell outside of the annual Southeast Banking Association meeting."

The screen cut to a video of a thin reporter with a microphone standing outside of an office building next to SouthPoint's much larger CEO.

"Mr. Cassell, to what do you attribute the remarkable bounce back in SouthPoint's share price following the shareholder meeting?"

The stress of the previous two months showed on Gary's round face. His eyes looked puffy from a lack of sleep, and his voice was hoarse from marathon phone calls with lawyers, employees, and shareholders. His resolve was never stronger, however, and he knew from the moment that he stood on the podium at the Four Season's Hotel that SouthPoint's future depended upon its honesty.

"Uh, well Travis, I think that when push comes to shove, shareholders really want a truthful assessment of the business. We are confident that our business model is sound even in these trying times for the financial industry. We admittedly made mistakes with the ICon acquisition, but we were open about the problems that we found and we are thankful that our shareholders have stood alongside us."

The reporter turned to the camera as Gary disappeared into the building behind them.

"Insiders say that it will not be so easy to brush aside the ICon debacle, and that there promises to be years of litigation and regulatory scrutiny over the acquisition. In the short term, however, SouthPoint sold ICon for a mere $75 million, and it hopes that the sale will help it move past this dark chapter. What lies ahead for SouthPoint is anyone's guess, but it seems to confirm the old adage that honesty is the best policy. This is Travis Thompson reporting for Channel 3 News."

The screen flashed back to the anchorman in the studio.

"Thanks Travis. SouthPoint announced today that Hunter McMillan, its longtime Chairman of the Board, has decided to resign from SouthPoint's Board of Directors in order to spend more time with his family. The company thanked Mr. McMillan for his leadership over the years and wishes him well. Florida authorities also are now reporting that a lawyer for ICon whose body was found in Key West shortly before SouthPoint's shareholder meeting was, in fact, murdered. However, authorities are not releasing any details yet or indicating whether this death is related to the fraud at ICon."

"Keep it tuned to Channel 3 for updates about this fascinating story. We'll be right back after this short break."

* * *

For a moment, all Jake could do was to stare at the computer screen on his desk. His fingers were still poised on the keyboard, but there were no more words – they all had been written. After a deep breath, Jake hit the *Save* button out of habit even though it had been only three minutes since the last time he saved the document and he had made no changes. Just seeing the tiny hourglass rotate and the document saved again gave him comfort.

Smiling pictures of his wife and son stood on either side of the computer monitor reminding him every day of why he worked so hard. Stacked precariously on his desk were three heaving three-ring binders littered with a forest of colored flags sticking out of the sides.

For weeks, Jake had poured over his interview notes, accounting entries, spreadsheets, and endless emails gathered during the internal investigation of ICon. Sifting through what was credible and what were likely fabrications or, at the very least, exaggerations, he balanced disparate versions and made judgments. It is much more an art than a science to turn the scattered facts of an investigation into a cogent story.

After sixty seven pages, Jake finally had finished his report of the ICon investigation. He gazed at the cover page on the screen with its intentionally colorless title: *Report of Investigation of Internet Connections, Inc. to the Board of Directors of SouthPoint Bank*. The report chronicled the investigation and described what happened and who was involved. The tone was antiseptic with legal caveats coloring each conclusion.

This report, however, was unlike any other he had written. For all the war stories that he boasted to the young associates in the lunch room, the ICon investigation stood above the rest . . . so far anyway. Money, sex, deceit, murder, and, just for good measure, the Russian mob. It might make a good book some day, Jake mused to himself.

It took weeks to calculate the financial impact of the cross-sell scheme. Ultimately, they concluded that more than a million people worldwide were duped into unwittingly subscribing to one or more adult websites to the tune of nearly $100 million. If not for the innocuous postscript on the back of Patti's exit questionnaire, the fraud may have gone unnoticed for years.

As he was straightening up the strewn papers on his desk, he saw something fall to the floor. He bent over and picked up Patti's security badge from ICon. That sandy blonde woman on the badge had no idea when she posed for the photograph that her life would be turned upside down in a matter of weeks. She had gone to work at ICon with hopes of making a better life for Aaron. Little did she know that she would end up making a better life for thousands.

Once the ICon story broke, she received invitations from companies across the country to speak about her experience and to help employees learn how and when to report wrongdoing. Her seminars drew hundreds of people and paid her handsomely. She had become a kind of folk hero among whistleblowers, and Jake smiled knowing that the once reserved woman with round glasses and hair pulled tightly in a bun was now being beckoned by executives of Fortune 100 companies. Patti dedicated her new-found career to making sure that the girl from Technyx who had so dearly paid the price for doing the right thing would not be forgotten.

Tragedy, however, oftentimes befalls scandal. So was the case for the Arnold family. After Cain's body was found in Key West, Alan could not cope with the guilt. His boat was found a week later drifting aimlessly off of the coast of Bimini about forty miles from Miami. The Coast Guard had been looking for the vessel for days after it failed to return to the marina. The *IConic* had not been damaged in any way, but they found its captain on the floor of the cabin with an empty bottle of sleeping pills rolling around nearby. Father and son were together again.

The search for Troy Vickerson took a little longer. When police broke down the door of his posh Coconut Grove home, they found only a deserted bachelor pad and an empty safe. They likewise were a step behind in freezing his bank accounts. He drained nearly two million dollars in cash just six hours before the presiding judge in Dade County finally got around to signing the freeze order. So his picture was added to a parade of other most wanted felons that marched its way through local police stations, airports, bus stops, and ports.

Three and a half weeks later, a local deputy in Maricopa County, Arizona ran the prints of a heavily built Caucasian male with a shaved head that he had detained after responding to a disorderly conduct call at a local bar. It turned out that five years earlier Troy had an altercation with a former girlfriend and he had been arrested. The charges were dropped, but his finger prints remained on file for posterity. The prints from Arizona came back a match, and twelve hours later Troy was sitting on an airplane between two federal marshals cuffed to the tray table. He would not leave federal custody for another seven and a half years.

When Neal Stein answered the call from the Assistant United States Attorney, he realized that his client had lied to him. He also knew that his client was in trouble. After two days of private hysterics, Jane Weaver finally took his advice and turned herself in. She appeared by his side at FBI Headquarters in Miami in a Valentino designer suit and Manolo Blahnik heels, the same outfit that she would wear ten months later at the opening arguments in her criminal trial. Stein spent four weeks by her side in a federal courtroom, but ultimately the jury of eight women and four men was not persuaded that she was coerced by the Russian mob into committing securities fraud. It would be twenty seven months before she wore those heels again.

By the time the authorities had landed in Grand Cayman, the officials at First Cayman Financial could only provide them with the date on which four million dollars had been withdrawn from the anonymous account. A grainy video from the week before showed a thin wiry guy in a Florida Marlins cap leaving the bank with a backpack and a smile. Mick Sertoff was never heard of again.

Months later, however, Cindy Dixon received an odd package about the size of a shoebox. There was no return address, but the brown paper wrap was embossed with foreign insignias and five large brightly colored stamps. For several moments, she just stared at the package on her kitchen table curious about the sender and wary of its contents. Finally, she carefully cut it open and slowly lifted the flaps of the box. Inside was a small note that said only *From Mick*. Underneath the note was half a million dollars in tightly wound stacks of bills.

Two days after SouthPoint's shareholder meeting, a bizarre anomaly seemed to occur for thousands of people on the Internet. At one moment, they were logged onto an adult website - then an instant later their computer screens went blank and a page appeared that said only *This Site Is No Longer Available*. All of the websites that had been secretly operated by Modos vanished into ether. All traces of the sites erased, all of the links terminated.

But two minutes later, before most people staring at their screens had even comprehended what had happened, links to new websites suddenly appeared. The names of the sites were new, but the content was exactly the same. It was as if the Internet had blinked. Of course, every one of those thousands of people then had to pull out their credit cards to re-subscribe to the new sites . . . and possibly unknowingly to other sites.

Jake was startled by a knock on his open door. He turned to see Alex standing in the threshold. The sleeves of his white dress shirt were rolled up and the knot of his tie had been loosened. His tan leather briefcase hung over his shoulder and his suit jacket was scrunched unceremoniously under his arm.

"Some of us are going to grab a drink downstairs. Are you game?"

Jake paused and then declined. "Nah thanks. I'm putting the final touches on the ICon report. I promised Thomas that he'd have it tonight. He needs some light reading for the board meeting on Wednesday."

Alex took a step into Jake's office. "Look if you want me to stay and read it over, I'll skip happy hour. Those guys will probably just bitch about their billable hours anyway."

Jake chuckled remembering the camaraderie of young lawyers sharing the pain of being overworked and the luxury of being overpaid.

"No you go ahead. You deserve a few drinks. I'm going to head home. That is, of course, unless my phone rings with the next emergency investigation," he added facetiously and winked at Alex.

"Well when it does, you know who to call."

Alex grinned and turned. Jake watched as he walked out of the office, his briefcase swinging behind him. He glimpsed himself many years ago. Not knowing what the future might hold, but knowing the direction that he was heading.

"Hey Alex," Jake called out.

Alex stopped at the door and looked back.

"You did a good job. A *really* good job."

The sincerity in Jake's eyes made up for the paucity of his accolade. He wanted to say more, but the words did not come. An irony not taught in law school is that lawyers often tend to be poor communicators, at least on a personal level. Jake was proud of Levi & Everett's newest associate, and he hoped that his few words conveyed his message.

"Thanks Jake. I appreciate it."

Alex disappeared from the doorway and again Jake's office was quiet. The slanted rays of the setting sun shimmered through his window and splashed across his desk. He turned towards the computer screen and sent the report to his client. Case closed.

Just as Jake stood his phone rang and the sound bounced around the empty office. He paused for a moment debating whether or not to answer the call or to let his assistant answer it. The phone rang again.

"Mary, can you get that?" Jake called out to his secretary as he grabbed his jacket.

Alex suddenly poked his head around the corner of the office door.

"Did I hear a phone ring? His eyes were beaming with excitement and his breath heavy from the sprint back.

Jake grinned at the eager young associate just as his secretary peeked into his office.

"Jake, it's some guy on the phone from Washington D.C. He says he has a problem that he needs to talk to you about right away."

Jake glanced over at Alex. "Are you ready for another one?" he asked with a smile.

"You bet," Alex said scampering into the office.

Jake tossed his jacket back onto the arm of his chair and lifted the headset.

THE END